Praise fo

'A story that connects across time,   'e
                and finding lights whe   ld
Sue Divin, award-winning author o

'A dynamic narrative, where two worlds collide in a story that is full of insight and integrity. An astonishingly authentic exploration of infertility and its impact on who we are and how we navigate our lives.'
Cathy Carson, author of *Becoming Marvellous,* winner of Saboteur Award for Best Spoken Word Show

'Imagine you are holding a piece of Irish oak in your hands and seeing that the tree rings testify to a catastrophe over four thousand years ago. The people living in Ireland would have suffered cruelly from cold and crop failure as a result of several years of diminished sunlight. Wouldn't you wonder what it would have meant to have lived in those times? Byddi Lee has taken that thought and created a deeply moving story. Two women, two eras that are over four thousand years apart. Yet the stories of Aisling and Zosime are entwined and they can help one another overcome grief. For Aisling, her loss is personal, a baby who would have been called Poppy. And for Zosime it is communal. Told in a highly original fashion, with beautiful, empathetic prose, Barren is filled with so much love that its tale of a journey through calamity and loss is a joy and a life-affirming one.'
Conor Kostick, award-winning historian and writer, author of the *Avatar Chronicles* trilogy.

'A story of connection across the millennia as well as between worlds: the world we know and the world we can only guess at. This book will be a gift to so many, a consolation and a comfort to those who have lost, who long to parent, and who still find a way to go on.'
Bernie McGill, winner of the 2023 Edge Hill Prize

'Barren is an engrossing, immersive and wonderfully constructed novel. Byddi's talent as a storyteller matches her astonishing ambition. This is a deeply impressive blend of the contemporary and the speculative; readers will be engrossed, moved, transported and left waiting impatiently for the next Byddi Lee book to land.'
Donal Ryan, EU Prize for Literature

Barren

Byddi Lee

ISBN: 978-0-9907695-8-3

Cover Art: Frances McKenna

In memory of Professor Mike Baillie,
Teacher, mentor, friend and the inspiration for this book.

"...2354 BC...The Earth experienced the effects of close-pass comets,
or cosmic swarms of cometary debris. Terrifying apparitions were seen
in the sky that were associated with optical, and possibly aural, effects.
Fireballs and associated atmospheric detonations gave rise to
frightening noise, earthquakes and tsunami. People experiencing these
phenomena identified them with the attributes of various deities."

Mike Baillie
Exodus to Arthur - Catastrophic Encounters With Comets
B.T. Batsford Ltd, London (1999)

For my own little Poppy Seed

CHAPTER 1

I love my mother—Aisling Breen, in tumbling magenta clouds, with washes of warm peach, shot through with sparkles of silver. Her happiness is the most important thing to me. I wish her the thrilling turquoise of joy, the soothing green of contentment, the bliss of an azure blue sky. Sometimes, my wish is granted. Sometimes it isn't. I have no control over wishes or emotions, but it doesn't stop me radiating my love to her, knowing she'll unconsciously absorb it.

She hums as she bends over the raised beds, tweaking out the newly germinated weed seedlings between her finger and thumb. The sun warms her back. Its energy radiates to me in a cocktail of light and joy. She straightens up, rubs her neck, and then the small of her back before bringing her hands to rest over her lower abdomen. Closing her eyes, she stops humming, turns her face skyward and listens to the familiar 'who, who?' of the wood pigeon.

'I need to find that birdsong app so I can teach you the names of the birds,' she tells me. There is so much she wants to show me in her world. I feel her swell of excitement.

'Lunchtime?' she asks, looking at the neat row of lettuce that has grown almost overnight. Five years after the move from Ireland to San Jose, she is still in awe of how fast the garden grows in April in California. She licks her lips, enjoying the prickle of salt on her tongue, tasting her own sweat. I taste it, too.

She picks up her bucket of pulled weeds and tosses the hori hori on top of it. She never needs the weeding tool since she is on those seedlings as soon as they appear, but she likes to have it – just in case. She takes a few steps towards the patio, then stops to look longingly at the bag of horse manure slumped against the fence. She can't risk lifting the bag. It's too heavy for a woman in her condition, but having the patience to wait until my father gets home requires a special kind of willpower. She sighs, pats her tummy and says, 'Come on, Poppy, let's get you fed.'

When she first realised she was pregnant, the doctor told her that I was the size of a poppy seed.

'My little Poppy Seed,' she whispered, her love swelling into a fiery ball. I felt it as pulsating waves of red and orange that warmed us both. The name had stuck and didn't change to lentil, blueberry or kidney bean; and I knew that grape was out of the question.

When the doorbell rings, my mother considers not answering it. Her headache ignited halfway through lunch. It's the first migraine she's had in her pregnancy. She recognised the tightening in her right temple, the sensation spidering across her cheekbone and tingling at the corner of her mouth. She's a little scared because she can't take her Sumatriptan now. That would normally sort it out, perhaps give her a sour stomach and a craving for sugary, salty snacks. Right now, she'll have to make do with a bath and a cold compress. It's disappointing because she was hoping the pregnancy hormones would keep the migraines at bay. She'd read up about that online, but maybe that wasn't to be the case.

The doorbell goes again. My mother pulls herself to her feet despite a gust of weariness. A soak in the tub is needed, she decides, once she sorts out whoever is at the door. Never mind the water shortages, this one time will be a little luxury for us both.

She opens the inner wooden door and peers through the decorative wrought-iron grille. Two clean-shaven men in dark suits with books in their hands beam at her. The taller of the two speaks in the accent my mother thinks of as 'cheesy American'.

'Hey, how are you today?' he asks, super chirpy.

The other one bobs his head, a plastic smile fixed in place.

She makes the mistake of smiling back. 'Fine, how are you?'

Immediately, she regrets asking as Cheesy leans in and says, 'Good, thank you. It sure is a beautiful day, isn't it?'

Cheesy waves a hand at my mother's front yard. Her California poppies run amok in a riot of orange, and her desert willow is resplendent with its mauve blossoms quivering in the light breeze.

Bobby-head pipes up, 'Perhaps we could come in and tell you about the Lord's good news.'

My mother steps back from the door. The grille door is locked. She gives one of the iron bars a tap. 'Sorry, lads. I don't let strangers in the house.'

They don't look 'laddish' at all, with their snappy suits, immaculate grooming and guileless expressions. My mother realises she's reverted to her 'Irish voice,' which makes her smile twitch as she chases away the urge to laugh.

'We don't mind sharing God's good news with you right here,' Cheesy says, casting an open hand toward the ornate bistro set my mother keeps in the front garden. She's never sat on the yellow tile mosaic chairs for longer than a few minutes. Now, she regrets having them there and wonders what the neighbours would think if they saw her sitting in her front garden with a couple of Jehovah's Witnesses.

'Crazy Irishwoman,' Ruby might tease.

'That's just for show,' my mother says. 'I don't think it can bear much weight.'

Her gaze drifts to the street behind the men. She thinks about how she'll phone to warn the neighbours not to answer their door when she gets rid of these guys.

Cheesy is spouting some nonsense about the Lord and final reckonings, but the words enter her ears and flutter past her brain without lodging as she tries to think of something to say to close the conversation down.

A sharp tug in the crease of her groin makes her gasp and sends adrenalin coursing through both of us. The sensation scoops out her chest.

Cheesy leans in, voice lowered. 'Ma'am, are you okay?'

'I have to go, sorry.' She closes the door in their faces. In the post-sun bright gloom of the hallway, a stab of pain doubles my mother over. She leans against the wall. Sweat breaks over her skin, slick in her armpits and in the creases of her elbows. But the trickle along her inner thigh isn't sweat.

She races to the bathroom, swallowing sobs and makes it in time to sit on the toilet as a violent contraction squeezes her like a giant hand wringing her out. This is the one. And though she prays that I am safe and tries to convince herself this is just spotting – that we'll both be fine with bed rest – with the next massive rush of blood, it's over. I move seamlessly, painlessly, blissfully through the gauze between the worlds to that place of light and enlightenment, not lost to my mother, but waiting for our reunion, specks of light rejoining endless light.

CHAPTER 2

2354 BC – IRELAND

My stomach cramps. A sour taste rises in my mouth. I swallow hard, but it doesn't help. I have my answer for another moon. Tears sting my eyes in the stench of the slop pit, but I wait until I'm outside to draw a deep breath and compose myself before walking back to our hut and Nereus, my husband.

My heart crumples with envy as I see Nereus swing Bion, his cousin's baby, high into the air, making the child screech with delight. The grin on Nereus's face lends a twinkle to his eyes, especially the left one, circled in charcoal. He wears our tribal Mark of Partholon with pride since he and Haemon left their coastal tribe at Mountain Gap and joined us eight summers ago. Only two summers younger, Nereus was Haemon's apprentice. Haemon taught Nereus his craft of weaving. When Haemon fell into companionship with Kallisto during trading, he wanted to move here. Not wishing to lose his teacher and best friend, Nereus came, too. Ironically, it is thanks to Kallisto that Nereus and I met. We fell into companionship, then love, then committed to partnership five summers ago, settling to live in our village, Seven Hills; so-called because huts and lands sprawl across seven hills clustered together like eggs in a bird's nest.

I remind myself to touch up my Mark of Paratholon where my tears may have smudged it, though it must not be too bad as Nereus doesn't seem to have noticed – yet. His attention is on Bion.

The baby gives another ear-piercing squeal as Nereus arcs him through the air.

'Be careful you don't make him sick,' I say, scanning the doorway to our hut to check that Nereus has lifted my bow, quiver, and wrist-guard out of the child's reach. On a high shelf on the back wall facing the door, I pick out sharp points on top of one of Nereus's half-finished baskets. At least he had the wit to stash the tools of our trade this time.

'He's fine, aren't you, Bion?' Nereus pulls the child close for a cuddle.

'Up, up!' The child points and wriggles. He is beautiful – huge, dark eyes light up above his dimpled smile. I'm not surprised that Nereus can't resist his pleas, but I'm irritated that the man won't listen to me. His thumbs and fingers touch as they wrap around Bion's chest beneath splayed, chubby arms. My husband lifts the child above his head. Bion shrieks with delight. This time, Nereus swoops the baby down low to the ground, then scoops him up again. The squeals stop as Bion inhales. He hiccups. I see his cheeks bulge, his lips part and white fluid spouts from his mouth, hitting Nereus in the chest.

Nereus scrunches his face and turns his head away, gagging, as he holds the baby at arm's length.

Bion wails.

The smell of curdled milk hits me as I reach for Bion, who nuzzles into my chest, grizzling.

'Shhh, ba ba, you're all right.' I rock gently, and he clings tighter.

Nereus disappears behind the hut to where the water carrier sits.

'If you empty that, you can refill it,' I call after him. Serves him right, but poor Nereus isn't the sharpest arrow in the quiver.

Bion screeches. He arches his back and stiffens his arms and legs, flinging them wide. I catch him before he slides off my knee.

'Shhh, ba ba,' I croon into his ear, rubbing his back.

'What's going on?'

I look up and see Kallisto, Bion's mother, marching towards me, her dark hair streaming behind her, bouncing with each footfall.

'He's had a little tummy upset,' I say.

Bion reaches for her, burbling. Kallisto tuts and sighs as she lifts him from my arms. He squirms to face me. Tears magnify his dark eyes, but a smile breaks. He points at the hut. 'Ne ne.'

'What did you give him?' Kallisto says, narrowing her eyes.

'I didn't give him anything.'

'Babies less than six moons can't eat grain mash yet.' She glares at the bowl by the fire.

'I didn't—'

'Kallisto! You're back already,' Nereus says, coming around the side of the hut, bare-chested, wringing water from his tunic.

Kallisto's eyebrows unknit. Her expression brightens as she drinks in my husband's physique. 'Yes. The dry weather meant we could cross the river without having to travel up to Old Ford. It's good I was able to get back sooner, evidently.' She casts her eyes in my direction.

'What's that supposed to mean?' I ask.

Nereus frowns and shakes his head at me just before Kallisto turns to face him.

'I was playing with him, bouncing him around too soon after his feed. Sorry.' Nereus pulls his damp tunic back over his head and covers up again.

'Well, it's not your fault,' Kallisto says smoothly, smiling and looking from Nereus to me. 'If you had children, you'd know that's not a good idea.'

There's a pounding in my ears. I want to run at her and rip fistfuls of that black mane from her head, but instead, I ball my hands into tight fists. My nails bite into my palms, helping distract me from the pain in my chest.

'Oh, I wouldn't say that,' Nereus says airily, though I can tell he feels the scorch of her words as keenly as I do. 'We have plenty of nieces and nephews.'

'It's not quite the same, though,' Kallisto says, walking away.

I'm too angry to meet Nereus's gaze, but I feel him watching me. I walk to the fire, pick up the grain mash, try not to cry. I feel his hand on my back. The warmth of his touch softens the tightness between my shoulders.

'When her time of mourning is over, I'll speak with her, ask her to be mindful of her words.'

'You think she will listen? She was like this before Haemon died. She's taking full advantage of her mourning rights.'

'Oh, Zosime, have some compassion. She lost her husband before Bion was born.'

'At least *her* baby was born. Where is her compassion for me?'

Nereus has no answer. I push past him into the hut and glare up at the half-woven basket holding my hunting kit on the high shelf. Nereus comes up beside me and hands me down the basket. I lift out my wrist guards and strap them on too tight, then release their leather strapping as the stone edges of the guard, dig into the heel of my hand. I hold up the second hand for Nereus to tie off. His touch is gentler than mine, and his fingers fit the guard without pinching my flesh.

'You're hunting today?' he asks in a low voice, handing me my arrows as I sling the bow across my back. 'Aren't you going to help round up the pigs?'

'Kallisto is the farmer. I prefer to hunt for my meat.'

'Zosime, don't be like that.'

'I'll be back before —' I turn my back, unable to finish. My plan to go hunting is an excuse to avoid the indignity of chasing after pigs with Kallisto, her sister Chloe, and a bunch of bumbling farmers. I yearn to fill my thoughts with nothing but tracking the prey and distract myself from thinking about how Nereus might walk away from me at tomorrow night's ceremony.

'Tonight?' He breathes a sigh. 'Please?'

I screw my eyes tight shut, bite my bottom lip before whispering, 'Yes.'

I was going to say I'd be back before the next night, in time for the Shortest Night Ceremony. The fact he wants me to be with him tonight sends my stomach tumbling – with joy that he seeks me out and fear that he may deliver bad news.

I open my eyes, blink the blur away and march out into the sunlight, stopping by the fire to fill my bowl with grain mash from the pot that warms there.

Nereus sets the basket by a pile of willow wattles stacked along the hut's outer wall and walks over to stand in front of me. I look up to meet his gaze. His eyes are so sad, it upends me.

Does he think of the coming ceremony as our last night together?

Our first Shortest Night together had been so joyful. We had happy news for the clan. My belly was already swollen with child. But within a week of the ceremony, it left my body still too small to survive. The Elders told me to be patient. My body would heal. More babies would grow. They showered me with the old wisdom, telling me that if I mated with Nereus under the shine of the first full moon after Longest Night, a child would surely arrive before the next Longest Night. So, on a shivering frosty night, Nereus and I braved the elements, but all we got were winter fevers.

The Elders had more rituals, and I tried every one. They even sent me to the Monarchs at Great Mound, who made me carry a squirming piglet against my breast for three days. It kicked, squealed and bit me. I was bruised and bloodied. A mother's sufferance, they called it. Then, on the third night, they sacrificed it to the Sun God and made me drink its still-warm blood. By our fourth Shortest Night, I had lost three more babies and had developed a guilty scepticism of our Elders' experience and wisdom, leaving me bitter and disengaged from our people.

Without a baby, we have the option to separate at the Shortest Night Ceremony. If one of us wants to, they can leave, move on and find a pairing that can produce children. Without a surviving child, our story will die. It will be as if we never existed.

I want to exist. I want Nereus to exist. I want *us* to exist.

Does he want to be free of me? His cousin Haemon had no surviving brothers, and Nereus might feel he should watch out for his widow, Kallisto. Does he want her as much as I sense she wants him? She has Chloe to help her. Chloe is young and not married yet, though I suspect she is in a companionship with a nice young cattle boy called Jaisun. He wants to learn hunting, but his family feels farming is a safer option. He sneaks out with me when he can. He's smart and quiet and will make an excellent hunter.

If Nereus leaves me tomorrow night, no man will pair with me. I'll move from maidenhood to Elder without earning the years and without anyone to carry my story.

'Perhaps it will be a good Shortest Night Ceremony this year?' Nereus's eyes drop to my belly.

I grind my teeth and press my lips together as his gaze rises to mine. He reads the expression on my face, and his eyes dampen. I can't bear it and turn away.

'I'm sorry,' I whisper.

I hear him walk away. My heart pounds at the thought that tonight could be my last night with him.

Shouts carry on the breeze from the hillside above the village and pull our attention. Three young cattle-boys call out and wave as they race down the pasture, leaping over tussocks like wild bucks. Their voices eventually form words.

'The Maiden! The Maiden is back. Come quick, you can see her from here.' Having caught the attention of the entire village, they stop and beckon us uphill, urging us to follow them, scrambling back the way they came.

One of them stops and waves at me. It's Jaisun, shouting, 'I saw her. Quickly, Zosime. She's up here.'

Around the village, people drop what they are doing and head for the hill. I lean my bow and quiver against my hut, abandoning my plan to hunt, and follow them. I'm keen to see this for myself, too. I've heard the Elders' stories of the last time she was here before I was born. In truth, I didn't believe the stories. Perhaps seeing her for myself will renew my faith.

Nereus is already ahead and running up the slope, winding in and out among friends, neighbours and family. I sprint up behind him, passing the older of my two brothers, Yani, who is laden down with his son, Claus. I should stop to help him, but curiosity and excitement drive me on. At the top of the hill, we reach the cattle-boys.

Then I see it, and it takes my breath away. Even now, as I blink away the glare of the Maiden's light, she seems too ethereal, too magical. On the far horizon where the sun disappears each evening, her pillar of light, nearly as bright as the sun, skims the horizon. The rest of the sky is clear blue. Not a cloud in sight.

Chloe arrives and joins Jaisun. Kallisto is not far behind her, with Bion in her arms. About a dozen people gather, with more streaming up from the village.

'It *is* the Maiden,' my sister-in-law Aleka says, appearing beside me with my youngest brother Agis, her husband. She's on her tiptoes and still comes only up to my chin. She slips an arm around my waist as mine snakes around her shoulders. I relax at her touch, and her gentle presence makes me smile.

'You think so?' I ask, pulling away to look at her before squinting at the presence in the sky. On a hunt, I can pick out a deer hiding amongst foliage. After stalking prey for hours, I can see a wild boar's beady eyes glinting from the undergrowth. But this brilliant light above the horizon looks more like the reflected flare of sunlight from my bronze axe head. I cannot distinguish a woman. But perhaps my talents lie in discerning game, not deities.

The cattle-boys said they had seen the Maiden the day before but that she was too faint for them to be sure what they'd seen. Rumours had rumbled through the village, and I wasn't sure what to believe. There's always some kind of story doing the rounds: about spirits visiting the living, evil mists bringing illness, deities appearing to deliver indecipherable messages in the form of unfavourable weather. But this time, whispering villagers say Geros the Wise is concerned. Geros is older than anyone I've ever known – the villagers say he's seen sixty summers. They say he's so old he can talk with the stars. I've seen how he comforts the dying and eases their fear as they pass over to become a star.

'It's definitely the Maiden,' Aleka says, breathless. Her cheeks are rosy. She seems vibrant, excited. 'Look. That's her hair. See? Flowing behind her. And that's her robes. She's full of sunlight.'

The Maiden is bright. Almost too bright to see. I raise my hand to shield my eyes, but that doesn't make her any clearer.

The villagers gather on the crest of the hill. Even Geros has joined us. His old limbs have more strength in them than I would expect. He comes up beside me and touches my elbow. His face crinkles into folds at the corners of his eyes and mouth. Linking onto his gnarled arm is like embracing a branch washed up by the river, smooth to touch but brittle if bent.

'Can you hear anything?' Geros asks.

'No,' I say. The skies have been dry for a couple of weeks. I only hear the strange sounds in my ears when rain is coming. 'How about you?'

'I always have the sounds, now. They come more with age.'

Nereus shifts from foot to foot beside me. He's uncomfortable with this talk of noises he cannot hear.

'Is the Maiden coming here?' he asks Geros. The people around us grow quiet. They too want to know.

Geros cranes his head forward, his eyes narrowed to slits. 'She looks closer since yesterday and definitely closer since she first visited.'

A murmur growls through the crowd as the information is relayed to those further away. We grew up listening to the Elders telling stories around the communal fire. Geros saw the Maiden with his own eyes as a child. Beautiful from a distance, he said, but she was a giant in far-off lands. Many travellers brought with them tales of the destruction she wreaked: how her hands gouged deep craters in the land; of her breath felling forests as if the tree trunks were no stronger than reeds; how her anger rained fire upon villages, setting everything alight; of her tears filling rivers that washed away entire settlements. She had, they said, vast armies and was at war with the Hag. Geros hadn't seen the Hag, but the stories told of her showing up at night with wild red and green hair, and fire shooting from her eyes, ears and mouth.

I've always found such stories hard to believe, though I know magical forces are at work in our world. Once, during my last winter of childhood, I watched the winter sky shimmer red and pink with my mother. She was frightened, saying it meant death would come. Death always comes. But it was another six winters before it came for my parents when a fever stole them away to the stars.

The Maiden and the Hag are different, but are they dangerous? I don't readily believe the stories. I've heard too many hunters exaggerate their tales – 'the stag was this big…' or 'the wolf was this close to me.'

Stories grow like ivy on the forest floor until they cover the truth completely. It seems to be how the best stories survive.

We often listened to the Hag and the Maiden story, captivated and terrified in equal measure by its drama. The two waged war. Their armies pummelled one another with showers of stones, which fell to Earth and killed many people and livestock, destroying cities. So, I understand why the appearance of the Maiden makes everyone nervous.

Geros says he knows a traveller named Egil who had visited Seven Hills to trade with them soon after the Maiden had left that time. Egil had come a long distance from lands beyond the sea. He had seen both the Maiden and the Hag, and heard the battle with his own ears. The booms had been so loud and terrible that they shook the ground beneath his feet. Egil had witnessed the Hag lift her axe into the sky and bring it down over the horizon. When he ventured there the next day, swaths of trees had been felled, huge forests cleared so the gods could make way. Bodies lay slain on every side. The crows had feasted on them.

Geros says Egil had trembled when he told that part of the story, so affected was he by the awful carnage he'd witnessed. But Egil said that the Maiden had prevailed. She raised a dagger made of bronze that shone in hues of yellow and pink. The Hag was so scared of this dagger that she disappeared at the mere sight of it, and the Maiden made her escape.

'I believe the Maiden will not bring us harm,' Geros says.

I clench my teeth despite the easing tension in the crowd. I want to trust Geros, but I don't know if I believe Egil.

'But we need to keep watch,' Geros continues in a voice that makes the tiny hairs on my arms stand, 'in case the Hag returns.'

That Geros is not taking Egil's word as oath brings me no relief. Now all I can think is: if she does exist, where does the Hag come from and where is she now?

CHAPTER 3

We don't come from nowhere, nor do we vanish into nothing. I always knew three facts. I was wanted – in bright shades of flashing yellow – desperately wanted. I was loved – in vibrant shades of swirling pinks and reds – unconditionally loved. And I'd never be forgotten – in shimmering waves of silver – always remembered.

My mother mourns me. She nurses me along with her other bereavements, placing her hopes for me alongside the cherished memories of her father and her friend Kate. I know my mother's thoughts but am fortunate not to be as enmeshed with her emotions as I was while a part of her. But now, I watch and listen, an observer safe from her pain on this side of the veil. She has kept the pregnancy test, and even six weeks after losing my physical form, she sits on the side of her bed for prolonged periods, staring at the blue line. It reassures her that she had me with her for those exquisite eight weeks when her little poppy seed had grown somewhere between kidney bean and grape.

Her mind replays the day she came back from the doctor's office. My father had decided to work from home, the next best thing to a day off from his job in Lick Observatory. If it weren't for a conference call, he'd have gone with her to get the doctor's confirmation.

She had been happy to go on her own but wished that her mother or Kate could have been a part of this moment in some way. When the doctor said, 'Congratulations,' she couldn't contain her joy and surprised the man with a bear hug. My mother drove the short journey home with her heart bursting. As she pulled the car into the drive, my father ran out of the house to meet her. She opened the car door, and they locked eyes; his brimming with the question, begging to be put out of the agony of waiting. A dip of her head and her slow smile spread joy to his face – a look she would never forget. He scooped her up in his arms. Their souls had entwined, reached out and touched the bliss we feel on this side of the veil.

I know that both my parents mourn the miscarriage in their own way. In the immediate aftermath, they had helped each other through. When one was up, the other was down; but it was hard when both were down together. They struggled on, hoping their grief would pass and that they'd see the world in a different light in the days that followed. Bitterness crept up on my mother. It was as though motherhood was some sort of club that she couldn't join, even though she'd filled out all the forms and had completed the initiation. It wasn't fair. She hadn't done anything wrong.

In the weeks following the miscarriage, my mother tried talking to my father, thinking that if they could put this pain into words, they could somehow make it better; but she could sense that her words wrung out his heart. Kate might have understood. And my grandmother? There was never an opportunity. In my grandmother's lucid moments, my mother preferred to chat about the easy things with her.

As time passes, and April gives way to May, my mother keeps her words to herself, doesn't bother my father with her sadness, and silently wonders if they are crying for the moon. Is parenthood too much to ask? I cannot answer her question.

From here, I am party to the thoughts of every living person, but most acutely to my parents – the ones who loved me most. I send them my love as energy vibrant in pink and scarlet. Sometimes, they feel it in the quiet moments and are comforted, but they have yet to learn how to listen for it.

My father tucks his loss into deep pockets. The youngest child from a sprawling Irish family of seven siblings who have migrated and are sprinkled around the globe, he never feels alone in the world the way my mother does. His parents, based in Belfast, have aged well, embrace their independence and travel widely. He sees a future like that for himself, and while he mourns now, he is one of life's optimists, believing things will work out okay.

But he feels helpless watching my mother's pain and worries about her while she seeks out the hollow place and yearns to fill it again. She misses dreaming of my future and talking to me.

I am never far from her, but she doesn't know that.

She misses Kate, but her friend's spirit is alongside me, watching over my mother.

Our spiritual presence is always more extensive than our physical one, especially when freed from the body. But my mother, like most people in a mortal body, is unaware of that, unaware of us in her day-to-day life. There are others here: ancestors who, like me, have passed on, or future descendants waiting to enter the mortal state. The people who love my mother most are very clear to me, like her father – my grandfather. He and I share so much that our souls merge in places, like puddles of coloured oils swirling together yet distinct. We feel only harmony on this side. The Universe is no longer a mystery. Everything makes sense, so there is no need for us to mourn.

This is housekeeping day, the day in the week my mother sets aside to 'clean the cage.' She starts with dusting the Greatroom, as the estate agent had called it – a living room, dining room and kitchen all in one. My mother dusts off a bronze axe head that she keeps on the mantelpiece.

As a teenager, broken-hearted over the death of her dog, Scruff, the young Aisling undertook the task of digging his grave in the crook of the roots of an Ash tree where its trunk splayed out, anchoring into the soil at the edge of their property. A metal clunk on her spade made her stop. She used her hands to scrape away the clay soil clotted around a wedge of metal: fifteen centimetres long, its width about half its length. One end was tubular, the other flattened, and there was an indented section where she later found out a handle would go. Her father – my grandfather – Jack Donnelly, brought her to the museum in Armagh, where they identified the object as a bronze axe head. My mother held her breath when my grandfather asked, 'Can Aisling keep it?'

'It's not made from a precious metal, so the landowner has title to it,' the museum curator said, turning to my mother with a smile. 'Are you the landowner?'

She squinted at her father and said, 'Kind of.'

The men laughed, and the curator offered to show them some polished-up replicas, saying, 'When first forged, some almost four thousand years, these bronze axe heads would have shone like gold.'

The young Aisling's eyes had widened in awe. 'They're *that* old?'

My mother stares now at the tarnished brown lump of metal in her hand. The dusting makes little difference to its appearance. She feels sad it has lost its lustre but keeps it as a testament to survival. Scruff returned to the soil, but my mother had unearthed something a human made thousands of years ago – still intact. Over the years, she's thrown out many things as she moved from house to house, continent to continent, but she keeps the bronze axe head.

She collects rocks, too, secreting them away in her rucksack from beaches and parks. On the hearth, she has a collection of obsidian, quartz, and a slice of rock with concentric circles of peach-coloured crystals – a polished geode.

Beside it sits what resembles a grey rock the size and shape of a goose egg, which my mother found in a tourist trap in a little mountain town in the Sierra Nevada.

'Who'd buy a random old rock like this?' my mother had said to my father in passing.

The wizened old shopkeeper overheard her. 'Ah, that's no ordinary rock. It's an unopened geode; you must crack it open with a hammer to see it. It's supposed to be a fertility symbol,' the shopkeeper said, winking at my father. 'But it's only potent when unopened.'

'Quite the sales pitch!' my father said. 'Might just be a dull old rock.'

'Think of it as a Schrödinger's rock. If you never open it, it can be whatever you want.'

My father laughed. 'You had me at Schrödinger's.'

'You're a physicist?'

'Astrophysicist,' my father said, handing over his credit card.

'A star man,' the shopkeeper said.

'A space cadet, more like,' my mother had said, tucking the unopened geode in her bag and giving my father a twinkling smile.

A month later, my mother discovered she was pregnant with me.

Hunkering down to dust the polished geode, she picks up the unopened one, cradles its egg form in one hand and says to the empty room, 'I never got to see what you were like.'

I feel the pull of a gossamer strand threading through the gauze between our worlds. I channel my love for her. Her face relaxes. She lifts her chin as if she's basking in the sun. It's all I can give her.

She sighs and sets the unopened geode on the hearth.

*

My mother doesn't enjoy the San Jose weather in late August. She is tired of the heat and longs for damp Irish summers. She dreams of mist lying in the hollows of fields in the early morning, of the sun whisking it away in tendrils until the morning lies clear and glistening with the jewels of dew. But she tells herself that she is romanticising and tries to remember the days of grey sky, rain and wind that drove them to California in the first place five years ago.

Still, she misses home. Ireland will always be home. She wishes she could visit her mother, my grandmother. Their phone calls are hit-and-miss as the dementia takes its toll on my grandmother. Some days, she is lucid, wise, and comforting; others, she is tragically absent, her mind wandering where my mother cannot reach her.

My mother sits at the ironing board in front of the mantelpiece. Her phone clamped between her ear and hunched shoulder, she waits for the ringtone to travel to her brother's phone in Ireland. The air-conditioning vents rumble, dropping cool, dry air into the room. She snaps the pillowcase to straighten the cloth and inhales the scent of laundry detergent as she runs the iron over it.

The first jolt feels like a truck has driven past at speed – impossible on this residential cul-de-sac. Then, the shaking comes in shuddering rolls. Pictures jangle from the walls. Doors clatter in their frames. Windows break in a crescendo of smashing glass. My mother drops the hot iron and grabs the ironing board, frozen with fear. It's not her first earthquake, but the others were mere shivers compared to this rattler. She tries to stand, wobbles and sinks to her knees, tucking her body into a ball. The mantelpiece buckles. The axe head falls, striking the egg-like geode below. With a brittle crack, the geode splits open into two halves, exposing their inner cavities, pink and glistening.

My mother cries out. Her fear is as raw and fresh as the day she miscarried me. I'm not supposed to sense her feelings once I pass on. But the gauze is suddenly thinner now. I experience a rush of panic-fuelled adrenaline. Emotions surge, kaleidoscoping around me in a storm of colours.

The shaking stops. I wait. Perhaps the intensity of the moment melted holes in the gauze? Something is different.

Her panic subsides from neon yellow to mustard, then floods purple with grief. She stares at the broken geode and sobs, 'No, no, no.'

She thinks this broken geode is a sign, the worst omen. In the wreckage of her living room, she crawls through broken glass, ignoring the splinters embedding into the flesh of her palms and knees.

It's okay. You're okay.

Her head snaps up. She looks around the room, then reaches for the phone she dropped.

'Jack?' she says, putting the phone to her ear. Hearing nothing, she pulls the phone in front of her face. The phone is dead, the screen cracked. She flings it away.

'Who's there?' she asks, looking around the room. 'Where are you? How did you get in?'

She heard me.

The idea comes in exhilarating flashes of gold interspersed with terrifying globs of dark purple. Emotions of my own are novel to me. For a moment, my thoughts jam. I think I've drifted back behind the safety of the gauze. I search for other spirits to forge a reconnection, but instead, I spiral and swirl. I have no anchor, no bind to either world.

Then my mother's hand hovers over a mean-looking shard of glass, larger than the rest, one that could do her serious damage if she were to lean on it. She doesn't see it. She's still looking up, trying to locate me, distracted. Her body tips forward as she shifts her weight. She still doesn't notice, and as her hand lowers to the shard, I send a thought as though I'm shouting: *Don't move.*

She freezes. Her eyes frantically scan the room.

Can you hear me? I ask.

'Yes,' she whimpers. 'Who are you?'

It's me, Mother, I send as gently as possible. *It's Poppy.*

CHAPTER 4

I sense Geros is desperate for a sign. That's why he had asked if I could hear the sounds in my ear. I hear noises for no reason that I know of. Geros is convinced it's either the stars or the gods trying to talk to me, but I don't think it's either. Why would the stars communicate with me when they have Geros as a willing listener? And as for the gods…why so cryptic? If they have all this power and magic, why would they make understanding a message so difficult?

I think it has to do with the weather. Perhaps my ears sense more than sound, the way birds know to fly to the sun when the days get shorter; the way buds on trees know when to unfurl; the way cattle cluster before the onset of a storm. The fact is, my ears never pop when we have glorious weather under an unblemished blue sky.

Ahead of us, the villagers drift in chattering huddles down the hillside. Anxiety pulsates off some groups, their voices high-pitched and rapid. Among them, I recognise some whom I know take delight in drama. They enjoy the worst news, ruminating over it the way cattle endlessly chew their cud. Other groups, mainly younger people, walk with a lighter step. They're more like me. The sagas from ages past are hard to imagine in these modern times. I'm sure I'm not the only one struggling to believe the Elders' stories.

Geros, along with the other Elders, Mela, Doah, Lan, and Aon, use their stories primarily to guide their governance. Mela, the eldest woman in the tribe, likes to use her stories to illustrate wisdom and forbearance, especially to the young mothers. Doah treats the sick; her stories contain the treatments and herbal remedies that heal us. Lan, Kallistos's uncle, is a great warrior and he favours the stories of other great warriors. Aon is excellent at settling debates with lessons from a story. Sometimes, he has them in such abundance, and so relevant, I think he must make them up on the spot, which is the greatest of skills, and our tribe respects that. Geros, as the most senior, a healer and also a mystic, tells the stories of gods, of stars, and the sun and the moon, and their children – the seasons. His stories are always more like riddles, and the hardest for me to understand.

Before I descend homeward from the hilltop, I take in the view of Seven Hills. The Ceremonial Hall atop the central hill, where we will meet for tomorrow's Shortest Night festivities, is decorated with garlands of flowers and ornamental wicker. Nereus, as master weaver, has created dramatic masks for the performers to tell their stories. I am proud of his skill. My favourites are the effigies of the forest animals. Each year, childish delight bubbles through me at the sight of the masks arranged around the doorway of the circular wooden structure, large enough to accommodate one hundred or so villagers for the ceremonies. A tall man could lie head to toe between each wooden post set into a stone wall foundation. The posts along each wall support rafters and a thatched roof. The walls are as thick as three or four foot-lengths and made of sod.

Geros lives in quarters at the back, separated from the main hall by a curtain of reeds, with his own hearth and a door leading directly outside. Some annexes, built onto the outside, house animals in winter and accommodate visitors in summer.

We villagers live in the round huts that orbit the main building in concentric rings. Circles within circles.

Each hut is thatched with reed over sod. Closest to the centre, the larger houses are built from split oak logs. The Elders assign these to the bigger families and those made up of many generations – each to their needs.

Nereus and I live in a smaller hut further from the centre, which is ample for us. Further out, the houses become less sturdy, with wattle and mud panels in place of oak. Dwellings at the periphery, fashioned with hides, belong to the clan's youngest, newest adults, or people travelling through and not planning to stay permanently. Around that is a fence made from split oak and laced with shrubs that grow fierce, sharp thorns. Some fields lying beyond the village, where Kallisto and the other farmers grow crops, have been enclosed with this fencing, keeping out wild animals, protecting crops from deer, and livestock from wolves.

But our fencing would provide no protection from the Hag.

With a few other volunteers, Nereus and I present ourselves at the Ceremonial Hall, and Geros divides the night into shifts. Anxiety pulls my shoulders tight to my neck. Three summers ago, we had to set watches after a trade dispute with the coastal village, Mountain Gap, where Nereus and Haemon come from. They still have family there. The coastal peoples wanted to increase their tariffs to carry cargoes of hides, cloth, flint, and other goods on their boats to the Warmer Lands. Heated words of protest turned into threats of attack, plunging me into a difficult position because, as a hunter, I have to help protect the tribe, but I couldn't bear to hurt another human, never mind Nereus's kin. Thankfully, Geros settled the discord without fighting, and no one was hurt.

This time, however, I'm unsure how we defend ourselves against the Hag should she appear. I'm not sure she exists at all. I doubt I saw a maiden, now the skies are clear again. What did I really see? My teeth clamp together so hard my ears feel hot.

Nereus and I take the third shift. Each one lasts as long as it takes the fire to burn three logs, and by the time ours ends, the sun will be rising. Sunrise is my favourite time of day. If it's to be my last day with Nereus, I want to watch the dawn with him.

He's smiling and thanking Geros, shaking the old man's hand as if Geros has gifted him. Affection swells in my chest. Nereus is affable, not clever, but dependable and more tolerant than I am. I know he'd happily sit on sentry duty the whole night through if he thought he'd be helping anyone.

I'm not so generous, and I take note of who else volunteers. Kallisto doesn't. Of course, Bion needs her, and Geros would never select her. Still, she doesn't step up in the ritual that many others make as a show of solidarity, even though they know they'll be turned down.

Chloe steps forward, and Jaisun offers to share that shift too, sparking nudges amongst the other cattle-boys and a flush of pink in Chloe's cheeks as she smiles at him. Kallisto glares at Jaisun, but he only has eyes for the younger sister. Geros gives the youngsters the first shift, when the sun still lights the sky, and there are a few chuckles from the older villagers as Jaisun looks a bit crestfallen.

Agis takes a shift with our cousin, Con, but Aleka doesn't step forward and won't meet my eye. Her shoulders slump. She looks tired. Sleep is hard at this time of year with such short nights. I try not to judge my friend. She's only been with Agis for one year, and the chances of them disengaging on Shortest Night are slim; but who knows what goes on behind a couple's smiles.

*

Con knocks on our hut and jolts me out of sleep. The sack I had filled with furs, cheese and apples sits where I left it by the door before I went to sleep. I secure the strap diagonally across my chest and gather up three logs. Flinging the door open and cradling our logs, I stride up the hill, leaving Nereus behind to shrug off sleep. I glance over my shoulder and grin as he struggles to catch up, still pulling on his tunic and lashing closed his waistband.

'Quick,' I tease. 'Before the fire dies!'

He bursts into a trot, closing the gap between us. He tugs my braid as he passes me, saying, 'What's keeping you?'

I quick-step to catch up and give him the logs.

Agis has prepared a warm grain mash for us, laced with honey and berries. We thank him for his generosity. As he disappears from the circle cast by the fire on the hilltop, Nereus rolls out our furs at the edge of the glow and sits cross-legged, facing both the flames and the dawn's horizon.

'Where do you think we'll see this Hag if she does turn up?' I ask, lifting the spiral twist of sheep horn resting on a slice of oak trunk nearby. My fingertips bump over the ridges that encircle the horn's hollow tube. I fit my first finger pad over one of the three holes near one end, then place the next finger over the hole beside it and set the third finger to cover the last hole. Nereus is better at making the horn sing than I am. I raise it level with, but not touching, my lips, lift the first finger off and pretend to blow into it.

'Let's hope we don't have to use it,' Nereus says, setting the hairs at the back of my neck on end. The last time the alarm sounded two years ago, a fire burnt a hut close to the village centre. Two of the family's youngest children perished.

I set the horn back on its wooden stand, its bend flowing with the curve of the rings in the oak – circles within circles, like our village.

'Do you think we'll actually see anything tonight?' I ask Nereus.

He shrugs.

I pivot, searching through the stars sparkling in the dark sky, scanning from where the sun rises, along the arc where the sun travels each day, to where it falls, then all the way to where the sun never travels, until I'm back where I started.

'Do you believe there is a Hag?'

'You don't?' Nereus says, shifting his gaze from the fire to me.

'I don't know.' I stretch my hands to feel the fire's heat. 'If I'm honest, I didn't believe the stories about the Maiden until I saw her.'

'And now you believe?'

I chew my lip and fold my arms. 'I suppose she is a deity, like the sun and the moon. But I didn't actually see a woman, did you?'

'You think too much, Zosime. What does it matter? What can we do? If the gods war, we're powerless to prevent it. We'll scan the sky tonight, and maybe something will happen. Maybe it won't. We have to live as best we can right now.'

I nod. He's right. Why worry until we have to?

I wish I could keep my thoughts as simple as Nereus keeps his.

'Sit.' He unfolds his legs and spreads them, knees bent, patting the triangle of earth in front of him. I settle before him and lean back with my head against his chest, tucked beneath his chin. I hook the crook of my elbows about his knees. He takes a mouthful of the grain mash and exaggerates his chewing so his chin dunts off the top of my head. It makes me laugh, but I dig him in the ribs. He pretend-spits and starts pulling little strands of my hair at the crown of my head, saying, 'Sorry, really, I am.'

'You better not have.' I turn and try to look up but find myself staring up into his black beard.

His laugh rumbles from his chest to my ear – a delicious sound. I untwist, square my back against his front and let out a long sigh. He sets down his grain mash and wraps both arms around me. I relax in the snugness of his hold. Then he uncurls one arm and points at the sky, saying, 'Look, our friends are out in full force tonight.'

There is no moon – the sky twinkles.

'Tell me a story,' I say. 'It's your turn.'

'In the beginning—'

'No, not that one.'

'Why not?'

'It's the same as our tribe's. Give me something fresh, something exotic. Something your tribe got from its travellers from across the sea.'

He goes quiet apart from his breathing, which he draws out into sighs, and it's like I can hear him thinking. I tap my fingertips together.

'Yes, yes, I'm getting there.' He clamps his hands on either side of mine, trapping them to stillness. 'All right. Old Saltbeard lies on his rushes in his cabin on the shore. His cabin is made from— '

'Is he sick or just sleeping?'

'He's sick. It's been many days since Old Saltbeard walked the length of the beach.'

'Is he dying?'

'Yes. Night is falling, and the moon rises from the ocean.'

'Why is he dying?'

'He's old.'

'So there's no hope for him.'

'No, not in this world.'

'Can we skip to the part where he dies then?'

'All the gods! Zosime, you have absolutely no patience. So he dies.' Nereus goes quiet again, and his silence stretches.

'Then?'

'You *do* want to hear the story?' Nereus says slowly.

'Yes, but can you make it faster, just get to the good bits? I don't care to hear the descriptions.' I try to make my tone contrite, but I know I won't fool Nereus. He's right – I have no patience.

'Old Saltbeard dies, and his spirit rises from his body and sees a shining pathway across the ocean to the full moon.'

'He dies at night?'

'Yes. Shh!'

'Just asking.'

'You told me to give less detail. Do you want me to stop altogether? You're making this too hard.'

'I'm sorry. Continue.' Smiling, I kiss Nereus's hand.

I sense he is smiling, too; it warms his voice as he goes on. 'Old Saltbeard's spirit starts off along the pathway, but the stars sing to him to stop....'

'What do they sing?'

Nereus clears his throat, pauses for a heavy moment, then says, 'No, you know I can't sing.'

My shoulders bounce as I chuckle, and he play-slaps my hand.

'So Old Saltbeard, I think he's going the wrong direction?' I prompt, knowing Nereus's ancestors' stories don't differ that much from ours – that when we pass away, our spirits follow the sun to its daily resting place.

'Yes, but the path looks so lovely, shimmering across the ocean, that Old Saltbeard's spirit keeps going. The moon rises higher, and the path gets narrower. The stars twinkle and call to Old Saltbeard's spirit, "Go where the sun dies and sets the Earth aflame so you can grab a light to find your way to life beyond the sky."

'"Let me be. Look. The moon has an easy path to the sky," Old Saltbeard's spirit calls back.

'"It is the wrong path," the stars cry out.

"'How would you know? You are only tiny stars,'" Old Saltbeard's spirit replies.

"'We followed the sun to her resting place, and she shared with us her heat so we could burn our way out of the sky into the afterlife,'" they tell him. "All you can see from Earth is our light shining through the holes. The moon has no fire, or it would warm the night. Don't follow the moon, or you will be lost to us that way.'"

Nereus looks at me, tilts his head to one side, and sighs. 'But Old Saltbeard's spirit doesn't listen, and as he climbs higher, a cloud falls across the moon. The path starts to disappear, but before it does, Old Saltbeard's spirit grabs a handful of its shiny light, but it's not strong enough to hold him up, and he falls into the sea and shatters on the waves. And that is why... can you guess?' Nereus asks.

'The sea tastes of salt?'

'No.' Nereus laughs. 'That's a completely different story. No, it is why the waves each carry a little of the light of Old Saltbeard's spirit to this very day.'

'Oh, yes! I remember the first time I saw the ocean. The surface never rested, and light danced upon it constantly. So Old Saltbeard had a hand in that?'

'Apparently so.' Nereus kisses the crown of my head.

I look up into the sky and feel swallowed by the night. So many stars! Does each one really represent an ancestor? My thoughts buckle under the scale of it. I sigh and snuggle backwards into Nereus's chest.

Our first log is burnt down to embers, and we add the second log to crackle with yellow and orange tongues.

'What can you see in the fire?' It's my turn to tell a story unless I can distract Nereus. I've had enough stories. 'I see dancers.'

Nereus leans forward. I wriggle to let him know he's too heavy on me. He shifts position, and I snuggle into him, enjoying his body heat though it is a summer night.

'I see fish swimming up a waterfall.'

'Really?' I squint and cock my head, but I don't see it. I think of how I could not see the Maiden where others could. Do we each see the world in a unique way? I know I hear the world differently from many.

One spark shoots high. I follow its arc into the night air over our heads and behind us. I rotate my head and shoulders to track it and ensure it fades before it lands. And there she is, coming over the black horizon – the Hag!

Her hair flames like our fire, but with bands of green and violet spinning into the sky. Her face is a black hole. Her arms flail and thrash. Even the stars have hidden from her, disappearing from the sky.

Nereus jumps up and stands between the Hag and me, though she is far off, still hovering over the horizon. There's no denying what I see with my own eyes, no refuting the Hag's violence compared to the shimmering light that enveloped the Maiden.

'Sound the alarm!' I shout.

As he draws the sheep horn to his lips, Nereus heaves in a breath, then blows a mournful blare. His fingers ripple, alternating the tone. I imagine the villagers in their huts sitting up in their beds. My skin contracts into bumps, my heart beats hard, and I try to slow my panting.

The sky where the sun arrives each day has lightened from black to deep blue. On the opposite horizon, the Hag slides down partly obscured behind the far hills. I stare at the burst of light that trails into the sky behind her. I search the skies for the Maiden but cannot see her. Where is she? So far, the Hag and the Maiden have not met. The sky is enormous. Perhaps they will not meet again. I hope they never do, at least not here.

Below us, people-shaped blotches leave huts and seem to float uphill. I'm amazed that Geros is among the first to arrive. In the light of our blazing fire, his skin is pale and his eyes wide.

'She's here,' he says. 'It is as I feared.'

The silence, with so many present, is eerie.

The sky lightens as the sun announces her arrival with brilliant yellow light. The Hag shrinks back.

'She's leaving!' people cry.

'The Hag is afraid of the sun.'

It makes sense. Jubilation and relief rise in me. Nereus scoops me up in his arms and hugs me. I breathe him in. He sets me back on my feet. I turn, looking for Geros, but instead, I catch Kallisto looking our way. Her expression is sharp, a predator eyeing prey. A shiver wriggles up my back. Nereus pulls me to his side, rubbing his hand up and down my arm to warm me. I can't banish the look on Kallisto's face from my mind despite the greater threat of gods battling in the skies above our home.

Geros raises his staff. Quiet descends. He extends his arm and raises his staff, signalling us to sit down.

There's a ripple of muffled noise as the villagers settle, trying to find comfort on the dewy grass. I'm glad we're still by the fire on our dry sheepskins.

Geros stands on the crest of the pasture hill, the fire in front, and most of the village sitting in a semi-circle before him. We know he has something important to say, or he'd have waited until the ceremony tonight.

'We need the bronze dagger Egil spoke of to protect us from the Hag,' he says.

'There is no such thing!' a voice calls out. Laced with fear and alarm, a medley of cries rises from the crowd.

Geros shouts over them, 'I know where such a dagger exists.'

An excited hiss ruffles through the crowd. Geros raises a hand. The people go quiet, and all faces turn to him. Chatter at the back is shushed.

'How do we wield such a thing against a god? Who has that strength?' one of the young cow-herders shouts from the throng.

'The dagger is made from bronze like the head of our ancient axe.' Geros looks at me, seated to his right-hand side. 'It shines with the colour of the sun. You saw yourselves how the Hag ran from the sun. But she may not run from the Maiden if they are evenly matched.'

I nod along with the villagers as understanding dawns. Egil told Geros that the sight of the Maiden's bronze dagger last time was enough to frighten the Hag away. It makes sense that displaying a great weapon infused with the light of the sun will be deterrent enough. Even stags won't fight with other bucks whose antlers outweigh theirs. Oftentimes, a show of strength is enough to determine a winner.

Our ancient axe has been handed down through my family, and as the eldest, it's *mine*, despite Geros holding it along with the treasures of the Seven Hills clan.

'Would my axe not protect us? Can't we use that?' I ask.

Kallisto pushes forward. Her lips are pressed into the thin line of a suppressed smile. She glances at me and draws a breath as if to say something.

'Later, Kallisto,' Geros says, and she deflates, retreats with her thin smile still in place and her head down.

Geros fixes his gaze on me and says, 'The axe does not have the same power as the dagger. Egil saw the dagger grow in size and strength once wielded against the Hag. It has to be this dagger.' Geros looks over the crowd and continues in a louder voice, 'But Egil told me how this dagger is buried in a tomb with a great warrior. We must send someone to retrieve it.'

The crowd seems to inhale as one creature and hold their breath – the hair on my scalp prickles. Only the Monarchs can enter a tomb, much less remove anything.

'But the curse?' a voice calls. The curse is no small matter – if you remove a treasure from a tomb, the Monarchs can curse you with enslavement or death.

'The Monarchs will have as much to gain from this action as we,' Geros says. 'I can intervene, and if the Monarchs grant permission, the curse will be lifted.' Geros closes his eyes. The people wait, huddled around like oak trees in a grove, silent, brooding. I wonder for a second if Geros has the power to commune with Monarchs right there. Usually, he needs to journey to the Great Mound to have any discourse with them. I went with him last autumn. They are a beautiful people, regal in robes of scarlet, with gold neckbands that shine like slices of the sun. The Monarchs look as if they are carved by the same craftsman. Their pale features are similar, with flowing white hair and pale blue eyes. They are a people set apart. Sisters married to brothers keep their lineage pure. They rule with a strict but fair hand. Breaking their rules incurs severe penalties. They are to be feared as much as admired.

Geros opens his eyes and stares beyond my shoulder.

I turn and see the last fiery tendrils of the Hag's head sliding below the horizon.

Geros watches too. He seems to have forgotten that Kallisto and I are there. A wave of fidgeting and whispering ripples through the remaining villagers.

Geros's eyes close. His body shakes, and words in a strange language tumble from his lips.

The crowd is stunned to silence. My scalp tingles as his eyes open and stare right at me.

Geros draws in a long breath, and his expression animates as he comes back to himself. The people gathered seem to exhale with him. It unnerves me, but most people seem enthralled. Many believe this is how he speaks with the stars – the spirits of our ancestors. Others say this is how he speaks directly with the gods. I haven't plucked up the courage to ask him. Someday, I will if I am to be his apprentice.

Geros opens his eyes. His gaze, tinged with sorrow or perhaps pity, rests on me. I frown, trying to decipher his body language, ignoring the tingle shivering over my scalp. Geros guards his expression as effectively as if he were pulling a mask over his face, looks around the crowd and says, 'Tonight is the Shortest Night Ceremony. You have much to do today in preparation. I will take the day to consult with the Elders' Council and consider our next course of action. I will present my decision at the ceremony tonight.'

I squint against the morning sunshine and try to catch Geros's eye, but the old man has turned his back on me to walk down the hill, stooped over as if carrying a weight. I feel a cool breeze at my side where Nereus had been standing. When I turn, the space is empty. Nereus stands several arms lengths away, looking into the fire's dying embers. Kallisto is there, too, talking with him. Nereus shakes his head, looks at me, and smiles. Kallisto scowls and stomps off.

As I approach, Nereus lifts some greenwood and says, 'We should keep this flame alive… at least until tonight.'

Tonight – when everything could change. My chest feels tight. Smoke billows from the newly added greenwood, tugged towards us by the breeze. Nereus takes my hand, looks into my face, concern thickening his voice, 'Are you crying?'

'It's just the smoke,' I say, ducking my head and swiping at my cheeks. He pulls me out of the smoke and slips his arm around my shoulder. As we walk to our hut, I wonder if it will still be our home after tonight.

CHAPTER 5

My mother can hear me!

She mouths the name she gave me as she shakes her head and searches the room for me, looking for the embodiment of the voice she thought she heard. But there is no body, nor even a voice. She heard me in her heart, in her thoughts and I, with my knowledge of the workings of this world and beyond, can't understand how this has happened.

The acrid scent of burning wool breaks through our frozen moment and jolts my mother into action. The iron! She let go of it during the shaking, and it fell to the rug. She sweeps it up in one swift lunge. A sludge of melted wool and polyester sticks to the hotplate. Smoke drifts in blue-grey curls. She stares, mesmerised.

Turn off the iron, I tell her.

She jerks her head around. 'Poppy?' Her voice trembles. 'How? What?'

The sludge on the iron's hotplate bubbles and crackles. It stinks.

Unplug the iron, I urge. The sensation of fear is alien, licking at me in flashes of orange and red. Something in the natural order is very wrong.

Now! I yell in my mother's head.

She pounces towards the socket, yanks the cord from the wall but drops the iron. It lands on its side, the edge searing a new brown scar into the red and gold rug.

My mother backs up against the wall, hands over her ears, eyes wide, breathing in sharp, shallow puffs. Her knees give way, and she slides down the wall in a huddle.

It's okay, I send.

She is out of danger, but her shock pierces me with silver shards. It makes me want to retreat back to the other side, the other world – my world – though that may not be possible. But I am drawn to the pure white love I feel, have always felt, from my mother, and surrender to it, luxuriate in it. Time rolls, tugging me in one direction like a riptide hidden beneath a lazy ocean. Before, when I was behind the gauze, I drifted, cocooned in contentment. I still sense my ancestors, but they are merely spectators, not caught in this current.

Time unfurls. I travel with it, in step with my mother.

Silence lolls between us.

'Poppy?' she whispers, cracking the quiet wide open again.

Her mind pops up a vision of my grandmother, sitting at the kitchen table, wagging a finger at an empty chair, arguing loudly with a man only she can see.

I see strands of crimson alarm thread through the mauve tendrils of my mother's grief, embroidery against the muddy-brown tapestry of her memory of my grandmother's confusion. I could stay silent and back away, but the thought curls through me like a lonely wind, slashing through my mother's emotions.

As she pushes the idea of me away from her thoughts, my disappointment stains patches of grey on the black fabric of her mourning. I am no longer an independent observer of her grief. Now, it drags at me too, painful and longing for relief. It is unbearable. I need to quench it. I realise the only way to do that is to connect with my mother, soak in her love for me and lavish my love upon her. How do living humans bear this maelstrom of emotion?

Yes, Mother, I'm here.

She gasps.

I rush to say, It's okay. You're okay.

'I'm going mad!' She beats the palm of her hand against the side of her head, her confusion crashing in on me in every colour at once.

Stop! Listen.

Her hands hover over her ears. She looks around, staring up at the ceiling, her gaze searching into the corners of the room.

'Where are you?' she whispers.

In the Light, the place of Enlightenment.

'What? Where?'

How can I explain that which a mortal mind has forgotten? I try again.

The spirit world.

She gulps and clamps a hand over her mouth, shaking her head. 'Is this how it starts?'

A memory surfaces in her mind – my Uncle Jack with his hands up protecting his face, stumbling back as my grandmother reaches up to

30

claw at him. Her face is twisted and snarling. Her five-foot-four is no match for his six-foot-three, but tears stream down his face as he pleads with her to stop.

'It's me, your son Jack.'

'You're the devil!' she screams.

My mother snaps the memory shut.

This is different.

'How can I be sure? You feel so … real,' my mother whispers. 'And I want it too much.'

Emptiness weighs heavy in her arms, as if her muscles can remember a child she has never held. Her eyes bring up a face she has never seen, and her nostrils inhale a scent she has never smelt.

She wraps her arms around her torso and remains slouched against the wall, breathing deeply – in for three, out for three. Her pulse beats slower. If I slipped away now, she could put our conversation down to her surge of adrenalin after the earthquake. Or maybe she'd think it was the first sign of the early-onset dementia that took hold of her mother.

I straddle worlds. The bliss of the Enlightenment is now tainted with the physical world's emotions. I sense the ancestors, but I am intoxicated with the two-way connection I have with my mother. Will staying here damage her and leave me stranded in this place where I should not exist?

Glimpses of the others in the Enlightenment tether me though our communion is attenuated. They are there, communicating that I have a purpose here in the physical world, but they don't elaborate. I don't understand what this purpose is. Not understanding is so alien to me that it envelops me in flashing colours.

If I am to stay, I need to make my mother understand. I need her to trust me, to believe that this is real and not in her mind.

I'm not sure why I can talk to you now. Usually, we can't, I tell her.

'We?' she asks.

I'm here with Granda. His spirit precipitates into a potent force transmitting from behind the gauze with his focus on my mother.

He sends his love. My words land, nibbling at her disbelief. Her spirit, swirling outside the bounds of her physical body, glows in vibrant oranges and reds.

'Dad?' she says on a breath. Tears glisten in her eyes. She looks around her, searching him out.

You won't hear his voice.

A spurt of dark purple disappointment quells the riot of colour.

There is a partition between our worlds, I continue, trying to make sense of what has happened. Words are not designed for such things. *I was able to pass through to your side.*

'The earthquake…' Her face turns towards the broken geode and the axe head. She jumps up and reaches for the axe head. As her fingers touch it, I feel peeled away. A bolt of fear crashes through my psyche. My mother and I share a vision of a woman on a hill looking over a waterlogged landscape amid a grey cloud of desolation.

Stop!

My mother drops the axe head as though she's been burnt.

'What happened?' Despite the California heat, my mother shivers and rubs her hands up her arms. The axe head lies at her feet. She steps back, frightened and confused.

I am firmly back in her world, but I know she felt the desolation I've drawn with me from the other place – the place the axe head came from. Questions build in her head. Some I can answer, others will take time to explain, and some I don't know the answers to. Those questions scare me.

It's something to do with the axe head, my mother says inside her head, reverting to talking to me the way she did when she was pregnant when she didn't expect an answer. *But I've handled that axe head all my life. So, what changed?*

She takes a deep breath and stares at the axe head on the floor beside the hearth. A glint of light reflecting from the broken geode's crystal interior catches her eye.

The geode! It broke open when the axe fell on it. She crouches beside it. *What will happen if I touch it?* She extends a hand, one finger out. Her translucent aura brushes against the pink amethyst crystals that line the concave inside of the rock.

I sense the presence of many kindred spirits, those of us cleaved from the same region of the Great Spirit. Our connections stretch across aeons on the physical side of the divide between worlds, but on the spiritual side, we pool together, our existence intertwined, flowing between a homogenous union and lobbing into autonomy – individuals and a collective at once – a more fluid version of the cells in a sea sponge that live and work as one but that survive alone, too.

I float between the worlds yet never fully in either place. I concentrate on joining them but get no closer, unable to escape the undertow of the physical world. Fluorescent-yellow panic churns through me. Why can't I go back?

The spirits voice encouragement, settling the yellow to a buttery hue. They are there for me when I return, but I have a task for now while the gauze is thin.

What is if? I ask them, but the ancestors do not answer me, do not reveal my task.

My mother rubs her hands through her hair. 'Maybe I banged my head during the earthquake?'

I stay quiet. She's had enough of a shock for now. I feel her relief as she rationalises that there is some kind of short-term physical reason for the voice she hears. She sets the geode down. I can still hear the spirits, but it is less intense. Is the geode my way back to them?

My mother straightens and walks to the kitchen counter, crunching across broken glass. When she opens a cupboard, a glass rolls out. She catches it before it lands on the countertop. The chopping boards stacked against the wall on the countertop have flopped over. She's afraid to open any more cupboards for now.

Twisting the taps at the sink delivers a sputter of water, then nothing more than a gurgling deep in the household plumbing. She turns off the taps, stares at the finger depth of water in the glass but doesn't fancy drinking it. In three strides, she's at the fridge, heaving the door open. A two-litre bottle of Coke tumbles out, hitting the wooden floor with a resounding thud. There's a high-pitched hiss followed by a beige fizzing fountain.

'Shit!' She picks up the bottle, trying to hold the plume of escaping Coke away from herself and runs to the sink. As the pressure decreases, she eases the lid off and pours herself a glass. She sinks a cold draught. It might be flatter than it was, but there's still enough gas to make her belch. She pats her fingertips to her lips, giggles, and goes at it once more before emptying the glass and setting it by the sink. She turns to survey the living room and kitchen, says to the dishevelled room, 'What the hell am I doing? Talking to my miscarried baby. That's crazy, or shock, or something.'

You're not crazy.

'You're still there?'

I am. Please, give me a chance to prove I'm real.

'How?'

I don't know. Sadness spreads in sepia smudges. *But I will find a way.*

'Please do.' She sighs. 'I need to clear this up.' She waves a hand at the toppled ironing board in the living room area. The rug is ruined with the melted patch from the iron. My mother checks her watch. It's only been fifteen minutes since the earthquake struck. Suddenly, her hands shake so much that she folds her arms, trapping her hands between her sides and upper arms. For the first time, she notices the blood caking her shin from a cut on one knee.

'The phone,' she says aloud and spins around, scanning the room, spotting it in a corner near the front door. In a few strides, she has reached it and picked it up. The screen is still cracked, but this time, when she presses the power-on button, the screen springs to life with a pixilated logo. It's working to some degree, but with the screen distortion, my mother can't figure out which icon to touch to bring up the phone call function. She nearly drops the phone when it vibrates. A feeble 'peep, peep' issues in place of a normal ringtone. She thumbs the screen and strikes lucky.

'Hello? Aisling, can you hear me?'

'Ben?' she says, so weak with relief that she kneels on the floor and slumps against the wall. 'I can hear you. Are you okay? Can you hear me?'

'Yes, yes. Are you hurt?'

My mother thinks of her conversation with me. Her previous dismissal of our interaction as her imagination still leaves me with a lingering ice-cold blue abandonment. I fight a strong urge to connect with her – to lay my case out, to tell her I am here – but her confusion hurts me as much as it hurts her. I stay silent despite the sense that she is probing for me, searching her mind to test if I was ever there.

'Aisling?' The urgency in his voice pulls at me. I can feel him in the same way I feel my mother, but only when she hears his voice through the phone. Before this, I was with him always, the same way I was with my mother. I miss his proximity.

'I'm okay,' my mother says.

Relief dampens his anxiety from electric to sky blue. 'Thank God! I've been trying to get through for ages. What's the damage there?'

'Just minor stuff.'

'Stay put. I'm on my way. I'll be with you in twenty minutes.'

'Ben,' my mother says, her heart thumping, 'I heard—'

'What? Wait, I can't hear you. Aisling. Ais—'

'I heard her talking to me, Ben. I heard her. It was—'

Fierce elation explodes in sunshine yellow as my mother whispers, 'Poppy.'

The silence on the phone line sizzles in her ears.

CHAPTER 6

I'm afraid to speak to Nereus all day, fearful that if he discloses his intent to leave me, I'll fall to begging him to stay. The gods know how much I want to continue to be his wife, but if I cannot give him children, it would be wrong for me to force him to stay. It will be too much to bear if he chooses to leave me and elects to be with Kallisto.

The preparations culminate in a feast at the Ceremonial Hall, where each villager brings something they value or have worked to provide. Nereus has already supplied the woven decorations, so I have joined with my brothers, Agis and Yani, to deliver two boars as our offering as hunters. Their wives, Aleka and Eleni, took Eleni's children to collect the herbs to dress the boars and prepare them for roasting. Con, our cousin who also hunts with us, has provided deerskin hides with his wife, Duna, for people to sit on. Between us, we turn the spit throughout the day so it will be ready for the feast.

Kallisto and her sister bring cheese. It is not yet harvest time, so much of what they produce is not yet ready. I like that this Shortest Night tradition goes further back than Kallisto's modern ways of farming. It proves how essential we hunters still are.

Jaisun leads the other cow-herders in a pulsing beat on their drums to gather the people together. Lan sounds the horn, three long blasts that reverberate through me. My pulse quickens as the sounds combine, and three young women play a haunting air on their flutes —hollow deer bones with holes along them to give them differing sounds. The rest of us have rattles made from a variety of sources. Mine is a tight woven ball of willow encasing small shells. It was a wedding present from Nereus, and I love its raspy sound. It's easy to jig it in time with Jaisun's drumming and my own heart rate.

The cacophony draws the whole village together at the ceremonial hut where we gather, upwards of two hundred of us, spilling out of the various entrances like bees around a hive. Young children run around outside close enough to be involved but with the freedom to play, supervised by their parents standing in the doorways, many holding the babies who will next year be scarpering around with their siblings and cousins.

Inside, in the centre of the hut, a raised wooden platform constructed for this occasion from the Elder's sleeping platforms holds the Elder Council a few feet off the ground. In the middle of the platform stands an ancient tree trunk. Its concentric rings are polished, showing how many years the tree lived before it was cut down by a bolt of lightning, or so the story goes – gifted to us by the gods. The oldest members of our village sit in concentric circles around the platform, gradually seating younger people, leaving a pathway from each of the four entrances so people can move to and from the centre as the ceremony progresses.

The tree trunk has been beautifully carved with notches and shelves that display our village's treasures. My axe is among them, its bronze head glowing in the warm evening sunlight streaming through the open doorways. It sits alongside one of six gold neck rings – the other five adorning the necks of the Elders. There are carved stones, chalices, and three bowls engraved with stories of our people. Polished rocks and gemstones of various colours twinkle and glisten. We must be a wealthy tribe to hold such beautiful treasures, I think, grateful for our bounty.

Five seats evenly spaced around the tree trunk's base provide a place for each Elder to sit. Mela and Doah, dressed in simple robes of finely woven wool, faded to soft cream from years of wearing and washing, smile at each other and to the people gathered before them, nodding to those they know well. Lan wears the leathers of a warrior, though his last battle was many summers ago. His expression is stern and aloof, his eyes focused somewhere above the heads of the people before him. Aon, in a tunic of bright colours, looks around smiling, his feet tapping with the beat of the drums. Geros also wears a tunic, though it is faded and a little tattered at the hem. He stands, faces the treasures and bows, walks around the tree trunk, and bows his head to each Elder until he is back in front of his seat.

Geros holds up a hand to call for silence and then commences by reading the names of the people who joined the stars since the last Shortest Night. We listen with respect. Nereus and I have not lost anyone close this year, but my heart is sad for the baby I lost before the winter. She didn't grow long enough inside me to have formed sufficiently to receive a name, but I think of her and her sisters that went before as if they had faces and names… and smiles. I always imagine them as girls, but I'll never know for sure.

After Geros says The Last Farewell, it is time to welcome the newcomers to our village. My heart still stings at the joyous parade of babies and parents because we should be among them but aren't. Nereus takes my hand and squeezes, sending a lump to my throat I find difficult to swallow away.

At the back of this line is a tall, golden-haired man, grinning and red-faced. We cheer when he steps onto the platform. His name is Dagfinn and he was a traveller from The Lands the Sun Abandons in Winter. He came to trade and fell in love with one of our villagers, and now he is asking to stay. Geros greets him with a hug and the crowd claps.

I find myself smiling at Nereus. He went through this too… for me. His beaming face is reassuring. Maybe there is hope for us yet, but I can't relax until we've gone through the matrimonial pledges. At least once that is decided, one way or another, I might be able to face eating the feast.

Geros gives each newcomer – usually a child – a piece of fabric their parents will fashion into a tunic. Dagfinn holds his up, a small square beside his broad chest, and the crowd laughs. Nereus sewed his into a larger cloth, which we sleep under. I wonder what Dagfinn will do with his.

Everyone expects the matrimonial pledges, but Geros sets aside his ceremonial staff and addresses the crowd.

'All day, the Elders and I have given deep thought to the appearance of the Maiden and the Hag. It has been decided that we shall send someone to the tomb of the great warrior to retrieve the bronze dagger that the Hag fears so much.'

A collective gasp from the crowd sets the hair at the back of my neck on end.

'How can they enter a tomb?' someone asks.

'What about the curse?' calls another voice.

'We have to wait to hear what the Monarchs say,' says Maga, an older woman sitting by the platform. She is awaiting her turn to be on the Elder Council and is growing impatient, or at least it looks that way to me.

Geros holds up his hand for silence once more. The villagers settle. It feels like everyone is holding their breath.

'There is no time. Great Mound is many days travel in the opposite direction to where the dagger lies. I will seek their permission, but we need a volunteer to go now – someone skilled in navigation.'

'Surely that is a task for a warrior?' Kallisto says, whipping her head up towards me. 'Or a hunter?'

'What if you don't get permission?' several voices ask at once so that the word 'permission' hisses.

Geros clears his throat. Speaking so loudly is making him hoarse. 'The Monarchs are not safe from the Hag either. I shall make them aware of that.'

'But what if you fail?' Maga asks.

'Are you more worried about one person suffering from the curse or the Hag destroying the whole land?' Kallisto asks.

Several people shout at once.

Geros shakes his head and holds up a hand. 'It is a long way. Whoever is selected won't be able to carry all the food they need. And visiting other villages to barter might prove counter-productive.'

'Surely it's in their interest to help us defeat the Hag,' my neighbour says. 'We all live beneath the same sky.'

'This is true, but these villages may not know of Egil's story the way we and the Monarchs already do,' Geros says. 'The villages might not listen to reason once you mention breaking into a tomb. You know how people feel about disturbing graves. You could make up another reason for your travel, but strangers caught telling lies are unsafe. Simpler to keep to yourself. A hunter to accompany them would be ideal – you can catch food as you go.'

Several people call out the names of suitable candidates.

'I suggest Zosime,' Kallisto's voice carries over the others, and a hush falls in its wake.

All eyes are on me. Fear wallops my chest. I don't want to enter a tomb, even with the Monarchs' permission. More terrifying is the idea that I might have to present the dagger to ward off the Hag if she returns. But I am too proud to show my fear.

Kallisto steps forward, 'Geros, you know Zosime is free to travel since she does not have a child relying on her like us parents do.'

Her words cut through that empty part of me I cannot fill. I know she's a mother. I never need reminding of that.

'Besides,' Kallisto continues with a sly smile, 'Zosime has such excellent hunting skills, and the Monarchs have already met her.

Geros's negotiations will fare much better if he is asking for permission for someone they know.'

The villagers break into a babble, discussing once more whose skills and situation match the task. Our village has less than a dozen who still follow the old tradition of hunting. Most other hunters are white-haired and tread with care, depending on stealth rather than speed. A journey such as this would be too demanding for them. The rest are my brothers and cousins who have children depending on them. I don't want them to go either.

But Kallisto has a point. Though I have resisted this new culture, right now, I wish I too were a farmer.

My heart sinks, knowing that this task will be placed on me. I can't claim motherhood to keep me in my village; I am fit and can feed myself along the way.

As for the Monarchs – Kallisto is right about that, too. Geros favours my company on journeys. He often tells me that I would make a suitable apprentice for him, which is why he has taken me to Great Mound several times. He always travels with a helper. The pride I used to take in being chosen has suddenly soured.

I'm trapped, unable to see a way to say no.

The crowd stares, boring holes into my skin. Sweat trickles down my back, yet I'm frozen, unable to speak, unable to move. Beside me, I feel Nereus shift forward from his sitting position to get his feet beneath him and stand.

He cannot go!

At least not alone. Nereus can barely navigate to the latrine and back without getting lost. He needs me. He stretches his hand to me.

'We will have a story that all children will tell,' he says. 'Our own story…'

I shake my head, but when he extends his hand to me, I reach up to grasp it. He pulls me to stand beside him, squeezing my hand as he looks into my eyes and smiles. He touches his thumb to my chin, the matrimonial gesture of taking me as his wife before the clan. He is choosing me again.

'Yes,' I say, past the lump in my throat. We are to stay married. I'm so relieved by this, I am trembling.

Nereus's face glows as he lifts our joint hands.

Over Geros's shoulder, I see Kallisto's smile wither as the villagers burst into applause. I look up at Nereus's face. He smiles at the crowd, puffed with pride that we've been 'selected.'

My surge of relief is short-lived. I can barely breathe. I look around, trying to relax my jaws and stop the furrowing of my brow.

Aleka beams at me, her hand on her tummy. She can't go. Of course, she can't. *She's with child.* This new knowledge is crippling. How it sears and penetrates my other concerns is beyond my comprehension. It's the same old thing – I'm happy for her but devastated for us again. Added to that crushing burden is the fact we have no choice but to accept this task of finding a bronze dagger that may or may not be real, in a tomb we have yet to locate, to scare off a Sky God whose very existence I doubt.

Beside me, Nereus soaks in the applause from the village. He sees his selection as an honour, as some great opportunity for us to prove ourselves.

Geros looks at me from beneath bushy white eyebrows. His eyes hold a hint of a question. I stretch my mouth into a smile with no heart. Fair enough, we are the best suited to the task. Others are as young and fit as we are, but they have dependents, or lack my hunting and navigation skills.

What if the Monarchs don't give Geros permission? Nereus and I will not know their answer when we take the bronze dagger, if we can find it. And what happens if we don't? But if we do, and with the Monach's permission, we stand to save not just our tribe but all the clans from the wrath of the Hag, resulting in our story being carved into a stone and kept with the tribe's treasures. This is important to Nereus. If I cannot give him children, I can give him a story that will last forever. We must find that dagger.

I need to vomit. I can't do this. I can't go into a tomb and take … take what exactly?

'How big is the dagger?' I ask Geros. 'If it's made of bronze, that's heavy. My axe is—'

'*Your* axe?' Kallisto asks.

'Yes. *My* axe.' We've had this out before. She thinks the decorative axe won't be mine until I have descendants to give it to. I disagree. It is mine until I die, whereupon *I* will bequeath it to my nephews. Kallisto argues that since they will inherit whatever is handed down from their parents, the axe should become the common property of the entire clan.

'You haven't explained the trade to her?' Kallisto says to Geros, a tight smile on her lips.

Geros closes his eyes, breathes a long exhalation through his nose and throws a scowl at Kallisto before saying, 'We need to trade the axe with Blackwater Ford.'

'What for?' I can't believe what I am hearing. The villagers look on, enthralled by the unfolding drama.

'Can't you sort that out when she gets back?' says Jaisun, running forward from the back.

'Don't worry, Jaisun. We'll sort this out.' Geros turns his back to the boy. Jaisun looks at me and shrugs before retreating, shaking his head.

'Zosime, your axe is needed in a village trade,' Geros says.

'You're giving away my axe?'

'It belongs to Seven Hills,' Kalisto says, feet planted wide, hands on hips.

'It's my inheritance.'

'She has no one to leave it to. We need a sow more than we need a decorative axe.'

'You're trading it for a *pig*?'

'The axe is just ceremonial. It's never used. It doesn't have magic powers. You can't eat an axe,' Kallisto says. 'We can expand the farm with this sow, grow more pigs from her, feed more people.'

'Huh! The lazy way of finding meat, keeping animals captive just to eat them, when we have hills full of wild boar and deer. There is plenty to eat out there – if you know how to hunt for it.'

'Right now, all that matters is finding the dagger,' Geros says. 'Zosime and Nereus will come to my quarters, and I will give them instructions to find it. Mela will finish the ceremony. But this can wait no longer.'

Aleka taps my arm and as I turn to her, she gazes at me with a furrowed brow.

'I believe in you.' She pulls me to her, and I inhale the scent of her hair, feel the press of her arms around my neck and feel the tears rise. I push the emotion away and let our affection and friendship soothe the aching crevasses of my heart.

'Thank you, my friend,' I say, then pull back and look her in the face. We smile at one another.

'Go, don't keep Geros waiting.' She lets go of me, and a cold breeze swoops in to replace the warmth of her body.

I fix my eyes on the ground and follow on Nereus's heels to Geros's quarters behind the reed curtains. His sleeping platform is gone to make up the stage in the centre of the Ceremonial Hall, and there is now more room for us three to sit on the sheepskins on the beaten clay floor by his hearth.

He gestures to Nereus and I to sit. The smell of human sweat and musty sheep mingle into an odour of childhood comfort. The fire is unlit. The days have been warm. Beyond the reed curtain, the rest of the Shortest Night Ceremony rumbles on without us.

'Geros,' I say with as much reverence as my anger allows. 'When were you going to tell me about trading my axe?'

'I have no song to teach you to make the way easy to remember. You will have to memorise the journey ahead, Zosime. Let us focus on that.'

'When is the trade taking place?'

'The day after tomorrow, but your axe will be of no consequence if the Hag is not beaten.'

'Surely it would help frighten off the Hag? It's made from the same—'

'You've asked this before, and my answer is the same. Moreover, it's not just about what it is made out of. The dagger is imbued with magical properties. Egil saw it work before now,' Geros says.

I frown and bite my lip.

'You doubt so much, daughter, and I know it's because you have a curious mind. Your curiosity is like water: too little, and your mind will dry up. Too much, and you will drown.'

'But—'

'Zosime,' Nereus says, taking my hand.

I try to wriggle it away, but he keeps a firm hold. I work hard not to appear churlish. I know Nereus depends on my respect for Geros to help me control my temper. I swallow hard.

It takes Geros a few moments to settle opposite us on the sheepskin. He groans with the bending of his limbs. I smell the fuggy scent of the animal fat he rubs into the skin at his heels and elbows, where it cracks and splits. He moves his head until the light from the door reaches his right hand, then sits with his eyes half shut as he concentrates on remembering the route.

'You need to learn the way and gather supplies, then go,' Geros begins. 'Do you need the rising sun to find the Orient?'

'I know where Orient is from here already.'

Nereus frowns. I think he worries that he won't learn the directions fast enough.

'To begin,' Geros says in the sing-song voice of storytelling, 'Orient by facing the rising sun and following your left hand to the sky where the sun does not go.'

My heart races. Geros tells us the directions as set pieces, leaving out none of the steps. We repeat the words several times, committing them to memory.

'Continue walking with the rising sun on your right.' Geros keeps his eyelids lowered.

Nereus squints in concentration.

'The trackway goes part of the way,' Geros continues. 'You're lucky. I remember when we didn't have it. The journey took twice as long.'

I'm stunned. I can't remember a time before the trackway. I've seen it being repaired. My father split the oak trees to replace rotten beams.

'Following the Noisy River to the Blackwater takes even longer – I know you know that way better, Zosime.' He looks up at me.

I nod. 'Hunting is good by the Noisy River.'

'You'll not need to hunt so soon,' Geros continues. 'Take the trackway to the ford over the Blackwater. Then follow its banks to the Sea-that-is-not-a-sea.'

We listen. We repeat.

'That's your first day's journey. You can camp there tomorrow night. Don't stay in a village. You don't have time to stay for the ritual welcome meal and don't want to insult them by refusing their hospitality. Besides, it's best not to tell anyone the purpose of your journey until you get permission from the Monarchs, in case they try to stop you.'

Nereus frowns and chews his lip. I imagine the directions scrambling around inside his head like blackbirds in a cage.

'We could make up another reason for our journey,' Nereus says.

'You're a horrible liar, Nereus,' I say. 'Geros is right – villages waste time. And we'd have to carry gifts, and we've no time to gather those or room to carry them. No, I usually avoid settlements when I hunt. Let's keep things simple.'

Geros nods and continues. After giving us time to repeat and learn each section, Geros covers the next set of instructions, which we commit to memory. Finally, Geros holds up a finger. 'Egil saw the dagger buried within the cairn that marks the great warrior's grave. The cairn is as tall as a man, with stones the size of a man's head. You will find it atop a hill, a half a day's journey along the biggest river. You will know it because this river leaves the Sea-that-is-not-a-sea.'

'A river *leaves* the sea?' I ask. I've visited Mountain Gap, or Gap as we call it, Nereus's village by the sea positioned in a gap in the mountains where they meet the sea. I spent a moon there the summer after we married. We walked the shoreline together, with me hunting on land and Nereus catching fish, which I had to kill for him. We laughed easily and often together in those days. 'I've never seen a river flow out of the sea unless the tides are rising. Is that what you mean?'

'There are no tides on this body of water. It is the Sea-that-is-*not*-a-sea. It is sweet water, like a lake, but you cannot see the far shore and this river flows *out* of it.' Geros finishes the directions, and we repeat them with a cadence that helps us keep them in our memory.

I lose track of time, but my stomach doesn't, and it grumbles while we recite. Eventually, my mouth seems to know the words without me having to think them.

It will take us four full days to reach the bronze dagger. And the same to return – if we're lucky. At least eight days away from the village, with my axe at the mercy of Kallisto. My heart sinks. I need to be back before my axe is traded.

Nereus is asking about the equipment we will need. I nod, only half following as I pick out the carved oak chests that store the clan's treasures next to Geros's sleeping area when the ceremony finishes.

'Pack, eat, then leave as soon as you can,' Geros says. 'Nereus, tell me the directions again.'

The chest with my axe has concentric circles carved into it. My axe will soon be packed away again, nestled inside and wrapped in leather. I peel my eyes away from it and focus on Nereus. He repeats the complete set of instructions once more without stopping. His eyes are glowing, and he sits taller.

The festivities move from the Ceremonial Hall outside to the fire as night falls. I smell the food and realise that I'm hungry. We'll eat and pack some of the feast to take with us. It grows quiet in Geros's quarters as we recite our instructions until Geros is happy we know the way.

'We won't let you down, Geros. We will find this dagger and defeat the Hag.' Nereus nods, convinced.

But I see too many holes in this reasoning. How do we know where and when the Hag will show up next? And if she does, how do we reach her? Is the sight of the dagger enough? Perhaps the lustre of the bronze will be enough to ward her off. I think again of the shine on my axe's head, and my heart fires up.

I'm not as sure as Nereus seems to be that we will find this dagger, but I do know one thing. I will not leave this village without my axe.

CHAPTER 7

'How…why are you here, Poppy?' my mother asks aloud, walking around the room straightening the things that have fallen during the tremor. I'm relieved that she is doing her best to believe in me, but I have no answer for her.

I just am. There may not be a reason.

'There has to be,' she says. 'Ha! Here I am asking you your purpose when I thought my purpose was to be your mother. But there must be a purpose to it, to all the—'

Pain… Loss… Longing?

She doesn't need to finish the sentence out loud.

I reach behind the gauze but can't connect with the other spirits. Have I been cast to this side alone now? Abandonment claws with arctic-blue talons. Being cut off from the Enlightenment feels askew and uncomfortable.

At birth, we transition slowly into the physical world. If I'd been born, I would have glided between both worlds for a time until I was comfortable enough to let go of the comprehensive knowledge we have on the spirit side. Then, if I'd lived, I would have been gently exposed to emotions. My enlightenment would have faded, and the need to learn and grow that the physical world demands would have blossomed in its place. But I'm not prepared for this swift untethering. I'm not used to having questions. Why am I here in this way? To what purpose? Does life need a purpose to fill this icy void? Maybe my mother is right. Maybe if I help her find purpose, I can connect to the other world where I am content. Perhaps that is my task.

I am always here. I never left you.

She squeezes her eyes shut, gasps short puffs of air.

'Really?' she says aloud. 'Dad, too?'

As she senses my affirmation, her muscles unclench, loosening a wash of buttery light in a sunrise.

We're here.

'Why can't I hear anyone else? Why don't they talk to me? To all of us? If I'm not imagining this, why can't people always do this?' She's at the sink in the bathroom, washing her hands and examining her palms for glass. There are a couple of scratches, but they aren't bleeding.

Remember Monday of last week when you were putting on your mascara? I give her a moment to draw up the memory. *Who did you think of?*

She looks at herself in the mirror of the bathroom cabinet. The corner of her mouth tweaks up as she remembers. 'I thought of Kate. She never left the house without her eyelashes done. Even when she was too ill to sit up, she needed her mascara on.' My mother's mind drifts back to sitting over coffee with her colleague, mentor and friend in the staff room at the school where they taught in Ireland before she'd moved to California. It felt like a lifetime ago to her now. 'Every time I put my mascara on, I think of her, but last Monday, I was filled with a nice sensation – like we were chatting over a cuppa the way we used to. I needed it. I was getting ready for that awful appointment to start my fertility treatment.'

*

The doctor's examination room had been over-chilled by the air-conditioning. My mother sat shivering in a disposable paper gown on the edge of the thin plastic-covered mattress of the bed. Her back ached from sitting still, feet dangling, but she didn't want to hop down and move around in case the doctor came in. Why that mattered, she didn't know. Wearing nothing but a pink gown that crackled when she moved left her feeling vulnerable. That and knowing she'd have to tell the doctor she was there because she'd lost me and wanted to have children, desperately wanted to be a mother. Admitting it felt like a failure already.

She wished she'd thought to lift her phone out of her bag. It would have given her something to pass the time. But she stayed where she was, perched on the bed, waiting. After a long twenty minutes, Dr Baker entered, head bent to the iPad he carried. My mother sat up straighter, a smile fixed in place, but the doctor didn't address her. He hummed tunelessly as he sat down, still reading the iPad.

'Is that tablet for your patients?' my mother asked.

He looked at her as if discovering her in his office by chance, then mumbled, 'Yes, indeed,' and delved back into the iPad.

She cringed inside and stashed this fresh embarrassment on top of the other indignities she knew would follow, chiding herself for even trying to engage him.

For several seconds, they sat there, her staring down through his thinning brown follicles, treated to shiny glimpses of his scalp, him oblivious to her scrutiny, humming away.

My mother imagined sharing this episode with Kate over coffee. She could almost hear Kate's throaty laugh as my mother described how lost in his head Dr Baker was. Kate got my mother's kooky sense of humour. She would have commiserated at how he'd failed to laugh at my mother's quip. They'd have fired up the puns and run with it for days. She could imagine Kate's face smiling. Her own smile had warmed from fixed to genuine by the time Dr Baker turned to her and said, 'So how are you today, Mrs Breen?'

*

'I felt like she was with me that day,' my mother says in a rush. 'As much as you are now. I think… Oh, I… God, I don't know. Oh, Poppy, I wish you could prove to me that you're really talking to me – that I'm not making you up.' Her longing engulfs me in a pewter haze.

She stops by the hall closet and lifts out the vacuum. She thinks of how she came home that day after the appointment and went to Kate's Facebook page, aching to be with her friend. There she found a short message from Adam, Kate's husband. The words still haunt her. Six months after his wife had died, Adam had written on her page, 'I miss you, Kate.' The thought of it still makes her want to weep.

'She's with Adam, too?' my mother asked.

Yes, she's always with anyone who's ever known her. Everyone you've ever known is with you, too, and more besides.

Her heart lifts in blooms of rosy pink.

'Even grumpy old Uncle Malcolm?'

Yes, him too.

'Good grief, that's a bit disconcerting… he was a right nasty old blighter.' She works her way around the Greatroom, broken glass clinking up through the vacuum hose.

He suffered terribly from arthritis. He was lonely. He didn't know how else to communicate with you, I tell her. From beyond the gauze, his spirit glows. I take strength from my reconnection – faint as it is; I can feel the other spirits when my mother thinks of them. It's like our combined effort amplifies my connection to them. I focus on Malcolm.

He had a good soul, and that's all that's left on this side. We leave the rest behind.

My mother nods, remembering an old man with a tweed cap and a stooped posture, bending to fill a bowl with water from a scratched plastic jug.

'He was so good to that Jack Russell of his. Pucker, he was called. I was sure he named him that to scandalise the wee old lady next door.' My mother's laugh is like a fireworks display that fades on the wind.

'I really needed Kate that day. I miss her so much.' Her longing radiates in mauve pulses.

She says you've no need to miss her. She says you need a new mascara.

Mauve blends to lavender swirls.

The sound of a car pulling into the driveway makes my mother drop everything and run to the front door.

'Ben!'

My father is out of the car and, in three strides, scoops my mother into a bear hug. She inhales the smell of his hair and registers the snug clench of his arms. She nuzzles against him before pulling away and asking, 'Are you okay?'

'Yes, you?'

She nods.

'The phone was cut off. All I heard was you saying that there was minor damage, and then the phone went dead.'

My mother realises he didn't hear her tell him that she'd been talking to me. She struggles to decide if she should revisit that. She sends me a thought. *Can he hear you?*

Dad?

He scrunches up his shoulders and shakes them loose.

My mother bites her bottom lip and searches his face. He kisses her furrowed brow.

'Don't worry, that was only a little shake.' His grin lifts her heart. 'By California standards. At least that's what the Californians keep telling me.'

'It was as big as I want to go,' she says, sliding her hand down his arm and grasping his fingers. She tugs at his hand and leads him into the house.

'Wow, I see what you mean,' he says. The axe head and geode lie on the hearth. Clean rectangles on the cream walls, where pictures used to be, make the rest of the wall look grimy. My father whistles through his teeth, shaking his head, then notices that my mother is pale and clammy. 'Are you okay?'

My mother drops his hand and runs her fingers through her hair, lifting it off her sweat-dampened neck. 'Don't freak out—'

'What is it?' His voice rises an octave.

'I said not to freak out, okay?'

'That's a surefire way to get me to freak out. Just tell me.' He searches her face, but she can't make eye contact.

'Poppy spoke to me,' she says. Her hands drift to cover her tummy.

Dad? I try again.

Hairs spring to standing at the nape of his neck. My father squints an eye and angles his head. 'Who?'

Dad, it's me, Poppy.

He doesn't hear me, but he rubs his neck.

My mother presses her lips together, dropping her gaze to her hands. 'Remember, our little Poppy Seed.'

He inhales sharply at the sting of red, raw grief.

It's okay.

Hope shines in my mother's eyes, but he can't hear me, at least not clearly. The hairs on his arms stand up now, and his scalp tingles. He shakes off a shiver, dousing me in a grey fog of despair.

'Aisling, are you alright?' he touches her chin, gently tipping her face up so he can see into her eyes.

'I know how it sounds. But our baby, she's talking to me—' A sob hiccups her words to a halt.

He pulls her into a hug and holds her, squashing her face to his chest. She listens to the pa-dub of his heart, torn between convincing him she's right and believing she's teetering on the edge of madness.

Talk to him, she says to me in her head.

I am.

He shivers again but interprets his reaction as worry about his wife's mental state. 'Aisling, this isn't good for you, for either of us.'

I'm sorry, she sends me.

I understand, I tell her and send my love to her in floods of turquoise.

Calmer, she relaxes against my father – my father, who cannot hear me but can sense my energy when I communicate, and it scares him.

'It's okay,' he says. 'It takes time to…' He clears his throat. 'You've had a shock. That was quite the shake. Are you hurt?' He holds her hands palm up and kisses the scratches and scrapes there. 'Do you need to see a doctor?'

My mother shakes her head, envisioning her own mother sitting vacant-eyed, curled in the foetal position in her chair in the dayroom of the care home. She knows she'll sound crazy if she persists in telling him about me. I know it, too. Besides, she isn't completely sold yet on the idea that it is me talking to her and not a disease preying on her mind.

I can't identify the emotions I feel. There are too many – all new. Colours blend, sharpen and merge too fast. I reach back to my ancestors but don't sense a communion with them. One colour intensifies from the melee – the slate grey of desolation.

*

My mother doesn't talk directly to me again while she makes and eats the evening meal. After dinner, she goes out to the garden to put the kitchen waste in the compost bin. She sets the small metal pail on the ground and kicks the side of the large black compost bin, then skips back, hoping the critters have scarpered. She's been startled by lizards on many occasions and is terrified that someday there'll be a snake in there. Tentatively, she flips the lid open and hops back.

'Did you feel the shake?' Andy calls from over the fence, making my mother jump. 'Sorry! Didn't mean to startle you.' Andy and Ruby are about the same age as my parents, and they have become friendly over the past five years as neighbours.

'You're okay,' my mother answers with an embarrassed laugh. She checks the bin to ensure it is clear before dumping the kitchen waste into it. A cloud of fruit flies lift into the evening air. 'We had some broken glass, and pictures fell off the wall. How about you?'

Andy huffs out a laugh and waves a hand. 'That was nothing! You shoulda been here in Eighty-Nine for the Loma Prieta earthquake. Now *that* was something to write home about.'

'I was nine and living in Northern Ireland,' my mother says. 'We'd more to worry about than earthquakes in California, believe me.'

'I was ten and terrified, but yeah, you win.' Andy holds up both hands. 'Do you want some zucchini? I got a basketful.'

'I can always use zucchini.' My mother reaches for the foot-long vegetable that Andy passes over the fence.

'Hang on. I have another one.' He bends down, disappearing from view, then pops up with two more.

'I think you're using me to offload this stuff,' she says, setting the three zucchini on the ground next to the metal pail. 'But I'll find some use for it. So, anything broken in your house?'

'A few bits and pieces. Great excuse to throw it out now. It'll kickstart the decluttering. Ruby will be delighted. Do you need glasses? I have boxes of crystal in the garage… at least I had.' He pulls a face, and my mother laughs. His garage is a treasure trove. He hasn't been able to park his car in his garage since he moved there eight years ago. Most of the boxes were never unpacked when they moved in with their newborn son, Toby. No point unpacking the delicate stuff with a baby in the house. Gwen arrived five years ago, and Rye two years ago. Ruby threatened to sell everything in a garage sale, but they never got around to it.

His sister got engaged, I tell her. *Ask about her.*

My parents met her when she'd visited recently from the East Coast.

'How's Jane?' My mother says aloud, and in her head, she asks me, *How do you know?*

We know all in the spirit world. It's the simple, if slightly inaccurate, answer.

'Great! The Beefcake proposed and she said, "Yes." So she's happy. And if she's happy, I'm happy.'

My mother is lost for words. Her head fills with wonder. She believes me, believes *in* me. Joy sparkles between us in golden flashes.

Oh, Poppy, she thinks, and her smile beams her happiness, which Andy attributes to his news.

'I should probably stop calling him Beefcake,' Andy says, filling the gap in the conversation. 'He's a hundred pounds soaking wet – one of those computer guys, all pale and skinny. You know the type? Squints in natural sunlight… But she loves him, and he's good to her, so… Anyway, let me know if you want those glasses.'

'Tell them congratulations from us.' My mother scrambles for composure. 'I'll do a stock check on the glasses, but I think you're just trying to fill up our garage now.'

'You won't get your citizenship until you can't park in yours, ya know!'

'We need to charge the car, so it's easier if we can park in the garage.' She says it the American way with two distinct syllables and softened at the end – 'gar aage'.

Andy shakes his head. 'You tree huggers! Those 'lectric cars are dangerous. One almost ran me down in the Safeway parking lot. Can't hear the darn thing coming.'

'Oh, but think of the carbon footprint.' She bends her knees, reaches down with her free hand, hooks the pail handle, and straightens up.

'You do know there's no point worrying about the greenhouse effect. Even if it did exist, all it'll take is a comet or an asteroid … ask Ben. Doesn't have to be that big.' Andy's eyes twinkle.

A memory of Uncle Malcolm referring to haemorrhoid cream as asteroid cream sets her aura radiating a warm orange.

'The greenhouse effect is very real, Andy – you're a gardener – you know how greenhouses work, right? It's shameful that we humans are causing it,' my mother says, batting the conversation deftly over the fence again.

'Or a supervolcano eruption,' Andy continues, sidestepping her point. 'That would end us. We're due one anytime now, so they say.'

'*They* say a lot of things.' My mother steps back from the fence.

'They sure do.' Andy mirrors her retreat. 'You tell that husband of yours to keep watching the skies now, ya hear!' He retreats inside, chuckling.

There's no point telling Andy that Ben only writes code for the Lick Observatory; he doesn't actually *look* at the stars. My mother hugs the zucchinis to her and smiles. A spectrum of pink through peach to warm orange radiates from her. She believes me.

Her aura is aglow as she steps in through the patio doors, her arms laden with what feels like five kilos of zucchini – or courgettes as she still thinks of them, though at this size, they'd be considered marrows back in Ireland. My father comes to help her as one slides off the top; he catches it just in time.

'So what was Andy saying?'

'Shhh, the window's open!' She drops her armful on the table.

'He's away inside,' my father says, clearing the table and helping my mother stack zucchini on the kitchen island. He leans against the island, folds his arms, then faces her. 'I'll bet he said that was only a small one, and you shoulda been here for the one in Eighty-Nine.'

'Yup. And his sister got engaged.' Her grin lights up my father. He reaches for her hand. She rolls in to lean against him. Contentment settles over them in a soft peach and cream haze. They savour the moment. I draw from it, too. The gauze thins, and I sense the spirits on the other side. Their strength oozes into me, and mine flows to them. I convey the peace I feel to my parents.

'Thanks,' my mother whispers.

'What for?' my father asks.

'Huh?'

She'd been talking to me.

'Thanks for—' She begins as he tips his head. 'For being here,' she says to both of us.

'Ah, sure, where else would I be?' He kisses the top of her head and then releases her to switch on the television before grabbing a can of root beer from the fridge and flopping down in front of the news. There's a report on the earthquake.

My mother settles in beside him on the sofa to watch. Her attention drifts to the axe head and the broken geode on the hearth. My father notices.

'I'll tidy this up.' He moves to the hearth and crouches, reaching for the axe head. As his hand connects, the three of us are ignited by an image flashing into our heads. It's the woman on the hill; her long black hair is flayed out behind her, and she's screaming: intense emotions of panic and fear blast in neon waves of violet and bright white.

My father drops the axe head, his mouth open in silent horror.

My mother recovers first. She dashes to his side and pulls him from the axe head but overbalances and plops down on her bum.

'What just happened?' he asks.

My mother looks at him from the side of her eyes. 'I don't know. What exactly do you mean?' She's afraid to admit she had a vision too. Added to her earlier claim of talking to her dead baby, it would sound crazy.

Tell her what you saw, I urge my father.

He jerks his head up, looks around him into the space above his head, almost as if he has heard my words in his head but doesn't comprehend where they are coming from.

Ask him to tell you what he saw, I tell my mother.

'Ben, it's okay.' She swallows hard. As the silence tightens around them, I realise she won't ask him. She thinks it's easier to pretend it never happened than to face having him deny it. She might have a point. His fear of the unknown is fast wiping the memory clear, erasing it.

You both saw the vision, I urge. *This might be your best opportunity to tell him.*

She draws a breath.

'Ben, listen.'

He locks eyes with her. Hope flares bright, but a flicker of muscle at the corners of his eyes, coupled with the tiniest shake of his head, sweeps that hope away.

'It's late, and we've had a rough day.' My mother is talking to both my father and me. I don't know how I know, but her energy is directed at me as much as her gaze is directed at him. 'Bedtime?'

I want them to revisit the vision. There's an urgency in me to find out what happened to the woman on the hill. I'm sure the woman there needs our help, but can't figure out why or how that is. But now I know the conduit for the visions.

If you touch the axe head, we'll see more, I tell them both.

No, my mother pushes back.

My father shivers and says, 'Someone just walked over my grave.'

Before she goes to bed, my mother puts on rubber gloves and tidies, puts the geode and the axe head on a shelf in the alcove to one side of the fireplace, still in view but not as prominent as before. My father notices but refuses to dwell on it, fear driving a wedge between what he saw and what he wants to discover. Like the geode and axe head, his curiosity is shelved, but my mother's blossoms, carrying her off to sleep thinking about the woman on the hill.

CHAPTER 8

Moonlight glimmers in the thatch of the village huts. Nereus and I watch from the shadows. I'm ready to bolt if anyone appears. My mind tumbles with excuses we could give for leaving our hut this late. Nereus fidgets. I dig him in the ribs and the air around us stills. Nereus glares at me. I grit my teeth and fling my gaze to the huts.

All is hushed, sleeping. What will Kallisto do when she finds out that the axe is gone? I'm pretty certain she set up the trade, and when the deal is broken, it will fall to her to explain why and strike a new deal.

'Do we *have* to steal the axe?' Nereus whispers.

Not this again! We've already spent too much time arguing about it as we gathered supplies for our journey. On top of the emotional exhaustion of the Shortest Night Ceremony, I'm shorter tempered with my husband than usual. But at least he's still my husband. He had nothing to declare at the pairing, nor did I. Kallisto skulked in the background and approached only to wish us well on our journey, saying she had to leave early to get Bion settled. I looked her in the eye and thanked her, keeping my plan to take the axe tucked away in my heart.

'It's not stealing,' I hiss. Why won't he listen to me instead of rehashing the same old argument?

'They need the livestock, too. What if we don't—'

'Shhh!'

For several heartbeats, I can't answer. I've held myself together so far by believing we will make it back to the village with the bronze dagger. We will save everyone, and everyone will be so happy that they will not care that we took a decorative axe. Ours will be a story to live long after us – a story everyone's children will tell.

Our people think because we have no children, no descendants, our story ends with us. The reality is that if no one carries on your story, no one remembers you. If no one remembers you, you never truly existed. If you don't exist, you don't need an inheritance.

That logic crushes me with grief and rage.

I want to know how a pig can be of more value to the village than a decorative axe — my axe — when the forests are full of wild pigs, yet there is only one axe?

I pray they don't punish Nereus. I love him. I do. He's a good man, strong and kind, even if he's as thick as leftover grain mash on a burnt-out fire.

'Wait here for me,' I say.

Nereus nods. I drop my deerskin wrap at his feet so it won't creak or rustle as I creep.

I run on tiptoes towards the Ceremonial Hall. Geros is half deaf, at least deaf to the sounds of this world. Yet he was roused easily by the alarm call earlier and was the first to climb the hill, so I need to be careful not to wake him.

'Zosime,' Nereus whisper-calls.

I ignore him and pray that he has the sense to shut up before he wakes the whole village.

Geros' quarters smell of the mint he chews to keep his stomach pains at bay. I lower the reeds behind me, plunging myself into blackness. In the time it takes me to swallow my fear, the blackness greys. My eyes adjust to the dim light. I listen, thankful that my ears are my own right now.

The rhythmic suck and push of air over lips comes from the corner. I can make out a dark lump on a platform against the wall. A glow in the fireplace winks from red to orange as the draft from my entrance fans the embers. Moonlight falls through the smoke hole and lies across the row of chests containing the village treasures, wrapped and stowed when not in use. I creep to the one with concentric circles carved on the outside and ease the lid off. The wood creaks and scrapes, making me flinch, but Geros's breathing remains steady as I slide my hand into the chest.

I know my axe. Its leather cover is sleek and sewn tight around the sharp head. Carved into its wooden handle is the story of my people's arrival on this island with six axes made from bronze that shines with the sun's brilliance. These axes helped them defeat the Fomorians, take this land from the demons in the sea and cut down trees to make shelter. The other five axes found homes in tribes in far-flung corners of this land, but one belonged to my grandmother's great-grandfather.

As I'm the eldest surviving child, it's mine, although it is held by Geros along with the other treasures of the tribe.

I know from watching him pack the axe away that Geros keeps it near the bottom. I crouch, trying to avoid the beam of moonlight. Sliding my hand into the pile, I feel under the soft hides that house the smooth gold discs of our tribe, the pinkish-grey soapstones that carry pictures of great battles, the wooden carvings that tell the story of my people's arrival on this island.

Geros snorts. I freeze – the muscles in my thighs quiver. Geros turns over. My heart judders in rhythm with my leg. Only when I hear the ebb and flow of his breath again do I move. I'm damp with sweat, legs cramping in my prolonged crouch, but my fingers find the handle. I ease the axe out of the box of treasures, coercing it around the other items until it is free.

As I squeeze back through the reed curtain, I look back at Geros lying with his face turned to me. His black charcoaled eye is like a hole in the white egg of his bald head. His eyes flash open. My heart ices over. I stand stock-still, my mind reeling.

'Follow the sky where the sun does not go,' Geros says softly, repeating his words from earlier like a mantra. 'Go beyond the sweet water that is as large as the ocean but is not the ocean, and find the river that flows the wrong way. The dagger is atop the highest hill.'

Frozen in place, I hardly breathe as Geros slowly stands, his joints cracking and popping into life. I could run, but he'd call upon the village to chase us down. I was hoping for the night to at least get a head start with the axe.

I could push him down, silence him with a crack to the head, but violence against Geros is not an option. I would rather die than hurt him.

'It's my birthright,' I say quietly.

'I know,' he says, walking over and standing to face me, the black charcoal around his left eye mirroring the circle I draw around my right eye.

'Take it.' Geros touches my right ear, the one where I hear the pop. 'You have the gift, and I know you will return.' He lowers his gaze to the axe in my hands. 'There may be greater worries than an axe in days to come. We both have journeys. But take heart. The stars whisper your story in circles that travel through time. Go well, child.' Geros lies back down as I struggle for something to say, then realise he needs no words from me. He seems to fall fast asleep in a beat.

My head swirls with riddles. I duck below the reeds, dash through the Ceremonial Hall and out the door, axe in hand, to my husband.

Nereus's face lights up when he sees me. A pit opens in my stomach, thinking of how he loves me and of how what I feel in return falls short. If we're caught with this axe and sent into exile, he'll lose more than I can bear to consider. Will we be banished as thieves? Or will finding the dagger exonerate us? And worse – what if the Monarchs don't grant us their permission? They'll turn us into their slaves or kill us. Or what if we don't find the dagger? I grab his hand and pull him into a jog beside me.

My heart squeezes at the prospect of never seeing the village again, of never slipping from our hut to my brother's to play with his children, to never smell the sweat from my baby nephew's hair as he sleeps in my arms while we adults chat around the fire. I chide myself for such maudlin thoughts. Surely, it won't come to exile.

We reach the meadow and keep our pace. Moonlight spills over us, silvering the sheen of sweat on our skin.

'At least it's not going to rain,' Nereus says, his words come in short bursts, staccato as he pants and gasps.

'My ears never lie,' I say with a flush of warmth for his optimism.

Nereus gives me a sideways glance. He is usually nervous when I talk about the sounds I hear inside my ears, those sounds that no one else can hear… except Geros. He claims they are the sounds from the other world.

Telling Geros was partly what got me into this, to begin with. He believes I am special, but I'm not sure that this variety of special appeals to me. Either it will rain or it won't, and I will know when. I will be prepared with an extra skin to gather the water, but it's not as if I have control of the sky to stop or start the water falling from it. *That* would be special.

*

I had seen ten summers when I first heard what I thought was a new bird in the forest. Its call came as a shrill pop, pop, pop. I searched the bushes; no need to look in the trees because the sound was never overhead, always hovering around at shoulder height. But I never saw the creature making the sound. It stayed to the right of me and moved as I moved. And always, it came before the rain. When the skies were blue, I heard nothing.

My mother feared that a spirit lodged in my ear. She took me to Geros and made me tell him what I heard.

'I hear sounds in my head, too,' he told us. 'Usually the high-pitched whine of wind in the treetops even on a still day. Many hear such invisible things. Sometimes, they feel dizzy. Do you get dizzy?'

I shook my head.

'Is it sound from other worlds or from the stars?' my mother asked. 'A message?'

'Perhaps.' Geros's eyes became sad. 'Little daughter, it may be a great gift you have, but such gifts require wide, strong shoulders,' he said. 'Let us see what develops.'

We left him, none the wiser.

*

Nereus doesn't like the connection I have with Geros, but that doesn't matter now.

Not everyone will feel like Geros does about my taking the axe. I hold it in my hand now and put my sack on one shoulder as we set off, travelling familiar paths to begin with, though that convenience will not last long. We put as much distance between ourselves and the village as we can.

Geros is the oldest person I have ever met, maybe the oldest in the world. He was old even when I was young. My mother could never recall him as young, and we guess he has seen as many as sixty summers, maybe more. And he knows so much. The village relies upon his knowledge and his comfort when life is ending, and we become stars.

When he said, 'The stars whisper your story in circles that travel through time,' was he referring to our ancestors sharing my story? I can unravel his riddles no better than I can understand the sounds in my ears.

I hear the pop, pop, pop, and then it rains – big deal. It rains a lot. If I stopped hearing the pop and it stopped raining, that would be nice on both counts, I figure. Geros says that life without rain is death. Many of the stories he tells are from ancient times and faraway lands where the rain stopped altogether. The plants died, the soil turned to dust and blew away, leaving only rocks. Those ancient people came here, Geros said, to find a place with rain. He warns us never to take our bounty for granted. I find it hard to believe we'd never have rain. It's always there, never far away. I wonder what our land would look like without the rain. Barren, Geros called it.

Barren is what the villagers have started to call me, too.

I used to take for granted the baby animals that appear each year. Seeds sprout on tilled soil with little effort. The Sun God times all with the cycle of the year.

I couldn't imagine how nothing would grow until I failed to make my own babies grow, and they left my body too soon. The first time it happened, I was tracking a buck of at least two summers. The forest was in full leaf. I remember thinking how clear my ears were as I listened to the birdsong. Life pulsated from every quarter. It made my spirits soar, but my body tired.

I lost sight of the buck and stopped to take some water. A spasm in my lower belly bent me double. The pain ripped into my back, making me weak. I dropped to my knees. Then I heard the pat-pat of drops landing on the forest floor. Blood dripped from my leg coverings. Grief crashed down so hard I couldn't rise. I limped back to the village and lay unmoving in my hut for days. Loss of blood made my body weak, but the sorrow in Nereus's eyes pinned me down for longer.

Barren is a hard place to be.

*

We travel quickly to begin. It's easy terrain following the wooden trackways, and pre-dawn, there are no other travellers to avoid. The sun creeps smoothly over the horizon into a cloudless sky. Nereus walks smiling, his mood lifting mine a little.

'What is making you so happy right now?' I ask.

'It's a glorious morning.' He lifts his hands up above his head, arms wide as if embracing the sky. 'Look at the sun, at the colours of the trees. Hear the birds, the river. It's just good to have this purpose, to be here with you.'

His simple outlook is so earnest, so pure, I feel tears prickle my eyes and I look away. I won't spoil this moment for him. He may as well feel good about the task for as long as he can. I swallow and find my voice again. 'I'm glad to be here with you, too. Thank you.'

'Thank me? What for?'

I shrug. Nereus puts an arm around my shoulder and squeezes me to him.

Ahead, off the trackway, leaves shiver, though there isn't a breath of wind. I stop our walk with the flick of one hand and pull an arrow with the other.

Nereus frowns but freezes.

A young buck noses onto the trackway twenty feet from us. I place the arrow in the bow with silent fluidity. Nereus places a hand on my elbow, shakes his head, pleads with his eyes.

He's right. We don't need the meat and can't carry it.

'Fine.'

The buck startles at my voice and crashes off into the undergrowth.

'Ah, we could have watched him for a while,' Nereus says.

I shake my head. 'We have to get going. It's easy now, but once we leave the trackway, we will be slower.'

'I'm looking forward to seeing new places,' Nereus says. 'Aren't you?'

'I'm curious, yes. But a bit scared about the tomb.'

Nereus chews his lip, and I'm sorry I mentioned it, but he nods and says, 'We don't have to worry about that until tomorrow, or the next day.'

'What if the Hag comes back?'

'Let's worry about that when she does.'

I see what he's doing. He's twisting my hunting philosophy – don't worry about the kill until you find the prey.

'So today we cover as much ground as we can and enjoy the sunshine?'

'I think that's a good idea,' he says, smiling.

I tuck the moment away with the feeling I will need to revisit it sometime in the future. When we leave the trackway, Nereus is in territory new to him but, for the first while, familiar to me. I point out the places along the way that feature in our hunting stories. The rocks where Con slipped and ended up in the river. The log that Yani tripped over chasing the boar. The bushes with berries that are delicious in the autumn. We don't look any farther forward than that day for as long as the day lasts.

At the end of the first day's walk, we see a large body of water from a treeless hill. It stretches and disappears without meeting land. I'm used to seeing lakes, seeing their edges curve, seeing the entirety of them, but this body of water is vast, like the ocean, with no far banks in sight.

'It's beautiful – more gentle than the sea,' I say, looking over the waves kissing the edges.

'I've seen the sea this calm,' Nereus says. 'You've only visited it a couple of times, and those times I brought you to my parent's home at the coast, the sea was angry; but it can be just like this, too. But it smells different, don't you think?'

I nod. 'If this water does not taste of tears, then we have come the right way, and we simply follow, keeping it on our right.'

Nerues scans the landscape. 'People must live nearby – someone keeps this hilltop clear for animals and crops. We better keep moving.'

We don't linger longer than we need to get our bearings. From this point on, other people can mean danger. We let strangers move unhindered through our land, provided they don't linger or hunt large game. 'The traveller's share,' we call it. We also expect them to spend an evening by the fire, exchanging news and information for provisions.

Our village may send a search party. At least we have a day's head start since the trader from the other village is not due to arrive until the next day. When Kallisto discovers the axe missing, she will not stay idle. She hates that I am a better hunter than she is. That's why she has turned to the new way – farming. But we've been rivals since we were old enough to run, so she'll set out after us. But she won't have the directions unless Geros gives them to her. I'm hoping he won't. I'm hoping he'll already have left for the Great Mound and not mention having seen me take the axe. But I can't be sure of what he will do.

The water is pure but not as sweet as promised in Geros's prediction. In deeper sections, it has a hint of the colour of an autumn leaf. It's a good feeling to be in the right place and know that Geros's instructions are accurate, though it is late. I'm grateful that the sun is taking so long to travel the sky. We sleep curled together in the hollow beneath a fallen oak trunk near the banks of the Black Water River, where it meets the bigger body of water. My ear is quiet, so I know we'll be safe from rising water in case the rivers flood; and we're high enough if there are tides in the same way the sea rises and falls each day.

In the morning, we eat cold grain mash, swatting away biting insects. We slept, but I still feel tired, irritable.

'We can head inland,' I say, pointing to a rise in the land in the distance. 'We can see the water easily from up there and we'll be able to follow Geros's instructions so long as we can see the water's edge.'

Nereus shrugs, mouth full.

'And we can catch fish now to take with us.' I glance at the sack of food, lighter now.

'You can.' Nereus pulls a face. 'I hate killing them.'

That man would starve without me.

I wander to a glassy eddy, off the main rush of the stream. The woman who looks up at me from the surface is pale and sad. I break the image, scoop a handful of water to my face and scrub. Black drips on my palms. I dash water on my skin until the drops run clear. I dry off using with my long black hair, then wind it up in a knot at the back of my head and feel it tickle between my shoulder blades.

'You're not going to stay like that?' Nereus touches a hand to his eye as if checking the charcoal is still on his own face.

'Why not?' I feel rebellious, pleased that I've scandalised my husband. 'We have no more charcoal, and besides, we are no longer Parthalon's people. They made us *leave.*'

'They didn't exactly *make* us leave.' Nereus sighs. 'And we *are* going back.' He's as tired of this now as I was a day ago, but I'm angry – this time at myself.

'You didn't have to come with me,' I say, and the double-take in his expression gives me twisted satisfaction. I've caught him off guard. 'At the Shortest Night Ceremony – you could have left. I can't have children, but perhaps you can. No one would have blamed you if you'd stayed to prove them right. I didn't fit in, but you could have… had someone to tell your story.'

'Stop!' He holds up both hands as if to push me away, warding off the thoughts that surely he must have already had. Or perhaps not – I'm the one who thinks too much. I'm not sure if Nereus thinks at all.

I turn back to the pool. The ripples flatten. My reflection floats, stretching and reshaping.

'There's time for you to go back,' I say softly. 'I'll find the bronze dagger and bring it back. Maybe you could plead on my behalf if they are angry about the axe.' My hand caresses the handle of my axe where it hangs from my belt.

'Don't be angry, Zosime. You only hurt yourself.' Nereus steps up beside me and strokes my back. 'I am here because I love you. Without you, there is no story worth telling.'

His words steal my voice. Tears burn my throat. I have seen many souls leave for the horizon, but the flames of my anguish over my invisible loss still lick hard and hot. Waves of sorrow rock me as I cling to Nereus. My nose runs, and the pop-pop-pop begins in my right ear.

Nereus steers me by my shoulders to face him. 'It is bad luck to stop wearing the mark of Parthalon,' he says, wiping his thumbs across my cheeks. 'You look like a little girl again.' He kisses my nose. I nuzzle into the warmth of his chest. His kindness pares away the irritation I've felt towards him since we left – the irritation, a result, I realise, of my anger with myself.

I twist back to look in the pool and see myself clean-faced and symmetrical. Nereus's charcoal is smudged. It could do with a touch up, but I don't tell him. It's going to rain soon, and that will make it worse.

'I'll put the mark back on when I need to,' I promise as the first spits of rain land.

CHAPTER 9

My mother stares out the window at the mockingbirds on her fence. The day before, she was sure she heard the raw squawk of a chick in a nest somewhere in the trees at the bottom of the garden. This morning, she found it eviscerated on the gravel at the base of her crepe myrtle. A sprinkle of pink blossoms covered the scaldy's body, a seemingly respectful token from Mother Nature if you could ignore the scavenging ants crawling over the once moist eye sockets and into the gaping yellow beak. The bird's death brought tears to my mother's eyes.

'Life is such a struggle, Poppy. It's a wonder anything gets born or manages to survive at all,' she'd whispered.

She's lost in thought, watching the birds, missing her mother, wishing she could talk to Kate when her phone rings and makes her jump. She answers the call from her brother when she sees the caller id.

'It's bucketing here,' Jack tells my mother. 'So much rain! It's bloody August, for God's sake, but the Callan burst its banks last night. We put the wellies on us and headed down the back field to have a look. D'you remember Dad used to do that?'

My grandfather's spirit glows. My mother's aura brightens and extends with the memory, almost touching that of my grandfather. She listens to her brother describe the drama of the walk to see the flooded fields. He missed the earthquake reports, and she has played it down because her brother would insist it's dangerous in California and urge her to come home.

'How's Mum?' she asks. Her aura retracts into a sky-blue outline, hugging close to her body.

'She's had a good week. The home says the new medication helps her sleep better.'

'Has she been asking for me?'

'No.'

'Okay. Well, that's good.'

'Aisling, I'm sorry.'

'No, really, it *is* good. If she doesn't ask about me, she isn't missing me, and she's not sad then. It's worse when she's asking for me, or Dad, or for her mum.'

'I know, I know,' Jack says, adding in a rush.

In flashes of scorched amber, my mother remembers that day six years ago when she told her mother about moving to San Jose with Ben, as newlyweds. It was one of the last fully lucid times Catherine, my grandmother, experienced before drifting into a pocket of space between worlds, her spirit straining against the flesh, trapped her in her mortal body.

'Go to California,' Catherine had urged. 'With my blessing. No one can tell the future, and you don't want to miss *any* opportunities – life's too short. Please, don't stay here for me. I love you too much to stop you from living as full a life as you can.'

But guilt still ravages my mother in tumbling billows of grey. She swallows hard to find her voice. 'I know she loves me.' She clears her throat. 'How are Emily and Fiona?'

Speaking their names lifts her aura to a light shade of blue.

'Great. Disappointed they didn't get a day off school because of the floods, but fine otherwise.'

'And Maureen?' My mother's aura dulls a shade at the mention of her sister-in-law.

'Grand, grand.'

Jack doesn't seem to be in the mood for sharing so instead asks after Ben. My mother decides against telling him about me. She hadn't told her brother about the pregnancy before the miscarriage happened, and as the months passed, it became more difficult. Would he think she had inherited her mother's early-onset dementia? She can't find the words to make it sound less crazy. She shuts me out too by not sending her thoughts directly to me. And though I still know her thoughts, I also know she has disengaged from me. From the other realm, the ancestors send me a warmth I feel less and less as time on this side of the veil goes on. I take comfort in sensing their presence despite how faint it is becoming.

There's a commotion in the background on Jack's end, high-pitched squealing through the phone.

'Sorry, Aisling, they're killing each other here! Gotta go.'

My mother hears Jack roaring, 'Stop pulling her hair—' before the line goes silent.

It makes her smile. He sounds so like her dad when he used to yell at them as kids. It must be a parent thing.

Would I have sounded like my mum if I shouted at you? she asks me in her head.

She has taken to surprising me with questions like this, puncturing long stretches of silence between us over the past couple of months.

Her home feels so empty compared to Jack's, with his girls squealing in the background.

In her garden, the mockingbirds squabble, flitting from the fence to the trees and back.

'Is your nest empty now, too?' my mother asks with a sigh.

She tries to fill her days, weeks, months with purpose, gardening, going to doctor's appointments, getting on with life. Chatting with her nieces on the telephone is a highlight. She yearns to travel back to Ireland to see them, but after seeing Dr Baker post-miscarriage, my parents began fertility treatment, and he advised against long-haul flights. She feels trapped in California as the blistering summer months roll into an equally hot and disappointingly rain-free autumn.

My mother can only think about one thing now – getting pregnant again. She believes she needs to be stress-free which includes her not engaging with me. I flutter in the fringes of her thoughts, like a butterfly batting at a window pane, caught in limbo.

The air-conditioning in Dr Baker's waiting room tightens my mother's skin into bumps. She rubs her hands up her bare arms and wishes she had thrown a cardigan over her shoulders but is grateful she and Ben are the only people here. She hates sharing the waiting room with other women. The sad-eyed, non-pregnant women bury their faces in magazines, while those with baby bumps seem to glow and look around with a smug satisfaction my mother longs to slap off their faces. She's long past worrying about these violent thoughts simmering over the low heat of an anger that has never quite petered out since the miscarriage four months ago.

She leans against my father, and he takes her hand. His other hand holds his phone, where he loses himself in an online article about the drought.

My mother feels pregnant – more so during this excruciating two-week wait than the previous times. Her breasts are tender, she tires easily, and she is convinced she's been feeling queasy in the mornings before a simple breakfast of tea and toast settles her stomach. But her rosy joy is laced cinnamon with fear.

This is the third round of intrauterine insemination, or 'artificial' insemination, as my dad calls it. Either way, the very name of the procedure makes her feel like one of Uncle Malcolm's heifers. Three months of Clomid – with timed intercourse, which just about ruined their sex life – has wreaked havoc with her hormones. Her mood swings have her dancing on the edge of sanity. Her conversations with me are sporadic. I know that for the sake of her mental health, I need to stay quiet and only speak to her when she asks me a direct question.

She edges her phone out of her pocket with her free hand and pulls up the photo she found online of newborn twins swaddled in a blanket and lying on a sheepskin rug.

Aren't they beautiful? she asks me now.

They're perfect.

Can you sense any souls in the before-life spirit world?

I'm sorry, I can only see the souls in the afterlife now. We've had this conversation a few times already in one shape or another. She seems to think if she phrases the question differently, she might get an answer she's happy with.

But you said the spirits were 'all-knowing' – don't you know how big our family will be?

I can't foretell the future. I don't mention that my 'all-knowingness' is fading, much as it does between physical birth and a child starting to talk.

My mother's frustration fizzles fluorescent green interspersed with pops of grey despair and bright silver flares of hope.

'What's wrong?' My father notices her frown.

She startles at his voice and almost drops her phone. 'Nothing.' She catches him looking at the twins on the screen. 'It's positive visualisation.' She switches off the screen and folds her arms.

'Whatever gets you through.' He kisses the top of her head. 'But you know I'll be happy with whatever comes along.'

'Me, too.' She smiles, but her feet and hands twitch. She needs to pee – she's been saving her first urine of the day to make sure she has the best possible sample for the pregnancy test.

It feels like hours to her before a nurse appears at the door and calls their name. My mother jumps up and makes it across the waiting area in three strides.

'Good morning, Mrs Breen. How are you?' The nurse has a soft voice that sounds caring but only irritates my mother with its professional insincerity.

'Good.' My mother forces a smile.

'We just need a sample.' The nurse nods at the toilet door, which opens directly off the waiting room, and a deadweight drops in my mother's stomach. She has a fear of the door opening while she's mid-flow and presenting her sitting on the loo to a room full of patients.

A noise at the main entrance grabs her attention. A burst of sunlight precedes a woman's entrance, backlighting her and casting her in silhouette. She's dressed in a sloppy tee, jeans and flip-flops and has her head down, rifling through a large handbag. The door bangs closed behind her, plunging them into the relative gloom from the tinted windows.

The woman looks up and catches my mother's eye at the same moment as the nurse hands the sample tub to my mother. Everyone knows what that tub is for.

'Set this in the hatch when you're done. Make sure to close the hatch and go back to the waiting area to be called for the results,' the nurse says, unfazed by my mother's beetroot cheeks.

'Thanks,' my mother mutters and heads to the toilet.

The door handle locks by lifting it. My mother checks twice that it's in the correct position but can't test to see if the locking mechanism works because it opens if she pulls down on it.

She pees into the tub, making sure to give the sample from mid-stream, which requires a lot of dexterity and well-honed abdominal muscles. Some pee splashes on her hand. Once, this would have grossed her out, but she's grown so used to collecting samples it doesn't bother her anymore. She's proud she's no longer so squeamish, considering it good practice for changing nappies.

My mother holds the tub in one hand as she wipes with the other, discards the toilet paper and reaches for the lid, balancing on top of the toilet roll dispenser.

The handle on the door rattles, making her jump. Her hand clenches. The tub pops up out from her grasp and lands upside down on the floor. The linoleum is saggy and uneven with age, so that her urine settles in three distinct puddles.

'Shit shit shit!'

The door handle jiggles again, this time more violently. A child's voice whines, 'Mommy, it's *locked*. I need to *go*.'

The handle rattles, holds, rattles again, and mercifully stays locked.

'Just a second!' My mother holds the tub below her and tries to relax, tries to squeeze out a few more drops, but now she has stage fright and is peed out. She can hear the child breathing on the other side of the door.

The two-week wait for this appointment has been unbearable. Dr Baker warned her not to do a test at home. Something to do with Clomid interfering with the result. But she can't wait another day, another hour, another moment. She pulls up her underwear, then scoops the largest puddle of urine into the tub and holds it up. There are at least two tablespoons in the tub – enough for a test. She sets the tub in the hatch, mops up the rest of the spilt pee, and washes her hands before exiting to sit with Ben and wait until they are called.

The kid is gone. Three women and Ben sit in the waiting room. She's dying to tell Ben what happened but is afraid the women will overhear. Anyway, she reckons Ben would tell her to wait until the next day and try again, and she can't do that. She has to know now.

Dr Baker's eyes are fixed on his computer screen as they enter. The nurse shows them to their seats and leaves. My father rests his hand on my mother's shoulder. Anxiety shimmers off them in magenta pulses, his slightly darker, merging with her neon tones.

Dr Baker hums as he reads the screen. Eventually, he pushes back from the desk and presses his fingertips together as he turns to them.

'So, the pregnancy test has come back negative.'

'I dropped the sample,' my mother says, sitting forward.

'Excuse me?' Dr Baker pulls his head back and raises his eyebrows.

'It spilt on the floor, and I – I couldn't do any more, so I scooped it up.'

My father bites his lower lip, but my mother can't read his reaction. She continues, 'Would that have affected the result?'

Dr Baker tilts his head to one side, and his gaze drifts over my mother's head. He narrows his eyes and shakes his head. 'It probably wouldn't. If HCG is present, the hormone produced by the placenta which we use to determine if there is a pregnancy, the test will detect it. In fact, I'd be more concerned that the sample was contaminated with someone else's HCG and giving you a false positive. But a false negative, at this time, is unlikely. We can check with a blood test if you like.'

'Will that cost more?' my father asks.

My mother stiffens. Their insurance is not covering the fertility treatment, and the cost is piling up.

'Yes, it's more expensive than a urine test. But it's also more accurate, and we can look at it qualitatively as well as quantitatively.'

My mother isn't sure what that means, but the idea of more accuracy appeals.

'Ben, let's do it. Please. I really think this is it.'

'And if it's not?' my father asks.

Desolation drops over my mother like a leaden cloak, bowing her head and dragging her shoulders forward.

My father clamps his lips tight together.

Dr Baker taps his keyboard, humming again, then sits back and says, 'I see here this is your sixth round of Clomid. The last three have been with IUI. If the blood test comes back negative, we can do another round with IUI.'

'What about IVF?' my mother says.

'It's a lot more expensive than IUI,' Dr Baker says.

'But the IUI hasn't worked,' my father says.

'As far as we know.' My mother catches my father's gaze and holds it with pleading eyes.

My father nods. He doesn't want her to think he's being negative, but he reckons if the test hasn't picked up the pregnancy hormone, then it wasn't there to begin with, spill or no spill. He knows that my mother will be heartbroken at the news…again, and it is wearing him down. 'Yes, hypothetically speaking, then *if* the blood test comes back negative, why waste more money on IUI. Can we go straight to IVF now?'

'Well, hypothetically speaking, yes, you could, but I would recommend another three rounds of IUI. We've had great results at this clinic.' Dr Baker waves a hand at the corkboard on the walls filled from edge to edge with photos of babies, interspersed with thank you cards.

My mother squashes the urge to rip the pictures into shreds. She doesn't care about these strangers' babies. She wants her own.

I love you, she sends a thought to me, *but I want a baby to hold, to smell, to hear giggle, to warm my lap. I want to be a mother in the fullest sense.*

I understand, I tell her. I'll never be enough for her now, and the thought slices me with ice-blue shards. This world has no place for a spirit with no flesh. I realise that my mother feels something similar – that her world has no place for mothers with no babies.

'Dr Baker, when I first came to you after my miscarriage, you told me that at forty, I didn't have a single month to lose. Why now are you telling me that a few more months of a treatment that has not worked will suddenly work?'

'Perhaps we should talk about this after we get the results of your blood test tomorrow.'

'Tomorrow?' my mother asks.

'Yes. We need to send it off to the labs, but it will be back in twenty-four hours.'

My mother groans. *Can't you sense if I'm pregnant?*

No, I can't tell if there is a spirit moving into the physical world or not.

I sense a swell of purple anger against me, against my futile presence here, and I counter with my own rising tide of grey-blue sorrow and frustration.

'So can we decide that we'll move to the next phase if the test is negative?' my father says.

'Well, let's wait and see what—'

'No,' my father cuts Dr Baker off. 'She's either pregnant, or she's not. If she isn't, I think three more rounds of IUIs would be a waste of our money. We need to go ahead with IVF.'

My mother nods vigorously, grateful to my father for cutting through Dr Baker's crap. She's been feeling strung along by him for the last six months, always being told to wait and see. She can't stand it any longer.

'As I say, our success rates—'

'IVF has a higher success rate than IUI,' my father says. 'I'm sure I read that.'

'Yes, Mr Breen, but here we do have higher than average—'

'I think we need to move to the next stage. Aisling?'

My mother nods.

'Well, if you're certain.' Dr Baker swallows.

'We are,' my parents reply.

'You'd have to go to a different clinic,' Dr Baker says. 'We don't do IVF here.'

'Ha! So that's why you've been stalling us.' My mother stands up. 'You'd rather milk another three months of IUI payments from us than let us get on with IVF.' Purple pulsing anger makes her voice shake. 'Give me the note for the blood test, and we'll be on our way.'

As they leave, they hear Dr Baker say, 'Perhaps we'll see you tomorrow if the results come back positive?'

Neither of my parents replies.

In strong words, my father arranges with the receptionist for the results to be given to us over the phone as he pays the bill, pointing out that this consultation cost him a hundred and fifty bucks, though there was no point to it. The insurance is not covering it, and surely a quick phone call would be a more economical way to go. He implies that he'll go elsewhere, hoping she's not aware of the conversation they had with Dr Baker and doesn't realise that they intend to leave the practice anyway.

Meanwhile, my mother nips next door to the onsite phlebotomist, who is gentle and reassuring as she draws her blood, and it restores my mother's optimism.

The next day the blood tests come back negative.

My mother cries as she searches online for the best IVF clinic within driving distance of their home. She doesn't connect with me at all. Although the ancestors shimmer faintly from the other place, I cannot return to them, nor can I comfort my mother; her bitter disappointment is a neon yellow, impenetrable shield.

CHAPTER 10

On our third day of travel, we come close to another settlement. We stay among the trees like ghosts and move with the silence of hunters. Summer holds the sun high. We don't need a fire. I don't replace the charcoal around my eye. Nereus's mark fades as the day goes on, so he looks younger.

We keep going – facing away from the sun at its highest point. Over these last two days, we've come to many rivers. Some are forded, others wadable, and one or two we need to swim across. Each of these bigger ones make me think they might be the one Geros mentioned, but they flow *into* the larger body of water called the Sea-that-is-not-the-sea, not from it. So, we push on through the day, at one point catching a glimpse of the Maiden on the horizon where the sun never goes. Although we don't see the Hag, the presence of the Maiden quickens our pace.

On the fourth morning after leaving our village, we see the biggest river we have come across yet. Its sluggish eddies curl into reed-lined banks on one side and whisper over shingle beaches on the other. A smooth expanse down the centre of the waterway tells of deep, strongly flowing currents. We've kept to higher ground to get the lay of the land. I raise my hand against the early morning sun and see the banks of the Sea-that-is-not-the-sea leading in that direction. Slicing away from the larger body of water is the river; and as I follow it, snaking across the landscape, I feel the sun's heat on my right shoulder.

'This better be it,' Nereus says. 'It looks difficult to cross.'

By the time we climb down to the shore, the sun warms my back as we follow the direction of the flow of the river, coming out of the big body of water. My heart quickens.

'It is as Geros predicted,' I say, breathless with excitement. 'I didn't think a river like this could exist. The streams always flow into our lakes. But this…' I wave a hand and grin at Nereus, who swivels on one heel to face me.

' …is a lake?' he says.

'I suppose. A Sea-that-is-not-a-sea. Who gives these things names?'

His eyes crinkle in a squinted smile as he looks down at me. 'If Geros's instructions are this accurate, then perhaps it is possible—'

'– to find the bronze dagger.'

He scoops me up and swings me around, planting a kiss on my lips that sears, hot as the sun. We sink into the heather and celebrate the rush with mutual fire.

My senses infuse with Nereus, his musky scent, the taste of salt on warm skin, his touch – tender giving way to urgent. Our bodies surge together. Our life forces entwine, stretching against the confines of our flesh, breaking free in glorious ecstasy.

In the contented sighs that follow, we lie facing each other, tracing each other's profiles with gentle kisses. Despite our past failures, I wonder if this is the time I'll prove fertile. The hope never truly dies. Each time, it ignites with a sweet longing that blisters.

As if reading my mind, Nereus's hand drifts to my belly. I feel the heat there, and my throat constricts. I sit up, push him away and say, 'Let's go.' I walk off, wincing at his slow sigh. No matter how hard I try, I cannot be what he needs nor give him what he wants. Anger fuels my pace.

Nereus trots up behind me. We continue in silence.

No pops sound in my ears as we make our way along the riverbank. Behind us, the sun climbs into a clear, blue sky. The banks are muddy and ensnared with brambles and willow, but the Sea-that-is-not-the-sea is so large we can walk a distance from the edge without losing sight of it. And we can avoid the other small settlements perched on higher ground. From this height, we can see the river flowing straight into the sunless horizon.

Follow the sky where the sun does not go.

The air is thick with the buzz of insects. We wrap our clothing around our exposed skin to prevent bites. Underfoot slurps and plops as we wade through mud, slowing our progress, and we leave the Sea-that-is-not-the-sea behind us.

We walk downriver all morning until the sun reaches its height. I catch a fish for our evening meal. Scanning the hilltops for a cairn, we move more slowly, afraid of missing the tomb.

Nereus points out the highest hill. 'I think I see something up there.'

I see a bump outlined against blue sky, but it's hard to tell if it's manmade or part of the hill.

'Geros said the highest hill,' Nereus says. 'He's been right about everything so far. I think this is it.'

We climb to higher ground, keeping sight of the river. Ahead, across a clearing, the trees grow tall and the understory dark. It looks like people used to graze livestock in this clearing, but the soil grew sour. Now, nothing grows.

The mound atop the hill is clearer now.

'It's a cairn,' I say.

'I see that. But it looks like quite a distance to go yet. Maybe we should rest and get to the cairn first thing in the morning.'

'I agree. There'll be very little shelter up there.' What I don't say is that I'd prefer not to sleep by a tomb.

We make camp early beneath a deep blue sky. The sun begins to slide towards the horizon, but at this time of year, it will be a while before it changes colour to match our campfire. When it does, we will extinguish our fire. No one cares about smoke during the day unless it is close to where they live – but a fire at night draws attention.

'We've been lucky,' Nereus says. 'It's easier not to have to explain our travels to the settlements. It's good they stay so high up the hills.'

'I think this river swells often,' I say, nodding at the black mud caked on my leg wrappings.

'I believe we will find the dagger,' Nereus says, looking at the hilltop. 'But I wonder if Geros has gotten permission.'

'I wonder how high the water gets.' I scan the hills and see the forests grow thick along the lower contours of the hill.

'Maybe the Monarchs won't be that particular.' Nereus is used to answering his own questions. 'It's in their interests, too.'

'What?'

'Well, surely the Monarchs want to be saved? The Hag would destroy all of us, by Geros's account.'

I shrug. Geros's account was, I think, vaguer, but it still did not sound pleasant.

A piercing fizzle like wood sap burning makes me look at the fire. I see no leaping flames, nor sparks, not even smoke. A roar overhead draws my eyes up.

Nereus looks up too, so I know it's not my ears.

'Gods preserve us!' he hisses. 'The Hag's attacking the sun!'

High above us, a fireball travels through the air. It splits the sky in two, leaving a trail of billowing white smoke.

'But the sun's over there.' I point, flinching as the sky rumbles and cracks with brittle pops and high-pitched sizzling.

Fear skitters through my chest, making me short of breath. Stunned, hands shading our brows, we track the fireball's trail until it disappears over the sunless horizon, leaving a smoky rip along the sky. Has the Hag torn the world open? Will the sky fall in? Is it a falling star?

'What was that?'

Before Nereus can answer me, a boom thunders through the air. The din hits me in the chest, passing through my flesh and bones like it could separate me from my skin. Staggering back, I grab my husband. We collapse to our knees, cowering and clutching each other as a grey cloud swells on the horizon where the fireball disappeared. The cloud grows and spreads. Hues of mauve edge the bulging bloom. Lower towards the horizon, orange and purple churn and blend as the cloud chugs upwards.

Inside my head, the pop, pop, pop begins, paced and certain. There are no rain clouds, but there is that monster cloud on the horizon. Rain will fill this river and make it flood.

'We need to go higher,' I say, standing up and dragging Nereus to his feet.

'What? Why?' The look on his face irritates me, but I force myself to be kind. He's as scared as I am.

'It's going to rain.'

Nereus nods, mute, and turns back to kick dirt over the fire.

'It's safe,' I say. 'Leave it.' I grab my axe and go up the hill. Nereus soon overtakes me. The gradient is gentle, and I'm able to trot to keep up with Nereus. The giant cloud hangs in the sky. It looks as far away as the sun. As I stare, the swirling edges tug and blend across blue sky, and the blaze of the sun dims.

I think the cloud is closer than the sun, like any other cloud, yet there is something different about this one. It billows like smoke from a fire but on a scale I cannot fathom. Eventually, the gradient tips and my breaths shorten as we gain height. On a ridge directly above us, I spot a cluster of huts.

Should we try to divert around this settlement? Surely, they are used to this river in full spate, so we'll be safe enough if we get to that height. I turn my head to the right to look at the cloud and don't see Nereus stop. I slam into his back, and we both stumble.

'What are you doing?' I snap.

He points downriver, his mouth open.

'Look!'

In the distance, a wall of black liquid charges upriver. At the bottom of the valley, the wave is higher than five mature oak trees end to end. Along its edges, treetops poke out of the water. Bushes, trees, rocks, and, to my horror, huts and livestock tumble and roll in the wall of water crashing upriver.

'Run,' I scream. And we do, but as the dark spread of water sweeps along the hillside towards us, I realise we are still on fairly low ground. The valley was wider than it looked. Above us, I see oak trees growing on flatter land above the settlement before the hill curves steeply upwards.

Gasping, we reach the village. Two women are outside a hut working at their fire. One looks up, runs into her hut and reappears with a stick.

'Go higher,' I call to the villagers, but they stare blankly at me from the door of their hut, terrified and perhaps unable to understand my words, my accent. I point at the advancing water, then point up the hill.

We keep running.

No one follows.

We are almost at the oaks when I glance downriver, where the wave is charging through the forest. The trees farther from the river are holding, their roots keeping them in place – the strength of the water peaking along the riverbed. We reach the dark understory of the oak forest when a blast of air topples us. I fall back and wriggle onto all fours. Nereus is on his knees beside me. The wind is strong and tears at our clothes, rips our hair, flings it in our faces, gouges tears from our eyes.

We can't stand.

So, we crawl.

'We have to climb a tree.' I grab Nereus and point to the nearest oak. The trunk is wide, strong and straight. I stagger to my feet, charge at it, and jump for the lowest branches, but I'm not tall enough. Nereus makes it on the first try, hauls himself up and reaches down for me, but I miss his hands. The wave is almost upon us.

The wind sucks the breath from my body.

My heart pounds.

I pull the axe off my belt and rip it from the sheath. I whack the oak tree, burying the axe head at an angle into the trunk.

It sticks.

I have a foothold.

Nereus catches my hand as I spring up. He hauls me into the tree. Bark gouges the bare skin on my stomach where my tunic rides up. It stings. I yelp, but I'm clear of the black water swirling underneath. The tree sways as we climb higher. We wrap our limbs around branches. I wail with the wind, my heart bursting, my cries lost in the crashing water.

The sun dims and dies.

Darkness descends.

My arms become numb as I press against the tree. Bark chafes my cheek, and tears sting the raw skin.

'Nereus?' My throat feels as ragged as it sounds.

Nereus doesn't answer, but I can feel his body quivering against my shoulder. The moon is behind clouds – if it is there at all. Even the stars are gone. At least Nereus's body is warm.

My right ear fills with the regular pulse of pop-pop-pop.

Rain is coming.

It's a long night in the tree, but mercifully, the rain holds off. In the darkness, I can't see the axe. It might be underwater. I'm not sure if the level is rising or falling, but I can hear the water's gurgles and whispers, curling around the tree trunks.

Shivers rack our limbs and keep us from falling asleep despite our fatigue. I make several attempts to talk, but Nereus doesn't respond with more than a grunt. I give up asking him questions and listen instead to his breathing: rapid, heavy, but not quite panting. Time stretches and condenses as my mind tosses through everything that has happened, making no sense of any of it.

The morning dawns in a blood-red glow, which spreads to orange as the sun moves higher. The sky doesn't clear. Instead, the light grows eerie, drenching the landscape in the colour of dried blood. The air smells of fish – sea fish like the merchants bring from the coast, dried in salt, not the lough fish we eat.

The axe sticks out of the tree trunk, a hand's span above the water. The flood is not receding but isn't rising anymore. The popping in my ear hasn't stopped all night. Rain is not far off – lots of rain. But what kind of rain will fall from these bloodstained clouds?

'Lower me down,' I say. Nereus gives me a hand.

Cold water bites my submerged skin all the way up my legs to above my knees. There's a tug in the water but not too strong, not as bad as when crossing the big river in low season. Nereus follows me to the ground and stands beside me, hugging his arms around his body. I balance against the drag in the water, grab the axe handle and yank it from the tree. I wobble as it comes away. Alarm blasts through my chest. I steady myself by grabbing a fistful of Nereus's tunic. He is solid, unmoving, his face as dark and foreboding as the water swirling about my thighs.

Groping with my foot, I find a firm place to stand. The next step trips me up. I fall face-first into the dirty water. It gets up my nose. I surface, coughing and spitting out the foul taste of tears and muck. Why does the water taste so salty?

'We need to go to the cairn,' I say, pulling myself up using Nereus's body.

Nereus nods, silent, wide-eyed and pale. He hasn't spoken a word since we went up the tree, only moving when I suggest it, as though he has relinquished all control to me.

We turn uphill and trudge through the trees, wading through water that becomes shallower the higher we go. I lose count of how often I fall, of how many times I choke on the rank-tasting water. Nereus seems to focus on keeping a steady plod. He doesn't fall.

My legs don't feel like they belong to me, keeping pace with Nereus as my mind unshackles. I can't make sense of it – the fireball, the cloud, the wave – so much water.

My ear pops, but the rain has not come. That scares me the most. What if the rain never comes, and we are left with this stinking water?

The trees thin out, and weak fingers of light push beneath their canopies. I stumble into the warmer air, squinting. Behind, the trees block our view of the valley. Above, I see the cairn. On the blade of the ridge, a blast of cold air nearly topples us. It's like nature is keeping us from the cairn, from the bronze dagger, from completing our story. Nereus will say this is punishment from the gods. But why now, before we've actually done anything wrong? He'll say it's because of my lack of faith, or because I stole my own axe. But why in this way, punishing so many for my wrongdoing? I stop arguing with him in my head. How would I know what he's thinking, especially now?

Nereus makes it to the cairn first. It's as tall as he is and as wide at the base as it is tall. Big enough so the rocks give him shelter from the wind that scours the hilltop. He turns to me, his eyes wide and mouth agape as he looks past my shoulder. I turn, and what I see leaves me stunned.

Water covers most of the land as far as we can see. Hilltops poke out – islands now in a vast expanse of muddy fluid. The village we passed is gone: no smoke, no huts, no people.

No one left.

Did the wave reach our lands, our village? Though it's a few days' travel away, could it too be submerged? Our home destroyed; our people dead - Geros, my brother and his family - I cannot bear the thought.

My ear pumps the rapid sound of pops through my head. Fat drops of rain begin to fall – and fall. I thump the side of my head, but still, it pops. I scream at the clouds blossoming in purple hues. But they drop more water. In a torrent of grief, I lift my eyes to the cruel sky and wonder, who will tell anyone's story now?

CHAPTER 11

Rain staccatos the garden shed's metal roof, filling my mother with a violet bubble of urgency. She suppresses the sensation, drops her shoulders from where they have bunched around her ears, and selects a large butternut squash. It takes both hands to lift it into the creaking basket alongside the leafy kale, garlic, onions, carrots, potatoes and some scabby late-season string beans.

The lightbulb sputters and goes out. My mother swears under her breath, waits a few seconds in the shadows to see if it will come back on, then gives up and heaves the basket handle into the crook of her elbow so she can carry it on one arm. She aims for the slash of brightness that falls through the door, crosses the floor and creases up along the far wall. If she hits a spider's web, she'll freak out. Keeping one hand in front of her face, she waves away sticky tendrils until she's outside. The rising sun crests the horizon, blasting bronze light through the rippling clouds, giving them a striped mauve and orange underbelly.

She casts an eye over the houses in the hollow and doesn't see a single light. A rainbow arcs against pewter clouds to the west, and she soaks it in, lets it warm her aura. It might be the only thing she's grateful for this Thanksgiving, and she wants to relish it.

I long to connect with her momentary luscious glow, draw from it, feed it – in symbiotic kinship, but she has shut me out since she began taking her daily injections to prepare her body for IVF at the end of September. She's angry that I won't tell her if the process will work. I can't do that. But I have nowhere else to go, so here I remain, watching, waiting from this place, stranded between worlds.

My father meets her as she reaches the patio doors.

'Electric's out!' he says, reaching for her basket. 'One wee spot of rain, and the whole place shuts down. And on Thanksgiving!'

'Poor Ruby! She'll be having a fit.' My mother kicks her wet shoes off and slides into her slippers. 'But at least we're getting water. We need it.' She follows my father to the kitchen sink, where he is already unloading the vegetables onto the draining board. Papery flakes of dried onion and garlic skin float to the floor.

My father's aura is mellow, with pastel turquoise hues radiating to infuse with my mother's. He bends and kisses the top of her head.

'These veggies look amazing,' he says. 'You're amazing.'

'Ah, thanks.' She pops a kiss on his cheek. 'You're not so bad yourself.'

Their glow strengthens, and I draw hungrily from it.

A dusting of mud sifts from the basket onto the granite countertop. Clean dirt, my mother thinks, something she'll brush up later after she has peeled and chopped the vegetables: her contribution to the Thanksgiving dinner potluck. A dinner she would happily miss, she thinks. It's like having two Christmases a year, and one is bad enough – a day where her empty table expands and mocks her with its minimalism. She dreams of Christmas Days with a tribe of kids around the table: but each year, that dream fades from an oil painting to a pencil sketching. She'd rather shut down and hide – ride the whole thing out behind closed doors with pizza and Cheetos and root beer, binge-watching *The Walking Dead*.

In their first year in California, my parents discovered that Americans couldn't bear the idea of anyone spending Thanksgiving alone. When my father mentioned they had no plans for the holiday, Andy and Ruby invited my parents to share in their gathering. It seemed like a nice idea, a party and an opportunity to make new friends.

Andy and Ruby grew up in neighbouring small towns in upstate New York. Both sets of parents were divorced and remarried, creating sprawling, complicated families. Andy, Ruby, and their three kids stay on the West Coast for Thanksgiving. They invite anyone who wants to travel west to join them from among their crew of parents, stepparents, siblings, half-siblings, step-siblings, nieces, nephews, cousins and friends. They, in turn, make the trek east for Christmas.

That first year had been fun. My mother had been full of optimism for her life in the new world. Ruby was good craic, if a little bossy: and her half-sister, a cousin and their spouses had been welcoming and friendly. My parents had a lovely day. My mother thought she'd connected with Ruby's half-sister, but she never heard from her after that initial gathering, though they were now friends on Facebook. Even after my mother had sent a cheery little message to check that they had safely made it back to the East Coast, there'd been no answer. In three years, they'd not met the same guests twice.

Now, my parents don't quite know how to turn down the invite each year without causing offence. This year, there would be five couples and twelve children.

And now there was no electricity.

My mother ran the tap, rinsed the butternut squash, and hoisted it back onto the draining board.

My father twiddled with the knobs on the hob. 'If I can find the barbeque-sparker-stick-thing, I'll get the cooktop going. It only needs electricity to ignite the gas.'

'I can steam the veggies, but how on earth will Ruby do the turkey?'

'That, my dear, is Ruby's problem.'

A grin sparkles between them, igniting a radiant outline around both of them.

*

My parents go next door to a house in chaos. Half the adults are outside in the rain, hunched under–but not wearing–raincoats, giving Andy conflicting advice on barbequing a turkey.

There's a clatter of feet amid a backdrop of squeals and laughter as a horde of children careens between the garage door, the den, and back again. The mingled smells of wet dog, wet wool, and a toddler's wet nappy push through the cooking aromas.

'Enough! Gwen, Toby, do what you're told!' Ruby shouts over her shoulder as she ushers us through the patio doors to the dining area. 'Crazy morning, but Andy says the turkey is well underway.' She pulls a face that indicates it's anything but. 'It's great you've managed to cook these. Thank you.'

'Gas hob,' my mother says, handing over her casserole dishes. 'Butternut squash steamed and mashed with butter, and the one on the bottom is stir-fried kale.'

'Oh, how very Californian,' says a wiry man with pattern balding.

'Brandon, meet Aisling and Ben,' Ruby says.

A cheer goes up as the lights flicker on.

'Thank God!' Andy appears at the patio doors, wearing oversized oven gloves, carrying a massive tinfoil covered mound. 'Quick – it's heavy!' He scuttles into the kitchen.

The eldest of the twelve children is a lanky, sullen teen called Chance. My mother can't decide if he's not smiling much because he has a mouth full of metal keeping his teeth in check, or if it's because his mother, a sharp-faced New Yorker called Melanie, has put Chance in charge of the rest of the kids. The youngest is Andy and Ruby's cute little two-year-old called Rye, who clutches a battered rabbit she calls Hop. She's besotted with her big cousin Chance and follows him everywhere, waddling in her engorged nappy. He, to his credit, is patient and charming with her and, it seems, the other kids. It's just adults he can't make eye contact with.

'Chance, herd those little 'uns to the den for their dinner. I'll change Rye.' Melanie lifts the toddler, who reaches with waggling fingers for Chance as she gets carried off.

My mother selects a seat beside my father. He's already engaged in conversation with Brandon.

'May I sit here?' says a woman, pulling out a seat beside her.

'Sure.' My mother smiles, taking in the blonde bob and wide-set blue eyes of the pretty, well-groomed woman in her early thirties.

'I'm Janice.'

My mother shakes the proffered hand, saying, 'Aisling. Nice to meet you.'

'Oh, I do love your accent. Ruby said there'd be Irish here, but you sound Scottish?'

'Really? I'm from the North, but I don't think—'

'Belfast?'

'Close enough.' My mother reckons Janice won't know where Armagh is.

'My grandmother was from Ireland.'

'Which part?'

'Oh, I can't remember. Em, let me see. Cardiff? Is that a place?'

'Yes, in Wales.' My mother tries to keep her face neutral.

'Is that in Ireland?'

'No, it's a separate country of its own.'

'Seriously? It was something beginning with "C".' Her eyes light up. 'Cork, that's it. Is that near you?'

'Other end of the country, I'm afraid.'

Janice looks deflated for a moment, then smiles and cocks her head. 'Anyway, I have to say, well done to you. Your English is really good.'

My mother is left open-mouthed when Andy grabs everyone's attention, bringing in a platter loaded with a glistening bronze turkey. Ruby and Melanie follow behind with an assortment of bowls containing the vegetables and side dishes.

The turkey tastes like sawdust, but my mother chews dutifully on it, listening in on my father's conversation with Brandon. She can't be bothered resuming the fluffy chat with Janice and is relieved to see her deep in discussion with someone further down.

Brandon is making my father's aura crackle with neon orange shards of frustration.

'I'm just sayin' that man's carbon emissions are nothing compared to what volcanoes are spewing out every single day. And have always done. How do you account for that?' Brandon shovels a forkful of sweet potato into his mouth.

Andy and Ruby, sitting opposite, abandon their conversation to tune in.

My father douses his irritation and clears his throat. 'Actually, that's not true. Volcanoes generate less than one per cent of the greenhouse gas emissions that human endeavours create today.'

'Oh yeah, says who?' Brandon smirks.

'That's data from an article in *Scientific American*.' My father smiles. He's been here many times before and has his snowballs lined up, ready to throw. 'In fact, the massive volcanic eruptions like Mt. St. Helens in 1980 led to short-term cooling because the gases and particles they throw into the stratosphere reflect the sun's energy... for up to a few years, actually.'

'Can't we trigger a few of those?'

'Not a good idea,' my mother says. 'We know from the historical record that volcanoes in Iceland have caused huge downturns in the weather in Northern Europe several times in the last ten thousand years.'

Brandon ignores her, but my father says, 'Aisling studied a degree in history. She knows all about it.'

Brandon turns to her and smiles, 'Well, there you go. Get volcanoes to cool the planet down; problem solved.'

'So you do admit there is a problem then?' my mother asks, without returning Brandon's smile.

'I was speaking hypothetically,' Brandon says.

'There's no need to be hypothetical, though, is there? The fact is humans have caused this warming by emitting too many greenhouse gases. Don't you think it will be easier to cut back on emissions than to attempt to harness volcanic eruptions?'

'Absolutely! No need to bring more variables into an already haphazard mix,' my father adds.

'Touché!' Andy says, with a slow clap. 'Brandon, I wouldn't mess with Ben and Aisling. We've had this out a few times. He's a scientist. Works up at Lick Observatory.'

'Ah, one of the nerds.' Brandon flicks his eyes up and nudges my dad good-naturedly with his elbow. 'We won't hold that against you.'

'What do you work at?' my father asks.

'I'm in finance.' Brandon looks past my father. 'And what about your lovely wife? What do you do now with that history degree?'

My mother's aura darkens and shrinks like an anemone startled by a shadow. She hates that question. Hates that she can't explain that she used to be a teacher, but she's not working because they are focusing on her conceiving, on building a family; that she makes her husband's life comfortable by doing everything for him but his job, the one he receives payment for.

'I'm in management,' she says.

Brandon nods and looks away, scanning the table for more food.

My father grins. Pride develops in a rosy haze as his foot slides up against hers.

My mother exhales, pushes the carrots she cooked earlier into a glob of gravy, then- onto the back of her fork and into her mouth.

'What kind of management?' Janice says.

My mother points to her mouth and chews.

Janice smiles, patiently waiting.

My mother, still chewing, points to her wedding ring and winks, then says from one side of her mouth, 'Lifestyle management.'

Janice squints as the penny drops. 'You're a housewife?'

My mother nods, smiling. 'And then some.'

'I like that description. I'm gonna use that, too.'

My mother relaxes.

When everyone has finished the main course, Ruby clinks a spoon against her glass. Silence falls on the group, and all eyes rest on her.

'Thank y'all for coming. We love having y'all here.'

'We love being here,' Janice says, and a ripple of agreement does the rounds.

Ruby holds up a hand. 'Before we bring out the pumpkin pie—'

'It better be Gramma's recipe,' someone quips to a gentle rumble of laughter.

'It is, it is.' Ruby extends a hand to Andy, and he stands up beside her as she continues, 'Every year we like to say what it is we're grateful for and this year especially.'

Ruby glows beside a radiantly smiling Andy.

My mother's skin tingles, and her pulse quickens. A hollow sensation flutters in her chest despite the big dinner she has eaten.

Ruby's hand drifts to cover her tummy, and the other pulls a black and white printout of an ultrasound from under her place setting and holds it up.

'Baby number four will be here by Easter!'

The table erupts with applause. The women stand and form a line to hug Ruby and Andy. My mother sits fractured – smiling outwardly for her friend's joyous news, but the intensity of her sorrow for her own loss triggers a rush of nausea. She swallows hard and turns to my father.

They share a glance, then slip impassive masks into place to hide the pain they each see mirrored in the other. My mother feels her chin wobble a little as she says to my father, 'Ah, that's wonderful. Four, a nice even number.' In her head, she's screaming – *One, all I want is one!*

I pour my love over them, trying to thaw out the ice blue of their shrinking, stippled auras. But they have pulled inwards to a place that I find hard to connect with. I cannot bear my loneliness. I reach for the spirit world, but there is nothing I can connect with there, either. Scarlet fear slashes through the leaden isolation. I cannot stay here forever. If I could figure out why I'm here, perhaps this solitude would end.

I await their unfurling, which happens slowly during the melee of congratulations and continues over dessert, like a daisy opening in the dawn. Eventually, my mother feels like she can breathe again, and my father covers her hand with his and squeezes. She nods. He smiles. She squeezes back.

A wail from the den is followed by a high-pitched howling, which gets louder as the den door is flung open. Chance runs into the hallway carrying a wriggling boy of about five years old with light brown curls. The child's screaming is only interrupted by a rasping inhale as he draws breath for the next crescendo. He claws the air with one hand, clutching a little toy car in the other.

'Joshua!' Melanie jumps up and runs to her children. 'What happened?'

'I don't know,' Chance says. 'He just started screaming!'

Josh scrabbles at the back of his head with one hand and reaches for his mother with the other, dropping his little car. His crying is loud, but the gaps between in-breaths get longer.

'His lips are blue!' Ruby says, her alarm adding to the neon flashes coming off Melanie and Chance. Josh's fear is a bolt of red slashing through it.

Ruby nearly steps on the little car, and my mother rushes to scoop it up. As soon as she touches it, I know what has happened.

There's a wasp down the back of his shirt. It's still stinging him!

My mother doesn't question me.

'Wasp – quick! Take his shirt off!' She reaches for Joshua's top and yanks it open, scattering buttons and ignoring the rip of the soft fabric. His crying is laced with sawing wheezes.

He's allergic to the sting.

'Ben, call 911.' My mother has the top off the child, and Melanie swipes away the bedraggled wasp from the waistband. A series of red welts has risen along Joshua's back from his hairline to his waist. Swollen eyelids have nearly shut, and his cheeks and lips are distended.

'Ambulance is coming,' Ben says.

My mother doesn't feel relief. Joshua is struggling to breathe. 'EpiPen? Anyone have an EpiPen?'

Melanie tries in vain to soothe the child, calm him down, and encourage him to breathe slowly and effectively. Panic pours off her in magenta torrents.

Ruby hands my mother an EpiPen.

'Where did you get this?' my mother stares at it for a second.

She hesitates. Joshua looks so small. He's too quiet.

'It's Gwen's,' Ruby says. 'Peanut allergy. But she's never used it. The needle's in the orange end. Pull off the blue activation cap. And inject.'

'Where's that ambulance?' Melanie asks.

'Five minutes away,' Ben replies, his phone still to his ear.

'Ask them if we can use the EpiPen?' Fear rips my mother in two. Use the pen and risk harming Joshua more with something not prescribed, or wait and run out of time?

Joshua lies limp, blue-faced, and barely wheezing.

You have to inject. He's out of time, I tell my mother.

She plunges the orange tip against his leg.

Melanie locks eyes with my mother as she withdraws the pen. There's a beat where time seems to stall, then it lurches forward as Joshua hauls in a lungful of air, and his crying returns with a gusto that has Melanie in tears as she clasps him to her. She mouths a thank you to my mother, who sits trembling with her own rush of adrenalin.

The paramedics arrive. A cocoon is drawn around Joshua and his parents as they are ushered to the ambulance. The other parents disappear to the den and various parts of the house where they reassure their own offspring, leaving my parents sitting alone at a huge table laden with the remains of pumpkin pie, melting ice cream, and cooling coffee.

'You were amazing,' my father says. 'How did you know?'

Buttery swirls of hope that she'll tell him about me melt to nothing as she shrugs.

'You'll be a wonderful mother.' His words sting as much as they salve.

She turns towards him, not trusting herself to speak, and they share a glance heavy with shared longing.

'Actually.' She swallows hard, licks dry lips. 'I knew because—' She glances at the little car now sitting where she left it on the table before grabbing the EpiPen. Hope surfaces. I don't understand this need to be known by both of them, but it tugs hard.

'Finally!' Ruby says, bursting into the dining room. 'Got my kids settled. That was intense, wasn't it?'

My connection to my mother ebbs again, and isolation engulfs me like a white shroud.

Andy is right behind Ruby with a fresh pot of coffee. 'Good job you had that EpiPen, Ruby. You saved Joshua's life.'

My father raises an eyebrow at my mother. She is used to being invisible in the company of mothers. As a non-mom, she reckons she's expected to not understand the stakes, to be a lesser empath because she has never known what it is to give birth and fear for a child. She hears it all the time, in news reports, memes, movies, those words that lend women credibility to sympathise more, mourn with others better, *As a mother...*

Janice joins them. 'God, that was awful. I hope he's okay.'

'He's in good hands. Hospital's the best place for him right now,' Andy says. 'More beer, anyone?' He disappears to the fridge in the garage as the rest of the party reconvenes around the abandoned desserts.

Ruby clears the empty plates. My mother and Janice help carry dishes to the kitchen. My mother scrapes and rinses, handing off to Janice, who stacks the dishwasher.

'This is lifestyle management at its most glamorous,' Janice says with a gruff laugh. 'Don't you think, Ruby?'

Ruby laughs. 'Yep, it's a fair description.'

'So, Aisling, do your kids go to the same school as Ruby's?' Janice asks.

'I, em, don't have any kids.' Air shrinks tight against my mother's skin.

Janice doesn't say anything, but the question *Why not?* hangs heavy between them. My mother can't make eye contact, can't bear either the judgement if Janice thinks she's a selfish cow for not wanting to be harnessed with children, or worse, the sympathy, the *Oh, you're one of those poor women.*

She lifts a casserole dish from the sink and swings it in Janice's direction, but it slips from her fingers before Janice has a hold of it. It tumbles to the floor and smashes.

'Sorry, so sorry,' they say together, both bending to pick up the larger shards.

Ruby is on it. 'Don't move. There's glass everywhere. Let me brush it up.'

Tears bubble behind my mother's eyes. The swell of emotion, of feeling stupid, useless, chokes her. She needs air. She rushes from the kitchen, through the garage, to the side garden. A crepe myrtle breaks the rainfall to a gentle plop and dollop. The smell of wet soil calms her jangled mind. She hears a footstep behind her and turns to face Ruby.

'Are you okay?'

The concern on Ruby's face is too much, and a tear escapes. My mother nods, clears her throat and wipes her face. 'Gosh, this rain! We needed it.'

'Yeah, we sure did.'

'I'm so sorry about your dish. Butterfingers, ya know?'

'Janice thinks she's upset you.'

'No, no. Not at all,' my mother lies.

'Maybe you just need a witty one-liner to explain why you don't have kids,' Ruby says.

My mother catches her breath. *A witty one-liner?* As if her fertility issues can be distilled into one line, witty or otherwise. She clenches her teeth, looks down, shakes her head.

'Just a suggestion.' Ruby pats her shoulder.

'Thanks,' my mother mutters.

'I'll see you inside. There's more pie!'

If my mother ever so much as sees pumpkin pie again, with its orange mush and too much cinnamon, she'll hurl. She wraps her arms around herself and shivers. 'I'll be in in a sec.'

A couple of minutes later, my father finds her beneath the crepe myrtle, blowing her nose into a paper napkin.

He folds her into his arms. Their auras combine, surging and ebbing red, orange, yellow.

I'm here, mother.

I know, she replies, thawing my grey isolation with a dusting of rose.

I send bronze ribbons of strength, and my parents draw tighter in their embrace, letting my fortitude encompass us.

'I'm happy for them. Really. I am,' she says into his ear. 'I'm just sad for us.'

'We'll be next. We're nearly done with these injections. You'll see.'

'What if IVF doesn't work?'

Her anguish dulls the bronze.

'Shush, it will be all right.' he holds her close, rubs her back, and polishes their hope to a yellow-pink glow.

CHAPTER 12

I stand with my back to the cairn and stare. The land stretches before me, drowned in murky liquid. I recheck the location where I expect to see the village we passed before the wave hit, but it is gone, covered in water pocked with eddies and twisted branches sticking up out of it. A floating mound swivels, producing legs as the body of a pig rotates in the water. Other mounds nearby are swaddled in wet cloth, black hair wafts alongside one. The realisation is a punch to my gut – this is a dead person! The other floating mounds are also corpses.

Pressure builds in my temple, buzzes in my ears, drowning out the *pop-pop-pop*. Tension tingles through me, converging on my hands, still clasping the rigid coldness of the bronze axe head, making it vibrate with otherworldly energy. This axe saved me from being washed away, from drowning – like those others. There's a snap in my head as panic surges through my chest.

I hear my screams but can't stop them; then I feel Nereus's arms around me. He clasps me to him, crushing my face to his chest. My screams stop. The warmth from his skin soothes me, and I breathe in great gulps of air. His arms tighten around me as I shake.

'It's all right,' he says, in the tone of voice he uses with my nephews when they cry. '*We're* all right.'

I wriggle out of his arms and step back. My breath catches in my throat. There's so much water. The landscape is unrecognisable, with so many landmarks gone – gone, just gone.

'All those people,' I whisper.

'We survived.' Nereus's fingers grip my shoulder. His simple statement gives me little comfort.

My chin wobbles as my vision blurs. I swipe the tears away, suck down a huge breath, reach for his hand and say, 'Yes, we survived.'

'Can we go home?' Nereus's eyes glitter. The rain has washed away the last of his charcoal, so he no longer bears Parthalon's mark. His ears stick out through wet hair plastered to his head. He looks like a lost little boy.

I can't bear to look at him, yet looking away forces me to view the devastation surrounding us. 'We have to find the dagger.'

Nereus nods and stares at the floodwaters.

'Our village?' The hitch in his voice hauls my heart over briars. 'You don't think—'

The idea of this wave reaching our village traps the air in my chest.

'No.' I look up into his face. 'We walked for four days. We are far from home. We live on higher ground.'

He nods again, chewing his bottom lip.

'If we go back with this story, they won't believe us. And we stole from them. Well, from ourselves, but they won't see it like that. We need to find the bronze dagger.'

We turn to stare at the stack of boulders that make up the cairn.

'If the dagger is here, we can go home,' I say.

'And if it's not?'

I shake my head. We hadn't discussed that. I don't want to consider it.

'You mean, if we can't find it, we aren't going back?' He swallows hard.

I shake my head. 'It's possible. If… we just…'

'Zosime.' Nereus draws a breath. I know how hard he finds it to go up against me. He hates arguing. 'You have to face up to what's happening. You can't pretend it will all go away if you ignore the problem.'

'I'm not ignoring anything – it's just … Look, let's get the damn dagger first.'

'And if it's not there?'

'Stars above, Nereus. We don't know that yet. Why worry until we know?'

Nereus lowers his gaze and shrugs. 'We will have to go back. There is nothing else. We have to warn them. And if there's no dagger, you have to give back your axe. It may be all we have to defend ourselves from the Hag.'

'How, Nereus? How will the dagger, or the axe, or anything defend us from the Hag?'

He flinches as I scream, but I can't stop. 'You saw the fire in the sky! It ripped the sky open. It swallowed the stars, and now this?' I fling my hand towards the flooded land.

'Geros knows how,' Nereus says softly. He nods as if reassuring himself. I feel sick at the thought of failure, though I don't believe it will do us any good. I hate myself for holding onto pride at a time like this. When all these people have died – whole villages – their stories wiped out. I'm selfish. Nereus's magnanimity always highlights this.

'Maybe the dagger *is* here,' I say, reaching towards the cairn.

The cairn is cone-shaped. Its base is three strides wide. Rocks the size of my head lie in layers of circles that get smaller towards the top, about the same height as Nereus. On top is one fist-sized rock.

'Let's have a look,' he says, stepping up to the cairn.

I follow. I can't reach the top-most rocks without climbing up on the bottom ones, but Nereus lifts them with ease and sets them in a neat pile near my feet until he comes to a much larger stone. It's heavy and his arm muscles bulge. He grunts with effort, pivots then drops the rock. It rolls a few times before it stops. He looks at me and raises his eyebrows.

'The village is gone,' I say. 'Who's going to care if the cairn is dismantled?'

'I will,' he says and reaches for the next stone.

*

When the cairn is low enough, I help. Most rocks are too heavy for me to lift, but I can dislodge them and let them tumble off. The rain has died down to a grey mizzle. Low clouds hug the hillside and obscure the view. I'm grateful for that.

With every new layer of the cairn pulled apart, I hope to see a bundle of cloth, or of leather, or even the dagger. As we continue, my despair deepens.

The last layer has the heaviest stones. We grunt as we push together to dislodge the final one. The bare ground turns to mud with the rain. I slip and land heavily on one knee. I dig my fingers into the muck as far down as my palms and drag them through the grit and sludge.

Nereus is on his knees, too, hands scrabbling in the mud, searching. 'It has to be here,' he mutters over and over.

Of course, there's no bronze dagger here. When has life ever been that simple?

Drizzle wafts over the brow of the hill. Droplets gather on Nereus's beard. Puffs of breath form in the air before his face. It feels more like autumn than summer. A shiver rattles my torso. Up to our shoulder, caked in mud, Nereus shuffles around on his knees in circles, still clawing at the ground, but I have given up. Drops fall from my jawline, and I'm not sure if it's tears or dampness.

'Stop,' I say, standing up and stepping back from the cairn.

Nereus looks at me with bland confusion that triggers irritation I find hard to quell.

'There's no dagger here.' I struggle to keep the edge from my voice.

'It doesn't make sense. Geros said—'

'Unless someone else took it,' I say, realising Nereus needs to believe in something. 'If Egil had mentioned it many years earlier to Geros, it's likely he told it to many other villages.'

'But the Monarchs would not permit it.'

'People do things without permission all the time. Think about it. This pile of rocks was too easy to take apart. The dagger must have been taken.' I shiver again.

Nereus glances across the hilltops as a gust of wind smears the mist across them. The large body of water and river we had been using to navigate are engorged beyond recognition. He stares at the settlement, now underwater.

'How far did the water go?'

I shrug. We can't tell from here. For all we know, it keeps on going – endless.

I can sense Nereus losing himself to panic as he says, 'How can we find our way home if the river banks and the lake are so flooded? Apart from the fact that our low-lying landmarks are gone, is there enough high ground to keep us above the level of the water? And what of the other rivers we crossed? Are they impassable?

'You want to go home without the dagger?' I ask, predicting his answer as relief loosens his shoulders and his frown relaxes.

'Yes,' he says, the word floating on a breath of fog between us.

I swallow the bitter taste of failure.

'Let's go back, then,' I say, sick to the pit of my stomach. 'We'll retrace our steps as best we can.' I don't know if this will work but it's a place to start.

I can't stop Nereus from rebuilding the cairn, so with aching arms, I help him. By the time he puts the last stone on the top, it looks like we never touched it, and I realise this might be a good thing despite the time it took.

*

We stumble like prey wounded in the hunt, in a frenzy of fear, running blind for home, hardly stopping to eat the dried meats and grain cakes we brought with us. When we try to rest, we can't sleep. Chunks of the day are missing. The sun is behind clouds, the sky unseasonably dark, and our summer wrappings do not hold the heat we need. It's hard to know if it is morning, noon, or evening; and by nightfall, we collapse shivering under a grove of oaks.

When I close my eyes, letting my body soften into its exhaustion, I jerk awake. Images rumble through my mind – the bodies of people and livestock rolling in murky water; the village levelled by the force of the wave; the sky ripping open and the blackness of the wave as it surged up the valley towards us. Judging by Nereus's hollow gaze, he too, is haunted. So, we walk through the night – a night that feels longer than it should.

The next day arrives with a line of red in the sky that bleeds into the clouds, allowing us to reorient with the flood to our left. The wave has raised the level of the Sea-that-is-not-a-sea and expanded its perimeters. We expect to see the sun before us, but the clouds are too thick. The sky doesn't clear, and the day holds an eerie gloom. The rain stops, but it is still cold.

The next night is equally devoid of rest. The next day dawns, dark and cold – too many clouds to see any colour. They hang so low, I feel I could touch them. If the sun was bleeding the day before, now it has nothing to give. Day blends into night. I lose count of how many nights and days pass like this: two maybe three, more? We cover more ground because we aren't stopping; but with the flooded landscape, it's hard to tell if we are always going in the right direction.

Navigation is easy – stay uphill from the water and keep it to our left-hand side. We manage to follow the swollen edges of the Sea-that-is-not-a-sea. We cannot retrace our steps as they are underwater. A river snakes off the Sea-that-is-not-a-sea to the horizon between Orient and where the sun sets. I think it is the Blackwater, though even at that distance, I can see that the river is now much wider and has spilt over its bank into lobes among the shrubs.

I slide my hand down to feel my axe. There will be no trade with Blackwater Ford. All that is left of the settlement is a tangle of wattle screens against some wooden posts and black swirling pools. A couple of crests of low hills rise as bare islands above the floodwater. No life found that sanctuary, if it could be called that.

With the Ford gone and the settlement wiped out, it's only the contours of the distant hills that guide me. I direct Nereus though we don't talk, merely stagger on. In what should be mid-morning, but which is more like a dull pre-dawn twilight, we arrive at what seems to be the furthest reach of the wave. Tree trunks and dead livestock lie piled in a row along a contour of a low hill where the wave dumped them before receding. Not that it has receded much, but it gives me hope, enough hope to speak and break the silence that has stretched between us for most of the return trip.

'If the wave stopped here, our village will be safe.'

Eyes haunted, Nereus stares at the bloated body of a cow. He can't bear the thought of anything suffering, part of the reason he is no good at hunting. I touch his arm. He springs away as if burnt.

Gently, as if talking to a child, I repeat what I said and add, 'Don't you think so?'

He mumbles in agreement. I take his hand. This time, he lets me. Exhaustion has smudged blue tones in the hollows between his eyes and nose.

'Come,' I say, leading him away from the debris. He follows. As I turn to face him, over his shoulder, I catch sight of a woman impaled on a branch. Her dark hair is snagged like a nest in the twigs; her face turned to the sky, eyes staring, a jagged stump like a cruel arm protruding from her abdomen trailing her innards to coil to the ground.

Nereus sees my expression and starts to turn.

'No,' I snap. 'Don't.'

His eyes widen. 'Another wave?'

'No.' I temper my voice. 'Not that. Please, trust me.'

'Always,' he whispers and squeezes my hand three times.

His simple trust almost makes me weep. I clench my jaw and push my legs to move, leaving the distended shore behind us.

We find the river that I think might be the Noisy River, which would lead us back to our village. It was called the Noisy River because of how the water babbles as it flows over the pebbles in its many rocky sections. Now, the water – deep, silent and foreboding – has broken its banks. I push away the thought that the wave might, in fact, have reached our village, or at least enough water has surged that far to have caused damage. Here, the murky water lies sluggish and swirling around the trunks of the willows and bushes that line the banks. In places, it has pooled into lobes, distorting my memory of the lie of the land.

'How will we cross it?' I ask.

Nereus doesn't answer.

Staying higher up on the way back meant the rivers were still streams – smaller, easier to cross – but we had to leave that higher ground to get home. Now, we're faced with crossing fast-flowing water in unfamiliar surroundings. We walk in the weird twilight that throws yellowed light over the landscape. Lakes have broken their boundaries, and the river follows new paths and meanders down long-forgotten channels. We have to cross it several times, turning back once when the depth and tug of water scare me.

Navigating the way feels like talking to a long-lost cousin who has returned from marriage in another clan. The foundations are familiar, but the current changes take getting used to. My heart lifts when I recognise our neighbouring village until I realise that we missed seeing a village we traded with for fish by the mouth of the river. It is simply gone.

Skirting the neighbouring village, we exploit the dim light to stay unseen, the urge to get home overpowering the need to gather information. Perhaps I should warn the villagers. Perhaps they could send out a party to find survivors. Perhaps there are no survivors. But I can't think straight, can't make sense of any of it. It's as though I need to escape what's happened, and in doing so, I create blank patches in my memory. This fugue is not unlike the time I lost my first baby. Disbelief pulled me out of this world to float untouched for vast stretches of time.

I know I'm making mistakes, being selfish and impatient, omitting critical actions that might save others, but I lurch homeward, dragged by a relentless urge to get back. These villages are close enough to return to within a half-day's journey. Perhaps later, when I've gathered my wits, I can be of more use.

Our relief is unspoken when the Ceremonial Hall of our village comes into view. The huts surrounding it are as we left them. The wave never got this far, and I tremble, letting go of the tension I'd stored. I pull Nereus back behind a bush and put a finger to my lips.

He scrunches his forehead and mouths, 'What?'

'Wait,' I signal as I would when hunting, hand open, fingertips raised.

He sighs and slides in beside me, and whispers. 'Why?'

'Kallisto will have worked out that I took the axe, and she'll be determined to turn the village against me,' I whisper.

'That will be forgotten when we tell them what has happened. All that with the axe – it's not important. Geros will help us.' Nereus attempts to stand up, but I grab his clothing and yank him back.

'Zosime!' His voice is louder now.

'She'll be happy to have me sent to another clan. You know she has her sights set on you.'

'You're being silly—'

'Shh!'

There's a shout from below, sharp and reprimanding. A toddler runs in a wobbly line between two huts, arms in the air, shrieking. I spot my oldest brother, Yani, and my heart warms at the sight of him chasing down my escapee nephew, Claus. I'm proud of his protests and glad of the strength in his lungs as he wails when Yani picks him up.

Nereus mirrors my grin and mutters, 'What a little demon.'

The normality is soothing.

'Maybe you're right. If we can get to Geros and explain, I know he will speak for us. This…' I wave my hand at the clouds. 'This is a bad omen. We need to be wary. He may not have returned from the Great Mound. He may not have received permission for… well, you know. We need our village. Even more now that so many are—'

He nods and chews his bottom lip.

We sneak behind the latrines, noses crinkling, past the pig pens, sliding between the huts and around to the door that leads to Geros's quarters in the Ceremonial Hall. Nereus's longer legs have carried him ahead of me. I snatch at his arm but miss. He blunders into Geros's quarters without waiting for me. I swear beneath my breath.

He turns with a quizzical look and shrugs. The place is empty. Geros's sleeping mat is still gone. None of the other Elders are here, either. They tend to prefer the company of their family when they have no ceremonial duties.

'So…' I whip around at the sound of the snide voice behind me. 'You're back,' Kallisto says with an air of triumph. She stands in the Ceremonial Hall with her feet hip-width apart, one hand snatching back the reed curtain, the other on her long spear, point up, planted on the ground, like Geros holds his staff at the council meeting.

'And you're as observant as ever.' I sense more than hear Nereus's sigh at my impertinence. 'Geros has not returned yet?'

Kallisto's eyes narrow. She looks over my head and eyes up Nereus, and though I can't see him, I can imagine him standing slack-jawed and wide-eyed in her scrutiny. Her eyes drop to my waist belt. Her lips curve to one side.

'The stolen axe,' she says.

'Huh, not that observant.' I drop my hand to the axe. 'It belongs to me.'

'That's debatable.' She tips her spear towards my forehead; even at two feet away, it's the ultimate gesture of bad manners.

Behind me, Nereus inhales sharply. A crowd has gathered outside the Ceremonial Hall. I see Yani among them, frowning and handing a squirming Claus to his mother, Eleni, who has arrived with Aleka, both of them carrying baskets of berries. There are plenty of witnesses.

'Relax,' I say. 'Geros would exile her for a full season if she used that on us.'

'If,' Kallisto says, 'Geros were here.'

'Where *is* Geros?' Nereus asks.

Agis pushes through the row of people in front of him and stands directly behind Kallisto. She twists around, sees him and steps back, keeping us both in her line of sight.

'Didn't you meet him?' Agis asks me. 'He and Jaisun came back from Great Mound four days ago and … left again. Alone. He said he was following you.'

Following us! Without an aide. He would have been right in the way of the flood. Four days ago, the wave hit. Or was that three or five days ago? I'm not sure. Why did he follow us? Did he fail to get permission from the Monarchs?

'Something terrible has happened,' I try to explain.

'We saw the fireball,' Kallisto said. 'Do you have the dagger?'

'No.'

'So you failed.' Kallisto's dark eyes glitter.

I don't know how to tell them of the devastation we witnessed. I look to Nereus. His mouth works to form words, but his face crumples, and he breaks down in a slather of uncontrollable sobs. Kallisto, Agis, and the gathered villagers watch his unravelling, terrified.

'Where is Jaisun now?' I ask, hoping he'll know how the meeting with the Monarch went.

'There's no point talking to him,' Kallisto sneers. 'He's only a cattle boy. He wasn't admitted to the Great Mound.'

'Listen to me. The fireball was just the start…' I try to explain, but I struggle not to follow Nereus into a pit of despair.

A white flake drifts from the sky and lands on Kallisto's black hair, followed by another and another, until the sky is filled with falling specks. It is the wrong time of year for snow, and the air smells wrong – sour, pungent.

Kallisto looks at the sky and says, 'And now we are defenceless.'

I lift my hand. White – no, grey – pale grey dust that doesn't melt but coats my skin in seconds and is gritty when I rub my fingers together. All the surfaces around us, grass, the leaves on trees, the thatch on the huts, the wooden trackways are already coated with dust as far as the eye can see. Our hair and clothes turn grey even as we shake it off. It fills my mouth and nostrils, rasping between my teeth. I cough, covering my nose and mouth with my hands. Nereus drops to his knees and curls in on himself. Yani lifts Claus from his mother, and they, along with Agis and Aleka, run to their hut.

The villagers, spluttering, scatter and run for cover as I pull Nereus to his feet so we can get to shelter, too.

'This is because you stole the axe,' Kallisto hisses at me as she backs away, 'and now you have weakened its power.'

CHAPTER 13

'Is this why you are here, Poppy? To save other people's children?'
I don't know.

'But you know *everything*. You knew there was a wasp in that little boy's shirt. You knew about Andy's sister getting married. And you talk with Dad, Kate and Uncle Malcolm, but you can't tell me anything about me? About this damn IVF treatment.' My mother's frustration pulses cyan as she pulls the underwear drawer open too hard. It snaps to the end of its runners. Her fingers slip off the handle, catching and breaking the nail on her forefinger.

'Fuck!' She nibbles the nail off where a sliver remains attached, wincing at the sting where it tears from the quick. She spits the nail into her palm and watches it curl like a new moon. She flicks it into the waste bin, stomps back to the drawer, selects a pair of white panties, then reconsiders, tosses them back, and grabs a pair of black ones – comfortable cotton ones, not the lacy wisps shoved to a forgotten back corner of the drawer.

'These won't show blood if there's any leakage after the egg retrieval. Will there be blood? Surely they'll provide a sanitary pad,' she says still speaking aloud, half talking to herself, half talking to me. 'Ten thousand dollars, they'd fecking better throw in a free pad!'

She's not sure what to expect. Her tummy flutters at the thought that this time next week, she could be carrying a baby, possibly two.

Sensible as they are, the black panties don't cover the chain of khaki bruises that encircle her abdomen. The first few injections made her feel like weeping. The injustice of the lengths to which she must go to have children when it came so easily to most people. Maureen and Jack planned exactly when they'd have their children. They complied, being born at beautifully spaced intervals. Whereas my parents tried for five years before they conceived me. Now they are well into their sixth year of TTC – trying to conceive – the abbreviation used in the online forum my mother consults.

She sits back and sighs with her entire body. There'd been that documentary she'd seen about a poor woman in Thailand who spent her days scavenging on a landfill site. The woman was pregnant with her seventh baby. My mother can't understand how it can be so difficult for her to produce just one, all the while eating the optimum diet and living in luxury. She hates her self-absorption, hates how her envy of that poor woman's fertility flares and displaces her sympathy for the woman's harsh circumstances. She hates that life is so unfair.

There has been what feels to my mother like endless rounds of medical preparation before they can start the IVF. Getting tested for sexually transmitted diseases and HIV had felt like an insult to my mother, but the medical team insisted it was protocol; and once the tests came back negative, she could proceed to the next stage. It hadn't helped that they had to navigate doctor's appointments and injection regimes around Thanksgiving, but she hopes to be pregnant for Christmas. What a joy that would be.

After three weeks of puncturing her belly each morning, my mother has built up a pragmatic hardiness. The tightness in her lower abdomen is rewarding. She reckons her ovaries must be swelling and growing the eggs she needs for fertilisation.

My father baulked at giving her the intramuscular injection – the hCG trigger shot – when my mother couldn't reach around to the top outer haunch of her buttocks.

'It's one injection,' she told him, amused and irritated in equal measure by the queasy pallor on his face. 'Well – seeing you're not getting poked and prodded left, right and centre.'

'I've to wank into a cup.'

'Seriously?'

He gave her the squint-eye.

'I suppose it's not easy,' she said, a rosy rush of sympathy tempering her agitation with him.

'It's not,' he replied, warming to her tone. 'It's not like it's for pleasure. It's like…' He grappled for the word. One that will impress upon her that he's not having fun, though compared to her, he's not suffering discomfort. 'It's a task. And the staff know exactly what I'm doing in there… like, they *know*.'

'Alright, alright. It's not ideal for either of us.' She bent over the back of the chair, pushed the waistband of her jeans down and picked up the instructions. 'Swab the injection site.'

They were both glad to have the injections finished with – for this round.

For the egg retrieval appointment this evening, she dresses in a long black and white paisley print jersey skirt that swirls at her calves as she walks. She chooses a sloppy black tee-shirt and a white cardigan over it in case the air-conditioning in the waiting room is too high.

My father arrives home from work at three o'clock on the dot. The timing is important. They can't be late, or it messes up the whole regime.

'Honey,' he calls as soon as he enters.

'Ready!' She meets him in the hallway. 'Let's do this.'

He hugs her tight, holding the embrace for a smidgen longer than usual. A lump forms in her throat that she can't speak past. She slips her hand into the comfort of his, and they leave the house in silence.

*

Leather armchairs, orchid floral arrangements, a drinks station with fruit, basil, and cucumbers floating in water jugs, and a vast selection of herbal teas make the waiting room feel as plush as the lobby of a five-star hotel. My mother thinks about how she would enjoy this room if she weren't so damn nervous. I try soothing her with soft lilac, but she barricades her mind from me.

My father paces. He stops at the TV, picks up the remote, turns it on, and switches through a few channels before turning it off again. He sits beside my mother and takes her hand, giving it a squeeze.

A woman in pink scrubs comes in with a clipboard and smiles. 'We're ready for you, Mrs Breen.'

'Please, call me Aisling.' My mother hops to her feet and follows the woman.

She changes in a large cubicle decorated with pink velvet cushions on a velvet padded bench and hangs her clothes in what she can only think of as a wardrobe. The gown she wears is plum and trimmed with the same shade of pink as the staff scrubs. The orchids in the hallway boast the same colour scheme. Tasteful, rich. And yet, my mother can't enjoy it any more than she can accept my overtures to help. She feels set apart, as though she isn't supposed to be here.

She hardly notices the stirrups on the chair in the procedure room. The young, immaculately groomed doctor greets her and introduces himself. She forgets his name – again.

Why does it have to be another man, Poppy?

Harder for women to get to the top.

Off having babies! Lucky them. Oh, I don't mean that! I hate the way I think sometimes.

She's annoyed at the tunnel visioning of her mindset that sends her thoughts spiralling uncontrollably along such uncharitable avenues.

Be kind to yourself, Mother. This is not easy.

'We're waiting on Mr Breen's sample to be washed,' the doctor says. He gives her a smile. 'Would you like him to join you?'

She nods, closes her eyes, and listens as the door whispers shut behind the doctor.

'Hey.'

She opens her eyes and gazes into my dad's face. 'It all feels so unreal,' she whispers.

'I know.'

'How did it go?'

'It… em…' He shrugs. 'I… I did my best, ya know…'

They laugh together at how absurd it seems.

'So, good news,' the doctor says, coming back. 'You have a high sperm count, good shape and excellent mobility.'

'Well done, Ben,' my mother says.

My father makes a clicking sound from the side of his mouth and says, 'That's my boys.' My mother puffs out a suppressed chuckle while the doctor and nurse position my father beside her shoulder so he can take her hand and watch the ultrasound screen. At the business end, my mother's feet are placed in the stirrups. She's instructed to relax and let her knees fall open.

She knows the drill and practises deep breathing to keep *everything* relaxed but still emits a sharp exhale as the ultrasound probe is inserted into her vagina. The pressure on her swollen ovaries translates to sharp pain, but she clamps down the groan and tightens her grip on my father's hand. They both keep their eyes on the screen, waiting to see the fuzzy whiteness yield the round black circles of follicles full of eggs.

Only one small round dark area emerges.

The doctor swings the probe to the other side, making my mother wince. The grainy picture is uniform – no black circles. Anxiety curls off my parents in neon green spirals.

'Is something wrong?' my mother asks.

'I would have expected to find more follicles.' The doctor swings the probe back.

My mother breaks into a cold sweat. She bites her lip, squeezes my father's hand.

He holds his breath.

'However, there is only this one and...' The doctor pauses to concentrate on measuring the follicle by dragging a white line across its diameter with a few clicks on the control panel. 'It's too small.'

He says something to the nurse about oocytes and gives her a number. She jots it down, nodding slowly, in a way my parents don't like because it's too sympathetic. Their anxiety blisters and peels to muddy beige disappointment.

In silence, the doctor removes the probe, takes the protective condom off and bins it. He uses scratchy paper towels to wipe the excess gel off my mother's nether regions. Missed gloop sticks the tops of her thighs together as she closes her knees and lifts her feet out of the stirrups. She sits up, feeling too vulnerable lying back.

'You have only one egg here,' the doctor says. 'Typically, in egg retrieval, we'd like to see at least six eggs. Statistically, we lose fifty per cent in retrieval, and then at least fifty per cent of those fail to fertilise. With only the one, it's much better to go with intrauterine insemination.'

'And if that doesn't work?' My mother says, dragging courage from the pit of her stomach. She doesn't want to know this answer, but she has to know, needs to know. 'Do we try again? Or is this likely to happen this way again?'

'The chances are you'll have the same result.' The doctor doesn't flinch. He holds her gaze steady.

'So IVF won't work for us?' my father asks. His aura throbs with the same muddy tone of yellow as my mother's. Where they connect, holding hands, the colours blend and strengthen.

'It won't, I'm sorry.'

My mother can't speak for a second, overwhelmed by a sense of being cast adrift, swirling, drowning. She inhales. Exhales. Repeats.

'Would you like to do the IUI?' the doctor prompts.

My parents nod.

Later, my mother can't remember the IUI procedure, the plush changing room, leaving the clinic, or driving home.

The only thing she remembers is stopping at the pedestrian crossing in Los Gatos as a mother and baby group, on some outing, crossed the road in front of them. My parents sat trapped at the crossing watching twenty strollers pass, my mother convinced the Universe was mocking her.

*

While she waits to see if the IUI worked, my mother is as cut off from her physical world as I am from the spirit world. We both wander lonely through swathes of empty time and space. She sits in the bath until the water goes cold before realising she has forgotten to wash. The sun sets while she prunes a rosebush, secateurs poised mid-air in gloved hands that have stopped moving. In these moments, her mind drifts to what will happen if this last desperate IUI doesn't work.

Or, to be more precise, what won't happen.

Her mind spools through little feet in baby grows, clutched teddies, nappy changes, night feeds, teething slobbers, toddler cuddles, birthday parties, cut knees, first day of school, Holy Communion, sandcastles, training wheels, exams, broken hearts, graduations, first job, wedding, grandchildren.

The hardest thing is this: knowing her stories stop with her. Who will want to hear about the adventures she's had in her life? Who will glean wisdom from the hard lessons – and there were some – she has learnt in life? If she has no one to pass this on to, what was the point of going through it? What is her purpose if this IUI doesn't work...?

*

My mother wakes up four days after the failed IVF to a bleed that soaks her pyjama bottoms and ruins the bedsheets. The water in the shower runs red as she stands under it, still wearing the pyjamas. Her period is heavy because of her whacked-out hormones. Her back aches, and a migraine puckers her right temple. It's nothing that a dose of Sumatriptan and two Panadol can't fix.

There is no tablet to fix the hollow pit in her chest.

I try to send her my love, but she pushes me away. Talking with me, the spirit of something she nearly had and so desperately wants is like another taunt from the Universe. I cannot tell her she is looking through a filtered lens of loss. She will come to that, but first, she must wade through her grief. I stay in the shadows and watch and wait and mourn, also.

Oh, Poppy! If I could just have had one day, held you, seen your face. My mother's grief is raw red.

I'm here. I love you.

But it's not the balm she seeks. She calls my father.

'The IUI didn't work.' There's no hello, no niceties, just this one fact.

'I'm coming home.'

'No, don't. There's no point.' She hangs up.

She's afraid he'll come home, and she'll go to pieces. In her mind's eye, she can see herself begging him to cross the line in the sand they'd agreed on when starting out, knowing that going back on her word, her reneging on what they agreed, would ruin their marriage.

If only she could call Kate, or her mother. She considers Ruby but pushes the idea away as quickly as it materialises – Ruby is pregnant, and my mother can't go there. She could call Jack, but where would she start, having not told him anything yet about trying to conceive? My mother wishes Maureen, her sister-in-law, had been the friend she'd once hoped for. No one understands her or what she is going through. My mother is lonely.

My parents have reached the end of the road. Exhausted emotionally, physically and financially, they always agreed on a point where they would stop, and here it is. No egg or sperm donation, no surrogates, no adoption.

The realisation that she may never carry her own baby guts my mother. Her sense of failure as a woman, as a wife, wafts from her in dull yellow and grey. My parents will never have their genes passed down. They'll never see themselves, their parents and grandparents, in their children's faces, personalities, and mannerisms. They see having children as a form of immortality.

'Housework,' her mother – my grandmother – used to say. 'Best therapy there is.' So, she strips the bed with a vigour approaching violence. Blood had soaked into the mattress topper too, but the under blanket did its work, and the mattress is unblemished. This brings her a spark of light that flickers briefly before it is blown out by the sight of the stained sheets. She gathers them up and brings them to the washing machine in the garage.

As she slams the washing machine door, the phone rings. It's her brother. She ignores his call. She knows she's been wallowing, but what can she say to him? Do infertile people get to make an announcement, like the opposite of the pregnancy announcements so popular on social media?

110

Should she post an ultrasound picture of her empty follicle ovaries and write, 'Guess who's never having babies?'

That would put the 'likes' across them!

She lifts the mail from the doormat as she passes through the hall.

Three cards. Fucking Christmas. She opens the first one. It's from Andy and Ruby, a photo of the family wearing themed outfits. They've posed their three children, wearing elf suits, sitting on a log with the parents standing behind them in Santa and Mrs Klaus costumes. Ruby is doing the pregnancy pose – tummy out, one hand resting on top, her other hand in the small of her back.

My mother's anger lights like a fuse, burning white-hot.

Though she's not religious, she thinks people have such a cheek to replace the Holy Family with their own on the front of Christmas cards. *Who the fuck do they think they are?*

She marches to the mantelpiece, tearing open the other two cards as she goes. They're from friends in Ireland, snowmen on one, robins on the other. As she sets them up, Andy and Ruby's card slides out of her hand and onto the hearth. It lands between the axe head and the geode halves, the latter's pink interiors sparkling in the winter sunlight. She remembers the hope she had when she bought it. Her anger explodes into a brilliant red fury.

My mother grabs one half of the geode and smashes it down onto the other half.

No!

My voice is too late, too quiet, too small against her crimson ferocity. Pieces of the geode fracture, flying in every direction. One shard flies off and slices the skin below her thumb knuckle. She doesn't feel the skin's edges sag away from each other; doesn't see the scarlet fluid drip down onto the axe head in her hand; can't see her blood soaking on a molecular level into the atoms of copper and tin of the bronze; oblivious to her blood splashing onto the crystals of the geode; unaware of the gliding between the worlds it holds together.

She strikes again, pulverising the geode. White dust puffs from the outer limestone shell and drifts in the air.

The veil between the worlds rips open wide, tipping us both into a maelstrom of colour: reds, pinks, purples and dust. So much dust, like falling ash, white and swirling high above the ground.

My mother freezes with the axe head held high, looking at the flying dust. Her aura changes from red fury to the purple throb of fear.

Around us, but looking through us, not seeing us, are people, their auras blending in fear and confusion as they run towards huts amid falling ash. One stops. She looks towards my mother, who is holding the axe head high in her outstretched arm, and speaks in a language that is not my mother's but which we both understand: 'This is because you stole the axe, and now you have weakened its power.'

My mother drops the axe head, and we're back in front of her fireplace in San Jose.

'We were in Ireland,' my mother says. 'I recognise the hill, the view, *something*. What the hell just happened?'

I'm also at a loss to explain it in any way a mortal would understand, but tell my mother, *I think it's either another world, or this one in another time.*

CHAPTER 14

I wake with sticky eyes and a bleary mind, unsure of where I am. Panic curls around me as the events of the past few days surface and break over me. I jolt up, then lean back onto one elbow and look around. I'm on my furs by our hearth. Nereus lies snoring gently behind me, the heat from his body soaking into my back through the early morning chill.

'We fell asleep!' I say, hardly believing my own words. I hear creaks and wonder if my ears are up to their old tricks again. But when I concentrate on the sound, I realise it is coming from the beams holding the roof. The roofing sod sags between the cut saplings that hold it.

Nereus's eyes open in a face caked with grey powder. He blinks and shakes his head, creating a cloud of dust that makes him cough again. A bitter smell irritates my nose and tickles my throat too.

I remember us both coughing and struggling to breathe as we ran uphill to our hut. Then, falling through the door, overcome with terror. We clung to each other, and this time, I was the one who cried while Nereus stroked my hair. The more he soothed, the more I mourned. The drowned villages, the floating bodies, the dead livestock, the lost dagger, Kallisto's anger, and Geros ... poor Geros, missing. How can we navigate this without him?

We must have been overcome by the physical and emotional toll from the last few days, for how else would we sleep? And for how long? My head and chest hurt. Nausea rolls my guts as I move onto all fours and push myself to stand.

The hut is dim. Early morning, perhaps? I stagger to the door and stare out at a landscape turned grey under a blanket of dust. Like dirty snow, it is ankle-deep, but at least it has stopped falling. Wind eddies the surface layers into drifts and ripples. The sky is heavy with clouds. But my ears are quiet. If there is no rain in these clouds, what *do* they contain?

I stare in the direction of the rising sun, but no light patch indicates the sun resting behind this cloud. I scan the sky and see a brighter area nearly overhead. Midday but with the pall of a winter's evening.

I hear her coming around the side of our hut before I see Yani's wife. She wears a stricken expression that reminds me of a baby deer I once caught in a trap – wild-eyed and skittish.

'Eleni, what are you doing here?' She jumps as if I've raised my hand to her. I temper my voice. 'Where are Yani and Agis?'

She takes a breath, rests her hand on her chest as though she is an Elder running uphill. 'They are at the meeting house. You must come to...' She stops, swallows, coughs and looks at the ground. '... To defend yourself. We are no match for Kallisto.'

Nereus is out the door and jogging down the path before I can reply. Eleni and I run after him, kicking up plumes with our feet.

*

Four Elders sit at one end of the meeting hall on a wooden platform rising between the fire pit and the wall as they do for formal rituals. Kallisto finishes saying something, and the Elders talk amongst themselves in low voices. There is a smattering of other people present. Chloe sits near Kallisto, but Jaisun sits apart from them. I wish I could talk to him, but I'm consumed with worry about Geros's absence.

Geros's living area near the door is tidy, his travel wrappings gone. His seat with the Elders lies empty and creates a void larger than the physical dimensions he usually takes up. The unlit fire is a pile of cold charcoal and ash. The space feels chilly and unwelcoming.

Coughs rattle around the hall in contrast to the low rumble of concerned conversation. Mela, the eldest woman in our tribe, shakes her head. She is known for wisdom and caution. Aon tugs at his beard, his hairy white eyebrows pulled together in concentration as he listens to Doah and Lan arguing. Aon is the thinker, the strategist. Geros relies on his advice to supplement his knowledge as story keeper and healer. Lan is Kallisto's direct kin, a great uncle, I think. He's brave and fought the Sea People during his youth. But he is short-tempered, and Kallisto inherited her mean streak from his lineage. Doah is usually the voice of reason and patience. She is fair and kind, and the village loves her dearly. I've no doubt she is countering whatever Kallisto and Lan are saying against us.

Dust covers everything, inside as well as outside, and my eyes itch. Nereus's broad back blocks my view of the area in front of the fire, but as we approach, a silence lands that frightens me. The hairs on my neck prickle.

What has she said?

In front of the fire, Kallisto and Yani square up to one another.

We present to the Elders, bow our heads. They nod. We step back.

'I'm sorry we missed the call to meet,' I say, watching Kallisto.

Her dark eyes are deep wells of hate.

I keep talking. 'Our journey took more from us than we realised. We didn't intend to sleep. There is much to report. But first, I must ask, has a search party been sent out for Geros. The village he visited has—' I stop.

Mela stands and raises a hand. She looks at me with a sad smile. 'Zosime, Nereus, you have lost your marks. Come replenish them at the fire.' She indicates with her hand that Nereus and I should sit by the fire; and we do, dipping our fingers in the dark charcoal at the edge and smearing the black ring of Parthalon around one eye, helping each other with touch-ups. It's ridiculous to spend the time on such trivia, but the Elders demand respect. If I rile them, they will never listen. I hardly know what I want to ask or say or defend anyway. I have no plan, no way forward. I'm cast adrift and floundering.

'May I sit, too?' Kallisto sounds inappropriately sullen. Chloe gasps and steps back into the shadows.

Nereus looks at Kallisto, surprised. I'm unnerved even more by her audacity.

'All right.' Mela sounds weary.

Kallisto moves to the other side of Nereus and sits.

'Now,' Mela begins. 'Kallisto tells me you stole the ancient axe *and* failed to bring back the bronze dagger. What have you to say?'

'The axe belongs to me. It was a good thing we did bring it, as it saved our lives.'

'Really?' Mela leans in.

Kallisto narrows her eyes.

I tell our story, how we followed Geros's instructions and saw the cairn to mark the great warrior's grave and how the fireball split the sky and exploded in a cloud on the horizon.

'Yes, we saw that, too.' Mela nods.

'Then a giant wave came down through the valley and swept away everything in its path,' Nereus says. He sounds like a boy making up a story. 'Water came up the hillside, and we had to climb into the trees to escape, except—' He looks ashamed. It tugs hard at me that he feels bad.

'I couldn't reach up into the tree, so I used the axe to get my first foothold. Nereus pulled me up the rest of the way.' I slide a glance in Kallisto's direction, but her face is a mask. 'So,' I say, 'I would have been swept away were it not for the axe. The water moved with a strong current, like a great river.'

Mela purses her lips. The heads of the other Elders bob.

'This wave,' Kallisto says. 'Where did it come from?'

Nereus shrugs.

'From the horizon where the sun never goes,' I say.

'Then what did you do?' Mela asks.

'We stayed up the tree until morning, then waded through the water to dry ground.'

'How did you wade through such water if, as you say, it had such a strong current,' Lan asks with narrowed eyes.

'By morning, the water had stopped moving. Its push was gone.'

'Really?' Lan sits back, raising an eyebrow in disbelief.

'Go on,' Doah says. 'In your own words.' She scowls at Lan. He sighs and shakes his head.

I swallow. 'The water tasted of tears.'

'Like the sea?' Mela asks.

I nod. 'We were a long way from the sea but that water, it came up over my knee. And when we saw that everything had been...' I falter, trembling at the memory of it. 'The water covered so much land. It was terrible. We decided to come straight home.'

Nereus opens his mouth. I drop my eyes to my left hand and make my hunting signal – wait. Only he can see it. Confusion flits across his face, but he stays quiet. His hand clenches three times – three squeezes – he trusts me.

I don't want to tell the Elders we dismantled the cairn in case Geros did not get permission. The less we admit to, the less we can be punished for. Either way, we have no dagger to give them.

'So you didn't bother to look for the bronze dagger?' Kallisto says.

'We wanted to warn you. There has been much devastation. It's too late for the dagger.' I address Mela. She is the least superstitious of the Elders, but not as sceptical as I am.

Lan slams his hand onto the bench beside him and glares at me. 'Who are you to decide such things? Geros sent you on a mission and you decide not to complete it? You decide to take a valuable axe with you. You have angered the gods. This.' He waves his hands above his head. 'This is their retribution, and we all suffer because *you* decide it?'

'Lan,' Doah says in a firm voice that belies her frail frame. 'The axe was not stolen, for Zosime has returned with it. And we always knew that her mission would be difficult. Did we not see the fireball the day she neared the cairn? Perhaps it was a warning to stay away from it.'

'Doah is right,' Mela says. 'We don't know what these signs mean. The Maiden and the Hag may not be at war. They may be allies against a greater foe. You draw too many assumptions and judge too harshly. This is a matter to take up with the Monarchs.'

'Which is what Geros did.' Lan stands up, paces in front of his seat.

I feel my scalp contract at the thought of Geros. I close my eyes only to revisit the image of the woman impaled on the tree.

'Aon, you've been very quiet,' Mela says.

Aon sighs. He takes his time answering and we wait.

After a long moment, he begins, 'This began when we saw the Maiden and the Hag. That has nothing to do with Nereus and Zosime.'

I hear Nereus exhale beside me.

'But,' Aon says. 'How do we know that the next action didn't trigger further displeasure from the gods – when Zosime took the axe.'

'The axe belongs to her,' Doah says.

'It belongs to the village. It is hers by tradition only.' Kallisto is too abrupt and even Lan seems agitated by her tone.

'Which is it?' Aon asks. 'Either she owns it, or she doesn't?'

It takes every drop of strength I have to stay quiet, to show humility. If this goes to a vote of the Elders, I need as many on my side as possible.

Kallisto's nostrils flare, but she realises, too late, that she may have overstepped the mark. I can sense her clamping down as she bows her head.

Mela clears her throat. 'So do you think the fireball came because Zosime and Nereus stole the axe?'

She is asking Aon, but before he can answer, Lan nods and says, 'The fireball and this dust, yes. And the wave they speak of. That, too.'

'Oh, come now.' Mela sighs as if to say she knows whose side Lan is on. 'If the gods reacted like this every time a human took something that wasn't theirs, there would be no world left, let alone a person taking something that *traditionally* belongs to them. It is a rather extreme repercussion.'

'Since when have the gods been measured or logical?' asks Aon, his eyes almost disappearing beneath his furrowed white eyebrows.

'May I add something?' I say with my eyes lowered.

'Go on,' Mela says.

'The village Kallisto wanted to trade the axe with is gone.'

'Gone?' Mela says. The Elders exchange looks. I hear gasps from those gathered.

'The wave washed it away.'

Many try to stifle their disbelief, but Kallisto snorts back a half laugh. 'This giant wave travelled all the way to the Blackwater Ford?'

'Yes,' I say.

Mela fixes her gaze on Kallisto. I can tell she is not impressed by Kallisto's sneer as she says in a low, stern voice, 'Kallisto, you bring this before the Elders, to what end?'

Kallisto shuffles her feet, shrugs and looks at Nereus. Anger rises hot within me.

'I would like an answer,' Mela says.

'I believe that Zosime has displeased the gods and has to make amends directly to them.'

A mummer skitters through the people gathered. Jaisun shakes his head. The Elders have probably asked him about his trip to the Mound with Geros; and as Kallisto said, he probably knows nothing about what was said to Geros. No one knows what is going on – least of all me.

Mela holds up her hand for silence. 'Are you suggesting a blood sacrifice?'

'Yes.' Kallisto can barely keep the smirk from her lips. She knows this will involve travelling to Great Mound and spending a moon cycle in penance, praying before the ceremony. Not to mention the time it will take me to capture a live animal to take with me for the blood sacrifice. That's plenty of time for her to work her way in with Nereus.

'I see,' Mela confers with Aon, and he nods before she turns back to the gathering. 'An animal blood sacrifice will be required. If the gods are displeased with Zosime to this great degree, then it is of utmost importance that she make this sacrifice as quickly as possible. Wouldn't you agree?'

The corners of Kallisto's mouth twitch. 'Yes, I agree.'

'So, to expedite the process, we will give Zosime a young beast from our herd rather than send her out to hunt for a live capture of a wild animal, which would take too long.'

'But—' Kallisto's eyes are round in shock.

'This is the best way. Let us progress now to the lower meadow and select a beast.' Mela turns her back on the gathering, and we are dismissed. There is no argument.

I'm not thrilled that I will have to make the journey to Great Mound and spend so much time there, but the sacrifice is to be taken from Kallisto's stock, which she has so lovingly bred and tended, while I depend on the old ways of hunting for my meat.

Outside the Ceremonial Hall, my cousin Con awaits with an oak drum in the crook of his elbow. He sounds out a bi-tonal beat, alternating with his thumb and the heel of his hand, as the village gathers for the procession to the lower meadow.

The four Elders take the lead, followed by Con, and the rest of us fall in behind. Con sets the pace with his drum. There is no conversation. Our footfalls echo the pa-dum of the drum, and we stir up a cloud of dust as we walk down the hill past the bigger huts. People hear the drumming and join the procession. There's the hiss and burble of suppressed voices as the reason for the procession is explained to those swelling the ranks behind us.

Beside me, Nereus' belly rumbles, and I realise that I'm hungry, too, though my insides churn at the idea of a blood sacrifice. It's not the blood but the fact that I don't want to waste my time and a pig's life for something I don't believe in. If our gods are so powerful, why would killing a pig keep them happy? And if they are so cruel, why would they keep any bargains with us mere mortals? You can't strike deals with people, much less gods. I think back to the suckling pig ritual to bring me children that didn't work.

We're passing by the last of the smaller huts, and the landscape stretches ahead of us, covered in dust to the horizon. The almost ripened cereal crops have flattened beneath the weight of the dust. It will be harder to harvest now, and removing the dust will be difficult since it covers everything and floats in the air when stirred.

In the crease of the landscape, the river is swollen and looks like a series of muddy slugs where it winds through the willows. We follow the trackway and turn towards the lower field, but the procession stops. Mela's hands fly to her mouth. A cry escapes Doah, and she slumps against Lan. He and Aon stop her from collapsing. The drumbeat dies away as Con stares at the fields below. I edge up beside him to see what has happened.

My jaw drops.

Every single pig lies motionless on its side. It is clear by the flies swarming over the glazed staring eyes that these beasts are dead, at least thirty animals snuffed out without a mark on them.

A squeak escapes Kallisto, then she pushes through the Elders, runs to the first animal and falls to her knees. She buries her head in her hands and sobs.

CHAPTER 15

A fry is the only thing my father can cook well. Getting the right bacon – proper back-bacon, not streaky – in San Jose is a challenge, but ever since they sourced it in a shop in Willow Glen, the full Ulster fry has been back on the menu. He carries a plate to the table, piled high with fried eggs, bacon, sausages, black pudding – or blood pudding, as it's called here – pancakes and potato bread. It's the bread that makes an Irish fry up into an Ulster fry.

'Here ya go,' he says, proud of his creation. 'Get this into ya.'

'Thanks.' My mother picks up her fork and gives him a ghost of a smile.

He kisses the top of her head and pushes away his unease. My mother retreats behind a beige cocoon to the sanctuary of an emotionless desert, while his helplessness hangs in a cerulean fog around them. He longs to bring her smile back; can't remember the last time she laughed.

It's been six months since they stopped trying to conceive. I float through time oblivious to its roll, aware only of the sorrow that hangs over my parents, and try my best to send them comfort, which each bats away in their own unique manner. My mother makes wishes, is offering her desires up to an impossible void, knows these wishes won't be granted; she wishes Kate were still alive to talk to; she wishes her mother wouldn't slide in and out of lucidity; she wishes she could hold me, if only, she pleads, for a moment.

My father, pragmatic and practical, wants something to do, some metric to measure, some way of knowing that they will get through this, over this devastating disappointment. He calls their infertility a 'disappointment,' but my mother has no words for it.

Sitting across the table from my mother, my father takes his time cutting up his sausages before forking a chunk and dipping it into the soft yolk of his fried egg. Molten gold oozes around the sausage and spills over the egg-white in slow motion. He savours the taste and watches as my mother pushes her food around the plate.

'I love you,' he says.

'I know.'

He looks at her, fork frozen in mid-air, waiting for her to follow up with, 'Thank you,' which always makes them laugh. But humour has taken a hike.

She senses him watching and looks up. 'Sorry, what?'

'Are you okay?'

'Hmm.' She shrugs, avoids eye contact.

'Should we get help?'

'Help? What would help?'

'Counselling?'

'What good will talking do?'

Her absolute defeat sends up neon blue spirals of alarm. My father sets down his fork and takes her hand. 'Talking might not do any good, but it wouldn't hurt to try.' He dips his head to try to catch her eye. 'You're not even talking to me.'

My father and I can both sense my mother's panic as repressed emotion froths up.

He's at a loss to know how to help her, and at the same time, he's considering his own grief. In the small forgotten moments of everyday living, he senses my presence, the way a smell can trigger a memory, some sense of how things could have been. But he has never responded to me the way my mother has. He's more robust than she is, allowing fragments of a new vision, a different future, to fill the void that childlessness has left. All she sees is the barren space she cannot fill.

She clings to me, then pushes me away in frustration. Ever since she smashed the geode, we have shared a stronger bond. Perhaps I am here because she needs me.

'Talking won't bring me a baby.' Her pain flares red raw.

'No, it won't. But you need to talk about how you feel.'

Talk to him. You both need it. I flood her aura with calming pinks.

She looks him in the eye.

'Are you sure you're ready to hear this?'

He nods.

She takes a deep breath, pushes away her plate. 'I feel ashamed that I want so badly to be pregnant when I already have so much. But I feel like a failure. I'm angry at my body, at my fucking ovaries for not doing their job. I just want to get it all ripped out, ovaries and uterus and have no more periods because, like, what the fuck's the point?'

'Ripped out?' He goes pale at the thought of it, horrified by the idea.

'Well, you know, under anaesthesia, of course.'

'Of course… but it's a bit extreme.'

'I knew you weren't ready to hear this. Forget it; I shouldn't have said anything.'

'No, no. You can talk to me. Please. You've been so distant.'

She stands up, the chair legs screeching against the wooden floor. 'Me, distant? You're the one who escapes into work, online, into every screen. You hardly touch me anymore.'

He rises from the table and steps towards her, stopping at arm's length. 'Don't—'

She stamps her foot. 'We wrecked sex. We made it a chore, and now I don't think I could ever be bothered again.'

Tears spill down her cheeks.

He opens his arms. She collapses against his chest.

'I'm sorry,' she whispers. 'I'm just useless, fucking useless. I've let you down. I'm a failure as a mother, as a wife, as a woman.'

'That's not true.' My father doesn't know what else to say. I focus my love on him and his skin puckers into goosebumps, but he doesn't understand why. He wraps his arms around my mother. They rock gently together until she wriggles and breaks away, wiping her eyes.

They sit back down to the now cold breakfast in an unspoken choreography. He tops up her coffee. She chews diligently on yolk-stained bacon.

As silence drapes between them, the urge to be known is overpowering. I can't stand watching them suffer. I send out as much love and compassion as I can, but it falls short. If only I could reach him, perhaps I could help them both heal.

'I want to be a mother so bad it hurts.' My mother raises a hand to her sternum and taps. 'Hurts here, you know?'

He nods, lays down his fork, and grasps her hand.

She grips back hard. 'Maybe we should think about adoption?' Hope glows from her in a golden burst that is lost in his pewtering blue.

'Honey, I thought we'd already decided. Adoption is not the answer for us.'

'For you?' she snaps.

'We talked about this.' He sighs. 'It's a long, hard process. There's no guarantee we'd have a child at the end of it. It's just…' He pulls his hand from hers and scrapes it through his hair.

'But that was before IVF. Before we knew I… this…'

'I'm exhausted, and so are you.'

'No more exhausted than I would be if I were pregnant.' Her shoulders sag. She already knows his stance, is running out of steam, but tries again. 'There are so many children who need parents. And we've so much to offer.'

'There's not that many children needing adoption nowadays.'

'Maybe, not as many, but still—'

'Raising a child is a lot of hard work, commitment, sacrifices – I could only do it for my own child.' His face hardens. He's not proud of what he considers to be a selfish stance, but this is his truth, one he cannot escape. 'How do you honestly feel about this?'

'I could totally do it. I know it would require sacrifice. I'm willing to do that. It would be worth it, so worth it.'

He presses his lips together, determined to let her speak, hoping she'll wind up in the same place as him.

Silence drapes between them.

Her heart pounds. She takes a breath and tries again. 'I was prepared to make those same sacrifices for my own child anyway. I don't have a job; I can stay at home and look after our children, and you can continue to further your career. It's no different with an adopted child.'

'I can't,' he says in a quiet voice. 'If fate had sent us a child, I'd have made the sacrifices, loved it.'

'What's the difference? Don't you see? To the child, it doesn't matter. We'd be their parents. The end result is the same – for me, for us.'

'There's the cost.'

'The cost? You're putting a price on parenthood?'

He's losing the argument, looking like a mean old bastard who won't help a kid out; but in his gut, he knows this isn't right for him. He can't do it.

He needs to justify it to himself as much as to her but can't find the words.

She thinks one more nudge in her direction might break his reasoning so far apart that he realigns his thoughts with hers.

He speaks first. 'It could take another ten years to adopt. We'd be hitting fifty. Would it be fair to saddle a kid with ageing parents? We can have a good life without children. There's so much to live for. And besides, we agreed. We talked this through before IVF. You know what I think about this. It's not fair to ask me to change.'

She pushes her chair back, and in her heart, she's pushing him back, disconnecting.

He senses it and feels icy.

I feel it as a fading. If my parents fall apart, do I disappear? Or do I need to heal this rift?

Perhaps that is what has me trapped on this side of the veil. My mother had asked me if my purpose was to save other children. But maybe *this* was my purpose – maybe I need to save *them*? And once my job is done here and they are happy, a portal will open and I can once more retreat to the bliss on the other side.

My mother is exhausted from the repeated cresting of optimism plunging into the depths of disappointment. She hasn't the strength to head up a crusade for adoption right now. Total defeat pops her last bubble of hope. Deep down, she agrees with him in principle, and adoption has to be a joint decision; but she can't bear that future. The years ahead look so empty, so bleak.

For both of us.

It's time to take a chance. If I get this wrong, I risk my mother banishing her thoughts from me, but it's worth it. I might disappear either way.

Tell him about me.

My mother swallows as if her throat is covered in cactus spines. *How will that help?*

I beam calming white light. *You won't be alone with my voice in your head. If he's even a little open to me, I can make him hear me, too. We can be more of a family. He might change his mind about adoption.*

Or he'll think I'm mad.

'Aisling?' His voice makes her jump.

'Yep?'

'Are you okay? You zoned right out.' He peers into her face with fresh alarm.

She directs her thoughts to me. *I've already tried. It didn't work.*

That was when my father picked up the axe head, and the vision broke through from another dimension. It frightened him, confused me. He had an experience, and if it happened again, he wouldn't be able to write it off as shock again. But when he touched the axe before, there wasn't exactly a connection to me.

The geode; try using that, I tell her. She'd scooped the broken pieces into a box and hidden them at the back of the closet after our last vision. Briefly she wanted to throw it out, but was both frightened and intrigued by its power. So, she kept it.

'We need to talk about Poppy.' My mother shifts forward.

My father rubs the hair prickling the nape of his neck. 'Poppy?'

'Our baby.'

'What about it?'

'Not it, her.'

'O-kay. What about her?' He shivers. The winter sun spilling in through the patio doors makes dust motes dance above the breakfast table.

'You believe in parallel universes, don't you?' My mother is so clever. She has to present this with as much hard science as possible.

He nods, relaxing into the theoretical tone of the conversation, relieved to be leaving behind the difficult topic of adoption; heartened also by the glow I am beaming to him, which he interprets as my mother's enthusiasm for looking forward in life.

'And you believe in heaven? That my father is in heaven?'

'Yeah, I think. Yeah.'

'What if the spirit world is a parallel place? Like a parallel universe.'

'Okay.' He nods, purses his lips, takes a deep breath. 'Maybe I could buy into that.'

'And what if a spirit travelled from one universe to another… somehow…'

'Nah. I don't think it would work like that.' He takes a draft of coffee and sets the empty mug on his plate beside the bacon rind.

'But what if that spirit could communicate? Would you try something with me?'

He raises his eyebrows. 'Sure.'

'Wait there.'

In the bedroom, she fishes out the box with the broken geode from the bottom of the wardrobe. There's a tingle in the newly healed cut where the geode fragment had sliced into her finger. She chews her lip. Her aura pulses dark red. I understand her fear. We don't know the rules – if there are any rules – governing this force we've stumbled upon.

My mother rubs the pink line on her finger, clasps the box to her, and brings it to the kitchen. The table is semi-cleared, the dirty dishes stacked on the countertop above the dishwasher now. As my father loads the dishwasher, he hums a tune he caught earlier on the radio that has stuck in his head.

How does this work? My mother asks me.

I don't know. But we should start with him holding a piece of the geode and see what happens.

She hesitates, picking up on the mauve ripple of anxiety I can't hold back.

I don't understand the geode's function, nor can I gauge its power. In my place in the spirit world, I am granted knowledge. It informs me of darkness in the other worlds, makes me aware of spirits with heavy souls that never make it to the light. They lose their colour to the blackness of despair and never gain the contrast of love, hope, or joy. They become the loneliness of the abandoned, the tortures of addiction, the horrors of war, emptying into the abyss of terror and hatred that plagues the physical world. But the innocence of my original world has protected me from their effect. Now, as I drift in the physical world, those shadows are apparent and manifest around fear and evil. Am I playing with forces I shouldn't?

I tune into my knowing and watch the kaleidoscope churn silver, purple, green, red until yellows and oranges pulse hardest. Like my father's 'gut feelings', I trust this cue.

'Come here.' My mother sets the box on a drying patch of the table and lifts the lid.

'Jeepers, what happened to the geode?' my father asks.

'Pick up a piece.'

He raises an eyebrow.

'Go on. Just do it.'

'Any piece?'

'Try that one.' She points to the second-largest piece, its pink crystals glistening in the sunlight.

He cradles it in his palm.

Father?

He hitches his shoulders towards his ears, settles back into his chair, and frowns.

It's me, Poppy.

'Is something supposed to happen?' The hairs on his arms stand, but he ignores them.

'Don't you hear her?'

'Hear who?'

'Poppy.'

I push harder. *Father!*

'Stop!' He shivers. 'This is crazy, Aisling.'

'Open your mind. Our daughter can talk to us. All you have to do is listen.'

'Enough. This is cruel and uncalled for.' He presses the piece of geode into my mother's hand.

She's transported.

*

A line of pig carcasses stretch across a field. All around are people dressed in skins and rough woven linen. They have their faces painted, each with one eye blacked out. Some are just joining the line. Others stand around watching, their faces solemn. A drumbeat tolls to a backdrop of keening. Three people in wicker masks move back and forth across the fields with smouldering clumps of herbaceous plants. Blue-grey smoke curls from them in spiralling patterns as the wicker-clad people wave their arms in a slow dance over the dead pigs.

My mother shares the overwhelming sentiment of the group, sorrow, confusion and an overarching fear deep in her core. She senses a presence behind her and turns her head.

A withered old man peers at her with eyes that hold ancient wisdom.

'I did not expect you to be here,' he says in a strange language that she can somehow understand. 'You have to return the axe to where you found it.'

'The axe?' she asks, but she knows he means the bronze axe head.

The strangest of these weird events is that we both know innately who this man is, despite the fact she has never seen nor heard of him. It's like she has tapped briefly into my universal knowledge. 'Geros,' she says, 'what is happening?'

'Go home, and I'll explain. Go.' Geros steps back, the colours lacklustre, the sounds of the people more distant than before. Everything fades. Their intense sorrow loosens its grip.

*

A hand on my mother's elbow pulls her back into the yellow-sunlit kitchen. She comes into herself as she would upon waking from a dream.

Fear makes my father sharp, aggressive almost. 'What the hell are you playing at?'

'I… I don't know…' Her face is wet with tears. She has dropped the geode piece into its box and she looks around, confused.

My father picks up his phone. 'I'm calling the doctor. You're scaring the shite out of me, Aisling. You need help.'

'No. I'm okay.' She puts her hand over his holding the phone. 'But I need to go.'

Dismay billows from him in purple and lilac. It rattles through me, but I don't fade as I did before. My mother is right; she needs to go home.

'What are you talking about?'

I counter my father's distress with pastel greens and yellows. His heart rate steadies until she says, 'I'm taking the next flight home.'

CHAPTER 16

I can't settle at home. I pace our hut. Three steps, turn, three steps, turn. A high-pitched whine fills my right ear. Rain is coming again. Nereus is outside, sweeping grey sludge from our roof in plump thwaps. Rain falling on the dust makes it heavy. Already, several huts have collapsed. The dust smells rotten when it is damp, like an egg that spoiled before its shell broke open; of flowers that call to flies rather than bees; of festering flesh.

Nereus wants me to keep away from the other villagers, at least until the cleansing ceremony is over. He thinks out of sight *is* out of mind. After finding the herd dead, Kallisto has been telling anyone who will listen that evil spirits came because I took the ceremonial axe. It's hard to refute that evil spirits are involved when faced with so many dead animals at once. It can't be the dust since that fell everywhere, on us, but only these pigs in the lower meadow have died. Sometimes, fish or frogs are afflicted by evil spirits that live in the water, and masses of them are found floating belly-up in a pond or side water. We are never certain why these evil spirits strike, but to see this in land animals, larger beasts?

Usually, when I find wild animals dead, they show signs of age, starvation, or injury. So, this must be malevolent magic indeed. Another horrific event to add to the recent toll; yes, Kallisto is happy to lay the blame on me. But I wonder if Kallisto made some mistake while tending to the pigs. Our tribe used to let them roam but she has kept them trapped in the low meadows. Could this anger the spirits? Or has Kallisto supplemented their feed with – who knows what? She left them unsupervised. Can she be the one to blame and not me?

Strangely, the cattle on the hill are spared. I haven't had a chance to go hunting in a couple of days since the pigs died, so I don't know if the deer and wild boar fare any better. But once this cleansing ceremony is over, I will take my quiver and venture out with the hunt that has been organised by my brother, Agis, and Con, our older cousin who taught us hunting along with our parents. It may be an old, waning tradition, but we hunters are a necessity again. With the pigs gone, what else will we eat?

The distant drumbeat changes pace and thrums low against the whine in my ears. This tells me the villagers have moved on from smouldering the herbs and have set the pigs on fire. Sure enough, the smell of the pigs burning sparks my appetite. But we cannot risk eating the pig meat in case the evil spirits make us sick. The cleansing ceremony will ensure that evil is driven far away. But still, I worry.

By Shortest Night, our crops were lush with foliage and building towards harvest. But now they too may be lost; the fields near the river are still flooded and the crops rotting, while a thick layer of fine grey dust has flattened those plants which escaped the floods. I worry that we won't have food this winter. We strain the water through cloth to take out the dust and mud, but it tastes strange, though it hasn't made us sick. Not yet.

A cough at our hut door makes me turn.

'Can I enter?'

'Geros! You're alive!' I'm so surprised, so relieved, I forget to invite him in, but he reads my tone of welcome and pushes aside the door flap. A lump forms in my throat and tears prick my eyes, making the light behind him blur and shimmer. But he is real, and he's alive. I stand mute, my arms wrapped around me, smiling at him like I've lost my senses.

He looks well, thinner, and dust covers his garments, but his eyes are as bright and full of wisdom as ever, though he looks puzzled.

'You know I'm alive,' he says. 'You should not have visited the ceremony,'

'I didn't.'

A frown creases his brow. 'No?'

'I was here the whole time, Geros. Nereus insisted.'

Doubt crosses his face. He shakes it off. 'That was wise. Forgive an old man his confusion. I'm glad to find you here.'

'Not as glad as I am to see you.' I take his hand and clasp it in both of mine when really I want to hug his frail bones to me, but that would be disrespectful. 'Terrible things are afoot.'

'I know,' he says. 'But first, tell me. Did you find the grave?'

'We found *a* grave, but we do not know if it was the right one.'

131

Geros's bony fingers grip my hand. 'Of course, you did not disturb the grave.' His eyes bore into mine. My heart thuds hard.

'Of course.' I cannot hold his gaze.

He lets go of my hand and indicates that we sit on the skins by our hearth. 'There are things we need to say, and…' He takes a moment to settle beside me. '…things we must not say. Do you understand?'

'Yes.' I'm scared. I cannot tell him we pulled the cairn to pieces. I pray that Nereus says nothing if Geros goes outside to ask him next. 'What is happening, Geros? The flood, the dust, the pigs? This can't be because I took the axe. Can it?'

'No, the Monarchs say it is the Hag. She ripped the sky open to let the dust fall from her world.'

'So you – they – saw the sky open too?'

Geros nods.

'And the wave?'

'We did not see that first-hand, but we heard about it from travellers. They came to ask for help. Many were lost to the gods.'

'I know.' Sorrow crushes me. 'I could not find the dagger.'

'I know.'

'How?'

'The Monarchs have it. Have always had it. The stories of its strength are false, and they knew that all along. I'm sorry I sent you on a fool's errand.'

I'm staggered by the weight of this. There is no protection from the Hag. Someone has lied, or at least exaggerated the story of the dagger. Nereus and I ventured out for nothing. What we did to the tomb was unnecessary. 'But what about—'

'Whatever you did in the execution of this errand lies with me. Any punishment from the gods will land on my head. You followed orders and did what you had to do at the cairn.'

I swallow hard and feel sick. I can no longer keep track of how our gods dole out their justice. Perhaps they are not just. After all, have I not learnt that even if you do everything right, you don't necessarily get what you deserve? Have I not seen good actions repaid with bad – or with nothing? Perhaps the gods seek no justice… perhaps they do not care for us. Perhaps the world is simply terribly indifferent.

Geros asks me for details of our journey. I tell him about the wave and the flood and the devastation. But he does not mention the cairn again. He listens, and when I am finished, he says, 'It was a mistake to take your axe.'

'It saved my life.'

'You would have found a way.'

'I'm not convinced,' I mumble. *And you didn't stop me from taking it when you woke up and caught me*, I think to myself, then wonder if Geros is saying this aloud in part to appease the tribe.

He ignores my insolence. He waves his hand, up, up. I stand and help him to his feet.

'You will need to atone in public. It will be called for if it hasn't been already.'

'You've not spoken to the council yet?' I ask. 'I thought you said you were at the cleansing ceremony.'

'I passed by it but stayed in the trees. I was only noticed by one person, and she was not of this…' he hesitates as if searching out the word, making me wonder if age is wearing him down. Finally, he says, 'Not of this place.'

He straightens his cloak around him. Clouds of fine dust puff off it and hang in the air like a ghostly shadow before drifting to the ground. There is no point in trying to sweep it away. This dust that has fallen from the Hag's world coats everything: the trees, the grass, the stones, the animals, the huts, even our clothes and our skin. It grits our teeth and fills underneath our fingernails. It is in our water, our food, and now, in us.

And I am the one who has to atone.

'Kallisto has already demanded my punishment.' I pull back the door flap.

We squint in the brighter light spilling in from outside though the sun is shrouded in cloud.

'That doesn't surprise me,' Geros says.

'But how do we know it is my fault, that the pigs didn't die through some fault of hers?' I hate that I sound desperate.

'She is not new to tending livestock. It's been handed down to her through generations just as hunting has been handed down to you.'

'But hunting is the older way. As we speak, Agis is organising a hunting trip to make up for the food we have lost.'

'Yes, that is true, Zosime. You are an important part of that. It is unlikely your actions caused the pigs to die, but there needs to be atonement for you taking the axe. That is undeniable. Don't you agree?'

'Yes. But there hasn't been an atonement since Torus cursed Rola three winters ago. How does taking an axe – which I returned – compare to killing with a curse?'

Geros stands with head bowed, unable to meet my eye. He gives no answer.

'Please, Geros, don't mark me as guilty. The village will always hold this disgrace against me.' I can't voice that I am already set apart because I have not given Nereus children. And if I *do* have children, this dishonour will now be handed down to them. How will I bear the shame? What the village will remember, is that I was marked in atonement when the pigs died, and they will say that the Elders think I am responsible for that when, really, we will never know who or what caused the spirits to take the pigs.

Geros turns to me with pain and compassion etched into his face. He does not want to do this either, but I realise neither of us has a choice. I took the axe. It was wrong.

I inhale deeply and nod.

Geros says softly, 'It will require a small blood sacrifice.'

'How small?'

'A few drops. From the heel of your hand.'

'From my hand? A human blood sacrifice? But—'

'It's just a nick,' Geros says in a soft voice that does nothing to soothe my panic. 'Symbolic.'

I'm breathing hard, trying to come to terms with this development. A human blood sacrifice has so much more weight, but I can see where he is coming from. There are too few animals to spare.

Geros keeps his voice soft, and this time I allow myself to take some comfort from it as he says, 'I suggest we use your axe.'

'But it's a ceremonial axe. It's never been used in battle. It's too blunt to cut flesh.'

'Then find your sharpening stone,' Geros says, stepping out into the daylight, leaving me alone in the gloom of my hut.

*

The drum beats out of time. I step onto the platform, head down, trying to block out the sea of faces watching. Agis, Aleka, Yani, Eleni and Con will be standing with Nereus in the front row, presenting a united front of support if I need it. But I can't bear to see Nereus. He hates this ritual. The idea of flesh being sliced nauseates him; living flesh, worse still.

Despite myself, I steal a glance upwards. Con is flint-eyed, a stone carving. Agis and Aleka stand together. His eyes burn with anger. Hers are wet with tears. Yani stares expressionless, stoic, but Elani's eyes soften with compassion. My shame affects them, but when they came

134

to my hut the night before they had only words of consolation, words that should have soothed my heart but didn't.

I tune everyone out, focus on the fizzling in my ears that tuck in behind the sounds of where I am: the crowd murmuring, people coughing, children at play, babies crying, Geros wheezing, my heart thumping. I lower my gaze from the line of Elders standing over the waist-high, flat-topped stone where my blood will drip. Three drops. Not much. It's the humiliation – Kallisto's gloating – that is hardest to bear. Lan, her uncle, is the Elder chosen to perform the ritual. Kallisto will enjoy that.

The sharpened axe edge shines brighter than the rest of the bronze. It mesmerises me as Lan slides it across my skin. I think of it biting into the oak tree, of the foothold it provided, of springing off it into the tree, of the wave bearing down on me, blasting everything in its path. Everything except me. In the tree.

The axe cuts. I bleed. Three drops.

I close my eyes and see a woman's face – kind, sad eyes, red lips, not quite smiling, with a bright light shining above her head. On my swift intake of breath, the vision vanishes. I open my eyes.

Lan says the words that keep the gods happy and the faithful happier. But I tune them out, enraged by their emptiness. The cut to my hand stings, but Doah – kind hearted Doah – applies the herbs that Geros has prepared to ensure rapid healing. My flesh will not suffer for long.

Geros lays the axe on the stone beside the blood so the blood can dry into both.

I feel steady enough to steal a glance towards Nereus. His stern expression lightens as we lock eyes. A lifted eyebrow from him, and I tilt my chin a fraction. His worry lines relax a little.

Geros steps forward. 'Witness all here today that this woman has paid a blood sacrifice for her wrongdoing. It is finished.'

Nereus claps slow, deliberate beats. Con joins in along with Agis and Aleka, and soon, half the village are voicing their support for me. Others stand silent, still siding with Kallisto. Chloe hesitates, looks at Jaisun standing nearby. He is clapping, too. Chloe stays with Kallisto, but with head bowed.

Kallisto has damaged me in the eyes of many, but in this moment, I decide that this does not matter. I am a hunter; I do not need her and her crops and her penned-up animals. I will be able to contribute to the communal pot, so I will always be a provider for my people. Everyone knows that I have always done more than my share, generously given. This will be forgotten in time.

As Geros says, 'We move on together.'

*

The gods pay us little heed, and the rain drives hard over the next moon cycle. I pay another blood sacrifice – in private this time – and let Nereus know he will have to wait a while longer to be a father.

'Perhaps it is as well,' he says the morning after I tell him. 'This year's harvest will be lean. I want you to have all you need.' He squeezes my hand. '...when the time comes.'

Lying beside him, curled up beneath our furs, I rest my head on his shoulder and inhale the scent of woodsmoke from his tunic. We shouldn't need a fire inside during this season, but it is cold and damp. So cold, it feels like we are closer to the Longest Night than the Shortest Night. The wind finds every crevice and whips through our hut mercilessly.

'Thank you,' I whisper. The fact Nereus is trying to make me feel better about it warms my heart.

'For what?'

'For your patience.'

'Not for the body heat?' He makes to move away.

I clasp him to me beneath the furs.

'Perhaps we should move back in with my parents?' he says.

'You're not serious?'

His laugh is a rumble to my ear pressed against his chest. 'No. I wouldn't take you to live with the coastal people. You are much too refined.' He breaks wind unreservedly.

'Good point.' I try to hold my breath until it is safe to inhale. 'Oh, that's bad!' I say as the smell creeps around me. 'Go outside the next time you have to do that. What was in the pot last night?'

'Not a lot.'

We sober up. In summer, the pot should be full to bursting. But it was more soup than stew, like an early spring pot, scanty from winter.

I stick a toe out. The air is frigid. I don't want to get up, but Nereus wriggles and, with a grim look, says, 'I may need to take this one outside.'

'Go,' I say, pushing him.

A draught of frigid air fills the void he leaves behind. I hug the furs tight around my body.

He pulls back the door flap. 'What in the gods?' The alarm in his voice makes me sit bolt upright.

I scramble to the door, still draped in our bedding, and peer out. Snow as deep as a man's knee covers our village. At least, I hope it is snow because if it isn't…

I stick my hand into its icy coldness and pull back a fistful of it, watching it melt with the heat of my hand, feeling the cold bite back. It's snow all right.

Outside, others emerge from their own huts. Snow in summer? It has never happened before in living memory. We make our way through the snow to the Ceremonial Hall, and as we wait for the Elders to convene, I look out over snow-covered fields. Ordinarily, I love how beautiful winter snow is, how it makes tracking animals easier and how it muffles sounds – making everything feel like a secret. But now I gaze upon this white-draped landscape and wonder if it is this cold in summer, what will winter bring?

CHAPTER 17

The cosy patchwork fields lift my mother's heart in a way she isn't expecting when the aeroplane breaks through the clouds on its approach to Dublin Airport. The greenery rolls out below like a carelessly strewn blanket, soothing her; a range of shades but mostly vibrant growth with the odd patch of blazing yellow where rapeseed blossoms fill random fields. Golden gorse, in full bloom, threads between some green patches. It's a balm after the yellow-grassed landscape of the Californian drought, already looking parched, although it's only early June.

'Home.' My mother inhales the word. Coming here is an itch she needs to scratch. Still, she misses my father and can't fathom what propels her away from him; this man she loves, needs, but who is oblivious to her connection to me, to a calling even she can't identify.

He has promised to join her in Ireland as soon as work allows, to holiday there, to accompany her on her return to California; but in this moment, she never wants to leave Ireland again. Homesickness, combined with grief, has mutated into a force she cannot battle. Ireland – home – is the only place she can nurse her broken spirit, her broken heart and search for... what? Her purpose in life? *My* purpose?

My father understands that he must give her space, but not for too long. His sadness paints more pastel shades on his heart than hers does. He's been sadder. Losing his dad when he was only sixteen, and his mother in his early thirties – my father has encountered grief and knows he'll get through this. Yes, he needs my mother, but he needs her to be happy more. His concern for my mother's mental health makes him think this trip home will be good for her.

He keeps returning to something she said the evening before she left for Ireland. He'd tried talking to her again about getting therapy.

'I don't need therapy,' my mother had insisted.

'We are grieving for our baby,' my father said gently. He took her by the hand and directed her to sit on the edge of the bed beside her half-packed suitcase.

'What would you say to her,' she asked him. 'If you could talk to her.'

'I'd ask if she knew me.' He hummed the first line of Eric Clapton's song 'Tears in Heaven.' His eyes glistened; he swallowed, unable to continue, and his own tears spilled over.

My mother wrapped her arms around him and rocked him, whispering my thoughts into his ear, 'She would know your name and hold your hand. She is with us always. More than you realise.'

Something about her confidence in saying that struck him then. He felt left out, abandoned by me, his child that he never had a chance to know; but he realised that my mother felt connected to me and there was comfort in that for him. I poured love over him. Some of it reached him, enough to reassure him my mother's faith in my presence, however strange or frightening it might be, kept her from falling apart. He had decided my mother's claims to hear me were her way of coping, and he wouldn't turn her away from that notion. He, in turn, imagined meeting me in heaven, imagined a little girl taking him by the hand and showing him around. While in his understanding this would not happen until many years from now, he didn't realise I had him firmly by the hand right now.

My father had felt that comfort enough to let my mother go back to Ireland to find her version of solace.

In her loneliness and bewilderment, she pulls me close in thickening tendrils of blue and violet that bind yet fortify me. Simultaneously, my connection to the spirit world thins, as if diluted by my closeness to my mother.

I delight in my mother's full attention as she focuses, for my sake, on things that give her joy: the Irish accents in the departure lounge in San Francisco; the empty seat beside her as good as a free upgrade letting her stretch out on the overnight flight; the sun rising to meet us, sending shards of light slicing through the cabin as passengers open their blinds on a new day, a new country, a new continent.

Protecting me from her sorrow's steely talons, she shares good memories, flashes from her life that glitter like precious gems on a sandy beach.

The first time I flew in a plane, I was four. This memory is swathed in a pink and mauve haze. *I was sure we would reach heaven. I thought I'd see angels with big white wings, playing golden harps, sitting on the clouds.*

She hopes the axe and the broken geode in her check-in luggage don't trigger a customs issue. As she waits for her bag, she shares how her dad loved collecting folk from the airport: his sisters back from holiday, cousin Bob from New York, even Uncle Malcolm once returning from a trip to London.

Dad would stop at the Carrickdale Hotel, and cousin Bob would always order a pint of Guinness and ask for an Ulster fry, no matter what time of day it was.

This recollection makes her puff out a laugh. The woman standing beside her, placating two tetchy children, gives her a funny look. My mother doesn't notice.

Her stories tether me to her world, giving texture and form to the shades and hues swirling around me: brittle silver – thoughts of visiting my grandmother – my mother's hopes that she is recognised – can have a decent conversation; sunshine yellow – Jack is picking her up – maybe he'll bring the girls; amber streaks – Maureen has already decreed that Emily and Fiona are not to miss choir practice – maybe she'll relent; bottle green tones simmer beneath the brighter tones – what will she say about my father's absence? Scratch deeper – slate grey – solid sorrow.

The bags arrive, customs wave her through, and in no time she's in the arrivals hall mobbed by Jack, Emily and Fiona. They form a huddle of pulsating peaches and pinks with sparks of silver and gold. She pulls out of the bear hug and looks at Jack; the corners of his eyes crinkle into lightly sun-kissed skin. In that moment, he's the double of their father, and we feel his spirit close by.

The girls take turns pushing the baggage cart to the car. Jack loads the suitcase and cabin bag into the hatchback of the black SUV.

'Can Aunty Aisling sit beside me?' Fiona asks, hope shining silver sparkles in her seven-year-old face.

Emily, the older by two years, is equally optimistic. Sitting in the front seat is the best thing, and she scored the coveted position on the way down. She might upgrade to a return journey in the front, but Jack is having none of it.

'Aunty Aisling is tired.'

The 'Ah, daddy, please?' in stereo makes Aisling laugh.

'No, Aisling's my sister. I want her beside me.'

Emily climbs in the back, mumbling that sitting beside sisters isn't a treat. But when she catches her father's narrow-eyed glare in the rearview mirror, she folds her arms and stares out the window.

There's silence in the car as Jack eases them through the car park pay barriers.

'Let me get this.' My mother lifts her handbag, digging around for her purse.

'All sorted. I use the credit card. *Mod-ren* or what?' Jack winds up the window and moves off. Sunshine pours into the car as they emerge outside.

My mother slips sunglasses over squinting, tired eyes. 'It's a beautiful day. Hardly feels like Ireland at all.'

'It's been the driest month since records began. Hasn't rained in nearly six weeks now.'

'Aunty Aisling?'

'Yes, darling.' A rosy glow ignites in my mother.

'Did youse see the big fires in California?'

My mother twists around to look at Fiona and is rewarded with the child's eyes rounded in wonder. Fiona's aura reflects my mother's, despite the grim topic.

'I didn't see the fire. But I *did* see the smoke in the sky.' My mother smiles at the child's mouthed but silent 'wow.'

'But don't worry, it was about a hundred miles away.'

'A hundred miles and you still saw the smoke?' Emily's curiosity propels her from her huff.

'Yep, but a hundred miles isn't far for smoke to travel. We had some of the ash from the fire fall in our garden.'

'We had dust from the Sahara Desert on daddy's car,' Emily says.

'They have camels there,' Fiona adds. 'They are like cows for desert people. You know, like daddy's cows.'

'How are your daddy's cows?' my mother asks.

Uncle Jack smiles. He knows it's code for 'How's the farm?'

'Spring was late. The grass crops are slow, and the later frosts impacted the apples.'

'That's climate change for you.' Everything about my mother dulls at the thought.

'I thought climate change is supposed to make it warmer?' Emily says.

'It does,' Jack says. 'I mean, the summer is stretching longer. October and November are definitely warmer; the frosts come later in autumn, and that's affecting the pests and infections. Like, in the cattle – we had more instances of pneumonia.' He stops talking as he navigates the car through the toll plaza and drops two euros into the basket.

The girls wave at the woman in the toll booth, and she smiles back with her wave.

He revs the car to speed and joins the flow of traffic heading north before taking up where he left off. 'I've noticed… this past few years, the natural cycle is off-kilter. There's a shift in the seasons, and it's affecting growth. Means I have to adapt, you know, plan differently. And it's only going to get harder for farmers with this new Climate Act. Here in the North alone, they're estimating half a million cattle and even more sheep would need to be lost to meet the new climate targets.'

My mother whistles through her lips. 'That's a big ask.' She admires his patience in explaining this to her and his girls, not speaking down to them.

I'd have treated you like that, too, she tells me, *but you already know everything.*

But I know less and less the longer I stay. My mother is not aware of this, and I intend to keep it this way.

'How many cattle would you need to lose?' she asks Jack.

'I don't know yet.'

'Oh, Aunty Aisling, we lost Mitzy,' Fiona says, feeling left out by the conversation.

'Oh no! Your daddy never said.' My mother is embarrassed by the tears that threaten for an aloof farmyard tabby.

'It's alright,' Emily says, giving Fiona a scathing look for her over-the-top drama. 'Mitzy came back a few weeks later with three kittens.'

This news washes through the car like turquoise foam, light and lovely.

'Let's talk more about the farm later,' she says. 'How's Mum?' She is scared of the answer, wants to put off seeing how diminished her mother has become, but she also yearns to see her, hear her voice, touch her skin, inhale her perfume.

'The same. Good days, bad days, in-between days. You never know what you'll get with Grammo.'

'I'll go see her tomorrow.' My mother smiles at the name my cousins gave my grandmother, a blend of the English word 'grandma' and the Irish 'mamo.' *You would have called her Grammo, too.*

Her having to tell me that is troubling. In the spiritual realm, I should know that, but here in my mother's world, I have forgotten. What else is slipping from me that I don't notice? How can you know what you forget?

'How's Ben?' Jack asks.

It's a light question that gives my mother as much space as she needs.

'The old tinnitus is playing up, but apart from that, he's good.'

Fiona asks what tinnitus is, and my mother explains that it's a sound in his ear that no one else can hear. Emily can't imagine how weird that would be. Fiona decides it's not worth thinking about, but remembers that poor Uncle Ben is an orphan and her sympathy wells again for him.

My mother chats with the girls. They enjoy her stories and beg her for more, directing the content with their questions: 'Was Daddy a good little boy?' – and favourite requests – 'Tell us about the day you fell in the mud.'

Uncle Jack listens but remains quiet, his questions unasked and unanswered. For now.

Ahead of them rises Slieve Gullion, solid, immovable; it looks like it's planted right in the middle of the M1, but after a few miles, the perspective changes and the mountain slides to the left as if giving way as they get closer.

'Are you hungry? Do you want to stop at the Carrickdale?' Jack asks.

'For a pint and potato bread?'

They laugh. The girls don't get the joke but giggle, too.

'Would you mind if we push on home?' she says.

'Not a bother.' Jack touches the accelerator and the car picks up pace.

*

Spatial proximity is unimportant where I am. There is no 'near' or 'far.' No traveling to be with, no sense of leaving. I'm caught betwixt worlds, yet I can sense more of other worlds in this place my mother calls home; like there is a confluence here and the veils that part realms are thinner, allowing worlds to swirl together like water in two rivers meeting.

You like it here too, Poppy, don't you? my mother asks me when she's alone in her room.

The pleasure I get from her noticing bathes us in buttery yellow and makes her smile. She intuits, like I do, a unique focus of energy here that draws realms tighter together, a buzz of vigour that infuses me with wonder and my mother with hope. Many souls congregate at this junction, but with my diminished knowledge from time spent in the physical world, I am not sure where it is leading me. The question of what will become of me is too much to contemplate. I do not know, and I am unused to not knowing.

When my mother has asked me questions about our different worlds, soothing lavender and jarring neon green intertwine when I can sometimes answer and sometimes can't. As time goes on there is more of the neon green, and I am unsettled by it.

In the wee dark hours, my mother lies awake, texting with my father. She worries that he's offended because she took off so quickly without explanation; but there isn't one that she can parcel up into words and deliver. She thinks about how he got upset when she asked what he would say to me, and her heart feels sore at the memory of his tears, yet comforted by the intimacy of the moment.

He felt your presence, Poppy.

It makes us both happy to know that.

He reassures her that he understands her need to be back home. When he sends her the message – *Do you want us to move back to Ireland someday?* – she stares at the text.

They never talked about moving back. My mother had given up a permanent teaching position to move to San Jose and allow my father to follow his career. They'd spent so much time and money securing green cards that it seemed ridiculous to contemplate moving home again. But the idea of it brightens her aura.

She types, *maybe,* deletes it and types, *someday.*

He replies with a smiley face with hearts for eyes. It's his code for 'need to work now, love you.'

Her smiley face to him blows a kiss. She envisions her lips kissing his goodnight; and five thousand miles away, he imagines her lips touching his. My parents smile at the same time, and I fill with golden light.

*

Released by sleep to wander the shadows of different worlds, my mother dreams of hard frosts and withering blossoms. Sedimented fear swirls up and partially obscures a woman's face looking at her with such unbearable sadness that it jolts my mother awake. She lies for a minute, surfacing from the dust of her dream. Birdsong guides her back to herself lying in bed, in her old bedroom, in what is now her brother's house.

She could be listening to the same rolling trills and peeps as her eight-year-old self, full of wonder; or fifteen, full of hormones and angst; or forty, full of what? Longing? Yet the birds sound the same.

She checks her phone. It's past nine. She's missed the girls leaving for school, but she pushes herself to get up and face the day, brittle sunlight thrusting around the edges of the blinds.

My mother is still bleary-minded when she enters the kitchen.

Maureen is there, wearing tee-shirt, leggings and trainers, high ponytail bouncing as she puts muesli in a bowl. Energy pounds from her in cobalt waves.

'Hi, Aisling. Good night's sleep?'

'Yes, thanks.' My mother slides onto a stool at the kitchen island, feeling self-conscious about her puffy legs and bloated belly beside Maureen's toned figure.

'I hit a PB on my run this morning.' Maureen sloshes almond milk into her muesli.

My mother isn't sure what a 'PB' is, but Maureen isn't waiting for her to talk. 'I'm knackered already, and I've a round of golf in an hour! Do you play?'

Shaking her head, my mother wonders if she needs to explain that she will never get into golf; the whole idea bores her. She's more of a hiking, biking, skiing girl. But then Maureen should already know that. They've known each other since they were eleven.

She sighs and forces a smile as Maureen faces her, bowl in hand.

'Oh well, that's a shame. Help yourself to coffee. You know where everything is. So feel free to make yourself at home.' Maureen walks past the kitchen island and sits at the table behind my mother.

My mother looks at the empty chair at the kitchen island beside her, then gets up to get herself a coffee. In her jet-lagged fog, she can't remember where the coffee or the mugs are kept in this rendition of her old family home. Of course, Jack and Maureen have remodelled. They have every right to. Maureen doesn't seem to notice my mother opening and closing cupboard doors as she assembles the coffee.

'So.' Maureen gets straight to it. 'Why didn't Ben come?'

'He has work.'

'Looks like your trip was pretty last minute.'

My mother can't dodge the implied question.

'I—' my mother pretends she's concentrating on pouring water from the kettle.

Tell her you came to visit Grammo, I prompt.

'I wanted to see Mum.'

Maureen smiles and my mother relaxes. Maureen has always loved Grammo, and my mother cannot imagine her being cruel about her.

'I was there last week,' Maureen says. 'Actually, she thought I was you. Imagine mixing us up!' She laughs.

I send my mother lavender to soothe her jarring jade, but her hurt overwhelms my effort. And it's nowhere near enough to override the rising guilt she has about moving to California and leaving Grammo in a home. Did that make Grammo worse, more lost and confused?

My mother takes a sip of her coffee, trying to ignore the scalding it gives her. She'll be mortified if the tears that threaten spill over.

She blinks hard, swallows more than coffee and listens to Maureen crunching cereal, hearing the *tink-tink* of her spoon as she chases the last of the oats around the bowl.

'Well, good luck with your visit,' Maureen says, getting up and putting dishes in the sink. 'Gotta go.'

When she hears the front door slam, my mother lowers her head to the cold granite of the kitchen island and lets the tears come.

*

My mother feels a cascade of silver light when she first sets eyes on Grammo. There is that rush of a child to its mother at the end of the day, when she picks her up from school, the unbidden joy of reunion after separation, or of accidentally bumping into a parent in the street as an adult. I savour it in the moment before my mother fully takes in how frail Grammo is – like a bird, bones held together with paper-thin skin stretched over swollen joints.

Recognition falls into Grammo's eyes as she looks towards my mother, glowing, not just from this world, but partially from where her spirit straddles the realms.

'My beautiful granddaughter,' Grammo whispers.

My mother's heart drops. 'No, it's me, Mum.' She kisses Grammo on the cheek. She can never get used to her mother not recognising her. It is another cruel cut this disease inflicts.

My mother wonders will Grammo get agitated if she corrects her but can't bear to pretend she's one of Jack's girls. It's too ridiculous. And what if she calls her 'Maureen'? My mother could not bear that. She decides on the truth. 'I'm Aisling, your daughter.'

'Yes, I know. But you brought her to me.' Grammo is shining, her eyes clear.

With a lurch in her heart, my mother realises at the exact moment as I do. 'You can see her?'

Their joy swells and unites, surrounding us in a silver bubble laced with an oil-on-water shimmering rainbow.

'I can't see her, but…' Grammo frowns as grey clouds gather. She looks around the room, unsure and a little afraid.

My mother reaches for Grammo's hand. 'It's okay, Mum, she's here.'

Grammo floods with relief. Feeling at home with her daughter, the clouds drift away from her thoughts. They sit quietly at first, neither expecting nor needing much from the other, happy with one another's presence.

I luxuriate in a buttery happiness. Grammo can see me. We share love, joy, contentment, each drawing strength from our interaction.

My mother chats away, choosing easy things: the sunny day outside, how quickly Jack's girls are growing, the flight from California, what's growing in her garden.

My mother wonders why Grammo isn't full of questions.

My grandmother knows this time with her daughter is precious. She can feel a draught tug at her mind and doesn't want to leave. But the gust increases until she must give way. I am her only clarity in the descending fog. I see through the mist, remain by her side.

My mother notices Grammo's gaze wandering, her eyes no longer showing recognition, avoiding her. A dusky curtain drops between them as Grammo twists her hand away from my mother's grasp, saying, 'I have to go now. My mother will be looking for me.' Grammo pulls her sleeves down over her hands. There are holes in the cuff where she's done this often.

'It's okay, you're okay.' Pushing back the lump in her throat, fighting the hot dampness in her eyes, my mother prays for Grammo's lucidity to return.

Instead, it wanders.

'Where are we? Whose house is this?' Grammo whispers, her eyes wide as she looks around the room.

'This is your room,' my mother tells her, keeping her voice as steady as she can. 'You live here now.' She has done this before and hates the haunted look on Grammo's face. She wants her back, the intelligent, funny gentle woman she knew; but for now, Grammo is out of my mother's reach.

But I feel my grandmother's presence on a different plane. With it, a soft lime green, and I am soothed even as I'm curious.

How are you here? I ask her. It's a shame I can't connect my mother to this conversation but I don't know how.

I'm not sure. It's as if I've been in one room for the longest time, but now I'm in a house with many rooms, Grammo tells me.

Different realms?

Yes, so, so many; but I flit between only a couple.

I understand, I tell her. *Can you choose which place to stay?* Perhaps she can guide me, teach me how to pass back to the world I came from and help me rediscover my universal knowledge.

Her lime green dims to pale olive. *No. I've only got the key for these two. There are times… like right now… I've left one room and the door has shut tight behind me. Sometimes, I do get back but it's changed, and I don't recognise any of it.*

Right now, in the physical world, Grammo is asking my mother to take her home, and my mother is trying hard not to cry as she placates her.

In this place, with me, Grammo says, *I desperately want to stay there. How can I leave those I love? Sometimes, I try the handle and it opens. I re-enter the room… only to forget what I went back for.*

My mother is soothing her, stroking her arms and hands, humming 'Danny Boy,' and eventually, Grammo's eyes close in sleep.

Can you sense others? I ask.

Yes. I feel my husband and my parents behind that one door. And there is evil behind some doors: war and depravity and loneliness and greed and, oh, so many things that I don't recognise. Then there are the wonderful things, surprises – like you – and that one door… well, I know it leads to death and to where the others are. I'm not afraid to go join them, but… I will be so sad to leave life. I'll miss my children.

You won't miss them. And you will no longer be sad. I promise.

Grammo brightens. *That's good to know. But my body is strong. It could be a while yet.* Her aura fades again. *I know it's hard for them when they see me like this.*

When you get here, it will be better. But we've no control over when.

In the room, time has passed, but I'm unable to gauge how much. Grammo wakes up and her gaze wanders around the room. Then she refocuses on my mother, and they both catch their breaths.

'Aisling?'

'I'm here, Mum.'

'I am, too. I'm so sorry.'

'Oh, Mum, it's not your fault.'

'It's too much, for you, for Jack – for me. I don't know how long I'll be—' Grammo shrugs. 'I will always be with you. In your heart. Just as Poppy is.'

My name is beautiful when she says it.

'How do you know her name?' my mother asks, beaming lemon light.

'I just… know.' Grammo smiles. 'She has a beautiful soul.'

I sparkle.

'How—' My mother can't articulate what she wants to ask, and it doesn't matter because neither Grammo nor I know how to answer.

'Maybe our dreams and our imagination take us to different places,' Grammo tries anyway with wonder in her voice.

'Or objects?' my mother says.

'Objects?'

As concisely as she can, my mother tells Grammo about how I connected with her after the geode was broken by the bronze axe head. She describes the visions when she touches the axe head, driven by a need to know what it means. She worries that it will be too much for Grammo's fragile state and fears that she might slip away. Yet, it is such a gift for my mother to talk this through. Grammo is the smartest person my mother has ever known.

I sense that my spirit is keeping Grammo present, keeping her in the room with my mother. I also feel that Grammo is tapping into a knowledge I cannot reach.

'Don't be frightened of the axe head, Aisling. It tells you a story. Listen.'

'But Mum, how do you know?'

'I just do. We tell our children stories from birth. Stories are important. They condense what it means to be human. They connect us to past lives, reach out to future peoples.'

Grammo closes her eyes and whispers, 'The marks we leave on the bark are signs a life was lived.'

My mother is confused by this, but she doesn't press. She watches her beloved mother slide into a deep, peaceful sleep – her face relaxed and beautiful to my mother's eye.

She sits listening to Grammo breathe, dozing a little herself until Uncle Jack arrives to collect her.

'How was she today?' he asks.

'Good. Really good. We had a nice chat. Lucid, you know?'

'I'm a bit jealous.' Jack hugs my mother and looks over at Grammo, still fast asleep. 'I won't wake her, though God knows I'm tempted if I thought I'd get a decent conversation out of her.' He pats his sister on the shoulder. 'C'mon, let's get you home for dinner. You must be starving.'

While Jack prepares dinner, my mother goes to her room to put on a cardigan. Even warm Irish weather is no match for body thermostats conditioned to Californian heat. As she rummages through her case, her hand hits the hard edge of the box that contains the bronze axe head. She takes the box out and goes to the window, looking out at the garden to the spot where she dug up the axe head thirty-five years ago. She eases the lid open and gently strokes the cold bronze. She closes her eyes and tries to connect, but she is suddenly cold and fiercely hungry.

Must be the jetlag, she thinks, closing the lid of the box with a shiver.

CHAPTER 18

My bones are cold. I can feel them ridged down my chest to where my skin scoops into my stomach and stretches between my hips. It has been a hard winter. Rivers froze. Fish died. We lost the pig herd. The crops failed. The cattle grow thinner. Our Elder Aon departed for the stars. It was sad. It was his time, but this winter, more of our people – especially those weakened by age or illness – died than is usual. There have been no more dust falls. Snow lies deep, but as the daylight lengthens, hope stirs. Spring will follow soon.

The Ceremonial Hall is a welcome refuge after spending the morning outside in the biting cold. I stamp the snow off my boots and clamp my fur-lined mitts under my armpits to slide my stiff hands out as I enter into the heat of the hall. To keep warm, Elders, children, and villagers who can bring their work with them, or whose work is impossible due to the weather, spend their days here. The air is damp, heavy with the fug of many bodies, woodsmoke, and the smell of the almost empty cooking pot. There's a dip in the chatter and bustle as everyone turns towards the door. I hold up my bulging hunting sac, and there's an added buzz as people voice approval.

I've had a successful morning visiting my traps and can provide meat for the communal pot from a young buck. It was smaller than I would have liked. I was surprised it got ensnared in the first place, but I could tell from its scrawniness that it had little energy to free itself. Still, it's better than nothing, and we badly need the meat to supplement the watery soup we've been relying on. It will reassure Nereus when I tell him I am entitled to a larger share. My heart speeds up at the thought I've not bled for two cycles.

Nereus gives a quick wave from the side of the main hall. He's surrounded by children about ten summers old, grappling with willow wattle and reeds, as he teaches them to weave. I'll tell him our good news tonight when we're alone. For now, I smile and nod back. It suits him well, being surrounded by children.

Lan guards the communal pot. He accepts the meat I bring with a smile. Nearby, Kallisto doesn't look up from where she prepares root vegetables for the pot with Chloe; but I can tell she can hear her uncle praise me. Bion sidles up and, keeping out of his mother's line of sight, wriggles his fingers at me with a twinkle in his eye. I tip my head and give him a coy smile.

Bion circles around behind me, popping up at my elbow so that my body shields him from his mother's view. He peers up at me, his eyes liquid brown pools in a grubby face, his expression unmistakable. *Anything for me?* I don't have anything edible this time, but I slip my hand beneath my wraps and pull out the boar's tusk I found. His eyes widen as he takes the tusk and turns it around in his hands. I've been slipping him some of my rations, and I'm gratified to see he's not as scraggy as his playmates. My brother's children get a hunter's ration, and though it's not a lot more, I know they are taken care of; but I worry for Bion. Kallisto's farming has not been going well. I wink at him as I hand him the tusk. He grins and mouths, 'Thank you.'

By Kallisto's stiffening body and increased focus on her task, I know she's making sure not to look up, loath to give me any gratitude or praise.

Others are not so coy, or stubborn, and come to see what we've brought in, smiling with shared relief when they see the buck, patting me on the back. We have been on tight rations since the beginning of winter. Lan's decision is not popular, but he is known for his justice, and the villagers trust him to keep order. He was clever enough to enlist the herders to help. With the cattle herds decreasing due to a lack of grass, and high demand for their meat now there are no pigs, the herders have less work. What's left of the herd is kept for milking and breeding, sheltered in the annexe to the Ceremonial Hall. The heat from the herd keeps that end of the building warmer, so the children play along that wall; their laughter and squeals adding another layer to the din.

The older children like to gather on the other side of the wall, with the beasts, away from the adults. Too young to be cattle herders out on a hillside, they can feed grain to the cattle and milk those cows still producing, freeing up older siblings who usually tend the cattle to help guard the pot. Lan says that giving these youths responsibility for securing our food means they are less likely to pilfer or waste it; and they'll have respect for how hard it is to procure. I agree. Jaisun was happy to switch to hunting full-time with me. Agis took on an apprentice too, but I know Kallisto hates losing her 'team' to us.

Aleka usually helps prepare the pot, but I don't see her. I scan the hall. Geros is in the far corner with his herbs and a smaller fire, making remedies for the queue of people beside him with coughs, sniffles and various other ailments. Doah helps administer the medicine under his guidance.

In another corner, people sit in a circle around a pile of skins and fleeces, making garments.

'Where is Aleka? Did she get her ration?' I ask Lan as he passes me a bowl of stew. The smell makes my mouth water and my stomach growl.

'She was tired. I think the baby is kicking her too much.' He smiles. Lan always says that the ones who kick will make good guards for the village. 'I sent her home with some smouldering wood. She needs her own fire beside which to rest. It was too noisy for her here.'

'Let me take her this bowl, and I'll return for mine.'

'Eat first, then go. You've been out since daybreak.'

'If you could call it that.' We're inside, using fire to see by. At this time of year, daybreak comes late, but it's been so overcast and grey that it hardly seems to brighten at all. If it wasn't for the blue whiteness cast by the snow, it would be hard to see even at midday.

My stomach growls so loudly Lan hears it, too. He raises a furry white eyebrow. 'Eat yours now. I'll fill this again for Aleka when you're finished.'

I eat. My belly might not be as empty as it looks, and I may not be the only one needing this stew. Jaisun sits with me. He's thrilled with what our snares caught, and I haven't the heart to tell him that in normal years, a buck this size is hardly worth bringing home. I remind myself we have good years and bad years and this is one of the bad years, albeit the worst I've ever seen – but spring will come.

'We might get a wild pig tomorrow,' Jaisun says.

'Maybe,' I say. But despite finding a decomposed boar, we haven't seen any wild pigs in a while. Whatever killed our pigs back in the summer did not afflict the wild pigs or those in the neighbouring villages, at least not at that time. A summer traveller told us that he'd heard tell – or perhaps he'd seen for himself, though travellers make many wild claims – that there was a mountain valley village where every breathing thing fell dead in their tracks, as if the life was washed from them like water over hot charcoal: people, pigs, cattle. He was cutting his journey short because it was already feeling like winter. That was in summer. Conditions have only worsened since.

We often laughed at how the travellers from the Warmer Lands wear furs here in the summer while we strip down to the thin cloth we make from plants. The travellers say they don't need furs where they come from, and that their cloth is finer and softer than ours. Geros says their blood is thinner and can't keep them warm the way ours does. But this winter, I fear that neither our furs nor our blood are as thick as we need them to be. These days, the cold is so piercing it hurts my bones. It's no wonder the travellers went back to the Warmer Lands early.

The stew warms my belly, making me sleepy; but I rouse myself and lift the bowl for Aleka. Lan tops it up, saying, 'I'm going to check with her that she gets it!' His warm tone and mock scowl tell me he's jesting. Kallisto's dirty look makes me wonder if she really thinks I'd stoop so low as to eat the food of a woman with child, or perhaps she's disgruntled that Lan is being friendly to me.

I beam a smile back at both of them before piling on my layers and heading out into the cold.

The sky is darkening already, yet we've just passed midday. The wind rattles bare branches, and thunks of snow drop into the drifts below. My breath lands in a white mist on the fur I pull up as far as I can over my face.

The paths through the village feel like a labyrinth of tunnels with walls of ice growing higher as each day passes. Usually, in winter, the snow falls, melts to soggy slush and disappears for a while before the next snowfall. Some years, the snow melts on contact with the ground. But this year, we'd had hard frost since late summer. There's been snowfall upon snowfall.

I can almost see over the snowbanks as I stomp to Aleka's hut.

'Aleka, it's me, Zosime.' I duck down by her hut door, ready to enter upon her invitation, but I only hear a low moan. 'Aleka?'

There it is again, hot with pain, crawling from the depths of a person.

'I'm coming in,' I say, pushing back the door flap. I'm met with the thick smell of blood. 'Aleka?'

And then, as my eyes adjust to the gloom, I see her. She lies panting on a pile of skins, blood pooling from beneath her legs. 'The baby's coming,' she whispers.

'But—' My eyes meet hers, and I swallow the words, *it's too soon.* Instead, I ask, 'Has Agis gone for Doah?' I didn't meet him, but there are lots of paths to the Ceremonial Hall, and it's hard to see over the snow drifts between the huts.

Aleka nods. Her face twists as another pain grips her. I take her hand. She squeezes, hard. I spill some stew on the floor but have little time to mourn the waste. I set the bowl safely to one side and turn back to Aleka. She is deathly pale. Her eyes roll back in her head with agony. She keens a low long wail as she exhales.

'Breathe,' I say. 'Doah will know what to do. She's brought many babies into this world. She has herbs—'

Running feet and the door flap opens. Doah appears, her eyes huge and sunken into a face sharpened by hunger. Her layers of clothing and furs belie how small her frame is. With grey hair scraped back into a braid, she is ready to work. I try to move away, but Aleka pulls me closer.

Doah sees this and nods for me to stay. She speaks to Aleka in such a soft, confident voice that I find myself believing that Aleka and her baby will be all right, even though the baby should not arrive for at least another two full moons.

Agis is right behind Doah, panting, trying to catch his breath in the tight, frosty air. Doah directs him to get more fuel and tend the fire. He leaves to find wood.

Doah strips Aleka from the waist down and parts her legs. I try not to look, to preserve Aleka's dignity, but I'm horrified by the wash of blood that comes as Aleka screams. She sits bolt upright, dragging my hand with such force that I lurch forward from where I'm squatting beside her onto my knees. My free hand lands in sticky, warm blood and as I scramble to get to my feet, I catch a glimpse of a glistening red glob in Doah's hands the size of a deer's heart. I gulp back my own guttural exclamation as I realise that it's Aleka's baby – or what should be her baby.

Aleka falls back onto her bedding. Her hand loosens in mine.

'Aleka?' I shake her hand gently.

She moans.

Doah lays a hand on my shoulder and says, 'There's something you must do.'

My hands shake as Doah gives me the bundle wrapped in cloth and woven rushes.

'It is so small.' My whole body feels the weight of sorrow for this lost little life.

'Not enough food for both of them. The gods made a choice,' Doah says.

'Is this what happens? When the gods choose?' I can't hide my anger. Why have the gods chosen to take away our sun in the first place?

Doah shakes her head, and her brow crinkles as she composes herself. She looks over her shoulder as Agis comes into the hut. He goes to Aleka, gently leans forward and kisses her forehead. She doesn't open her eyes but whimpers. He soothes her, whispering something I can't hear. Then he rises and comes to where Doah and I stand watching him.

'The baby?' he asks, then sees the bundle in my hands. He swallows hard. 'I'll take it, Zosime. I need to be the one to…'

I hand it over.

'Stay with her until I get back.' Agis leaves.

Doah is cleaning up the blood and laying out fresh bedding. She lifts what's left of the bowl of stew. 'Eat, there is little to spare.'

'I've eaten,' I tell her, though my stomach grumbles again.

'Aleka won't be fit to eat yet, and I don't need it. You have it.'

'Are you sure?' I feel bad giving in. but I won't waste it.

'Our village is lucky to have you. I was at Old Ford yesterday. Their hunters are elderly, and their hunger is greater than ours. They have lost three babies this way.'

'That's so sad.'

'Many of their women are so thin, their cycles have stopped.'

A chill creeps over me. 'Stopped? And they aren't with child?'

The compassion in Doah's wise old eyes is unbearable. It's as if she can read my mind; as if she can sense the sickening feeling creeping into my throat and making it hard for me to breathe.

'No, they are not with child. When we do not get enough nourishment, our bodies shut down. There won't be many children for a while, I think.'

'I see.' Hope shrivels and dies, leaving a hollow ache in my chest, though it is my belly that is empty, despite the extra stew.

'Where has our sun gone?' Doah says.

I can't speak but Doah doesn't wait for an answer. 'I was hoping we'd have word from travelling traders at Old Ford, but no one has passed that way in some time. The last one came through around the autumn before the river froze. He said the sun still appeared in the Warmer Lands. But since then it's been too hard to travel with the snow. We have no idea what is happening.' Doah hands me a damp cloth and nods toward Aleka. 'She has a fever. Use this. Add snow if you need to.'

I sit with Aleka, pressing cold compresses to her head. Her skin is scorching, but she shivers beneath her wraps. When she mutters, I lower my ear to her lips, and that is when I see a flat, blotchy area of raised, reddened skin on her neck.

'Doah, she has a rash!'

'Show me.'

I move back to let Doah see.

'Herder-rash,' Doah says.

I exhale a small sigh of relief. 'I had that as a child. She'll be okay, won't she?'

Doah's silence fills my heart with ice.

'If this is the cow-herders' rash, she will recover. I did.'

'You were strong, well fed,' Doah says.

I look at Aleka. Her face is so white it looks grey, darker around the eyes, and her lips are tinged blue.

'The fever does the damage, not the rash,' Doah says, stopping as Agis and Nereus come into the hut. Silence drapes the air.

'What is it?' Agis looks from Doah to me to Aleka, his eyes red-rimmed.

'She is ill with herders' rash. It's probably why the baby came early,' Doah says. 'I will get snow for this and ask Geros to make her herbs to give strength.'

She doesn't mention to Agis what cannot help; that Aleka is too thin, too hungry, weakened by losing blood. I realise that Doah cares for our hearts and minds as much as Geros looks after our bodies.

'You stay, Doah,' Nereus says. 'I'll get Geros.' He leaves and I hear the muted thud thud thud of his running feet on compacted snow.

Doah takes the compress from me and goes outside, returning with it full of snow and hands it to me.

Aleka pulls her head to one side, trying to escape the icy cold of the compress, but she is too weak. It feels cruel, but Doah is right. I need to cool her skin down because this burning is dangerous.

Agis and I sit with Aleka and wait for Geros to bring his healing remedies. Doah rests at the back of the hut, safe from the brittle cold of nightfall.

It is pitch dark outside when Nereus pulls back the door flap. His beard is white with frost though he has only walked from the

Ceremonial Hall. His head and shoulders host a layer of fat white flakes that are already losing shape and melting. He pulls a pot out from where he has tucked it beneath his furs.

'Geros sent this,' Nereus says. 'Aleka must drink it.'

'Geros is not coming?'

'He can't. There are many others at the Ceremonial Hall with the rash.' His face crumples and his lips press together as he fights for control. 'So many children have it.'

'They'll be okay. We had it as children and survived.' I guide him to a seat beside the fire, trying not to think about what Doah said about needing strength to fight disease.

Nereus nods at Agis and hands him the pot before folding himself to sit. Agis tries to coax Aleka to drink.

'I didn't have it,' Nereus says. 'Nobody in the coastal tribes had it until we started keeping cattle.'

'Usually, we only have it once, but Aleka's had it before, I think.' I raise an eyebrow at Agis.

He shakes his head. 'I don't know. It's not something we've talked about.'

'The children will be okay.' I take Nereus's hand and massage some warmth into it.

Aleka groans. Her legs straighten and her feet kick out. Her back goes rigid, throwing her head back. She grinds her teeth.

'Aleka!' Agis tries to wipe her brow with the compress, but she shudders, her body writhing.

'Shush,' I soothe, trying to uncurl her balled fists, but she is clenching tight. Nereus goes to the back of the hut to wake Doah in urgent but hushed tones.

Aleka's limbs flop. Her head lolls. Agis whispers to her, wiping her skin, kissing her fingers. Then her arms and legs tighten, straightening again, making her whole body shake so violently that her head bangs off the bed.

'Aleka!' Agis cries, trying to hold her.

She convulses twice more, then falls limp.

'Doah, quick.' I hear the panic in my voice and try to steady myself, but Aleka's breathing is shallow, her eyes only half-open. Fear pierces me. She's too young, too good, too precious to me, to my brother.

By the time Doah reaches us, Aleka's breathing has stopped. Her eyes glaze over, staring, but only seeing into the next world.

My brother bellows like a wounded buck, clutching his wife to his chest. He buries his face in her hair and sobs. Tears drip down my face. Nereus's hand rests on my shoulder. I curl into him and weep.

As the first rush of sorrow crashes through me, I hear Agis wailing Aleka's name over and over, begging her to come back to him, to not leave him. But it's too late – she has left.

My chest hurts as I breathe. It has happened so quickly. My gaze falls on the cold stew bowl by the fire.

I was bringing her stew. I was excited, hopeful for her baby, for my baby.

The bowl lies on its side empty.

Aleka was supposed to eat that stew.

I brought it. For her. For her baby.

Now the stew is wasted.

She would have been happy I brought her stew. We would have sat a while together talking, sharing secrets, as she ate from that bowl.

The stew is gone.

And so is she.

I will no longer walk with her and share my secrets and my dreams. Who will laugh with me about my daft brother who made us sisters with his love for her? What will we do without her? I cannot bear such a future, and the gods only know how Agis feels.

They know because they did this!

Rage rises in my throat, so hot I fear I will scream and never stop. I force it back and tell myself this is not my time to be lost in grief. Agis needs me.

We let his sobs subside. As his strength ebbs, his grip on his dead wife loosens. Between us, Doah, Nereus and I gently ease Aleka from Agis's arms. She has no weight; like a feather found in a meadow, she has wafted away from us. Nereus lays her on her furs. Doah wraps her. I arrange her hair. Agis sits at her feet as if hewn from stone, staring.

Nereus touches my elbow. His breath is warm in my ear. 'I'm going to tell Geros.'

'I'll come.'

Doah nods as I glance her way and cock my head in Agis's direction. I don't want to leave him, but his pain is unbearable to watch. My mind, my heart can't take it. I need the distraction of doing something – anything.

Layered against the cold, I follow Nereus out of the hut. Once outside, he pulls me to him and almost smothers me in our furs. I squeeze him, then pull back and look up into his face. Despite the freezing air around us, his eyes burn into mine, pulling me to a place where I am warm and loved and held.

'You are my everything,' I whisper.

His face crumples. Tears spill into his beard. 'You,' he whispers, 'are all I need in this world.'

The cold forces us to break our embrace. As we trudge through the snow in the darkness, guided only by the stone lamp Nereus holds up to light our way, I have an eerie sensation that someone – something – is following me.

I look behind but see only our flickering shadows against grey-whiteness.

I drop back, hold my breath, and listen hard beyond the usual pop and buzz of my ears. If a deer, or any other game, has wandered into our village, we could do with the extra meat. This snow has disoriented them and though it's unlikely they'd come so close, I can't shake the prickling sensation at the back of my neck. Then the sounds in my ears arrange themselves into voices.

The marks we leave on the bark are signs a life was lived.

Spinning full circle, I cannot see anything other than Nereus ahead with the lamp.

I catch my breath as I smell summer flowers, minty herbs, rain on warm soil.

'Zosime? Are you alright?'

Nereus's voice brings me back to myself.

The voice goes quiet. The smells vanish. Freezing air gnaws at the exposed skin on my face.

'I'm fine,' I say and hurry to catch up.

We plunge into the fetid warmth of the Ceremonial Hall. The atmosphere is more subdued than when I left it earlier. People sleep in rows by the fire while others tiptoe through them, looking for a spot to settle for the night. Many have relocated to sleep here to save fuel.

We find Geros dozing in a seat beside a sick child. He wakes as we approach.

'Aleka—' The word sticks in my throat. I only manage a strangled squeal.

'She has passed over,' Nereus says gently.

As Nereus's words land, Geros closes his eyes as if he's absorbing them somewhere deep inside. He takes a couple of breaths, then flicks his eyes open again. 'I'm sorry for your loss. I know what she means to you.'

I swallow and nod, not trusting myself to speak.

'Was it herders' rash?'

We both nod. Nereus is as choked up as I am.

Geros rubs his face with both hands then looks at us, weary with sorrow. He points at a row of children lying beside him. 'They have it.'

I count five little ones.

Beside me, Nereus inhales sharply. 'I don't understand. They were fine this morning.'

'They are weak from lack of food. They cannot fight the rash as normal,' Geros says. 'I saw this when I was a young man after the clan war. We had not been able to spare people to plant and gather crops, and there was little to go around that year. What the battle didn't kill, sickness finished.'

'This is your fault, Zosime.' A voice hisses behind me.

I turn to see Kallisto, her face twisted in rage. Bion stands behind her with eyes rounded in fear, looking from his mother to me. I'm too stunned to react.

'You took the ancient axe and set this in motion.' Kallisto steps closer, teeth clenched.

I shake my head.

'It's all right, Bion.' Nereus stretches a hand out to the child. 'Your mother is tired.'

Bion's mouth quivers, but he takes the proffered hand, and Nereus lifts him into his arms. Bion snuggles into the space beneath Nereus's chin and heaves a sigh.

Geros stares at Kallisto for a moment. I can almost feel his mind trying to decide how to handle this. I'm too weary for another go-round.

'Kallisto,' Geros says slowly. 'I recall that it was your decision to bring the cattle into the annexe. The children that have been playing in there have the sickness, and it will spread. I've seen it before. Those who have had it before stand a better chance, but those new to this sickness are unlikely to make it through.'

Panic swells in my chest. I look at Nereus. A terrifying thought takes hold. If this sickness spreads to Nereus, will he survive it? Would I survive losing him? He has not had herder's rash before, and although he's more robust than a child, he is skin-and-bones compared to the man he usually is. I've seen him give his portions to the smaller children when they cry with hunger. I take in Nereus's sharpened features and limbs, so thin the joints stick out like the knots in his weaving.

As if he can read my thoughts, he turns to me, frowns, then steps closer and grips my chin in his hand, turning my cheek to the light. His frown deepens as he leans in then drops my chin and clasps me to him.

His voice is hoarse and thick with emotion as he says in my ear, 'You have the rash, too.'

I shove him from me. 'But I've had it before.'

He lifts his hands to his hair and buries his fingers, breathing hard, repeating, 'No, not you.'

Geros stands up and gestures to Nereus to step away. But Nereus stands his ground, holding his head, panting hard.

'Zosime,' Geros says in a calm, even tone. 'It looks like herder's rash. I've seen people who have had it before get it again, but only if...' He stops and looks around the hall, pulling on his beard. 'Only if they were old or... severely underfed.'

CHAPTER 19

My mother doesn't register scratching the nettle rash on her wrist near her watchband as she checks the time. The rhubarb patch needs a good weeding. Nettles run amok around the edges as if guarding the tasty red stems.

The range in the kitchen still works the way my mother remembers it did back when my grandmother taught her to bake. Uncle Jack has kept Grammo's recipes in a folder in the tiny nook-shelf built to fill the gap between the old range and the new units when the kitchen was refitted. Maureen never used the shelf, dubbing it 'useless' because of its small size and awkward position. Jack stores the old recipes alongside the lone surviving cup and saucer from my grandparents' wedding china.

This shelf is like a gap in the space-time continuum connecting me to my memories of a golden era with your Grammo, my mother tells me.

I feel like I, too, have dropped into such a place – a gap between my world and yours.

I'm glad you're here, Poppy. But are you happy?

I'm not sure how to answer. I want to be with my mother but fear it is dangerous for me to stay with my knowledge – my existence – peeling back and dropping off like rose petals. I cannot tell her this; she will worry. Instead, I tell her another truth and hope it satisfies her curiosity.

I come from the light, a place of pure contentment. You could not hope for more.

Her watch beeps. Time's up.

My mother smiles, lifting the rhubarb tart out of the oven with mitted hands. She sniffs, and the fruity tang transports her back to those days with Grammo so vividly it almost makes her cry. The tart's crust is the perfect shade of gold, and pink syrup oozes from the slit she made in the centre. A sprinkle of caster sugar makes it look professional, she thinks, admiring her creation. Contentment and pride roll from her in a range of tones from rhubarb-pink to deep lilac.

'Ah, that smells great,' Uncle Jack says as he arrives at the front door with my cousins, Emily and Fiona, who are on their toes, dancing. Ripples of cyan joy fan from them at the sight of their favourite aunty baking their favourite tart.

'Can we have some now?' Fiona asks, clasping her hands together at her chest.

'You sure can,' my mother says. 'If it's okay with your dad?'

Jack laughs. 'I can hardly say no and deny myself a piece, now can I?'

'Ice cream!' Emily whacks a tub down on the table beside the rhubarb tart. They cheer.

'Right, assembly line,' my mother says. 'I'll cut the tart, Fiona, you get the plates and the forks—'

'Spoons.' Fiona dances off towards the cutlery drawer. 'For ice cream.'

'Of course, silly me. And Emily, will you serve the ice cream, please?'

'Sure thing. What will daddy do?'

'Make sure it's not poisoned.' Jack nips off a corner of the crust and pops it in his mouth then rolls his eyes, clutches his throat and groans as he sinks down behind the kitchen island.

My cousins shake their heads, battling to keep straight faces. Silence descends as they devour the treat. It is broken by the sound of spoons tinkling off plates as they scrape every last piece into their mouths.

'Please, can I have some more?' Fiona holds her plate out in her best Oliver Twist impression.

'I'm saving some to bring to Grammo, but when I was out picking the rhubarb, I noticed a big lavender in full bloom. You know what that means?' My mother tilts her head, waiting to see if they make the connection.

'Lavender shortbread!' Jack says. 'Were you out at the old herb garden by the pet graveyard?'

'Yes. There's still plenty growing there – lots of mint, too. I'm surprised you let it loose.'

'Yeah, I saw that. We kept the mint in terracotta containers; but I think one smashed in the move to the new growing grounds by the river, and it took hold. I need to get down there and clear it out.' Jack exhales, a flicker of exhaustion sags his face, and his aura dims.

'Let me do it. It will give me a sense of purpose.' The last word catches in my mother's throat.

'Okay, girls, homework.' Jack says, laying a hand on my mother's shoulder to let her know she's not going anywhere. He quells the girls' moans, and they leave him and my mother alone in the kitchen.

'Are you okay?' Jack asks. 'You say you're home to visit Mum, and I get that, but there's more, isn't there?'

My mother shrugs. 'Everything's fine, really.'

'Is it Ben? Are you two okay?'

'Yes.' She sounds sharp, and she realises Jack won't buy it.

'I know it's your own business, but you're my sister, and I can tell you're...' Jack presses his lips together, reaching for the right word, then settles for, 'Sad. Deeply sad. About more than just Mum's illness.'

'We can't have children.' It comes out in a rush, saturating the space between them with bleak greyness.

'Have you tried—'

'Yes, we've tried everything we can.'

'But surely there's—'

'There's nothing more we can do. We just have to accept it now.'

'My friend's sister had problems, but they—'

'Stop it, Jack!' My mother puts her hand up, pushing his words away. Her emotions crawl over each other in a jumble of greys and blues and greens. She searches for a kinder tone before she speaks. 'I know you mean well, Jack. Everyone has that story for me... someone they know who had a miracle baby against the odds. But sometimes the miracles don't happen.' She thinks of me and adds, 'At least not the way you'd think.'

Jack's heart lurches. He can't bear to think of a world without Fiona and Emily. He can't fathom the pain his sister is in and wants to take it away for her, give her hope. But the small silver glimmer he has to share will not flare into the hot orange flames she needs right now. He turns her words over in his head before he speaks again. 'Jesus, Aisling, I didn't realise. I'm gutted for you.'

My mother stands mute. She wants to tell him how it is for her, how she sees her future, rattling around an empty house with my father, too quiet, too tidy. How she feels old already. How she has done nothing with her life because she thought being a mother would be enough for her. How she feels there is no point in doing anything. After all, she has no one to pass it on to; and at forty, she's too old to build toward a new dream. It comes back to this one idea that she cannot get past – what use is she?

She plasters on a brave smile.

'Saves us a fortune in college fees, though, doesn't it?' she says.

Jack meets her halfway.

'Never mind college fees. Mine are bankrupting me with the cost of designer trainers.'

Unbeknownst to the other, each pushes away the same memory; their father saying, 'If you can solve a problem with money, it's not a problem.'

The kitchen door is flung open. Maureen comes in weighed down with Hobbs and Ted Baker shopping bags.

'Hello, you two.' She heaps the bags onto the kitchen island. 'Who died?'

'No one,' Jack says. 'Apart from you slaughtering the credit card! How was your trip to Belfast?'

'Great. I think I made some good business contacts. What's this?'

'I made rhubarb tart,' my mother says, forcing a smile. 'Want some?'

'Yuck.' Maureen does an exaggerated shudder. 'Can't stand rhubarb, gives me the runs.' She folds her arms and leans back against the counter. 'Jack, did you give Aisling her bag?'

'My bag?'

'Hang on,' Jack jumps up and heads upstairs.

'Stick on the kettle, will ya? You're closer.' Maureen slips off her shoes and sits on the stool at the kitchen island.

'There's tea in the pot,' my mother says, lifting the teapot.

'Too strong. I'd rather have a fresh pot. Nice and hot, mind,' Maureen says, rubbing her foot without looking up.

My mother fills the kettle and flicks it on, then transfers what is left of the rhubarb tart to a plastic box, ready for the fridge. The kettle rumbles to the boil, but now Maureen is closer to it. My mother moves towards the kitchen door.

'Milk, no sugar,' Maureen says, massaging her other foot.

'Black, no sugar for me,' my mother says, reaching the doorway. 'Actually, don't worry about me. I've just finished a cup. See you later, Maureen. Enjoy.'

Maureen whips her head around to see my mother leave the room. 'Right,' Maureen says. 'Sure, I'll make it myself then.'

*

166

Jack finds my mother in her room putting away her laundry. He knocks their knock, a little rhythm my grandfather taught them, and she calls out, 'Come on in.'

'I found this in the attic,' he says, handing her an old leather satchel.

'Oh my god, my old schoolbag!' My mother takes it. The smell transports her back to the day she went with my grandfather to buy it at the Saddlers in Thomas Street. The shop had racks for belts and bags and all kinds of leather goods that she didn't know the name of. Behind the counter were laces that she recognised as whangs. They were the whole rage in school. Friends would plait them into bracelets for each other. She'd practised on wool and was pretty sure she could do it with leather – the real deal.

'Can I get one of those, Dad?' she'd said, pointing them out.

'How much are they?'

She doesn't recall how much they were, but whatever it was, my grandfather had been happy to buy her one. She plaited it into a bracelet and gave it to Maureen, her best friend at the time. Maureen never wore it, nor gave her one in return. The memory dislodges hurt that shimmers off my mother in a green haze. She shrugs the feeling off, wanting to enjoy the memory of her father buying the satchel and the whang.

'Mmmm – the smell.' She forces a smile for Jack's benefit. He leans against the door jamb and folds his arms, smiling.

'What's in it?' he asks.

Inside the satchel are several school jotters my mother used to write stories in, and seeing them ignites a yellow thrum of pleasure. But she says to Jack in a neutral voice, 'It's just old school books.'

She pulls out a jotter to show that there's nothing exciting about the plain green cover, but a red rosette – stuck to the back of it – falls off and flutters to the floor.

'Oops,' my mother says, swooping down to scoop it off the floor.

'What did you win the rosette for?'

'A short story at the county fair.' She is befuddled and embarrassed about the stories.

'We had county fairs?'

'God, I've been living in America too long. It was called the Apple Blossom Festival back then. I remember a tent with drawings and embroidered cushion covers. Our teacher entered our efforts.'

'You did embroidery?' Jack is grinning, and my mother is torn between wanting to laugh and feeling jeered at.

'Yeah, wasn't much good at it.' She pushes the rosette into the satchel.

'But you did well in the story writing,' Jack says, smiling, his aura welcoming and steady, but my mother doesn't read it, barricading herself behind her lack of confidence.

'I suppose so.'

'What was the story about?'

'A bratty older brother who comes to a bad end.'

'Seriously? Was it?'

'Yeah. The judges loved it.' My mother turns away, hoping Jack will leave it be.

He gives her the stink eye, but she doesn't see it. She doesn't want to tell him that the story is about a mother searching for her lost child in a supermarket.

'And the jotters? Are those other stories?' His voice is gentle.

My mother feels able to breathe again.

'Yes.'

'I loved the stories you told the girls when they were younger.'

She hesitates, feels heat in her cheeks. 'You remember them?'

'Of course I do. They're brilliant. The girls loved them. They still talk about Snuffy, the polar bear.'

Heart thudding, she looks up to check if he's joking and realises he's being sincere.

'Thanks,' she mumbles.

'Why did you stop?' he asks.

She shrugs.

'Life. I needed to earn a living, get qualifications.'

'Think how much more you have to say now with your life experience.'

'Life experience?' She snorts.

'You've lived abroad. It's more than I've done.'

My mother thinks about how she gave up her teaching post to follow Ben to America. Or did she give up teaching to be a mother? And look how that turned out. Now she can't go back to teaching, can't bear to be with all those children, reminders that she failed to produce her own. She remembers now how every time a parent asked her if she had children of her own – as if that was what would have been a better qualification for teaching history and geography to teenagers than the four years she'd spent at university – she used to reply, 'Not yet.' Back then, when there was still hope.

Now, she has no hope, no future, nothing to offer. She hauls her mind out of that muddy black pit.

'Did you want to live abroad, Jack? Do other things?'

'I never considered it, actually. I always wanted to farm and live here.'

Rage flares in her, red hot and unwelcome. She doesn't want to be angry at Jack, who has always had simple needs, easy choices and lots of opportunities. She's had opportunities in her life, certainly, but she's also had choices denied her that most people take for granted. That one choice, her most important one, the choice to carry a child, to be a mother – she knows now that that was never an option for her. She's angry and doesn't know why it's hammering down on her so hard right now. Nor does she know why she wants to direct it at her poor, unassuming brother. She harnesses her emotions and reels in the fury.

'Aisling, are you okay?'

'Yeah. I just… I wasn't expecting to see these again.' She nods at the jotters.

'Tell you what.' Jack takes a step backwards out the door. 'You have a read of these, and I'll give you a shout when dinner's ready.'

*

After dinner, my mother excuses herself and goes to her room. The satchel lies on her desk beside the box where she stores the axe head and geode. The box doesn't fit into the satchel, but she wants to keep the axe head with the jotters. This organising of her childhood memorabilia into one place feels ordered and calming. She opens the box and tips the axe head into the satchel.

A bronze ray of evening sun, projected through a hole in the clouds, lights up her room, bathing it in rich light, saturated with invitation. She needs to be outside – loves these warm bright summer nights. Dusk won't arrive for another three hours. Grabbing the satchel and an old blanket, she leaves her bedroom.

Wind ripples across the barley field, stirring up waves on a sea of green tinged with gold. My mother gazes at the blue sky dressed with voluptuous white clouds. She has missed cloud-watching in California, where the sky is mostly a solid sheet of blue. Moisture from this afternoon's rain, still clinging to blades of grass, seeps into the toes of her trainers. With the sun out in full force, steam rises from the road and fence posts; tiny individual water particles ascending in wisps to form the bulging thermals above her.

She breathes in the scent of the damp soil, brushing her hand through the mint and lavender to release their aromas, too. Bees jostle for position as the flowers swing back into place, the air heavy with a busy hum. Lavender reminds her of Kate, and she wonders what has become of Kate's beautiful garden now Kate is not there to tend it. She pulls her thoughts back to this place, this garden.

The old satchel, slung across my mother's body, thumps against her hip, weighed down by the axe head. She pats the bag and smiles to herself, setting the blanket against the diamond-shaped bark ridges of the trunk of a solitary ash tree. Sitting down, she unbuckles the satchel and takes out the jotters and a pencil.

A rosy glow of contentment surrounds her as she reads the stories scribbled in her handwriting; a flow of words marching across grey-lined pages, delivering up a colourful mash of teenage angst, romance and drama.

One of the jotters is half empty and another not used. My mother skips two pages from the last story she'd written as a sixteen-year-old and starts to write again about the little polar bear called Snow Flake by his mother, though his friends called him Snuffy for short.

She'd told these stories to her nieces when they were tots, before she'd moved to California. My cousins had loved hearing about the little bear's trips to find an ecosystem that would support him despite the melting ice-caps, not least because both girls appeared as characters in the story. My mother kept it as real as she had dared, insisting that Snuffy eat only ringed seals and not children, no matter how hungry he became or how appetising the children's soft skin seemed. The girls squealed in fear as my mother read to them how Snuffy would see his friends and his mouth would water, but he'd resist … for now.

Now, she loses herself in her creating until Snuffy's world expands outside the limits of her own. When she runs aground on a plot point, she looks up and takes a breath, registering and re-entering her own world: the sun, now lower, cooler and casting rich light oozing gold and copper onto the undersides of the pinkening clouds; the air cooler and damper; the lavender scent; the birdsong.

She is completely in the moment, alive and appreciating her existence. Heart full and easy, she embraces the moment. She has not felt this free of grief in a long time. It is like a golden bubble inside her. It will pop, but as she looks at the jotter, she knows where she will find it again.

'If I hadn't lost you, I would have written these for you,' my mother says aloud.

You haven't lost me, mother. I'd love to hear your stories. The creative fire of her story-making fizzes with hope and potential.

'I'll write you a book of stories, Poppy.' Smoothing her fingers over the rough jotter paper, she notices the flecks in the wood pulp that make up the page. She remembers Grammo's words, '…The marks we leave on the bark are signs a life was lived …'

She twists around to look at the bark of the ash tree and sees its regular ridged pattern. She's not surprised to see that it has no scars or carved initials. Grammo taught them not to write on trees, that it was vandalism, and that too many scars on bark could kill a tree.

'So what did she mean? Did she mean marks on paper? That I should write? Is that what she was trying to tell me?'

Think about how writing makes you feel.

'It makes me feel free …like anything is possible.' My mother caresses the knobby bark tenderly and lets out a sigh before turning around and sitting back against the tree. Then she's off, her pencil galloping across the page, the story building to a climax; and she doesn't stop until, several pages later, she's finished. She doesn't know if she's been working on the story for ten minutes or ten hours, sliding into a world of her creation, a place of magic under her control and bursting with any and every emotion she chooses to inject it with. Aware it needs more moulding into shape, she flips back to the start of the story and starts reading it again.

Her phone buzzes from her pocket. She knows it's my father even before she sees his caller ID.

'Hi honey, how's it going?' He sounds happy.

'Great. I'm sitting in the garden, watching a gorgeous sunset.'

There is a lull, then a crackle on the line, then my father saying, 'Hello, can you hear me?'

'Yes, I said, I'm watching the sunset.'

'Sounds wonderful, darling.'

A honeyed light surrounds them, drawing me into it with them. My mother beams a smile that my father can't see but knows is there. She doesn't want to share that she's been writing, not knowing how to explain it without sounding silly.

'So what have you been up to?'

'Nothing much.' He answers too quickly.

'Oh. Really?'

'Look, I'm on the one-oh-one and coming up to patchy cell coverage, so I'll make it quick. I bought a ticket to Ireland. We need to talk …'

My mother's stomach plunges. 'What? Why?'

'My flight leaves at 1 p.m. I'll see you in the morning.'

'Should I be worried?' She clambers to her feet, checks the time – five in the afternoon, minus eight hours for California time. She tries to do the mental maths to work out what time it is for my father. Nine a.m. That fits. He has three hours to check in for the flight.

The line crackles.

'… layover in Paris for three …'

'Ben? Three what? Three hours?'

'… I'm hiring a car in Dublin. I'll see you in Armagh first thing in the morning.'

'Ben, wait!'

The line goes dead.

'Jesus! What the hell? Poppy, what's going on? Do you know?' My mother is sweating and panting. 'Is he leaving me, but doesn't want to tell me over the phone? Please, Poppy, what do you know?'

Please, Mother, be patient. Whatever he wants to tell you, he wants to tell you in his own way.

'Is it bad news?'

I don't know.

'How can you not know? You told me yourself you're all-knowing, but really, you know nothing!'

I can't always interpret what I know. I will have to tell her at some point that parts of my knowledge are fading, that I am fading. But now is not the time; she's fragile and scared. Her confidence is flayed because of the hormone treatments and the failed IVF. Talking to me in her head is probably not helping her, but neither of us can let go of the other. Not yet.

She senses my introspection. 'Poppy, I'm sorry. I'm just …'

Scared?

'Yes.'

It's all right. I understand.

I'm scared, too, but telling her that will not help.

She turns her phone over in her hands, contemplates calling my father back then decides against it. She slips the phone into the satchel and picks out the jotter she was working on. She wants to ease back into Snuffy's world, lose herself in her imagination. The pencil has fallen off the jotter inside the satchel. Still standing, she rummages around in the bottom of the bag, inhales the leathery aroma and closes her eyes. Her fingers touch a hard coldness. Before she realises what she is doing, she has grasped the axe head and pulled it from the satchel. She holds the cool metal to her cheek, feeling suddenly flushed.

*

The smell of woodsmoke makes her open her eyes. It's dark and cold, and she's no longer under the ash tree but standing in a dim hut. Shadowy figures surround her, but curiosity quells my mother's fear, and she is filled with a strange sense of calm. On the ground at her feet, she sees the woman from her vision; the woman we both register as Zosime. Her black hair fans out on a pillow of furs. Her eyes are closed. She is deathly pale, sweating and murmuring.

My mother bends over her, clutching the axe head to her breast.

Zosime's eyes open suddenly. 'Who are you?'

It's a strange language but we both understand it.

'I'm Aisling.'

But all Zosime can hear is the pop and fizz in her head that her ears make when it rains. And I wonder how I can know this, but not why my father is coming to Ireland.

'I can't hear you!' Zosime says, rising up on her elbows. Hands reach to calm her. Voices speak words of comfort to her in the strange language.

'What do you want?' Zosime reaches for my mother and grabs her hand, knocking the axe head to the floor. 'Wait, come back…'

*

A bolt of lightning and we are back under the ash tree, the axe head at our feet. Plops of rain land on my mother as she stares at the axe head beneath pewter clouds. She jumps at the boom of thunder and then hears her brother shout from the back doorstep.

'Come in outta that before you get hit by lightning!'

My mother takes another look at the axe head and decides not to touch it. She leaves it lying in the grass under the ash tree, closes the satchel slung over her shoulder and runs to join Jack at the back door as the sky opens, unleashing a torrential downpour.

It's only when she's in the kitchen towelling off her hair that she realises she left the axe head lying in the spot where she first found it twenty-five years ago.

CHAPTER 20

My ear buzzes like bees in ivy. Or maybe it's the hailstones hitting the thatch. I claw my way through the fog of fever to see Geros beside me, wringing out a cloth and pressing it to my cheek.

'Where is Nereus?' I nuzzle into the coolness of the wet cloth.

'Sleeping.' Geros looks like he should be the one resting.

'Is he sick, too?' I try to sit up. My body is so weak I can barely lift my head.

'You need to rest.'

'Tell me. You're scaring me.'

'He's alive.' Geros moves to one side. I'm in Geros's quarters. The reed curtain is scooped back, so the area is one with the Ceremonial Hall. Beyond Geros, I see Nereus curled up beneath furs nearer the fire. Sweat glistens on his forehead. His eyes are shut. Violent shivers make his sleep look anything but restful.

'How is he?' I whisper.

'His fever is high. It hasn't broken yet. Yours only broke this morning. Here.' Geros picks up a cup of broth. 'You need to build your strength.'

'But Nereus—'

'Stop. Put your worry aside. You can do nothing for him when you're so weak yourself.' Geros glares at me.

I have no strength to fight his will. I breathe deeply until the air catches in my chest, making me cough. My chest, my head, even my eyes hurt.

'How long have I been sick?'

'Half a moon cycle, but your rash has gone.'

As I try to speak, another cough rattles through me. When it settles, I focus on Geros. Though he looks tired, I don't see the angry red herder's rash that I had, that Aleka had. Oh, sacred goddess – Aleka!

Hot tears trickle down my temples and into my hair. I'm helpless to stop them.

'Are you ill?' I ask Geros.

'I'm fine. You concentrate on getting better.'

'But how come you didn't get sick?'

'There are a small number of us who never catch herder's rash. I don't know why, but thank the gods, there are some of us left to take care of the others.'

'Yani? Agis?' I ask, hearing the panic in my voice.

'We're here, sister,' Yani says from the other side of the fire.

There are others here. The buzzing in my ear clears, replaced by muttering, moans, low voices. So many are sick, it sounds like the whole village has been crammed into the Ceremonial Hall. Of course, it is easier for Geros to tend to the ill and keep us warm when we're together rather than have him move around outside in the snow.

'Who was that woman?' I ask, remembering the strange visitor.

'Doah?' Geros asks.

'No, a stranger. She didn't wear Partholon's mark.'

Geros frowns and leans in. 'Can you describe her?'

'She wore strange colours and carried a light: a bright white light.'

'This light, was it in a vessel, like our torch lamps? Or did it shine from her?'

I close my eyes and try to remember. 'Neither,' I say, opening my eyes. 'The light was apart from her, like a star at her shoulder.'

Geros sits back on his heels, thinking hard. 'Was it a vision of the Maiden?'

'No.' Of this, I am certain. 'She didn't have long golden hair, and she looked frightened.'

'What did she say?'

'They spoke to me, though the words were not clear, as if coming from a great distance.'

'They? There was more than one?'

'Yes. But ...' I'm confused now. I saw one person yet felt two. 'I can't explain it. Maybe it was a dream.' Yet something about it felt different from the dream world, but how? Exhaustion swoops over me like a shadow. I fight to keep my eyes open. Geros's smooth fingertip traces my eyebrows, and as he shushes me, I surrender to sleep.

*

'Nereus!' I jump awake. My head hurts, but this time, I'm able to sit, propped up on my elbow. Thirst scrapes my tongue. Where is Nereus?

175

At the far end of the hall, Geros is talking to a group. Heads nod, people mumble, but I can't make it out clearly. I can see Doah and Lan moving about also, but there is no sign of Mela.

Closer, there are rows of people under furs. Some are turning, restless with fever, kicking off their covers to shiver; others snore, and one is dreadfully still, with the covers pulled up over the face and head. I catch my breath.

'Nereus? Where are you?'

My name sounds like a rustle of a hand through reeds, he whispers it so weakly. 'Zo-sim-aye?'

And then I see him, by the wall, under a fur that doesn't cover his feet. Poor Nereus. He hates having cold feet. I pull myself up to kneel. Sway. Drop to all fours and crawl to him, dragging my furs with me.

His face is wet with perspiration and tears. I hug him to me, inhaling his scent, a welcome homecoming despite the hum of sweat and illness. Pulling back, I search his face. He raises one hand. His fingertips trace my temple. The gentlest tickle but filled with the energy of a loved one's touch. I absorb it. His Mark of Partholon is smudged over his cheek and down into his beard. His eyes glisten, releasing a drip down his temple when he smiles.

'Thank the gods, you're better.' His voice is only a croak. 'I thought you were going to—' His face crumples. He buries his hand into my hair at the back of my head, pulling us forehead to forehead. As he succumbs to shuddering sobs, I clasp him to me.

'I'm here.' I dapple kisses over his face until he gains control.

I crawl under his wraps and snuggle against his body for heat, arranging the wraps over our feet. We lie face to face, holding hands, too weak to move much, our bodies too achy to wrap around one another, dozing in a haze of semi-sleep until thirst wakes me up.

I'm used to hunger, but this deep thirst is something else.

Nereus feels me wriggle and lets go of my hand. I shiver at the draught as the covers shift. He sits up, stretches his arms, and yawns.

'Stay here,' he says, bundling me up again. He stands up with slow, deliberate movements, revealing his own weakened state. I watch him walk to the firepit and come back with a skin of water and a bowl of soup. He helps me sit up. My head spins. I slump against Nereus as he holds the skin to my lips. I slake my thirst in sucking gulps, feeling the chill of the water travel to my belly. The soup warms me. I feel fuller and a little stronger – enough to swing my legs around and cross them in front of me so I can face the firepit and feel its warmth.

On the other side of the Ceremonial Hall, Geros looks towards us. He finishes up what he is doing and makes his way through the rows to join us. 'It is good to see you both up. How are you feeling?'

'Stronger,' Nereus says.

'How's Agis?' I ask, thinking of him on his own without… Grief thumps into me again. I wobble as I draw in a deep breath.

'He didn't get sick. He's hunting with Yani and Con,' Geros tell us. 'Their families are well.'

I'm relieved to hear that, but thinking about Aleka is dagger-sharp. Tears start again.

Nereus puts his arm around my shoulder and pulls me to his chest.

'You missed the funeral. We couldn't risk waiting. There were so many funerals,' Geros says. 'So many children.'

Nereus grips my hand and whispers. 'Bion?'

'He's sick, but his fever broke last night. He's been sleeping since. We're hoping he will wake up soon. He's over there.' Geros points to the far end of the Ceremonial Hall, centred on the larger ceremonial fireplace. It looks like they have set up a cooking station and a gathering place for people healthy enough to care for the rest of us. I wonder how Bion can sleep with all this activity.

'Can I see him?' Nereus asks.

This is usually where my pangs of jealousy would ignite – Nereus investing so much of himself in his cousin's child, in another woman's child – but I'm beyond that now. Too much has been lost.

'Please do,' Geros says. 'He might hear your voice and follow it from the land of sleep.'

Geros walks with us to see Bion. When I wobble, he links his gnarled arm through mine, and I feel strength in his grip. Nereus takes my other arm.

In better days, there would be a buzz of excitement when we'd gather in the meeting hall. It might be to see visitors and share stories of their travels; to celebrate the passing of seasons, unions, births, festivals; to hear the council discuss lawmaking, or on rare occasions, lawbreaking. But now the air is heavy with dread. Even the solemn funeral ceremonies, where life is celebrated and spirits are sent off to join the stars, did not press down with this feeling of hopelessness.

With so many dead, the funeral fires outside have been burning without the ceremonial aromatic herbs that normally mask the burning of our dead; supplies have run out. I can smell the rancid aromas of burning hair, flesh and bones that foul the air and saturate the hair and clothes of the mourners. No one escapes the stench. The charring flesh lends a disquieting smell of meat roasting that I know does not come from our cooking. We've not had the luxury of a spit roast in several moons. I will never be able to stomach it after this.

Instead, a soup pot simmers, tended by a young woman I recognise as a cousin's child. We nod acknowledgement, but there is no conversation with the sallow-eyed girl. Another sits nearby, stripping willow branches and passing the bark to a man who grinds it for medicine. There is no chatter about the weather, no asking after the health of each other's kin. The answers are the same – 'It's too cold' – or unbearable, 'They're starving; sick; dead.'

Bion sleeps soundly on a bench behind the line for soup. Chloe, his aunt, sits cross-legged on the floor at his head, watching the to-and-fro of people.

'Has he been awake?' Geros asks.

Chloe shakes her head, dull-eyed. 'Kallisto is in the soup line. She'll be back soon.' She keeps her head down, her thoughts withdrawn.

Nereus kneels on the other side of the bench. 'Go, rest. We'll wait with him.'

Chloe unfolds as if she has the joints of one twice her age, stands up and shuffles away.

Nereus takes Bion's hand in his. 'Wake up, little man.'

I rub Nereus's shoulder. 'Bion survived the fever. He will live, won't he, Geros?'

Geros doesn't answer.

'He is a strong little boy,' I say.

'He was weakened by lack of food, like all of us.' Geros is trying to prepare us for the worst, but I can't bear to see the pain on Nereus's face.

'He's stronger than you think,' I say. 'We shared our rations with him. That must have helped.'

Geros gives me a strange look, almost as if he is angry. I rush to explain, 'Haemon is not here to help, and Nereus is his closest male relative.'

There is movement behind me, and I hear Kallisto say, 'You shared your rations with Bion, Zosime?'

I turn and face her. 'Yes.'

She holds my gaze. Neither of us have words to share, but there is a frisson of understanding, a flicker of connection despite her clenched teeth and lifted chin.

'That was foolhardy,' Geros says in a hard, cold voice.

'But—'

'You risked more than just your life.'

I shake my head.

Kallisto narrows her eyes and says, 'Surely Zosime saved his life? That extra food kept him strong, didn't it?'

'It did,' Geros said. 'But our village depends on Zosime as one of our best hunters. The needs of the many were at risk because she fed Bion. People go hungry while you recover, Zosime.'

Kallisto presses her lips together and shoots a narrow-eyed glance at Geros. He raises an eyebrow at her defiance, then turns his back and walks away. She looks at me, her lips a bloodless line. Is this where she will blame me again for the pigs dying last year? Will she bring up the axe? Will I have to defend my actions – again? But instead, she takes a step back, lowers her head and says, 'I thank you, Zosime.'

It is a thaw of sorts, but at what cost? As I watch her sit down by Chloe and watch her son in silence, fatigue wraps around me, squeezing hard. I lower myself to the floor with shaking limbs. The warmth of the thin soup is leaving, and though my belly is full of fluid, I do not feel the nourishment a full meal would give. Geros is right. I need to return to hunting as quickly as I can.

Nereus talks to the child, coaxing him to wake up, jiggling his hands, and tickling his toes. At last, Bion responds. His eyes open and he stares at the wattled ceiling. There is no expression on his face, an emptiness in his gaze.

'Mama's here,' Kallisto says.

The child doesn't move, save for the rise and fall of his chest.

Kallisto picks him up, but his body is floppy. His head tilts back. Kallisto holds it up with one hand and tries to gather his arms and legs with her other arm. They loll from her grasp.

Nereus calls Geros over. The old healer's face drops when he sees Bion sprawled in his mother's arms.

'Try giving him water.' He hands a cup to Nereus.

Kallisto is murmuring, 'Come on, Bion, sit up. Be a good boy.' She arranges him into a sitting position on her lap, facing Nereus. 'Ne Ne has water for you.'

Nereus lifts the cup to Bion's lips. The child stares past it. Nereus touches the cup to Bion's lips, hoping to trigger a reaction… but nothing. He tips it to wet the lips, but the water dribbles down the child's chin. There is a gurgle as some enters the child's mouth and bubbles. We expect Bion to cough, but instead, we hear a wet wheeze.

'Stop!' Kallisto says.

There is still a lot of water in the cup Nereus holds, but Bion's gurgled breath sounds like a fish on a river bank. Kallisto tips the child forward, clearing his mouth and airway. His breathing sounds more natural now; but if Bion doesn't swallow, we cannot get the water into him. We look from one to another, wide-eyed and scared.

'Do something, Geros, please.' Kallisto is panting hard, clinging to her boy.

Geros shakes his head. 'Even a newborn knows how to swallow.'

'But he'll be okay?' Kallisto urges.

Geros takes a deep breath. 'I don't know.'

*

The next day, I force myself up despite a pounding headache. My legs tremble as I dress, Geros's words from the day before bouncing around my head.

People go hungry while you recover, Zosime.

The thin soup warms me, the headache subsides, and I feel stronger. I can walk. And if I can walk, I can hunt; so despite Nereus protesting, I take my quiver and bow and head out with Agis, Yani and Con. We can't bear to talk about Aleka, so we focus on the hunt. The dawn chill chews mercilessly through my furs and wraps. The nights have shortened, but the sky stays grey. The sun has not come back with any strength and the snow still lies.

I tug at a twig in my way and examine its tip. 'I would have expected the bulge to have begun already,' I say with a sigh.

'Too cold.' Agis nudges me from behind. I keep moving, stepping out from the deer run onto the trackway that leads to the Great Mound. Every step requires effort. I'm panting on the flat. What will going up the hill do to me?

'Con and I have had to travel further to find anything worth hunting,' Yani says, dropping back with me as Agis and Con pair up and stride ahead. Already, I am tiring. It's this brisk walking. Once we are tracking prey, treading stealthily, I hope my skills kick in and I will not hold the others back so much.

Going up the hill, I slow to catch my breath. Yani keeps pace with me, telling me the plan. 'We'll follow the trackway towards the Blackwater River and start our hunt after the ford.'

'That pushes us right up against The Crossing's hunting lands.' I remember a dispute when I was young. If it wasn't for Lan's diplomacy, there would have been war.

'We heard their hunters are dead,' Yani says quietly.

'Herder's rash?'

Yani grunts and keeps his gaze down. Ahead, Con and Agis widen the distance between us. I cannot push my legs to walk faster.

'What is The Crossing doing for food now?' I ask.

'They left.'

'Left? The whole village?'

'There aren't that many of them anymore. Twenty, give or take. They passed us on the tracks heading to the Great Mound. They think the Monarchs will have food to give them.' Yani shakes his head and casts his eyes up.

'How long ago was this?'

'Before the last full moon – if there was a full moon.' Yani looks up at the grey sky. 'How do we know anymore?'

His question sets my scalp tingling. We know how many days a moon cycle takes, and without seeing the moon, we assume the cycle is the same. I scowl at him, avoiding talk about the moon disappearing. 'Did you tell the Elders about people abandoning The Crossing?'

'Of course.'

'And?'

'And what? They never tell us anything. All this.' Yani waves his hand at the sky. 'We've never had such terrible weather for so long. If the gods are so unhappy with us, why don't they kill us and be done with it? This drawn-out punishment is cruel. I have no respect for gods who have less compassion than a human. I wouldn't let an animal suffer the way they have been toying with us – even a wasp's nest deserves better. And if—'

'Shush!' I stop walking.

'What? You're afraid the gods will hear me?'

'No. But he might,' I point up the trackway. Ahead, Agis and Con have stopped to talk to a tall man wrapped in thick white furs, his long hair the colour of dried grain stalks. He is a head and shoulders taller than my brother and cousin. They stand looking up at him, engrossed in what he says.

As we approach, I hear the stranger using words in our language but in tones and inflexions that require focus to understand their meaning.

Con introduces us and says, 'This is Arne. We met a couple of summers ago when I travelled to the coast where the sun sets. He is a travelling storyteller. He's been to many faraway lands and has many great tales to tell of them.'

'And of you, my friend, from our times together – those were good times.' Arne claps Con on the shoulders and addresses us with, 'Hallo.' He has a kind, open face and a ready smile.

As we greet him, Con updates us on what we missed in their conversation.

'Arne says he is journeying to the Warmer Lands to find the sun.'

'Have you been there before?' I ask.

'Ja, many times. But only in winter. It is usually too hot for me. I'm from a land of ice, but this season, phew, this winter, there has been too much. I want to see blue sky again.'

Blue sky.

The last time I saw a blue sky was when it ripped open. The memory gives me a strange tingle of longing mixed with fear.

Arne continues in his strange accent, 'Our plants will not grow without sun. Where I am from, the sun is with us in the summer but for long days, long, long days. No night. In the winter, it is dark all day. We need the sun.'

'How will you get there? To the Warmer Lands?' I ask, my mind stretching to try to imagine the darkness he describes. It sounds worse than the winter we have just had, yet Arnes speaks of it like it is normal.

'Last time, there was a boat that went from … Moontancoop? Near your mountains that meet the sunrise, where the sea comes up into the valley, not far from here now. Two more days walk at most.'

I nod, recognising the description of Nereus's hometown of Mountain Gap. With Arne's strange accent, I can hear how he's mispronouncing it, but I don't bother to correct him. It has many industries like jewellery-makers, stone masons, weavers, fishing, and trade with travellers from across the sea. I have made that walk in a day, but it was a long day, and I was fit and well-fed.

'Zosime, accompany Arne back to our village. He needs someplace to rest tonight,' Yani says.

I need the rest every bit as much, if not more; and if any of the four of us can be spared from hunting, it is me. The walk has left me exhausted.

'Of course,' I say with a smile. I have many questions for this gentle giant.

Arne agrees to eat with us in our hut, away from the din of the Gathering Hall. We have taken our share from the communal pot and split it with Arne. He has foraged along his way and can add some root vegetables and some dried meat from his pack to that thin soup. The dried meat looks suspiciously like rat, but the small, dried-up leathery strips are smoke-cured and add flavour and sustenance to our little feast.

The ringing in my ears tells me that rain or sleet is close, but we are cosy in our hut with our guest.

'Arne tells me he is travelling to the Warmer Lands,' I say to Nereus as they stretch out in front of the heat, their long legs flanking the fire pit. 'To find the sun.'

'You think we need to go overseas to find the sun?' Nereus asks.

'Yes, this island is too small. The sun is further away than your land stretches.'

That surprises neither of us. We've heard that a person can walk the length of the land in one moon and sail around it in the same time.

'Where do you sail from?' Nereus asks.

'Mountain Gap.' Arne pronounces it more clearly this time. 'You know it?'

'I do. I was brought up close by.'

'Do you still have family there?'

'Distant relatives, yes.'

The two men share the names of the people they know and find they might have a mutual acquaintance, but the connection is vague. It's what we do – try to find the connections – even with travellers.

I steer the conversation back to Arne's trip. 'So you think you will find the sun again on your voyage?'

'Yes, I'm sure of it. We've had word from our clansmen who travel there each year. Those who cannot bear the dark months that follow the sun but return when the sun returns to our land every summer.'

'Every year?' I think travelling on the ocean must be difficult and take time, yet these men routinely take that journey. 'How long does it take?'

'From Mountain Gap?' Arne shrugs as he thinks. 'Less half a moon cycle; at best, seven days, but much more if conditions are difficult.'

'A hard enough journey, I would imagine.'

Nereus shakes his head. 'No, not necessarily, if you have the right vessel and crew. Many of my people have taken that trip.'

'So do you think if the sun doesn't return, we could follow the sun to the Warmer Lands too?' I direct the question to Arne but keep an eye on Nereus's reaction.

Nereus frowns. 'You think the sun won't return?'

'It should have returned by now, but the days have stayed dull.'

Arne nods in agreement with me.

'Maybe it's just late,' Nereus says.

'Maybe,' says Arne. 'But if it doesn't, nothing grows in the dark and the cold. I have had enough of that for a while.'

Nereus purses his lips, thinking about what Arne has said, then tips his head towards him, conceding, 'It is very dark in your land. That is understandable.'

'It has been dark here, too,' I say. 'More so than is normal.'

'True,' Nereus says.

'Would you be prepared to travel to the Warmer Lands if the sun didn't return?' I ask.

'The sun will come back,' Nereus says.

Arne looks sceptical. The first drops of rain patter off our roof.

'But let's say it didn't,' I push.

'Ever?' Nereus's eyes widen.

I quickly add, 'Say it took longer than usual. Would you go to the Warmer Lands then?'

'If nothing was growing, yes,' Nereus says.

I feel an odd sense of relief.

Arne smiles as if his trip has been vindicated.

'But that will never happen. The sun always returns, always.' A burst of heavy rain almost drowns out Nereus's words.

Arne laughs. 'I think the Gods are arguing on mine and Zosime's side tonight!'

We laugh together, but deep down, I think the gods have never been on our side, or anyone's for that matter.

'So,' I say, turning to Arne. 'Tell us about how you travel to the Warmer Lands then.'

CHAPTER 21

My mother wrestles on a pair of Marigolds to retrieve the axe head before the house awakens. The increasing number of things I do not know tug on me and dissipate, like branches shredding mist in treetops. What are these visions that appear when my mother holds the axe head? We share a sense that what we see is important – enough to break the barriers between worlds. Is it connected with my breaching the barriers between the physical world and the spirit world? Or is it a message? If so, it is one we have yet to decipher.

In the mornings, fresh from dreamtime, my mother feels especially close to me. Our cosy communion is swathed in tinges of rose gold. We share a knowing, speaking without words, in a way that is fluid and fulfilling for me. She is not as aware that it is happening and sometimes believes that my thoughts are hers until she questions how she knows things; like now, as she stands beneath the ash tree, with the morning sun making the dewdrops glisten, she knows that this axe head belongs to Zosime, a woman from another time. She knows that many questions will arise, some answered and more generated by those answers when she has the time and can build up the courage to hold the axe head to her skin. She doesn't know if she can grow tolerant of the axe head's effect, doesn't realise she can't simply switch it on to communicate with the past the way she would switch on an electronic device. I don't know how to explain it to her, though; and if she asks me too many questions, she'll grow frustrated and concerned. It is enough that I worry about my enlightenment slipping away. What can she do if she realises this is happening? No point in us both worrying.

She slips the axe head into her satchel as the tiny thunks of raindrops hitting leaves alert her to another oncoming shower. Back in her room, she sets the satchel on her bed. She lingers, watching the rain gush in sheets down the windowpanes, thankful to have a strong house and roof to protect her from the deluge. Then hunger sends her to the kitchen, where she finds Jack preparing for the casual chaos of school-day breakfast.

'It's like a tropical downpour, isn't it?' Jack says, nodding at the window.

'I don't remember anything like this when we were young,' my mother answers, thinking how the Irish love to discuss the weather. 'I can't get used to *warm* rain here, or anywhere for that matter.' She thinks of the first trip she took to Florida. How she'd worn warm layers beneath a waterproof jacket – as she would in Ireland – when rain was forecast. She'd ended up soaked with sweat instead of rain.

'The fields need it,' Jack says. 'But when it comes down this hard, it knocks the apple blossoms off, washes the topsoil away.' He takes a long slug of coffee.

My mother's phone chirps.

'Ben's landed at Dublin,' she says, reading quickly. Jack doesn't notice her trepidation, the sheen of violet rippling her aura. 'He'll be here in an hour and a half, two max.'

'It's great he could get over. Maybe we'll get a wee night out at the weekend.'

'That would be lovely.' My mother doesn't understand why my father has decided to come on such short notice. She's frustrated with me for not being able to tell her, but I can't reach my father. Another fading, a diminishing of my essence. Will this continue until I peter out to nothing?

'We could get a babysitter.'

'Babysitter?' Emily asks, whipping through the kitchen and out to the utility room, returning with a lumpy plastic bag. She clambers onto the stool beside my mother at the kitchen island.

'Never you mind.' Jack ruffles her hair and nods at the bag. 'What's this?'

'Science project.' Emily pours milk into a bowl of cereal with one hand and, with the other, extracts a plastic food takeout box from the plastic bag. 'We had to leave food in plastic boxes for two weeks to see what happens to it.' She sets down the milk and reaches to lever the lid off the box.

'No!'

Emily freezes at her dad's sharp tone. A frisson of hurt puffs from her like mauve powder.

'Not in the kitchen,' Jack says in a kinder tone.

'Eugh, that's disgusting, Emily,' Fiona says, entering the kitchen. 'It smells rank!'

'Did the teacher tell you to do this?' Jack asks.

'She set one up in the classroom for the whole class to see, but I wanted one for myself, so I made my own here at home,' Emily says. 'Mine are better. I'm taking them in to show the teacher.'

'How many boxes do you have?' Jack says, lifting the bag and looking inside.

'Five.'

'Five! And where did you get this?' Jack is trying not to laugh but can't hide a smile.

'Leftovers for one day. You know, from when we eat. Before you put it in the brown bin.' Emily spoons cereal into her mouth. Everyone listens to her crunch, crunch, crunch.

Jack puts the box back, closes the bag and says, 'Jesus. One day? I didn't realise we wasted so much food.'

Emily shrugs, still crunching away.

'Aunty Aisling,' Fiona says, coming up beside my mother. 'Will Uncle Ben be here when we get home?'

Nothing gets past her, my mother thinks. 'Yes, darling.'

'Goody, I can't wait to see him.'

'Me, too.' My mother puts her arm around Fiona's shoulders and gives her a squeeze, kissing the top of her head. 'Quick now, eat your breakfast. It's nearly time to go.'

By the time the girls have eaten and Jack has herded them out to the car, my mother has about half an hour to load the dishwasher and wipe down the counters. Peace unfurls in the kitchen as she sets it to order, leaving a place set on the kitchen island for Maureen's breakfast. She's out for an early jog, so my mother has the place to herself for a while yet. Morning sunshine topples in the window and lolls across the sink as the sun crests the hawthorn hedgerow outside. The double glazing is no match for the morning conversation of the resident chattering birds.

Though it has changed since she was a girl rushing out to school, my mother can still conjure up the memory of sitting at a wooden table where the kitchen island now sits. In her mind's eye, she sees her dad lifting the plate to wash it as soon as she picks up the last piece of toast. Her dad wanted a tidy kitchen for her mum coming home from the night shift in St Luke's.

They worked so hard for us, she tells me in her mind, to give us every opportunity in life. *What am I doing with that now?*

Not being able to answer her fills me with a violet, oily dread. My mother senses my fear and shivers. *Is being with me harming you? Is that why you know less and less as time goes on?*

Even if I wanted to go back, I don't know how to.

What does this mean for you, Poppy? How can I help?

I cannot tell her. I don't know if I am kept this side of the veil because I crave her or because she needs me. If I ask her to cut me loose, will I lose my last anchor before I'm cast into the void? Could she cut me loose if she thought it would help? Would she?

My mother is distracted by the gravel crunching under tyres in the driveway and the sound of a car engine shutting down. She runs to the front door, aglow in pulses of pink, tinged with muddy beige trepidation. My father's aura reaches out, wisps of pink and full of joy, spanning the gap between them, connecting with my mother's aura before he is completely out of the car and standing straight. She rushes to him, finding home in his embrace.

Suddenly, I know why he's home. The knowledge floods in like lights in a stadium and informs my mother, too, with no effort from me.

'You applied to the Planetarium?' my mother says. 'You really want to move back?'

My father pulls back to search her face. 'How did you know? Did you see the job advertised? I wanted to surprise you.'

'Oh, you did.' She snuggles into him and knows the interview is the day after tomorrow. She thinks she's getting the information from me, but actually, upon touching him, she knew the story without me relaying it. Unable to explain it to him, so she lets him think she saw the advertisement and pieced it together herself. He tells her about his flight; that he's planning to stay for a week.

'Work doesn't know yet that I applied to the post here in Armagh. There's no need to ruffle any feathers until I know if I'm in with a shout. You sure you want to do this? Move back?'

'One hundred per cent,' she says and means it. The thought of moving home fills her with crisp turquoise light. 'We both need this.'

And she's right. It's such a simple decision, it's hardly a decision at all.

Now he's here, and my mother has reconnected her aura to his, I reconnect to my father. But I'm concerned by the gap between us, by the fact that my enlightenment is fading so quickly. Is it passing to my mother? If so, what happens to me?

She helps him take his bags into the house and up to her room.

'What's that?' my father asks, spotting the old leather satchel on her pillow.

'My old school bag. Jack found it. There were some old stories I'd written in it.' My mother shrugs off a tingle of self-consciousness.

'Will you read them to me?'

'You're tired. Do you want to catch a quick nap?'

'I slept on the plane for a couple of hours.' He looks out the window at the sun breaking through the clouds. 'I'd love a walk. Clear the cobwebs.' He lifts the satchel. 'C'mon. Take your bag, and we'll sit in the old orchard at the derelict farmhouse, and you can read me a story. How about that?'

Grinning, she lifts up on her tiptoes and pecks his cheek. 'Okay, let's go.'

*

White cow parsley lines the narrow lane with a layer of frothy lace. They walk holding hands, one on each side of the tuft of grass that grows up the middle. Branches stretch overhead, forming a leafy tree tunnel. The dappled shade chills as they approach the bridge, where the temperature around the river dips. They stop on the stone bridge, prop their elbows on the rough blocks of limestone and look downriver. The stream is as low as my mother has ever seen it.

A flash of blue darts from beneath them and streaks out of sight upstream.

'Did you see it?' my father asks.

'Gorgeous – a kingfisher!'

They sigh and laugh. They've called this the 'Bridge of Sighs' ever since they had their first kiss here. They never cross it without at least a peck.

'I love you,' my father says.

'I know.'

'And?'

'Thank you.'

He tickles her and she cries, 'Okay, I love you, too, I love you, too.'

They fold into each other with a luxurious kiss that fizzes through them, infusing me with the energy of their reconnection. Time ticks by as they stand there, lost in each other, until she shifts to one foot, and it's enough to break the spell, naturally, easily. From the river, it's uphill to the old farmhouse, now a shell, providing shelter for livestock in the winter.

The stone wall merges into a vertical grassy bank strewn with ferns and topped with a tree trunk running parallel to the road at shoulder height. Tiers of fungus grow on its bark, little cream and brown tutus.

'Look.' My mother points to a wild strawberry about knee-high in the undergrowth. She picks it and finds another for my father. The intense sweetness puckers the insides of their cheeks.

'Oh god, they're divine,' my father says with a groan of pleasure. He moves further up the lane, foraging. 'There's more here.'

'So tiny and so sweet,' my mother. 'Mind the nettles.'

They are still smacking their lips when they arrive at the flat rock in what was once the garden, between the small orchard and the old house. My father sits down and pats the spot beside him. My mother settles in, lies back against him, closes her eyes to the sunlight, listens to the drone of bees and lets the sweet chirp of wrens fill her heart.

'We could buy this from Jack and build a house here,' my mother says dreamily. 'I mean, look at that view.'

She opens her eyes to gaze down through the apple trees at the river meandering across green fields, disappearing under the bridge and a jumble of trees to reappear glittering over a shallow gravel bed. Fluffy white clouds build on the horizon, stark and bulbous against the blue summer sky.

'Hmmm.' My father is noncommittal, knowing full well she might prefer a place in town, an easy walk to the city centre. They're building castles in the air, and he knows air is not the most solid foundation. But it's okay; it's a process, their process. Rippling with golden contentment in the summer sun, he takes my mother's hands. He intertwines their fingers, bringing the clasped hands to his mouth, kissing her knuckles. 'What about reading me a story?'

'Okay.' She slides her hand into the satchel and gropes for the notebook, but the axe head gets in the way. Her hand closes around it. Suddenly, her vision blurs. It clears almost at once, and though they are standing in the same spot when she looks around, she sees that the garden, farmhouse, orchard, road, and bridge have disappeared. There are structures along the crest of the far hill, huts maybe.

*

The temperature has dropped. They both shiver.

'Jesus Christ!' My father is agape.

My mother experiences a flicker of relief, knowing that it's not just her. But this fleeting yellow glimmer quickly stains to sepia of alarm as she takes in the scene on the hill.

Beneath a leaden sky, haggard people huddle in groups around raised platforms bearing layers of twigs and sticks. These are topped with elongated bundles wrapped in cloth. Tongues of yellow and orange flames lick up through the wood, spewing smoke in rollicking curls into the air. Keening, a wail of soul-shredding misery, carries on the breeze, lonely and hopeless. My mother stifles a sob as the smell of burning meat, hair, and bone hits them.

'Dear God, they're burning bodies.' My father, still clasping my mother's hand, tries to stand but can't get his legs working.

My mother grips the axe head hard. She wants to see more, know more, though the scene is harrowing, the people desolate, thin. How can she help them? But my parents are snapped back to their own world, sitting near the crest of the hill in front of the derelict farmhouse. My mother draws the axe head from the satchel and holds it up.

'Why did it stop working?' she mumbles.

The axe head is still as powerful as ever, but you build more resistance to it every time you use it, I tell her.

I have to find out what it is trying to tell me before it stops working completely, she answers.

She is gripped with an urgency to get my father on board and figure out what she is experiencing and why.

'What just happened?' My father stands, turns in a circle to check that what they saw is really gone. The acrid smell lingers in their nostrils, in their memory, but it, too, is passing. He is trembling and pale; my mother composed, by comparison.

'It's the axe head,' she says to him. 'It's happened before. Remember, you saw something, too. After the earthquake?'

My father has erased that memory.

'What are you talking about?'

Tell him about me. I want him to know me, recognise me, hear me.

'Ever since the earthquake, I've been able to hear things, see things, talk to …' she draws a breath. 'Please try to believe me, please.'

'What? Believe what?'

'I can talk to our daughter Poppy.'

Tears sting his eyes. 'Aisling, don't do this.' His loss plumes.

'Mum sensed her, too.'

He shakes his head. 'That's hardly a validation now, Aisling, is it?'

'Ben!'

He softens his tone, 'It's just…' He searches for the right words. 'Your mother sees lots of things that aren't there.'

'You saw a field full of people. Right here, with me. We both saw that, smelt it, felt it!' She waves the axe head at the space, hoping to conjure up the vision – something – again.

'Maybe it's jetlag.'

'I'm not jet-lagged.'

'There has to be an explanation.'

'The axe head. It's a connection to the past,' she says. 'Ben, we both saw it. We looked back in time… to the famine or something.'

'No. We shared a hallucination, that's all. It's not real. Maybe we ate something. Those strawberries?'

'Strawberries don't do that.' My mother puts the axe head back in the bag. She is close to tears, frustrated. 'It's not the strawberries, Ben. It's something special. Talking to Poppy – it's a good thing. You should try—'

'Stop!' He holds up one hand to her, the other to his chest like he's winded. 'The baby is gone. This is too hard, Aisling. I can't…' He rubs his face and shakes his head. 'The fungus.'

'What?'

'That's it! The fungus on the old tree trunk. The spores must have landed on the strawberries.'

'No.'

'And we ingested them.'

Their auras shrink and shrivel in cold tones of blue and violet. My mother shivers again despite the warm day. Loneliness spills from her in muddy greys.

'That's not what happened,' she says, desperately needing him to open his mind.

'There's no other logical explanation,' he shouts, startling her.

Tears of frustration blur her vision. 'Not everything is logical,' she shouts back. 'Wanting a baby is not logical. Love is not logical. Life is not fucking logical.'

'Oh, come on!'

'*No*! Life – not logical! You wake up, get out of bed, piss, brush your teeth, eat, work, eat, work, eat, sleep – and again, the same shite the next morning. In fact, the same old shite every damn day for eighty or ninety years – if you're lucky. What's the point if it's only about logic?'

They stand panting, glaring at one another. My mother leans on the rock.

'Ben, look, if we'd had some psychedelic mushroom trip, we wouldn't have seen the same things, would we?'

'I don't know.' My father sits beside her. He tries to take her hand, but she shrugs him off. 'I've never done LSD or mushrooms,' he says more gently. 'I don't know. But I'm worried about you.' He reconsiders how my mother sees me, questions how healthy this approach is if it means they have these visions, yet can't accept that he has actually seen anything. He attempts to block it out, but somewhere deep down, wants me to be there – for both of them.

'I'm fine,' my mother insists.

'You're talking to—' He rubs his face, not knowing how to reference me.

Father, it's okay. I send this thought to him with so much energy I feel I'm waning as a result.

It lands softly as a flash of insight, something he can manage that makes sense to him. He thinks of how, when sitting exams, he prayed to his grandpa, who had died when my father was a teenager. Infrequently, he'd dream of his grandpa, giving a cosy feeling he'd wake with and carry all day.

My father's thoughts turn to me, recharging my energy, and he sends me a simple message in his mind, *Look after her, please. Look after us both.*

This is the best he can do, and it is enough. My love for him pours from me. I see it reach him as his aura glows vibrant peach.

'I think I know what you mean by talking to Poppy.' His voice hitches on my name. 'It brings you comfort.' He reaches for my mother's hand, and she lets him fold his fingers around hers. 'I'm sorry it comforts you more than I can.'

'Oh, Ben.' She rolls against him. 'It's not like that. You do comfort me. But there's a lot going on.'

'I know, I know.' He gives her a squeeze. 'Do you really think—' He swallows a lump of fear. '…There's no point to life?'

'God, no!' My mother hesitates. 'I just think that if you make life about logic, you strip away the wonder, the beauty, the magic that makes it worthwhile.'

'Hold you onto that magic.' He kisses her forehead.

'I love you, Ben Breen,' she says softly.

'You're right, Aisling Breen. That is not logical.'

Their auras soften and entwine in warm oranges and pinks.

My mother pulls me in as she thinks, 'I'm sorry, Poppy.'

All is well. My father knows me in his own way. Be gentle with him. He cannot handle the visions. We are on our own with that.

Whatever *that* may be. I'm curious. Maybe my purpose is to explore it, but fear snakes around my curiosity like grey smoke around yellow flames.

My father moves on, still convinced the mushrooms are to blame for their hallucination. My mother lets it be, deciding I'm right – this is something she and I must figure out alone.

'Are you still up for moving back to Ireland?' he says, tugging her to her feet. They set off down the hill beneath the gnarled apple trees. The blossoms have dropped from swellings that will ripen into apples. The trees are as old as the house but still full of life. The barley in the field beyond is already ripening, holding the gold from the June sunshine in its nodding green heads.

'Yes,' she answers. 'Absolutely.'

'Are you sure you won't miss San Jose?'

She thinks of Ruby and how the friendship is superficial, nothing like what she had with Kate. Between setting up a new home and garden, and not working because she was preparing to be a stay-at-home mother, then running to hospital appointments, she hadn't had the chance to make new friendships. Her peers were too heavily involved with raising their own brood. But there was no point raking over this with my father, she reckoned, so instead, she said, 'California's too hot and too dry. Climate change has made Ireland more bearable, don't you think?'

They walk out from under the shade of the trees into the heat of the day, the sun blasting from a clear blue sky.

'Yeah, but at what cost to the rest of the planet?' he asks.

'You're making me feel guilty. But you're right. Everywhere else is either burning or flooding. And how long can Ireland avoid the worst of it? Where will it end?'

'God only knows. But I suppose Ireland is as good a place as any to ride it out.'

'So you want to come home?' She likes the idea more and more.

'Yes.' He nods firmly.

'Are you ready for your interview?'

'I think so.' He pauses. 'If I don't get the job—'

'We'll cross that bridge,' she says, smiling as they stop in the middle of the stone bridge and she pulls him in for a kiss.

CHAPTER 22

The sodden soil is disturbingly slimy and smells sour, like the mead the Elders make for festivals. I rub my thumb against my palm to thin out the clod of earth and turn up the grain seeds within. They are nothing but outer husks with white mush inside. Nothing has germinated. The field is awash with muck, the seeds rotting.

'Shall we call Kallisto?' Jaisun asks.

I look to Chloe, Kallisto's sister and the second in charge of farming, but she shakes her head. 'Kallisto cannot leave Bion.'

Dropping the mud, I wipe my hands on a rag, staring at the field. Too weak to hunt, I thought I'd help Jaisun and Chloe with the crops. The days pass slowly, with too much time to think. Everyone has suffered so much loss – friends, family, lovers, children – that words are useless for carrying our anguish to and from each other. The catharsis of mourning our dead one at a time is a luxury we cannot afford as multiple funeral pyres burn daily. There is nowhere to lay our grief.

'When do you usually plant?' I ask.

'A moon, maybe two before now. This is late.' Jaisun shakes his head and sighs heavily. There are not enough livestock to keep him as a cattle boy. He wanted to switch his apprenticeship from farming with Kallisto to hunting with me, but Agis and Con have no time to train him, and Yani thinks a novice will hinder them. They must find food – training will come later. Jaisun is trying to be useful in the fields and, I suspect, spend more time with Chloe.

'But usually, we go by when the Earth warms up,' Chloe adds. 'Except it hasn't warmed enough yet.'

I know what she means. At the end of each day, it grows dark, and at the end of each night, it brightens; but we have not seen the sun or the blue sky since the flood. The noises in my ears are as unrelenting as the grey skies. Although the thicker snows of winter have thawed, we had another dusting of snow last night. It melted with daybreak, but the chill clings to the air.

I think back to the conversation I had with Arne, the travelling storyteller, a couple of days ago. He was going to find the sun, following it to its horizon. Perhaps he's found it. Maybe the sun is already warming his face, kissing his skin, turning it golden. Longing swells within me.

'We planted half the grain seed. It's gone,' Jaisun says. 'We'll have no crop from this. We need to call a meeting.'

Poor Jaisun. Hunger nags at him more than the rest of us. He's growing from boy to man, every day taller but thinner. His eyes grow huge in a bony face. A leader is developing from this youth, with his level head and patience. He steadies me when it should be the other way around.

'Yes, we need a meeting. But listen to me first,' I say. 'We need to find the sun.'

'How is that possible?' Jaisun asks.

I tell them what Arne told me of his plans and the journey he is on. Chloe frowns. Jaisun nods. At least one of them might be on my side.

'I, too, have heard of villages leaving,' Jaisun tells us.

'The Crossing?' I ask.

'Yes,' he says. 'And others. We met travellers out on the back pastures. They told us the same.'

'We need to convince the village that we must go to the sun, too,' I say.

'The whole village?' Chloe asks.

'Everyone.'

*

'Everyone? Even the children, the sick, the elderly?' Doah asks.

There's a fragile silence stretched across the villagers as I search for the best way to answer.

'We cannot leave them,' I say. 'There is no food here. I cannot bear to think of how hard the journey will be for the ill, but if we leave them behind, they will not survive.'

'Either way, they will not survive,' Doah says gently. The compassion in her face clogs my throat. 'It might be kinder to let them stay, have comfort before their last journey to the sun's horizon.'

I swallow hard.

Doah is right. The dying need their dignity. Not to mention the fact that they would slow everybody else down and make it impossible to travel the distances needed.

The faces of those gathered are already hollow-eyed and gaunt. Yet these are our strongest people – fifty standing here at most – from a village that numbered at least two hundred a year ago. It is the first time I have taken stock like this. The reality leaves me devastated, speechless.

Doah puts her hand on my shoulder. 'We are both right. Leaving will not be easy. Nor will staying. Ultimately, we will shortly be on a journey – the first for some, the last for others. Go, Zosime, with our blessing, and take anyone who wants to go.'

'What would we eat?' a voice asks from the back of the crowd.

'We're hardly eating now,' I say, finding my words in some dim glimmer of hope. 'We bring as much as we can carry. Trade what we can along the way. Hunt, too, where we can.'

But there's a chorus of questions.

'You're right. We hardly have enough to eat now. How can we walk and carry everything with no food?'

'Where are we going?'

'You don't know where you are going or what you'll find. How will we cross the ocean?'

'There will be boats at the coast,' Nereus says, his voice straining as he projects over the growing noise.

'We can't afford passage,' Lan tells us. 'I travelled to the Warmer Lands as a lad. It can be a hard crossing. You need big, strong boats and navigators who can read the waves.'

'We can work for passage,' Jaisun shouts.

This is met with bitter laughter.

'Work, son? I can barely stand.'

'They'll make us into slaves.'

'My grandparents were freed slaves. I'm not about to go back.'

'If we stay here, we will die,' I roar with as much force as I muster. A lull falls.

'Spring will come,' says a girl at the back. There is a wane murmur of agreement.

'The time for spring has passed. We should have warm breezes and leaves on the trees. But we have snowfalls and twigs. Nothing is growing. Nothing!' My voice breaks. My hopes rise as Geros steps forward. He is Geros the Wise. He will know this is the only way.

Geros holds up a hand and waits for complete silence. I wish I had done that, but I don't garner the same respect. I'd probably have been ignored, left standing there like a fool with my hand in the air while everyone talked around me.

Geros gets everyone's attention. 'Like Lan, I've been to the Warmer Lands. Yes, it is over the ocean and a hard journey. But when I was there, it was barren. They'd had no rain for two winters, and nothing was growing. Many of them came here. It is what people do when their land dies. They move. But it is not easy. There is hardship, sacrifice, slavery, war.'

People chatter at the mention of war. Geros holds his hand up again and gets the quiet he needs. 'Partholon came from the Warmer Lands to this place. His people came in boats and fought back the demons who lived here. The story is told through the ages and is recorded on the decorative axe.'

The mention of my axe sets the hairs on my arms bristling. I think of the symbols carved into its handle. Pictures of a story handed down so we would never forget where we came from.

Geros continues. 'Partholon and his people freed this land for crops and livestock so we could live here. But now it has become impossible. Perhaps our time here is over. Perhaps it is time to leave.'

Lan stands beside Geros. 'My friend, my clansman, my brother. You may be right, but I will not go. I cannot bear to undertake such a journey. For though I am younger than you, my bones hurt too much, and my final journey is near. I am staying. The people have heard us both. Let them decide. Those who wish to go are free to leave. But I will be here for those who want to stay.'

'My friend, my clansman, my brother,' Geros replies in the formal address. 'Staying is death.'

'As is leaving.' Lan places his hand on Geros's shoulder.

They stare into one another's faces with grave expressions. The only sound is the crack of the fire and a stifled cough. I hardly dare breathe. A fracture is coming that will never mend, and we all know it.

'We each choose our own end.' Geros's voice is thick with sorrow. 'Each villager will decide if they will come with me to travel to the sun or stay here with you. Let those who intend to leave gather at the lower end of the hall so we can make plans.'

'So be it, brother. We will part with no hard feelings.' Lan embraces Geros as a fissure rips through the villagers. A sob from the crowd triggers a rumble of voices that rises to a roar as couples argue, friends debate, youngsters plead with parents.

Nereus takes my hand, and we follow Geros to the gathering point. I'm afraid to look behind me, afraid that I will not see my loved ones behind us, but also terrified that we have condemned them to a terrible fate by leaving.

I hear Agis talking behind me. Yani answers. I release the breath I've been holding. Turning, I see that Con is also with them. There are about thirty people in the group who gather with Geros. Most are young, with Nereus, Yani, and I amongst the eldest, having seen no more than thirty summers or so. Geros and Mela are the only Elders to join those of us who want to go to the Warmer Lands.

'Where is Doah?' Agis asks.

'She's staying,' Yani says in a flat voice, nodding towards the old woman standing at the edge of the group gathering at the other end of the meeting hall.

I'm gutted. Apart from missing her, Doah will be a loss to us; but if Geros is leaving, they will need a healer to stay. I know Doah suffers from aches in her joints. The constant movement of travel would be torture – but so would starvation.

Guilt creeps through my bones. All of my hunting party is coming with us, including Jaisun. But there is little left here to actually hunt with the animals dying off. Only one hunter is staying. He is old and limps, and he relies entirely on traps and snares now. His arms are not strong enough to pull back a bow. Our departure will hasten their spiral into starvation. Perhaps I should try again, try to reason with them and show them they *need* to get out of this place, find somewhere better, find the sun.

I turn back to go to the other group, but a hand on my arm stops me.

'No, Zosime.' Geros steps up beside me. 'You must leave them. It is the lesser cruelty.' His eyes glisten as he turns and looks at the group staying.

'Kallisto is staying, too?' Nereus whispers to me. 'That can't be right.'

I'm surprised at Kallisto. She, more than most, knows how bad the growth is this year. Standing in the midst of the other group with Bion wrapped up in a sling and tied to her, she rocks from foot to foot, rubbing the child's back. Her lips move as she murmurs comfort to him. He's too big for a sling, but he has not eaten in many days, and it is unclear if he is taking in water. His eyes never focus. His body is limp. If it weren't for the sling, his head would roll back like a newborn's.

Nereus takes a step towards her.

'Where are you going?' Cold fingers of fear grip my belly. What if he won't come with me? What if he chooses her?

'She has to come with us,' he says, 'for Bion's sake.'

Geros has a hand on each of our shoulders. Gently steering us to one side, he says in a whisper we can barely make out, 'Bion won't be coming.'

I look over at the child clasped against Kallisto's breast. The boy's face holds no expression. I stare a moment at his greying skin and blue-black lips. Then the truth hits me and I gasp. My scalp prickles. The fear in my belly turns to nausea.

Nereus buries his fingers in his hair and cradles his face, groaning.

'When?' I whisper.

'This morning,' Geros says, his voice hoarse.

Nereus shifts his weight to take another step towards Kallisto, but Geros grabs Nereus's wrist. 'Shhh. You must give her space to say her farewell.'

'She knows?' I ask, looking at Kallisto rocking the child's body, jostling as if to calm it.

'Her ears know, but her spirit is refusing to listen,' Geros says.

My throat tightens as I press the crying feeling down. Shards of pain shred my chest. I squeeze my eyes shut in a slow blink, take a deep breath, then reach for Nereus. His eyes are drenched with devastation. His lips press tight, his eyebrows pulled together. He has no words. His breath comes in sharp tugs as he drops forward, hands onto knees.

'Geros, please, tell people there is no time to waste. We just need … We'll be with you when …' I don't know what we need or what 'when' is … When we have gotten past our shock? When we have mourned this child's passing? When we can think straight?

I know one thing for certain. We have to go. There is nothing for us here. If we stay, our stories will drown in the cold rain, sucked into barren mud under a grey and desolate sky.

CHAPTER 23

The noise of splattering water jolts my mother from her sleep. She lies on her back, motionless, scarcely breathing, trying to work out what she's hearing. Beside her, my father's snores are a deep buzz. Quickly and with relief, she realises the sound of gushing water is not coming from inside the house. It is a violent torrent backed by an orchestra of erratic tinkles, drips and splashes.

She sits up, ears straining. A deluge of water falling from a height smacks the concrete below the bedroom window. She can make out the familiar purr of rain on the roof and the higher timbre of it on the foliage outside, but this gushing water is disconcerting.

'What is that noise?' my father mumbles, surfacing from sleep.

'I don't know. Might be a broken pipe outside.' She slides her legs from under the quilt and over the edge of the bed, sitting up as her feet search for their slippers.

'Jack probably needs to clear the gutters,' my father says, settling down again. 'Come back to bed. You can't fix it now.'

But my mother needs to know what's making the noise. She looks out the window. It's too dark to see anything. From this angle, she can't see the guttering. She's amazed the downpour hasn't triggered the motion sensor spotlight mounted above the back door. Perhaps if she sticks her arm out the window and waves, she'll get some light on the situation. She opens the window. Rain spits in on her, and she pulls it closed quickly. Outside, the rain falls straight down in sheets. It's a weird rustle of billions of drops landing on leaves and grass, but with that strange splattering to the forefront.

My father is fast asleep again, and my mother is glad. He's exhausted from jet lag and has his interview in the morning. She knows she won't sleep until she's figured out what's causing the gushing. She worries it will damage the house, lead to lying water, or a flood or structural damage. Even if Jack now owns the property, it's still her old home.

She knows the house so well that she can make her way downstairs without turning on a light. When she gets to the front hall, she sees a light in the kitchen. Jack is already downstairs, so she walks through the kitchen to find him lifting a foot-long Maglite torch from the utility room cupboard. He's wearing a waterproof coat over his pyjamas and wellies.

'You heard the water then, Jack?'

'Yeah, I think it's the joint in the downpipe where I added in a rainwater collection pipe.' He pulls up his hood and heads for the back door.

My mother follows him as far as the doorway. She sticks her head out but keeps as much of her body as she can inside, balancing on her tiptoes to watch her brother in the backyard. The floodlight flares, making them both squint, but the light is directed down and doesn't reach high enough up the wall to show the problem.

Hunch-shouldered, Uncle Jack shines the torch up to the roof. The shaft of light from the Maglite picks up the rain, slicing through the dark sky in silver streaks until Jack readjusts the beam to hit the guttering at the edge of the roof. He follows along the white PVC until he locates the downspout. About a quarter of the way from the top, water jets out with such force it squirts horizontally for a metre before dropping to the concrete below.

Jack comes back to the utility room. 'There must be some volume of water falling on the roof. It's being channelled down into this spout and it's cracked the pipe branching off to feed my rain barrel,' he says, sloughing off his raincoat. 'The rain barrel is full already.'

'Wow.' My mother remembers the thousand-litre rain barrel was almost empty the previous morning. Even the recent thunderstorms hadn't filled it. Jack had been using it around the garden and in his greenhouses almost constantly because of the hosepipe bans. 'Will this damage the house?'

'Nah, I don't think so. It's just happened,' Jack says. 'I'll fix it tomorrow. Go on back to bed. Don't be worrying. But...' he ruffles my mother's hair. 'I'm glad you were here for backup.'

'Always.' My mother smiles. She knows he'd be thrilled if she were to move home. She hasn't told him about my father's job interview. She doesn't want Jack to get his hopes up, too.

She goes back to bed, but the slapping water keeps her awake and staring into a monochrome room. Uncle Jack's assurances don't quell her rising panic. She knows, in theory, they'll be fine. They're in an elevated position, far enough from the Callan River to be unaffected if it bursts its banks, which happens from time to time. Her mind flits to the news images she's seen of people in flooded Pakistan, crammed onto high ground not much wider than a single-lane road, their few remaining possessions with them in small, bedraggled piles.

She thinks of the footage of families on rooftops in Missouri awaiting rescue; the inundated villages in Mozambique; the landslides caused by rain-soaked land in Portugal; communities in Australia evacuated because of rising waters. She pulls her thoughts closer to home, to the streets of Strabane, people in despair at homes underwater yet again, while their kids kayak on their flooded football pitches.

What a terror it must be for them to lie listening to the rain falling, knowing the flood waters are rising. She imagines families in locations unused to such high volumes of rain, cowering in flat-roofed buildings not constructed to withstand such downpours, with buckets placed to catch drips, or water levels rising and seeping in under doors, murky liquid reaching window level, and people on the upper storeys praying for the rain to stop. Or – worse still – sheltering beneath tarpaulins, having seen their homes swept away by mudslides or submerged by floodwaters flowing with such ferocity that they swallow bodies, trees, livestock, vehicles and structures without mercy.

Oh, Poppy, she thinks, pale grey shades of despair shimmering in her aura. *What are we doing to the planet? Poor Jack is trying to be green with his rain barrels, but now it's backfired on him. It's such extra hassle and probably useless. What is it all for?*

I try my best to answer her. Life is a struggle but so many keep going. That must mean the struggle is worth it. It must mean there is a purpose to it.

I feel as if I once knew the answer to her question, that when I was in the Enlightenment, I understood what life meant. Yet here, trapped between worlds, I hold on to something that lasts even in the most dire and dreadful places.

Hope, I tell my mother, *hope is what keeps us moving forward and reaching for purpose. Hope makes us fight for life.*

My mother's aura softens from grey to dusky pink. Outside, the rain stops, and, as if a tap has been turned off, the splattering of water ceases. The silence is luxurious. In that first instance of relief, my mother feels dry, warm and safe.

Oh, Poppy, I wish I could spread this feeling to people who need it, my mother tells me. Although guilt dampens the edges of her comfort, she is cosy enough for sleep to seep in. She drifts off, leaving me alone to ponder her words.

My abilities are limited in this plane, but I channel the energy of her sentiment into the Universe. It may be a minuscule joule of energy, but somewhere, someone who needs it will pick it up. Somewhere, someone in despair will feel a brightening. Somewhere, the purpose of life will be glimpsed with enough hope for someone to keep going, because hope is a form of energy, and energy can never be destroyed.

*

My father's interview is in the Armagh Observatory, a beautiful Georgian building complete with a circular tower capped by a green-weathered copper roof. I convince my mother to take a walk in the grounds nearby so I can be close to my father should he need me. However, I'm not sure anymore how I can help, sliding as I am further from the Enlightenment as time passes.

They part in the car park with a gentle squeeze of hands.

'No kissing,' my father had pre-warned, 'It's unprofessional!'

I'm cleaved from him and left clinging to my mother, frightened by the sense of abandonment. What happens if I keep fading from them and am someday untethered from her, too? Anxiety builds with pops and shards and fizzles of silver, making the world a cold, lonely place. What if I can no longer feel love? Is this what mortality feels like? Always this nipping fear that all you hold dear can be taken away? If so, I envy the bliss of souls passing straight from the prelife to the afterlife, missing the mortal life as I did, as I was supposed to. And yet, I'm glad not to have missed experiencing my mother's interaction, her knowing me and I her, the extremes of emotion, the kaleidoscope of colour. But I miss the Enlightenment.

Foliage provides cool shade over the path from the car park to the observatory. My mother watches my father disappear out of sight at the top of the path before she turns right towards the Astropark, curious to see the scale model of the solar system.

Two little dogs with squashed faces wander along beside an elderly man, who looks up and smiles at my mother.

'Lovely day,' he says.

'It is, isn't it?'

Both their auras expand and pulse yellow as they pass one another, smiling. A wood pigeon coos, and my mother inhales a deep sigh, enjoying the scent of the freshly mown grass.

The main path borders a long, gravelled rectangle, but a smaller path spirals off down to a white metal archway. The archway is set into a circular paved area with concentric circles detailed in the brickwork.

'This must be the sun,' my mother says aloud, standing under the arch. She has the place to herself and enjoys taking her time to explore the solar system. A metal rail on the ground that reminds my mother of a train track passes through the centre of the paved area. It leads to the far end of the gravel, about a hundred metres away and disappears into the undergrowth. Metal spheres of different sizes are placed at intervals along this track. My mother rakes her memory for the order of the planets, identifying Earth – a tennis ball-sized sphere – third one along. She follows the metal rail out into the gravel area to the biggest sphere, the size of an exercise ball, big enough to sit on. She reads the label out loud: 'Jupiter'. She walks on to the next one, which is slightly smaller. 'I find it hard to tell Saturn from Jupiter without the rings.' She looks back at the arches. 'Gosh, it's so far away.'

At the end of the gravel, she goes back up onto the path. To her left, the trees give way to a wide, open space rising up into a hill. On her right, she passes shrubbery, then a little patch of grass with another shiny metal sphere. She wishes my father was with her so she could point it out and say to him, 'Look, there's Uranus!'

Beyond that, my mother sees a cube-shaped framework, with two successively smaller cubes suspended inside one another. She stops at the sign that says 'Hypercube', and reads a granite inset at the edge of the platform beneath the cubes with an explanation about the great distances in the Universe:

'YOU ARE NOW ENTERING A REGION WITH A LOGARITHMIC SCALE.

For each 10 metres you advance from this point your distance from the solar system will be multiplied by 10.'

She shakes her head, but her aura tingles with neon blue and silver sparks, dimming when she reads the bit about logarithmic scale. 'I never could understand that in maths class. It says here the nested cubes explain it. So, let me see. The smallest cube has sides eight centimetres long. The one surrounding it has sides eighty centimetres long. Hmmm … okay.' She stares at the cubes for a second, then goes back to the sign. 'So, the second one has sides ten times longer than the first. Okay, I got that. Ah, and the third one's sides are eight metres long – so that's eight hundred centimetres long. So it has sides that are ten times longer than the second one, and the next one up would be eighty metres long – halfway up the hill – wow!'

She stands for a second, gazing at the succession of cubes, and suddenly, the logarithmic scale makes sense to her. 'You'd need a park bigger than Ireland to show the next nearest star using the same scale.'

Plumes of lilac emanate from her as she says, 'I never understood that before and now I feel like a secret of the Universe has been unlocked. It's wonderful.' She does a full pirouette, looking up at the cubes. 'I can't imagine how you must feel knowing everything. The Enlightenment must be so, so wonderful!' She sighs as she gazes up at the 'Hill of Infinity,' a mown area with inserted granite pavers, the grass, vibrant green against the blue sky after the rain.

It is wonderful, I send her, but I can't hold back the dusky blue.

You're sad, she sends back.

You can tell?

Oh, Poppy. You don't know? A wave of violet splashes through the lilac. *Are you alright? Are you leaving me?*

I... don't... know.

No, I need you. My mother walks up the hill, unsure if the pain she feels is a stitch in her side or the idea of losing me. 'But Poppy … is staying here safe for you?' she says out loud again.

Her perception of my thoughts and feelings has become stronger, clearer, and I can no longer hide my fears as her aura intuits mine.

She has her head down, trudging up the hill, reading the granite pavers, passing the marker for Proxima Centauri, Polaris, through the Orion Nebula, and then stops at the centre of the galaxy to catch her breath.

'The axe head,' she says aloud. 'The axe head is where it started, so it must have our answers.' She peers up at the blue sky, squeezed between bulging thermals. As if forging some kind of pact with the Universe, she closes her eyes, reaching through the layers of time and space, trying to connect without the axe head.

She feels the woman Zosime, senses her beside her. My mother opens her eyes, looks downhill and sees huts in a cluster with the fires smouldering in small piles on the outskirts. She panics and the vision fades. Her sense of the other woman lingers long enough for her to speak her name. Then, the feeling slips underneath her own reality, like a rock beneath an incoming tide.

'Dammit.' My mother is more frustrated than scared this time. 'I need the axe head. We'll do this, Poppy,' my mother promises. 'We both need answers, don't we?'

She sets off uphill again, at a pace that takes her breath away, concentrating on the ground a few feet ahead, keeping the view as a surprise for when she gets to the top. Once there, she reads the final sign: 'The edge of the Universe'.

She looks up again. Not far from her are two women with prams at the Stone Circle, an arrangement of black granite monoliths on the top of the Hill of Infinity.

My mother stops, not wanting to be near babies, but one of the women sees her and says, 'Miss Donnelly! Hello.'

The use of her maiden name lets my mother know it's most likely a past pupil. She'd only been teaching as Mrs Breen for less than a year before she'd given up the post to move to California. She squints, trying to match the young woman's face to an array of past pupils, taking in the blonde bob, blue eyes, freckles sprinkled across the bridge of the nose where foundation has worn thin. A similar height to my mother, the younger woman is heavier, with a voluptuous post-baby body.

'Ah, you probably don't recognise me – Fran Hughes – you taught me history many moons ago.'

Her late-twentyish features rearrange themselves in my mother's head as those of a slim, straw-haired teen in a green school uniform.

'Ach, Frances, of course. My goodness, look at you, all grown up!' My mother flushes pink with fondness for the girl, remembering her as a sweet, beautiful child. She nods at the pram. 'And who's this?'

This time, Frances is the one who flushes pink. 'She's called Aisling.'

'Really? That's my name.'

'I know. Stevie insisted.'

'Stevie?' My mother's aura churns from peach to mauve as she remembers a chubby boy with cut knees and a muddy face, crying behind the canteen with a bottle of his mother's painkillers in his hand. Her sorrow cuts as hard today as it did fifteen years ago. 'Stevie O'Hara?'

'Yep, he's my husband and Aisling's dad.' Frances holds my mother's gaze, intense but steady. 'Stevie's grateful to you for helping him when he was bullied.'

'I only did what anyone would do. It wasn't much.'

'Actually, most adults looked past him, found his situation too painful. You noticed. You got the school to switch up the classes, split up the bullies and take them out of Stevie's class. It gave him the space he needed.'

'And he ended up marrying the prettiest girl in the class,' my mother says. 'And smart too, I remember. What did you do before Aisling arrived?'

'I'm a social worker, but on maternity leave now.'

'And what's Stevie doing now?'

'He's an astrophysicist here in the observatory. Dr O'Hara, if you don't mind.' Pride rolls off Frances in sparkling magenta. 'Here, this is how he looks now.' Frances holds out her phone and shows my mother a picture of them standing together.

My mother takes in the handsome young man, almost unrecognisable, taller, leaner, but she finds the little boy in his smile, lingering in his eyes. It crunches my mother's heart. 'Oh, that's so wonderful. Tell him I said well done.'

'He'll be thrilled I met you. You really changed his story, miss. If you hadn't stepped in…' They nod, suddenly mute, the alternative story unspeakable. In the awkward silence that descends, my mother smiles towards the other woman, standing politely a little distance away, a willowy woman who looks older by about five or six years, with doe eyes and dark hair tucked beneath a burgundy hijab.

'Gosh, where's my manners!' Frances jumps back and pulls her friend forward. 'This is Nour.'

My mother shakes her hand. 'It's lovely to meet you, Nour.'

Nour smiles, her reply jamming in her throat. My mother has spoken too quickly and Nour hasn't caught her phrasing, expecting a simpler greeting. It takes her a few seconds to line the words up straight in her head. 'Hello, I am pleased to meet you, too.'

'Are you from Armagh?' my mother says more slowly. It's a normal question amongst locals. Sorting out breed, seed and generation is a full-time hobby for some, but my mother hopes it is an inoffensive way to give Nour space to say as much or as little as she wants about where she is from.

'I'm from Syria,' Nour says.

Grey-blue washes over my mother. 'I'm so sorry about what has happened there. Do you have family there still?'

Nour shakes her head, brown eyes heavy with sadness.

'Her mum and sister are living in Turkey,' Frances says, patting her friend's shoulder. 'But Nour just got her citizenship, so she'll be able to travel to see them soon, won't you?' Frances doesn't tell my mother that Nour's brother and father were killed in a Russian air strike. But the thought of not being able to go home for a visit is enough to trigger a welling of emotion that floods my mother's eyes.

'I'm sorry,' my mother tries to explain, embarrassed by the overreaction. 'It's just I appreciate being able to come home for a visit. I live in America now, and I find homesickness hard, but I can come home whenever I want. I can't imagine how you must feel.'

Nour meets her gaze, touched by my mother's compassion for her. Tears globe along her lower eyelids. 'Thank you.' She wants to say more but doesn't have the words in English to hand.

My mother nods to the bundle in the pram and, forcing brightness into her voice, says, 'And who's this little one?'

'This is Polla.' Nour pushes back the pram's shade so my mother can see the baby, fast asleep, oblivious to the world.

'She's beautiful,' my mother says on a breath. 'How old are they?'

'Three months, both of them,' Frances says. 'Nour and I met in the maternity ward. These pair are twins.'

'Yes, twins!' Humour sparkles in Nour's eyes as they gaze at the two babies, one dark with a mop of black hair, the other pink and bald. Baby Aisling opens one eye and creaks her mouth open at one side in a mewl. She sees me and reaches out a hand, but her enlightenment is fast fading as she grows into her physical world. She can only convey her thoughts as pulses of colour in her aura, a complex shifting pattern of light and hope, bursting with the potential of her life.

'Oops, it's getting near to dinner time for this one,' Frances says, letting off the brake on the pram. 'It was wonderful to see you again, Miss.'

'Please, call me Aisling.'

'Ah, sure, that would be confusing, now,' Frances says with a wink and a nod towards her daughter.

'Lovely to see you, Frances. Take care, Nour.'

My mother watches the two friends push their prams off down the path. She sits on one of the rocks to settle the swirl of emotions that meeting the women has fired up. Putting the cramp of baby envy back on its shelf, she polishes up the joy that she's made a difference in Stevie's life.

'You really changed his story …'

The sun warms her. The breeze cools her. The green hills soothe her. The blue sky makes her wistful. In the distance, the majestic cathedral with its twin spires dominating the landscape faces across to the square tower of the older, equally beautiful cathedral. Armagh City lies slung between the cathedral-topped hills. My mother tries to identify the seven hills that Armagh is said to be built on. She picks out the old windmill on the horizon and, orienting herself, scans across to the far hills, one of which is home.

'Home,' she thinks in a calming pink blush, seeing the two women and their babies reach the bottom of the Hill of Infinity and pass a man walking in the opposite direction, coming uphill. My mother smiles as my father sees her and raises a hand to wave at her. She gathers up her scattered emotions and runs from the edge of the Universe down the path towards him, wondering if he knows yet if they'll be moving home.

CHAPTER 24

I will never see these hills again. Knowing this brings a dull ache that throbs deep below my hunger, bloating my grief. How much there is to bear! Huddled in furs, I lean against the flat-topped rock near the summit of the hill and look down on our valley, where the funeral pyres are now more plentiful than huts. The river still surges beyond its banks, the field's muck and mire empty of plants and animals. There was a time when this valley was verdant, the river a gentle caress through the folds of the hills, when the breeze carried music, children's laughter, cattle lowing.

Geros packs the tribe's treasures to buy passage. There is bronze and gold. Gold, while softer and heavier than the bronze in my axe, is more valuable. We can make it into neck ornaments and bracelets. The Elders have said we must take those for trade.

Geros has given me my axe and asked if it is worth bringing. I sit here, looking down on my home, and turn the axe over in my hands. When polished with sand, it gleams like the sun, but no one has taken the time to do that in a while, and like the sun, it has dulled. My fingers trace the carvings on the wooden handle, telling the stories of our forefathers coming to this place. How will we tell the story of our leaving? Will there be anyone left to carry those tales? Whose ears will hear them?

The axe has little value outside our clan. Geros has left the decision about the axe up to me. This axe – once so precious to me – is heavy and of little use. Wrapping it up in its leather sheath, I know what I must do. I must leave its stories here because they are of this place. If any of the villagers who stay survive, they can carry on these stories. Once I leave, my stories will no longer be of this place. My story may never be told.

Sighing deeply, I let my head fall back and gaze up at the ashen sky. A yearning to see blue soaks right to my core. I try to bore through the grey clouds to find the sun. Then I feel her presence. Aisling. I don't know how I know her name. I sense her more than see her. I lower my gaze from the sky to her gently as if approaching a deer. She has a bright light by her head, like a star. She looks past me at the village. Fear flashes in her eyes. She fades but not before I hear her say my name. I reach for her, but she is gone. There is no one there. Perhaps hunger is giving me visions. But the feeling stays with me; she came to either guide me or warn me. I don't know which, and this is a problem.

I make my way with a heavy heart to the village to find Kallisto at the Ceremonial Hall with Bion still in his sling. She has covered his face, a sign she has begun her final farewell to her baby son.

'Kallisto,' I say gently.

She turns, her face haggard, her eyes haunted.

I flick my gaze to the bundle at her breast. 'I tried—'

'I know.' She strokes the top of the bundle.

'I'm sorry.'

'I know.'

I search her face and find no anger or accusation, only defeat.

'Will you come with us?'

Kallisto shakes her head. 'I must lay my son to rest with his father. My place is here. I cannot leave him. I will help Doah ease the pain of those who stay.'

I open my mouth, then close it. What point is there in telling her she will die if she stays? I suspect she would welcome death right now. My grief for Aleka is an unbearable ache, and she was my sister-in-law, not my child. How much more agony must Kallisto feel? I take her hand in mine and lay the wrapped-up axe in her hands.

Kallisto's eyes widen. She unwraps the axe and stares at it. Tears drip down her face.

'It belongs here,' I say. 'With Bion.' I don't mention that I'm leaving something of myself here with him. This axe drew my blood.

Blood is persistent.

Blood stains.

Kallisto takes a fat leather pouch from her belt and presses it into my hand. 'Take these. If you get to the sun, plant them. They will grow.'

The pouch contains grain seed, enough to make the pouch as heavy as the bronze axe head. Enough to feed a family for a season if it were to grow.

'But you can grow this next spring.' I push it back towards her. 'As a wise woman once told me, you can't eat an axe.'

Kallisto shakes her head. 'We won't survive until next spring. My story ends here, with my boy. I was fortunate to have my story extended so.' She grips my forearm. 'Your story is still being told. Don't give up. And this…' Kallisto takes the axe, '…has always been yours. You are the true owner. It will always carry your story, and someday, someone will tell it. Your story will not need children to carry it.'

My heart snags on this, like skin in a bramble thicket. I pull away and feel it tear a little.

Kallisto holds my gaze. 'But I will lay this axe with Bion. He will take our collective story to the stars.'

'Thank you. I wish we—'

'We were night to each other's day, Zosime. You were the best opponent I could wish for. We kept each other strong, but now I would make us weak. My courage for living is gone. Besides, you have plenty to overcome without me.' Kallisto smiles. 'I trained you up well. Look after Nereus. You are his day and his night.'

I embrace the woman who was once my adversary but who, I realise, I have a profound respect for. I often wished for her strength, her beauty, her child, and now I wish she finds peace. We were never that different. The same things make us happy. And the same things break our hearts, too.

*

I don't tell anyone I have the grain seed, not even Nereus. It is for planting, not eating, and temptation is a terrible curse. I wrap the leather pouch in two more layers of oiled leather to keep out water. This is our start in a new place.

Nereus and I walk at the back of the procession of thirty or so bedraggled people who decide to come with us. My brother Yani, his wife Eleni, and their two girls walk ahead of us. Alarmed, I look for their son, Claus, but see him sleeping in his uncle Agis's arms up ahead. Our cousin, Con, and his wife Duna and their children have come. Jaisun is with them, his parents having passed away. Chloe walks with Jaisun; she has her head covered. I can hear her weeping for Bion and her sister, Kallisto. She stumbles, and Jaisun puts his arm around her for support.

Geros sets a pace that is steady but slow, so slow it will take what can usually be walked in a day as long as two days, minimum.

'I am proud of you for leaving the axe with Kallisto,' Nereus says.

I nod. Nereus takes my hand and pulls me closer, burying my hand in the warmth under the furs at his chest. I can't speak about those we lost, but Nereus possesses courage I have never witnessed in him before. He absorbs every blow and yet stands tall.

'When we get to the coast, we will look up my kin. They will guide us to the best boatsmen,' Nereus says.

I believe him. He grew up with the ways of the seafarers. Geros has faith in him, too.

We pass no other travellers coming inland, but we see smaller groups ahead walking in the same direction. The trackway leads up over the hills that encircle our home. Night drops before we reach the highest point. The wind moans through the trees and attacks like shards of ice, cutting through our wraps and sapping what little strength we have.

We huddle in a dip of the hill, trying to escape the worst of the rising storm. My ears squeal and pop. There will be rain soon.

'We need to find shelter before it gets too dark to see,' I say to Geros.

'There is a small village not far off the track. They have sheltered me before now. In better days.' Geros frowns. 'But we have nothing to gift.'

I am glad I have not told him of our seeds.

'I've traded with them,' Nereus says. 'I can offer to weave and repair huts if they need that.'

'It will cost us time,' I say. 'And delay our departure tomorrow.'

'It is all downhill from this point. Our journey will be faster,' Geros glances skyward as white specks drift on the wind. 'We may have to wait anyway if this lies.'

Con and Yani say they know the village and will leave us to circle around to see if there is any hunting in the area, in the hopes we can bring something to the village pot.

By the time we reach the village, we are cold, wet and bedraggled. The last light of the day leaches from the sky. Some of the villagers accompany one of their Elders to greet us with a warm welcome. They look healthy and haven't lost as much weight as we have. Their relative proximity to the sea, compared to our village, might give them more opportunities for trade, and of course they could fish.

The people here have moved to their Ceremonial Hall to stay warm, as we'd done, but there is not enough room for us. There are, however, three abandoned huts at the edge of the village, with enough space to house all of us. Their Elder tells Geros that Nereus can report to the Ceremonial Hall at first light to fix the thatch. We split into three groups and prepare to settle down for the night. We have no fire, so we let the children chew slivers of dried meat our hosts have kindly given them. The adults soak herbs in the cold water as best they can.

'We will have fish tomorrow,' Nereus promises, 'and shellfish and sea greens.'

People wrinkle their noses at the latter two, but I know they will eat these foreign foods if Con and Yani cannot find game.

I wonder where they are. There won't be much hunting now that night has fallen. They may find it hard to navigate to the village in the dark.

'I'm going to signal Con and Yani,' I say to Nereus. 'You stay here. You will need your strength for tomorrow. I won't be long.'

It has stopped raining, and the wind has died down. I am grateful for that small mercy as I cup my hand around my mouth to make my hunting call, the whirring chirp of a nightbird that penetrates the darkness but which doesn't upset nature. As I make the call, voices from a few huts over catch my attention. Their words carry in the cool, still night.

'... And should any die, that will be more for our pot.'

They must still have livestock. Perhaps I can barter – perhaps they will take some of Geros's treasure. I check it out before raising our hopes. I don't mean to sneak up on them, but I move like a hunter with little noise. As I round a sapling fence, I see a fire. My eyes, accustomed to the dark, pick out every detail in the light from the flames.

There are three men by a dilapidated hut. One lies on the ground under a rough woven fabric; the other two stand over him. I hesitate; the man lying down must be ill. Shrinking back into the shadows, I'm about to turn away as one man lifts the covering, leaving the man on the ground naked. He'll freeze to death in this temperature. What are they thinking?

The younger of the two says, 'I-I don't think I can do this.'

'He's dead. You can't hurt him.'

'He was my friend.'

'You're useless!' The older man raises his arm, swearing under his breath. The firelight catches the stone axe head held high. He brings his arm down in one swift stroke. The axe embeds in the man's neck.

My gasp is masked by the muffled yelp from the younger man, which gives way to swallowed sobs. There's no arc of blood. I realise

215

the woven sheet is a funeral wrap, the same as those we use to bundle bodies before cremation. But why would anyone cut off a dead man's head?

The older man hacks a couple more times, crunching through neck bone. He uses his foot to roll the dismembered head onto the funeral wrap.

'Now,' he sets down the axe and picks up a skinning knife. 'Just like with the deer. Okay, son?' He holds out the knife.

The younger man dries his eyes and sniffs but takes the knife and drops to his feet beside the body, mumbling, 'I'm so sorry.'

He cuts a line down the dead man's belly, from the base of the chest and ribs to the hips, then opens the body cavity the same way you would gut a deer. He lifts the innards out carefully onto the funeral sheet. Glistening in the firelight, they could belong to a deer; they look so similar.

'That's it,' the older man says, adjusting the cloth around the pile. 'I'll add some old furs to contain the juices so we can set the remains alight. His family won't know any different.'

'But I will.'

'And you'll say nothing and eat your stew like everyone else.'

The younger man gags.

'Let me do the meat if you're going to be sick all over it.' The older man shoves the younger off towards the wood pile, dry-retching on an already empty stomach.

I slide back, deeper into the shadows, panting shallow breaths. My hair stands on end. They are eating their dead. I can hear the rip of sinew and skin peeling from flesh. My gorge rises. I swallow hard and move away as quietly as I arrived.

I stand outside our hut, trying to breathe normally, to control my shaking hands, and to think clearly. Nereus meets me as I enter. 'What's wrong?'

'Where's Geros?' I ask, pulling Nereus away from the throng of bodies.

'I'm here, child.' Geros appears from the shadows.

I tell them what happened and finish with, 'They are eating their dead, and they would eat ours, too.'

'But none of us has died,' Nereus says.

'Yet.' I stare at him.

Nereus's eyes widen. 'You think they would hunt us?'

I shrug.

'But killing?' Nereus shakes his head. 'We don't know for sure that the man died of natural causes or was killed.'

Geros and I exchange a look, and Geros answers, 'They have already crossed one line, eating their own people. Perhaps eating outsiders would be easier.'

I wish for a second that I had Nereus's faith in people, and as quickly, I thank the gods that one of us has a sense of the bitter reality we face. Shivers rattle my arms.

Nereus pulls me against him, rubbing his hand up and down my back, tucking his furs around my shoulders. 'You stood out in the cold too long.'

I sink into the heat of his body and close my eyes, but my mind turns to the sucking sound of skin pulling from flesh. I push back and look up at him.

'It's not safe here,' I hiss.

Heads turn towards our hushed conversation.

Geros scowls and lowers his voice a notch. 'We could let the people rest for a short while, but we must keep our guard up and leave well before the village rises.'

'But we said I would mend their thatch,' Nereus says. 'We had a deal.'

'It's not much of a deal,' I say. 'They didn't give us food, and these huts were already empty. They didn't even give us a fire.'

Curiosity has silenced the people sharing our hut. I bite my lip and tip my head in their direction. 'No one is resting. We're wasting time. The rain has stopped, and the wind has settled. It's as good a time to leave as any.'

'What about Yani and Con?' Nereus asks. 'They haven't come back yet.'

'I'll find them.' Agis steps forward from where he's been eavesdropping. It's what hunters do. 'I can circle round the area, hidden so the village won't find me.'

'That settles it.' Geros turns and clears his throat, but the adults in the hut are already wide awake, expecting him to speak. 'We cannot rest here any longer. Carry those children small enough and wake the others. We leave now.'

'Why? What is it?' one of the women asks, adjusting the sleeping child on her lap. He's malnourished – skin loose on fragile bones, like an old man – too small for his age and yet, that's probably fortunate for

217

him right now. His mother won't need to wake him. I envy his comfort, his ignorance of the horrors around him.

Geros takes a deep breath and sighs, shaking his head. 'You must trust me. I haven't time now, but I will explain when we get to the coast. Right now, all you need to know is that we must leave in silence… Absolute silence.'

One of the older children whimpers as he claws his way from sleep.

'Shush,' his father says. The child protests louder. His father clamps a hand over his mouth, startling the child. Fear does the rest.

'Nereus,' Geros says, 'lead them directly away from the village, up the slope. When it flattens out, you will know you are on the top, then it goes down the other side until you pick up the trackway. Turn left and keep walking. Zosime and I will rouse our people in the other huts. Don't wait for us. We will catch up. Do not stop for anyone.'

The hut stinks of sweat, the pungency that arises not from heat or running but from fear. Apprehension vibrates in the air, in the whispering of the parents to their children, in the shared looks, the stumbled steps, the hunched shoulders. They have borne so much; I'm proud of my people's courage in the face of their unknown terror. Their hushed rustle melts into the darkness, away from the village.

As Geros and I creep to the other huts, I hear our hunting call in the near distance, and further away, it's answer. Agis has found Yani and Con. One less worry, I hope.

At the next hut, Geros delivers his message. Though it is met with grave concern, the people wordlessly obey and creep out, following the same directions that Geros gave Nereus. Have they, too, sensed danger in this village?

At the last hut, we go through the same procedure and meet the same compliance. Tension tightens the air as people gather themselves and their children until a wail rips from the back of the hut. All heads turn. A woman bends over a motionless young man with skin the colour of whey. She collapses onto his chest, crying, 'No, No.' A man pulls her back, but she wrenches from his grasp and flings herself onto the dead boy.

Before panic can take full hold, Geros singles out an older woman, giving her the same directions in a swift, curt tone. 'Take everyone else.' Turning to me, he says, 'Zosime and I will deal with these parents and their son.'

Geros lets the father console the mother to the point where her wails subside to weeping. I stand at the door, fear pricking my skin as I watch for lights from the main village. They are bound to hear the woman's cries. Will they guess what has happened? My guts churn, repulsed by the words from earlier.

…And should any of them die …

I refuse to let that happen. I send out our hunting call, looping it up at the end, a signal for help, hoping that my brothers and cousin can figure out the direction it came from. There is no reply. I try again.

'We will take him with us,' I tell the parents. If Yani, Agis and Con can follow my call as we move, they will be able to help carry the body.

'No.' The father stands up to face me. 'We will stay here, and we will send him on his journey to the stars where he died.'

The mother nods, sniffing, unable to tear her eyes from her dead boy.

How do I tell them that if they stay, this village will add their beloved child to their communal pot? I look to Geros. He is calm, as if he does this every day.

'I understand the way of travelling is to send off those who pass from where their spirit leaves the body. But there is an exception to this because we are so near to the sea. In daylight, we can see the ocean from here. And it will give you more time to prepare his spirit,' Geros says, taking the mother's hand. 'The coastal people will build us a raft, and your son will have his lifelong wish – to travel across the sea.'

I am amazed at how well Geros knows everyone in our village. I can read a trail, tell you which animals have passed this way and when, but I find it hard to remember faces and names, even of those who are kin. Geros knows how to connect with people. He convinces these parents that we need to carry their son to the coast for his send-off.

'We must go right away,' he says.

A shiver ripples across my back. Time is rolling past. I help bundle the body in spare wraps. It is lighter than a boy in his early teens should be. Still, he is heavy to us, weakened because we haven't eaten since we left, and the quality of what we've eaten has been poor for several moons now. I hoist the body onto the shoulders of his father and banish the thought of a hunter carrying home a small buck. Thank the gods we don't need to tie the body to saplings and carry it between the two of us.

As we step out around the back of the hut, heading for the dark slope ahead, the two men I saw earlier block our path.

'Where are you going? Do you not appreciate our hospitality?' the older one says in a friendly tone.

'We thank you, but we need to go,' Geros says.

'Leave him,' the older one nods at our dead clansman.

'No, we must take our dead.' Geros stands in front of the father carrying his son's body.

I slide my hand under my wraps to my belt, wishing for a moment I had my axe but then realising it would not do. I find my hunting knife and draw it slowly, keeping my hand hidden below the wrap.

'You are free to go, but you leave the body here. We will take care of it.'

'Maybe we should stay.' The mother rests her hand on her dead son's wrapped-up head.

The father, stooped under the weight of the body, turns slowly to face Geros.

'Go,' Geros says in a firm, low voice.

'Leave the body!' The older man pulls out a knife and waves it in front of him.

The younger man is slender and around my height. Despite the biting chill of night, sweat pops at his temple. I can smell him – a nervous animal. His attention is on the older man who watches Geros and the parents of the dead boy, huddled together, sharing the weight of their son.

I spring with the knife, grabbing the younger man's hair from behind and encircling his neck with the other arm, holding the knife to his throat.

'Let them go.' I spit through clenched teeth.

The younger man wriggles. I press the skin below his jaw with the knife, hard enough to bring pain and a bead of blood. He stops resisting and says, 'Let them go, Ori.'

The older man throws him a look of utter disdain. 'You are too weak. This is about survival.'

'You've crossed a dangerous line,' Geros says with a calm voice. 'We don't eat human flesh.'

A strangled yelp comes from the mother; the father backs away, stumbling and almost dropping his burden before the mother helps him steady it.

'There is nothing else to eat. And what harm is done? We burn the flesh anyway. It is wasted.' The man called Ori holds Geros's gaze, but his beard trembles where his lips press and flex. He steps toward the couple, waving his knife.

The dead boy's parents stand mute with terror.

My heart thumps in my throat. My arms are weak. I don't know how long I can keep holding the younger man. He doesn't struggle. I feel him sag a little, but I stay alert.

Finally, Geros breaks the silence.

'What happens when there are no more dead to provide flesh for you? People will still be ill. Do you assist their death?'

Ori shakes his head. 'Of course not!'

'Are you sure you wouldn't just help them along a little? I mean, it would end their suffering sooner, fill your pot quicker?'

'Gods, no! We would never do a thing like that.'

'But this time last year, did you think you would eat human flesh?'

Ori opens his mouth to speak then stops, drops his gaze and wraps his arms around himself. I feel the younger man tremble beneath me. His nose sucks in a wet sniff.

He is crying. So is Ori.

Compassion undermines my anger.

A year ago, we were different people. A year ago, I would never have held a knife to a young man's throat. A year ago, I was grieving for a tiny life that never made it into our world; and now I am mourning the loss of our entire world as we know it. These men have been doing the best they can to keep their village alive. A part of me admires their resourcefulness, even as it makes me gag.

'Let him go, Zosime,' Geros says. 'Ori will let us leave together. Won't you?'

Ori hangs his head, defeated, waves a hand as if swatting away a fly, and steps aside to let our people stumble past with their burden.

Geros waits for me.

I let go of the young man. He stumbles forward, standing with his back to me, shoulders heaving out his sobs. I'm shaking so much I can barely put one foot in front of the other, but already the dead boy's parents are walking up the incline out of the village. Geros has his hand at my elbow, guiding me after them.

When we get to the top of the bank, I look back to see the younger man fall to his knees and pitch forward onto his hands. A traitorous thought crosses my mind. If I hadn't found them butchering the body, we would not have known. We'd have left the dead boy and his family here. There would have been meat in the pot and they would never have known any better. As a group, we would have been safe because there would have been no need to kill when someone had already died.

Part of me wishes I'd never seen the men by their fire, wishes I was as blissfully ignorant as I'd been this morning. Another part wonders how far I would go to stay alive. Would I eat human flesh? Has my interference condemned these villagers to death when they might have survived long enough to grow crops?

The sky in front of us lightens – a sheen through clouds – throwing the boulder-strewn hillsides into layers of soft greys that sweep down to a strip of shimmering water. Geros was right; we are close to the sea. It stretches to the horizon. I wonder how far away that is and how far we will have to go to find the sun.

CHAPTER 25

'Remember when we were trying to decide if we wanted to move to California, we did a daily mark out of ten?' my father asks, admiring my mother in her pretty blue summer dress that makes her eyes twinkle.

My mother gives a soft laugh. 'Yeah, when it rained, it was a hard eleven! It was November… it was eleven often. God, I yearned for the California sunshine.'

'If we stayed here, would you miss the sun?' My father's gaze drops to his phone resting on the patio table between their cups of coffee, willing it to ring. He wants the job, but more than that, he wants the waiting to end.

Squinting, my mother looks around the garden, stretches her arms in the sun's warmth and says, 'I don't think I'll miss the California sun if Irish summers continue like this. We sit outside here more now than we do in San Jose. Sure, it's too hot to sit outside there most of the time.'

'And then it gets too cold at night.'

'It's weird. It wasn't how I'd imagined it would be in the end, what with San Fran so bloody cold and us too hot in San Jose – except for nights; and the beaches so disappointing because the water was Baltic.'

'Arctic, actually,' he says. 'Straight down from Alaska – that's worse than Baltic.'

She takes a sip of her coffee. 'I do miss home, Ben.'

They hold one another's gaze and he nods.

Heartened, she goes on. 'It would be nice to be near Jack and the girls, and Mum, too.'

'Of course.' He slides his hand across the table and squeezes hers.

His phone rings, making them both jump.

'Armagh Observatory?' she asks, straining to see the caller ID.

'Nah, it's Lick.' He lifts the phone. 'I'll just be a minute.'

She hears him answer, his voice fading as he paces to the other side of the patio. His voice is steady, but something about the way he holds

223

his shoulders closer to his ears, shoves one hand in his pocket, rocks back and forth, signals to her the tension that I also pick up in the neon green that ripples through his aura. He strolls to the patio doors, talking as he disappears inside.

She doesn't want to force him to come back to Ireland if he's happy in California.

He wants to move back, too. It's not all on you, I tell my mother.

Her aura glows with a buttery hue. I couldn't see myself as a little old lady in San Jose, my mother sends. But I can see us growing old here, taking walks to the bridge every day, dodging the rain showers. She smiles.

'You look happy.' Maureen appears at the patio doors.

'Good morning. I'm just enjoying the sunshine.'

'Love the dress. I have a cardigan that would be lovely with it. Hang on.' Maureen disappears and returns a minute later with a blue cotton cardigan, the collar and cuffs trimmed with little white daisies. 'See perfect colour match.'

'It's lovely, thanks.' My mother slips it on. It feels expensive.

'Ach, it's old now. Your mum got it for me before she got sick. Feel free to borrow it today. A jacket is too heavy, but you might want something to cover your arms if it turns chilly.'

'Thanks, though I think it will stay warm.' My mother touches the daisy-shaped buttons, and her aura warms as she remembers what lovely taste in clothes Grammo had.

'Yeah, it's a great forecast.' Maureen tips her head to one side. 'So look, I was wondering if you would mind cancelling your trip with the girls to the museum today, maybe move it to another day. Today's more of a picnic at the seaside kind of a day.'

'That's a lovely idea. Where are we heading?'

Maureen blushes. 'Ah, well, actually, it was just me and Clare and the three girls. I hope you don't mind.'

My mother pauses. Her aura dulls and shrinks.

Maureen says, 'It's just, well, Clare and I do this mothers-daughters thing where we meet up and play Uno; and we thought this time, we'd have a day out, and it's just…'

Hurt blooms red and billows from my mother.

Guilt tinges Maureen's aura with taupe. Flashes of brittle lemon show she's annoyed that my mother is making her feel bad.

Maureen clears her throat. 'We thought you'd probably not want to come because it's…' She lifts her hands, palms up, and shrugs. 'You know, mothers and daughters.'

Gutted, my mother breaks eye contact and nods, not trusting herself to speak.

'Oh good, you do understand,' Maureen gushes. 'I'll tell the girls. You can go to the museum another time.'

Maureen registers my mother's hurt feelings. Baffled, she refuses to accept that it's her fault. Irritation fans the brittle lemon to slashing red. Maureen looks away from my mother's bowed head, adding, 'It's not the end of the world.'

Not for you, my mother says in her head. Her heart thumps the pain through her veins. She considers Maureen's words, not wanting this to escalate into an argument she can never win. My mother knows Maureen doesn't understand because if she did, Maureen would not sweep my mother's grief under the carpet with those words.

Finally, my mother manages, 'Okay.'

Maureen backs away and disappears into the kitchen, leaving my mother nursing a hollowed-out heart.

Returning from his phone call, my father takes in the expression on my mother's face.

'Are you okay?'

'No, actually, no, I'm not.' She bursts into tears. 'It's stupid, really. I want to go with Maureen and the girls to spend the day with Clare and her daughter. I was Clare's friend first. Maureen met Clare through me. I know that sounds so silly, so childish. But now Clare and Maureen and their three girls are a unit. Apparently, they meet up and play Uno, but now they're going to the seaside, and Maureen says I can't go because I've no daughter.'

My mother feels ridiculous and that compounds her upset.

My father, angry at Maureen's carelessness, rubs my mother's shoulders. 'Would you really want to be round at Clare's playing Uno? What the fuck even is Uno?'

'I don't know. That's not the point! And yes, I would. I love spending time with Emily and Fiona, and in a couple of years, they won't want to hang out with the grown-ups.'

'Did you tell Maureen that?'

'No. It sounds stupid.'

'So you're hurt because they left you out?'

'Yes, and because Maureen thinks she can ride roughshod over me and my plans.' But not just that, my mother thinks. Maureen's dismissal haunts her – *Not the end of the world*. It is the hidden nature of her grief, how people like Maureen think that you can't mourn for what you've never had. If I had lived, taken even one breath and then passed over, there would be all kinds of support for my parents, but this hidden loss leaves my mother alone in her bereavement. It swaddles her in suffocating grey mists, isolating her from the world she sees around her with people taking their children for granted, some envying her freedom from the shackles of motherhood.

My father is more pragmatic. His loss is different. He doesn't understand how alone a non-mother is in a world where women are expected to be mothers before all else. He considers my mother's distress and is upset for her. Trying to make her feel better, he says, 'But I thought you said you had nothing in common with Maureen and Clare.'

'Well, yeah, I know. I hear myself, and it sounds so stupid, so petulant, but when I'm with the pair of them, they just talk about the kids – where to get school uniforms, what shoes they need for P.E., their ballet and Irish dancing and Saturday football, and I have nothing to contribute, so I sit there saying nothing, the whole time.'

'Neither of them has much else going on in their lives. What else can they talk about? Clare hates her husband and Maureen can't very well talk about her husband since he's your brother.'

'They could talk about … I dunno … current affairs, the floods in Pakistan, the fires in Australia, climate change.'

My father chuckles. 'Seriously? Maureen worrying about climate change?'

'I feel so left out. Everywhere, not just with Maureen. I don't fit in. Do you realise that nearly every woman we know who is my age or within five years of my age has children? It's like I don't have a tribe.'

'It's harder for you. I'm sorry.' He tries to wrap his arms around her, but she doesn't want that, can't bear the comfort he has to offer. She steps away, needing to find her own strength, her own way of holding herself together.

'I'm always the odd one out, and they don't get me.'

'I get you.'

She softens and melts towards him, leaning her body against his, their auras swirling, blending, warming.

'Thank you,' my mother whispers. She can't tell him it's not enough; she feels devoid of purpose and useless.

He tightens his arms around her waist and says, 'And Fiona and Emily get you, too, you know – in a different way, but they're tuned into you.'

She pulls back and looks into his face. 'You think so?'

'I know so.' He kisses her forehead and then the tip of her nose.

She tries to let his comfort in, tries to make it easy, resolved. She's wrestled with this hurt many times before, but the sting lingers, compounded by the fact that it's Maureen who delivered it.

My mother leaves my father in the garden and goes to their room, trying to pack away the pain that Maureen has unfolded in her. It flares hot today. I can't see past the white heat of it into my mother's heart. I try to quench the fire with my love, but I can't seem to make a difference. I'm surprised when my mother sends, *I don't think you can reach this pain and fix it for me, Poppy.*

You feel me try?

Yes, but I also feel you weakening.

I'm sorry I cannot help.

You shouldn't have to. You're my child. I should be helping you, protecting you, but…

There is a surge of ultraviolet as her realisation that I am weakening crystallises and lands.

Oh, mother.

She creeps up on the idea that she might not have me forever, frizzing her aura with neon blue. Her pain reaches me. I ask her, *Why has Maureen upset you so much?*

My mother struggles to explain to me how stupid she feels about being so hurt. She knows Maureen is careless with people's feelings. She learnt that when they were teenagers and Maureen failed to return the friendship my mother so readily gave her.

My mother takes a deep breath and tries to set her thoughts straight. Her courage is iridescent green as she peels back the most painful layer of her grief to scrutinise what she now considers the most critical issue we have, which we have both tried to ignore.

I love having you with me, but you must go back to where you are supposed to be.

Perhaps I am supposed to be here.

Is that really true? Do you think you'd be losing your strength if this place wasn't somehow toxic to you? Your place is in the Enlightenment, with my dad, your … grandfather.

My mother chokes back a sob, thinking about how much she would have loved to see us together. An image flits through her mind of us both alive; him with me as a toddler, walking with me hand-in-hand, matching his stride to the stretch of my short legs. It's saccharine and acerbic in one bite. Her tears flow freely.

She grabs a tissue and dabs at her face. *You asked me why Maureen has upset me so much. That's the first time you've needed to ask me a question. Usually, you know things.*

She calms her heart rate with more deep breaths before continuing out loud, 'When we lost you, it felt like the end of my world. Then I got you back, but we both know you cannot stay here. That knowledge has been creeping up on me, and now I can't ignore it. I love you too much, Poppy, to let you fizzle out to nothing. Either way, I'll lose you. And Maureen doesn't realise it, nobody does, but it feels like the end of the world all over again to me.'

You're right. I must go back. It will be easier for me to be there than for you to be here without me. The Enlightenment is bliss. I'll not feel these emotions that burden you in this world. But leaving you feels like the end of the world to me, too.

'Oh, Poppy.' She covers her face with her hands. We are both buffeted by blue-grey desolation. She rides it out, then inhales deeply and forces the exhale through pursed lips. In her head, she tells herself that it's not the end of the world really, that her tiny, inner world is not so important in the scheme of things – her mother lost in dementia, a wider planet with people homeless from floods, climate catastrophes and famines and wars.

But still, it hurts.

How do we get you back to safety, Poppy? My mother drags orange tendrils of courage and strength from the depths of her being.

When the axe head hit the geode during the earthquake, the veil between the worlds thinned. Perhaps the axe head is the way back. Or the geode? The axe head seems to connect us with Zosime, but is this my way back to the spirit world?

I think that's why I wanted to visit the museum, she tells me. *They helped advise my father back when we found the axe head. Perhaps being there will give you some ideas?*

It's worth trying.

We might find out how to send you back, and then … then, you'd be gone from me.

I know.

The orange tendrils shrivel and wither, leaving my mother shaking with anguish.

But I won't be gone. I'll always be there with you, and someday you'll join me and we'll be together in the Enlightenment.

'Oh Poppy, Poppy, Poppy,' she says as if repeating my name aloud pulls me closer to her. 'We should try dropping the axe head on the geode now. Before it's too late, but I just…' She exhales hard, fully, caving forward, collapsing in on herself, pulling her legs up, knees to chest, her body rounded in a capital 'G' for grief. She switches back to sending me her thoughts. *I don't know how to let you go.*

It will be okay, I tell her, but she is swathed in impenetrable dark maroon. *You will be okay.*

I'm thinking. I want … It's just … I'm trying to remember if I've told you everything I want to tell you. To make sure I've said the things I want to, oh God, Poppy. It feels so sudden. But she knows it's not that sudden. She remembers how I've changed, from having all the answers, to the times I wouldn't give her answers for her own good, to when I didn't have the answers, to now, when I'm the one asking questions.

You won't leave anything unsaid, I tell her. I will still hear you from the Enlightenment. Better, in fact, because I'll hear your heart. Even if you can no longer hear me.

I love you, Poppy. I always have and always will.

I love you.

I have nothing left to tell her and she knows that.

I'll miss you.

I know. But I'll be with you. You'll feel me – in the softer moments – you'll feel me there with you.

I believe you. She puts her hand to her heart.

I flush the space between us with reds and oranges and yellows.

She smiles, feeling the warmth of my love.

My mother lifts the axe head out from the satchel, finds the box with the broken geode and opens it. The geode has broken up more in transit – fracturing along the brittle interface between the crystals – twisting sunlight into rainbows flung against the sides of the box.

She drops the axe head into the remains of the geode, but nothing happens.

When my mother tries to lift the axe head, a sharp edge of crystal slices into her finger. It is nothing more than a paper cut, but as a drop of blood drips onto the axe head, my mother sees Geros standing on a hill overlooking the ocean, saying, 'I know the way.'

The vision ends so quickly that my mother wonders if she actually saw the old man this time, or if a thought of him has passed through her mind. Either way, she understands that the axe head holds the key to all that has happened since I entered her realm, that her connection to Zosime began at the same time as her connection to me.

We should go to the museum without the girls, she tells me. Perhaps we've used up the energy in this axe head, but the museum is full of bronze axe heads. Maybe being there will increase the strength of whatever energy is needed to send you back.

She uses these words to mask her uncertainty from me, but we both know that if her plan fails, the alternative will be too hard to consider.

CHAPTER 26

After only two days away from our village, I miss Kallisto. That's a strange thought for me. We were never close, always tugging at each other, rarely pulling together. When one was the sapling – bending, flexing, the other was the gale – challenging, pushing. We drove each other on, measuring our strengths against each other. Switching places as necessary. But a sapling will not budge without the wind. And how will the wind know its strength without the sapling?

From the mountaintop, we have a view of the sea. There is a gap in the mountains that gives the port its name and allows the sea to cut inland. As we drop down from the hills toward the Gap, the roads become busy with groups of dishevelled travellers like us, shambling in the same direction with bowed heads and empty faces. Boats of all shapes and sizes dot the estuary and litter the shoreline. The noise meets us at about the same time as the reek of seaweed and fish.

I twitch my nose, and Nereus, seeing this, smiles. He doesn't find the stink as distasteful as I do, having grown up with it. Drawing nearer to the town, the crowds grow. Our group of thirty squeezes together. I worry that some of the frailer people will get separated from us. But Nereus guides us off the main trackway along a muddy path to a relatively quieter area against a rocky outcrop; it's behind a large thatched wooden structure that resembles our Ceremonial Hall, with wider door openings, so it looks like it has no wall along the front. Inside, people stand by wooden stalls. Others wander up and down. Nereus nods, smiles and uses words that belong to these people. They reply without the usual smiles and welcome. In better days, this market would have had dozens of stalls piled high with meats, cheeses, grain, edible roots and skins. Nereus used to sell his baskets and masks here before I met him.

I see only a few sellers with some fish and shellfish. There's a stall piled high with seaweed, but their business is not brisk. No one has any grain or vegetables to trade for this food. There is no livestock or meat. Beggars plead with the fishermen for scraps, and loud disputes flash into violence. Our people cower beside me. If we didn't need to buy passage on a boat, I would buy the fat, silver fish lined up on the trader's cart. My mouth waters at the thought of it baked in a fire pit with herbs and grain mash.

Geros addresses the villagers, 'Nereus knows this town and its people. I will let him take the lead today.'

No one protests.

'Geros and I will go talk to the boatmen about our voyage,' Nereus says. 'Agis, come with us. I will show you who to talk to for the boy's funeral.' Nereus nods toward the body the villagers have carried between them from last night, a burden even though it is pitifully light. The dead boy's parents stand over his body, their faces masks of anguish and exhaustion. 'I will have my cousins take care of it. We can trust them.'

'Wait for us here.' Geros turns to go.

Nereus pulls me to him in a quick embrace, saying, 'Keep everyone together, and keep to yourselves.'

He doesn't say this place is dangerous. It never has been on previous trips we've taken to the coast, but I can't ignore the desperation hanging in the salty air. I climb on top of the rocks beside us and watch as Nereus, Geros, and Agis leave.

I pivot, look out to sea and see three ships. Closer now, they look much bigger. The largest is built from two giant tree trunks hollowed into dugouts the length of twenty tall men lying head to toe, and as wide as one of those men with his arms spread open. Each dugout could easily carry our party. The two dugouts are strapped together with logs, and a platform spans the area between them. A narrow, thatched hut runs the length of each platform. At the front, three long posts pierce skyward with folds of material at their base and a slew of ropes along their length. I don't understand how the pieces will work together, but I have seen smaller versions of these types of vessels before – without the hut – bringing livestock to shore.

The scale of this vessel is impressive. Beside it are two smaller versions of the same craft. It looks like a seaworthy fleet, and my heart lifts. When Arne described his travels to me, he talked of these ships. Many people voyaged across the oceans in them, he had said.

There are smaller boats, too, for fishing or transporting goods. The sea looks calm, sheltered between mountains on both sides. The people here must have had an easier time, being able to fish; but even with that, I can see they are thin, and wreckage above the tide line tells a story of violent storms and crazed waves. I shiver at the thought of being at sea when the water becomes angry.

After a little while, Agis returns with two local men.

'Nereus says he has arranged for a floating pyre for your son. You must give the body to these men.' Some of the villagers protest, but the dead boy's father stops them. 'I trust Nereus. Our boy will be in good hands. Thank you.'

The men gently take possession of the wrapped body. I wonder if anyone else recognises the armlet one of them wears. It is the armlet Geros has worn for years, a gift from the Monarchs when he finished his service with them. It is valuable. But then, if it cannot fill a belly, how valuable is it?

I sit on my perch atop the rock and stare out to sea. It is still morning, and though the sky is grey, there seems to be more light, with waves glistening as far as the horizon. The sea is so vast I cannot comprehend what it will be like to cross it. When we meet the horizon, will we see the other land?

Nereus and Geros are gone for longer than expected. Some of the older and weaker people hunker against the rocky outcrop while the rest stand around them, shielding their vulnerability. Yani and Eleni keep Claus and his sisters close by. The children stand round-eyed and wary, far too thin, lacking the exuberance that children have when well-fed and full of mischief.

Agis beckons me down from the rock and pulls me off to one side. 'Haven't Nereus and Geros returned yet? They left me with these people and went off to secure the passage, but I thought they'd be back by now.'

My brother is impatient at the best of times. Though I share his trepidation, I try to calm his fears. 'Nereus knows his way around. He knows these people. I trust him.'

'It's not him I'm worried about. You saw the armlet?'

'I assume Geros used that as payment.'

'Yeah, he did. I was there. But my point is, Geros has all our wealth. If he were attacked—'

'Don't.' I cut him off because I can't bear to think about it. Agis has identified that which has me unsettled: a sense of lawlessness. Like our own village, many of the Elders here are gone, judging by the lack of greyheads. The strong rather than the wise have been left in charge.

Worry creeps in on me the longer Geros and Nereus are gone, with every skirmish in the marketplace, with every beggar that approaches us and is turned away empty-handed, with every stranger who tries to sell us passage, with every sick and dying person carried past us. All I have of any real value are Kallisto's seeds in a waterproof pouch hidden beneath my furs. I press it against my belly, comforted by its lumpy presence.

'Will I go and look for them?' Jaisun asks, overhearing our conversation.

'No!' Chloe says, pulling on his arm. 'Tell him, Zosime.'

'We stay together.' I fix him with a scowl that doesn't ground him for long. He shrugs Chloe off and climbs up on the rocks to watch for the men. Chloe sighs and folds her arms.

My relief at spotting Nereus pushing his way through the throng is short-lived when I meet the grim expression in his eyes. I look around for Geros but don't see him.

'What happened?' I ask.

'We need to go now,' Nereus says, helping a woman to her feet. 'Right now. We're going with this tide.'

This is it. We're leaving. My limbs feel wooden. My heart jumps in my chest. I cast around for my brothers and see them helping people to get moving.

'Where is Geros?' I say in a low voice to Nereus, leading everyone towards the dock.

'He's making sure the boat doesn't leave with the payment.'

'How much did it cost?'

'Everything.'

'*Everything?*' I'm horrified. What will we use to trade with when we get to the Warmer Lands?

'Everything, and more.' Nereus doesn't hide the bitterness in his voice.

'More? How can we give more if we don't have it?'

'Some of us will have to work off the rest when we get there. Geros wants to clear it with our people first.'

'Of course.'

I swallow back the rising lump in my throat. This will split our group further. Some may not go, and others will be as good as slaves. I think of the seed secreted in my pocket. I take Nereus's hand. 'We'll have sun and food, and we'll be alive. That is what matters.'

234

'Getting on that boat is what matters,' he says, squeezing my hand and ushering the rest of the village ahead of us.

Geros is waiting by the jetty. It looks like the trackways we use to join our villages, but it juts out above the water, supported by tree trunks and wooden struts. Boats ranging in size from ten to thirty foot-lengths are moored alongside it.

When Geros sees us approaching, he steps off the jetty and beckons us to follow him to a sloped, pebbled area on the shore. It doesn't take him long to explain how much the passage costs: all of our treasure and two years of labour by ten of our people. I'm sure he has had to bargain intensely. Our group of thirty only has ten people fit for the type of work that would be defined as labour – the hardest, heaviest work that no one else wants to do: building roads and temples; cutting trees; clearing land. I do not relish it, and though Nereus is strong, he is creative. He works with his hands and his heart. These will be long, hard years for anyone taking on the task. Those of us physically able to do this hard labour know who we are. Agis, Yan, and I catch each other's eyes with grim acceptance.

When Geros finishes speaking, the group falls silent.

The dead boy's father speaks first. 'I'll stay. That will be one less passage to buy. Will that help?'

Geros shakes his head. 'My friend, I think these men require the labour regardless. And we'd have to give you your share of the valuables. But most of all, there is no life left in this place. You will die here of starvation.'

'Geros is right,' I say. 'It is impossible to stay. I will do it. I will work for them.'

'Me, too,' Nereus says.

'I will work, too,' Agis says, followed by Yani, Eleni and my cousin Con. When Jaisun and Chloe step up my heart aches for their lost youth; but still, they'll live. Before too long, at least ten people agree to the deal.

'To be clear,' Geros says, 'Ten workers and our village treasures for thirty people's passage to the Warmer Lands. They think it will take seven or eight days. It will be uncomfortable, but they have seen the sun at our destination.' He smiles at our reaction; a slight lift of heads, nods, clasping of hands. Then his face closes as he adds, 'Be aware that once we leave on their boats, our lives are in their hands.'

He is met with solemn nods. We have no choice but to go, whatever the risk.

We follow Geros to the jetty, and our village is broken into three groups. Each group is assigned to small vessels made from two dugouts strapped together, similar to the huge ship I saw in the estuary. The well-fed sailors wear warm clothes, waxed with animal fat to keep them dry and have fur-lined hats and gloved hands. Compared to us, they are well equipped for the cold, wet conditions we will meet. Each has a dagger in his belt. I try to tell myself they need such tools for sailing, that we have paid a fair price, and these men are helping us find a better life. But it's hard to believe the things I tell myself as they roar instructions at us. Our people, harried and panicked, try to comply but stumble and rear back from the shifting boats. The sailors, their hands drifting to the hilts of sheathed knives, shove our people forward, snarling commands which we can't quite understand. I have seen livestock treated with more compassion.

We can barely fit into our boat and crouch in rows in the hollow of the dugouts in fear as it settles low to the water. Supplies are strapped in piles on the platform joining the two dugouts, leaving no room for anyone there other than the crew. Waxed skins, tightened over the front of the dugouts, stop them from being swamped by waves that slap over every so often, causing the children in our group to squeal in terror. I don't know how we stay afloat, but thank the gods, we do.

Nereus and I are in the same boat as Agis. Yan, Eleni and their three children are in the second boat. My cousin Con, his family, Jaisun and Geros are in the last boat. Chloe is with us, upset that she has been separated from Jaisun. Each boat has two crew members who work with sails and oars to make the vessels move us into the bay. But they don't take us towards any of the three larger ships, as I had expected.

'How do we get onto our ship?' I ask the man who has been giving orders to the other sailors.

He laughs. 'This is your ship.' His accent is strange, and I wonder if he misunderstood my question. I stare at him, waiting for an explanation.

'It is too small,' I say.

'You don't like it?' The man's laughter turns cruel. 'You want to swim?'

'Zosime, hush,' Nereus says in a low voice in my ear.

I glare at him, but he flicks a glance at their knives, and that, along with the resignation in his eyes, causes me to back down.

'We'll fall out of this,' I say in a small voice.

'Only if you don't hold on tight,' the sailor says with a nasty grin.

*

The estuary is calm, but I don't realise that until we hit the open sea. It is no longer flat water but a mass of moving rounded humps that we summit and slide down, over and over again. As we leave the land behind, we shrink in comparison to the waves, the sky, and the vastness of the ocean. The sailors roll out the sails, hanging sheets of cloth that catch the wind and pull us along with it. It is magnificent and terrifying at the same time. Some of our party become seasick and retch over the side of the boat.

Nereus smiles as we glide along with the wind. From the crest of a swell, I realise that I cannot see the land in any direction. Night steals the light from the sky. The sea turns black, ominous. We lose sight of the boats ahead of us.

'How does he know where we are going without the sun or the moon and stars?' I ask Nereus.

'They can tell from the wind and the patterns in the waves. My cousins could do it, but I never understood it.'

It strikes me that Nereus has cousins for every eventuality. I accept his explanation without any more questions. I suppose it's like how he knows when the willow is ready to harvest for making a mask when those branches look the same to me, or how I know that a buck may have crossed our path from the signs it has left behind, but which Nereus can never discern. These sailors are on this same voyage as we are. I must trust they wouldn't have undertaken it without knowing what they are doing.

I fall asleep sometime during the night and awaken slumped against Nereus. We are still moving, whispering along through waves. On our left, there is a white line, and after a moment, I realise it is the horizon, with day breaking. That makes sense – we want to travel toward where the sun is most of the time, and that would mean we would orient sunrise to our left. Figuring this out brings me comfort, or perhaps it is the brightening skies and the sight of the other boats and the people in them sleeping.

The large boats are dots ahead of us in the distance, but we are close enough to the other smaller boats to wave at Geros, Jaisun and Yani. Our crew is handing out food: dried meat, which we gnaw on, and hard rocks of dried grain mash, which we soften with spittle in our mouths before chewing. It's not much, but it's better than nothing – more than we have been used to in recent months. My water skin is still half full, and the crew tells us to top up our water from the barrel they keep by the mast. They tell us rain will fill it again soon. My ears agree. The popping has started up, and I dread the coming rain. We have little or no cover, and we will suffer from the cold more when we are wet.

When the rain falls, it soaks us. We huddle in the cavity of the dugouts, bailing with wooden scoops, trying to stay warm. The cold is painful and so are the cramped conditions. We take turns stretching a limb at a time. Seven days of this ahead of us. Already, I'm sore, though not as pitiful as those who can't stand the rocking motion and continue to vomit. But as the day unfolds and the rain passes, we move with the wind. I feel a warming in the air, and the rain is not as frigid. The sails pull us harder, dragging us up waves that seem even bigger, plunging us into deep troughs so fast, it feels like I've scooped out my chest and left it behind.

We lose sight of the larger ships and only spot Geros's and Yani's ships when we crest a swell. The second night closes in and passes, suspending me between a dazed sleep and an exhausted trance.

Over the next couple of days, conditions settle. The larger ships come back into view but are so far ahead they are specks in the vast expanse of grey ocean. I lose count of how many days we've been huddled on these boats. When we ask for more food or water, the sailors lose patience and threaten to strike us. The kinsman next to me whispers that we should fight back and stand up for ourselves, but Nereus warns us to be cautious. These men know how to sail. Without them, we're at the mercy of the wind and waves. So we hunker down, wait it out, and pray for land.

Then, one day, the wind is much warmer, but it is wilder and can't seem to choose which direction it wants to blow. Thunder booms. Lightning splits the sky to our right. It is far away, the sailors tell us.

'It is often like this at this point in the voyage. Hold on tight,' one of them says. 'The gods will not catch us.'

But the gods do catch us and unleash their fury around us as though they are angry at our escape. Night slams in with the thunder and is ripped apart by the lightning. There is no sleep for anyone. The sailors work with the sheets and ropes to lower the sails. They tie the supplies down, lash our three small boats together – ours in the middle – and secure themselves to their boats. The waves are like raging beasts, lifting us high on their backs, then hurling us into dark, churning pits. I scream myself hoarse, cling to Nereus and plead for the gods to make it stop.

Eventually, the waves lose their anger, and we meet the dawning day in a haze of terror and exhaustion. As it becomes brighter, we realise our three small boats are alone. There is no sign of the larger vessels that we'd been following.

'Are you okay?' Nereus asks.

I nod; others do, too, when Nereus checks them.

'Geros?' I call.

He raises a hand from his boat, seems too spent to shout, but he's alive. There is a gap where the food sat on the platforms of the two outer boats. I count heads, trying to pick out my family, Geros and Jaisun. Everyone is still here, but over the cacophony of splashing waves, shouting sailors, crying children and groaning injured, I realise Jaisun is screaming, holding up a mangled hand. I try to stand up. A sailor tells me to stay put. He clambers across the lashed-together dugouts and speaks to Jaisun. I can't hear what he says but Jaisun's screams quieten.

'Jaisun!' Chloe sobs, too exhausted to shout to him.

I try to take her hand, but she's out of reach. I shake my head, trying to clear my own tears.

'It looks like the sailor is taking care of him.' Nereus soothes me. 'Perhaps he is a healer.'

I swallow hard and nod, taking in the drawn faces around me. Many have bruises blooming. Some bleed. The moans from our people compete with the wind screeching through the empty ropes strung along the masts. At the back of our boat, a wail rises above other sounds and sets my hair standing. Another death.

The sea has settled from a rollick to an easier roll, and the crewmen hop across and meet in the middle platform of our boat. Soon, their interaction becomes heated. One is shaking his head, pointing to the sky and waving his other hand while the others shout at him.

'What are they saying?' I ask Nereus.

'They don't know where we are,' he says in a low voice, so only I hear him. 'The storm has blown us off course, and they don't know how far we've travelled. They fear that we might go too far and miss the Warmer Lands.'

'What is beyond the Warmer Lands?' I dread his answer. He holds a finger to his lips.

He concentrates. The sailors are speaking too fast for me to grasp their words. Nereus listens hard, grimacing at parts, before whispering to me, 'And we've lost the food and water from two boats. I didn't catch the next part.'

One of the sailors from our boat has seen that Nereus is listening and nudges the others. They lower their voices and choose words that are harder for us to understand. After some back and forth and much waving of hands and scanning the horizon, they seem to reach an agreement.

'Hurt, sick, old here.' A sailor points at Geros's boat. There's already Geros and two others who are very frail there. 'Bring food.' He points at the sacks on the other platforms and motions for them to move the food to the empty platform of Geros's boat.

'Move!' The sailor kicks Agis who jumps up and stares the sailor down. The sailor grabs his knife. Agis backs away and sits down.

'What are they doing?' I ask.

'I think they must have a healer. They are putting the sick and injured in one boat with the food,' Nereus says, watching the sailors pass the food to the same boat. The worst injured are already on that boat, so it makes sense not to have to move them. Six ill or injured people transfer to the healer's boat. Con and his family of three and five others are distributed between our boat and Yani's, making it a bigger squeeze in our dugouts. I wonder what will happen to the dead person at the back of ours, but say nothing. The sailors are in the one dugout with the sick people, settling them in and affixing the ropes and sheets.

A sailor comes on the platform on our dugout, still in the middle of the three vessels.

'Eat now,' the sailor says, drawing out his knife and using it to open this last sac filled with dried meat. 'Eat.' He steps back off our boat, knife still drawn.

I am busy helping people pass food across when I hear the snap of a sail and look behind me. The sailors have unfurled the sails above the sick. As the wind catches and fills the sheets, I brace for the tug on the vessels but feel nothing. The straps are severed between our boats and the boat containing the sailors and the injured. Our boat and Yani's boat are left behind, still lashed together.

'Wait!' I cry with a voice too hoarse to make more than a squeak.

As the sailor's vessel picks up speed, Geros jumps up and tries to pull down the sail. The sailor closest to him elbows him out of the way. Geros loses his balance, falling overboard a good twenty feet from our boat.

I jump in after him. I'm not a strong swimmer. The water pulls at me, making my clothes heavy. The cold steals my breath, my coordination, my wits. I hear shouting. Nereus throws something. A rope lands beside me. I grab for it, kick hard enough to raise myself in the water and see Geros splashing an arm's length away. I lunge and grab him with one hand. The rope tightens in the other. Nereus drags us both back to the two boats that are left behind. Agis and Nereus haul us into the dugout. I endure a violent bout of coughing before I can catch my breath. Geros gasps beside me, but no one is paying us any attention.

All eyes are on the sailors in their boat speeding away with the wind, with our food and with our sick and frail. We watch in horrified disbelief at being abandoned like this as two sailors work the sails, taking their boat further away from ours. Another sailor, the healer perhaps, tends to the sick and injured. He leans over Jaisun, then beckons another crew member over to help. The healer lifts Jaisun under his armpits. Jaisun shrieks in pain and struggles, but another sailor grabs him by the ankles. What are they doing to him? They are hurting him. He wriggles and squeals, but the thin youth is no match for the brawny sailors.

They swing him out over the water and drop him. He hits the waves with a splash, quickly disappearing underwater.

'No!' I scream.

Chloe wails Jaisun's name and leans over the edge, reaching out to him. I grab hold of her waist and scan the water, but he doesn't reappear.

Men on our craft are fumbling with oars but are not coordinated enough. Jaisun's gone. We can't see him nor find the place where they dropped him.

The sailors not manning the sails work in pairs, pick up people by the wrists and feet, swing them over the side and let go, systematically throwing each and every one of our sick and frail overboard.

It happens quickly. Those thrown overboard are too far away. We can neither swim to them nor move the boats in any coordinated fashion. Too weak to swim, some float momentarily, then sink; others splash and struggle before sliding under the surface.

The thing that strikes me is their silence. Those drowning are too busy fighting for their lives to call for help.

CHAPTER 27

The Mall is resplendent in the June sunshine with horse chestnut trees towering over the path, providing shade and a sprinkle of crusted cream petals underfoot as they shed the last of their blossom in the heat. The Armagh County Museum sits on the west side of the Mall. My mother stands in the summer heat gazing at the building, with its three long, narrow, round arch-topped windows peeking from between four grand pillars. It's warm enough for my mother to not need Maureen's cardigan. She carries it in her hand in case the museum is air-conditioned or chilly, as old buildings sometimes are.

When I was a child, she tells me, *I thought this place looked like a palace. Her aura is stained with a deep navy. I wish I could have taken you here. I wish I could let you run on the Mall's lawns and play with your cousins and a puppy ... yes, definitely a puppy.*

She turns her back to the museum to look at the Mall and sees a mother pushing a stroller along the shady path. At first glance, the child inside looks too old to be in a stroller. Then my mother notices that the child's head is supported by a brace, spots the feeding tube up his nose and the limp set to the child's limbs and understands that this mother will never see her child run on the Mall's grass either.

None of us ever had guarantees, I tell my mother. *We are not broken promises. There is much heartache here, and much love.*

The woman pushing the stroller has a strong yellow aura. It has been a good morning for her. Her child is fed and hasn't choked on reflux or brought up his feed. She is relishing this walk in the sun, thinking how lucky she is that her little boy made it through his last chest cold. The child enjoys the vibrations of the wheels on the tarmacadam path. He absorbs the energy of his mother's aura and wriggles his fingers at the sky. His discomforts are forgotten in this moment. But it is only a moment.

There are in-between times, too. I'm not sure my mother needs to know about that; not now while she is experiencing her own in-between time.

My mother turns back towards the museum, takes a deep breath and tells me, *You're right, Poppy. You're not a broken promise. You are a gift.*

A gift she thinks she needs to return to save me.

Is it too much to ask of her? Of us?

Her steps slow. She almost stops walking. She places a hand over the heavy throb that has developed across her chest. Thoughts tumble and crash, making her scrunch up her face and bow her head. She hauls in a long breath, holds it and feels her panic subside to a dull ache. She is swathed in pale blues and pinks like a summer sunset taking its leave.

Her love for me overcomes her urge to hang on to me. It is the hardest thing she's ever chosen to do – give me back to the Enlightenment.

I feel a mix of relief and sadness laced through with longing for the Enlightenment where I won't be buffeted by the extremes of emotion I feel here. I yearn for the rest, the sanctuary, the bliss.

I may not be destined to go back. This may be my place. Here with you.

But we both know she has to try.

My mother has always loved the museum, luxuriating in its quiet stillness as if it holds its own reverence for the past. It's cooler inside and she slips on Maureen's cardigan, glad she has it now. The museum is busier than she expected it to be; she's used to having it to herself on previous trips. Ahead, a group of three older women climb the stairs to the exhibition galleries. They stop at the turn in the staircase to stare up at the Timothy Lennox painting of the buildings of Armagh. One of the women, in an expensive-looking beige trench coat, reads the museum signage out loud while the other two try to squint over her shoulder. They nudge each other and point, picking out the cathedrals, the museum, familiar landmarks. Their voices rise, ricocheting off the stairwell, in conflicting guesses as to which streets they can make out. My mother stands quietly, waiting for them to move on, staring up at the giant antlers of the Irish Deer that went extinct eleven thousand years ago.

Eleven thousand years ago, she thinks.

Not so long, really; we predate this by aeons, our souls derived from the energy of
…

Of what? I've lost the knowledge, and I find myself on the edge of an empty black void where once I knew these things: ignorance and an abyss.

What did Ireland look like then? my mother muses.

Trees, lots of trees. I find it strange that I know that, yet have lost so much of my enlightenment. Fragments of knowledge are caught like sheep's wool on barbed wire. Where does it end for me? Will I be tugged apart piece by piece on the barbs of this physical world until there is nothing left? Extinct, too?

'Extinct,' my mother says on an exhale, with a shiver, and I wonder if she has tapped into where my thoughts are kept.

The woman in front of her startles when my mother speaks.

'So sorry,' the woman says, nodding at the other two, still debating a detail of the painting. She holds her hand up in a fake stage whisper and says, 'They don't get out much,' then taps on the arm of the woman nearest her. 'Yer holding everyone up!'

'It's okay,' my mother says, smiling. 'I'm not in a hurry.'

'But I am,' says the woman, tugging her friend's arm. 'C'mon, the talk starts in five minutes.'

'I didn't realise there was a talk,' my mother says, thinking she would like to have the museum to herself so she can say her final goodbye to me. Maybe once the talk is over, everyone will leave, and she'll have that space she needs.

'It's Professor Baillie from The Queen's University, talking about tree rings.' The woman smiles and nudges my mother. 'I'm sure there's room for one more.'

'I think I know him, if it's the same Professor Baillie from my undergrad days,' my mother says, following the women up the stairs.

As she heads through the main exhibition gallery towards the rows of chairs set out for the talk, she passes stone and bronze axe heads on display in cabinets. She's drawn to them and stops to stare. Thinking about who might have made them and what stories they must carry causes a sizzle in her veins, an effervescence that makes her a little lightheaded. She decides to stay for the talk, even if it's only to adjust to this strange sensation that is also somehow pleasant.

My mother sits in the back row. The event is well attended for a Wednesday afternoon in June with the sun splitting the sky. The museum is a cool sanctuary, and my mother is again glad to have the extra layer of the cardigan that Maureen lent her.

The speaker is the same Professor Baillie who taught the archaeology module she did as a history undergrad. My mother remembers him fondly. The years have been kind to him, his hair and beard marginally whiter than she remembers, but he has the same engaging twinkle in his smile. His voice is warm and welcoming, a storyteller's voice. She remembers how she enjoyed his lectures, how he could keep the student's attention as he wove a story out of the way they built an oak tree-ring chronology going back seven thousand years.

His talk refreshes her memory. The professor describes how the cross-section of an oak tree trunk reveals concentric growth rings that the tree adds each year. She remembers being fascinated by how the width of each annual ring reflects the growing conditions for the tree so that the tree keeps a record of climatic conditions. She had loved the simplicity of that – still does – and remembers with fondness the tour of the Paleoecology lab back in her undergrad days, where they were shown how the wood was prepared and then counted using a microscope attached to a computer. The researchers would turn a handle that moved the stage the sample was mounted on so that crosshairs moved across each ring. They'd press a button, making a high-pitched pop each time a ring was measured to send the data to the computer – an Apple IIe. The lab sounded like strange birds conversing, especially if two researchers were counting in adjacent cubicles. When she had described the sound to Ben, whom she'd just started dating, he'd said it reminded him of his tinnitus.

Professor Baillie is a skilled storyteller and teacher. He explains the laborious construction of the seven-thousand-years-long oak chronology in a few simple sentences so that no one in the audience is left behind. None of it is new to my mother, but she appreciates the recap of how living oak tree patterns were cross-matched and then extended back with overlaps from archaeological samples and then further back to subfossil oaks found in bogs, known as bog oaks. The audience members give a collective murmur of suppressed awe when he says the oak tree-ring chronology stretches back to 5470 BC.

My mother glows in peachy light, content to let her mind be filled with this talk. I understand her embracing the respite from her thoughts about letting me go.

Professor Baillie shifts his story to focus on periods in history highlighted by points in the chronology where the tree rings become narrow, or 'downturns for Irish oak', as he put it.

'Extreme events stood out in clusters of very narrow rings, and they appeared to be related to other things going on. These were compared to the layers in the Greenland ice cores. If there is a big volcanic eruption, it dumps sulphuric acid on the ice and is recorded in the ice record. Several of these dates coincide with the narrowing events in the Irish trees, such as one that occurred from 3199 until 3193 BC, another starting at 2354 BC and running to 2345 BC, and the one that starts in 1159 BC and runs to 1141 BC, eighteen years in duration.'

My mother feels the hairs on the back of her neck rising when he says, 'And you have to ask yourself, what was happening to people in Ireland when that was going on? Things may well have been pretty rough here.'

She listens to the Professor describe what he believes happened during the 540 AD event that showed up in tree rings around the world: the dry fogs, which he attributes to dust clouds; the terrible famines in China; plagues in Europe – possibly as a result of massive volcanic eruptions in Iceland.

The audience, my mother included, is engrossed in the story. Something in my residual enlightenment tells me the Professor is on the mark. The tree rings have recorded the story of our past climates, marking them down in the annual timescale of Earth, backed up by the Danish ice core records from Greenland. The Professor's curiosity and intelligence have pieced together the events of a volcanic nightmare scenario with stunning accuracy.

A hand goes up. It's the woman she met in the stairway. The Professor invites her question with a patient smile.

'So are you saying this is like the volcano that went off in Iceland in 2010, you know, the one that stopped all the flights?'

There's a murmur through the audience as people remember the event. A couple nudges each other and nods. They'd had their holiday cancelled – they remember it well.

'Yes, except in comparison, that was a squib.' The Professor enjoys the collective gasp. 'And,' he adds, 'we now know there was probably not just one big volcano in 536 AD but several, probably at least three. And if it happened again, it would almost certainly be a civilisation-stopping event.'

He lets silence drape over his audience for a couple of seconds as they digest that information. Then he says, 'That event was fundamentally volcanic, but some of the BC events could have had a cometary element.' With this statement, Professor Baillie moves on to talk about how he'd taken a side-step into looking into how stories of King Arthur, Cúchulainn and other Celtic deities like Lugh are told.

'Perhaps they are the stories of comets that came too close to the Earth. Their lights, colours flashing in the sky, or as bright as the sun in the sky – as Lugh was described – would have terrified people. People who had no other way to explain these happenings had to account for the extraordinary events they were witnessing.'

The Professor goes on to explain the possibility of the Earth traversing the tail of one of these close comets, resulting in extraterrestrial debris hitting the Earth and causing cataclysmic climate events.

My mother feels a tingle creep over her skin, which neither of us can explain. I can sense an awakening of her own enlightenment. I'm not sure if her connection to me is the conduit or if it's the axe head in her bag – vibrating with a strange new energy – sending a message to her.

My mother raises her hand as if on auto-pilot and finds herself surprised by her forwardness as Professor Baillie invites her question.

'Could a cometary strike trigger a volcano?' she asks.

'I wouldn't rule it out,' Professor Baillie says before launching smoothly into his next theory. 'The tree-ring chronology shows a decade-long narrow rings event spanning 2354 BC to 2345 BC.'

My mother feels cold. The axe head thrums. She holds her breath as she listens to the Professor speak.

'This narrow ring episode also coincides with stories from around the world dating to that time period, such as the Chinese Emperor Yao who reigned during a series of catastrophes, including floods, in 2346 BC. In fact, in the sixteenth century, Archbishop Ussher dated the Biblical flood to around this time, and it even shows up in the Mayan calendar, dating the birth of three deities. Something happened in the sky that had memorable consequences for people on the ground. We have tree samples that indicate an inundation of Lough Neagh at that time.'

Professor Baillie opens a box and brings out a wedge of wood. It is polished. The ring patterns have been highlighted with chalk. On one side, the rings are even rows, but on the other side, the rows are contorted and deformed about a scar. As he holds it up, my mother and I feel a ripple, a heightening energy flow that no one else notices.

The Professor continues, 'This sample, Q9172, was taken from a peat bog west of the river Bann and ten kilometres north of Lough Neagh. This scar would have been about one metre above ground when the tree was alive, and when dated, it appears the scar was inflicted in 2354 BC. It's possible that this damage was inflicted by rafting debris during a flood that happened at the base of the trees.'

The axe head, I say, but my mother already knows that it was not floating debris or an act of nature but a human wielding an axe, the axe head in her bag, that caused this damage.

When the talk is finished, there is a resounding round of applause before everyone moves to the refreshments table, where they mill about, helping themselves to tea and coffee. My mother sits watching as the Professor is drawn away from the podium, answering questions. Her attention shifts to the table beside the podium with the scarred oak wood less than ten feet from her. She stands.

Everyone else's attention is on their cup or the Professor.

Sample Q9172 draws her closer. She slips one hand into the satchel to rest on the axe head. It is warm with a power she has never experienced before. She glances around the museum gallery. No one is looking her way. Extending her other hand, she reaches out with her index finger and touches the scar on sample Q9172.

It's like a circuit completing. There is a rush of energy bubbling in her veins, fizzing in her head, popping her ears, blurring her vision.

And in that moment, my mother sees it all.

She sees Zosime and Nereus living here, where my mother grew up, but thousands of years before she was born. She sees meteors burning through the atmosphere as the Earth passes through a long-since sun-eaten comet's tail. She sees the largest meteor strike off the coast of Iceland, sending a wall of water toward Ireland and triggering the Heckla Four volcano. She sees Zosime standing on the slopes of a hill, axe in hand, watching the tsunami thunder down the Bann valley towards Lough Neagh. She sees the axe head biting into the tree to cause the scar my mother's finger now touches.

Like looking at a detailed photograph on a computer, every time my mother zooms closer, she not only sees more detail, she understands it: the volcanic cloud changing the weather for nine years; the ash covering the neolithic Irish landscape, freshly deforested by the advance of agriculture; the famine caused by plummeting temperatures; the plague of measles that jumped species from close contact between the cattle they kept and Zosime's people; people dying and survivors fleeing; people desperate with hunger; the exodus across the ocean to find the sun; the people traffickers leaving them to die at sea. Then, suddenly, at the most close-up point, my mother finds herself in a boat face to face with Zosime, Nereus and Geros.

CHAPTER 28

It's hard to gauge how long we sit in shock, watching the sailors until we can no longer see them. Through all the terrible things that have happened to us since the gods ripped the sky open and hid the sun: the flooding, the pigs dying, the crops failing, the plague. All of that we endured, but the selfishness, the injustice, and intentional brutality handed out by other humans have broken us.

I sit with Geros's head on my lap, tucked under furs that have dried stiff and salty in the sea breeze. His eyes are closed, his breathing shallow.

'He will rest and be stronger soon. I know it,' I say. No one seems to listen. They are destroyed in their grief, their desolation as grey and solid as the sky above us. My heart is so raw after losing Jaisun that I cannot bear to think of losing Geros, too.

The light leaves the day, plunging us into the darkest night. The sea is absurdly gentle, like a child repenting for its earlier bad behaviour. We lie paralysed by grief and hopelessness, no one moving, the only sound the sniffing, weeping and coughing of those left in the two boats lashed together. We rock in a black void; no land, no horizon, just sea and sky merged into one colossal darkness. There is no light, none. I cannot see my hand in front of my face.

My ears make their own noise. At first, I think it's signalling more rain and wonder if this will finish us. I'm too numb to care if it does. But this noise is different. It is like the sound of people clapping, far away, but in my head, only in my head, because out here on the ocean, we are silent.

Then words, foreign words which somehow assemble themselves into sense, come to my ears.

'Don't give up, Zosime.'

Geros moves. His hand finds mine and squeezes.

'I hear it, too,' he whispers, 'the sounds are from other worlds. We've always had that in common.'

'Shush,' I soothe him, worried he is feverish and rambling. But there is a spark of light hovering in the air above us.

I blink.

It stays there, expanding, becoming less dazzling, illuminating a woman standing beside it. She reaches out her hand. I lift mine to touch it and feel a surge of energy – a swelling of joy and sorrow at once.

It is unbearable.

I snatch my hand back, but the woman is still there, with a star shining beside her. She is sitting as if in a trance, not seeing me, perhaps not even seeing this world.

I reach out. This time, we touch. Our fingers are cold, but together, warmth spreads into my palm. The woman looks around as if waking from a dream.

'Who are you?' I ask.

The woman smiles. 'I'm Aisling. And you're Zosime.'

CHAPTER 29

While my mother connects with Zosime, I am drawn to Geros's aura. His body is weak, but he glows with enlightenment. Some individuals are gifted with this all their lives. They have been called mystics, savants, clairvoyants, witches – the name depends upon the culture they live in. Although Geros's body is weak, his spirit connects with mine.

'Poppy?' he says.

Yes. My words fill my mother's, Zosime's and Geros's thoughts simultaneously.

Zosime gasps. Her eyes widen. 'You can speak with the stars?' She stares at Geros in awe.

'We are all stars,' Geros says. 'You can speak with them, too.'

'No.' Zosime shrinks back, thinking of the holes in the fabric of the night that have been burnt by the souls of her ancestors. She shakes her head, thrumming with red and violet. The sounds in her ears grow louder, different to the usual sound she hears, crisper than the 'pop, pop' she is used to. She moves her head around and finds the noise originates with my mother.

'What is that?' Zosime is frightened, overwhelmed by terror of the unknown. I try to send her comfort but I'm too weak.

'Fear not, my child,' Geros says. 'It is the language of the future telling the story of our time. The translation is difficult but worth the effort.'

Zosime tries to push the fear away, putting her trust in the wise old man, although she is numb from the accumulation of shock and horror of recent events. I see her courage pulsing through her fear – saffron, crimson, magenta.

The sound reaches my mother's ears now – a paced 'pop, pop' – like a heart monitor. How can that be? The cadence is familiar. Then it dawns on her. It's not a cardiac output machine. It's the noise of the dendrochronologists counting the tree rings in the Paleoecology lab. Of all the bizarre things she needs to explain, this is the most challenging. How can Zosime grasp the concept of a machine that makes a popping beep, never mind the rest of this strange meeting? Yet, it makes sense to my mother. The story was written in the tree rings as they grew, affected as they were by the weather. The measurement of their widths told of the downturn in the climate. The energy from that story, and how it impacted the people living there, carried in the axe head. When the axe head hit the geode during the earthquake, that energy moved in unprecedented ways. She comprehends yet cannot describe it.

I understand how difficult this is, I tell my mother. *When I was gifted with full enlightenment, there was so much I wanted to tell you but could not explain. You had no perception of it.*

The cracks in my enlightenment now feed an ever-widening emptiness, a quiet nothingness that makes me long for the comprehension I once had.

Geros coughs, recovers and speaks with a hoarse voice. 'You are here for a reason. We all are.'

You are close to Enlightenment?

'Yes, closer now than ever,' Geros says. 'I will show you the way back if that is what you desire?'

I feel prickles of excitement, like discharges of static from a woollen garment, then a tug, like a current running towards Geros. *He* is my way back to the Enlightenment.

As soon as I know this, my mother knows it, too. She sucks in a half sob as her world darkens. Her heart twists hard, but she fights back her sorrow, using her love for me to ease the pain of losing me; an ache that reverberates through every cell in her body.

'Does this mean you must go?' she whispers, each word searing her heart. 'But …' She hesitates, wondering if she will be stuck here.

Zosime puts my mother's question into words. 'We are cast adrift here. How do we get home?'

'You will never get home, Zosime,' Geros says.

Pain ripples in cyan and navy across the auras of both women.

'What will we do if you leave us, Geros?' Zosime cries. 'We don't know which way to go, even if we knew how to harness the wind. We need you.'

'You have watched how the sailors harnessed the wind,' Geros says. 'Nereus has a basic knowledge of it that will get you by.'

Beyond our circle of Poppy's light, the others in the boats look dull-eyed and vacant, staring past the version of Zosime and Geros interacting with us, seeing only their inert outer shells, blind to them in this bubble of energy. In this pocket between the worlds, time is static.

'But where is the land? Where are we now? Where do we go?' Panic rises in Zosime's voice.

'I know your story,' my mother says. 'I can help you.'

'How?' Zosime asks past a lump in her throat. Having her story known means more to her than she realised. She's become used to the idea that without children, her story will die, yet here is a woman who has heard her story in the strange language of the future.

'I know where the land is. I can work out where you are now,' my mother tells her. 'You left Ireland.' Zosime looks confused, and my mother adds, 'Your island … and you sailed for warmer lands, right?'

'Yes.'

'So you must have sailed south.' My mother is speaking as much to herself as to the others now. 'No matter how far west or south the storm has blown you, the chances are there will be land closer to the east.' She thinks of the map of the world and places Zosime's boats somewhere in the Atlantic, hopefully in the Bay of Biscay, or at most, further south, off the coast of Portugal.

'East?' Zosime asks.

'Where the sun rises.'

'I must follow the Orient?'

'Yes. The wind across the large ocean usually blows that direction, but you should check each morning.' She doesn't know how she knows this; it's information she has gathered up over her life without realising it, but she is sure that the trade winds blow from west to east, because of the earth's rotation, something that hasn't changed since Zosime's time.

'We haven't seen the sun in a long time, but we can tell where it is behind the clouds by the brightness in the sky in the morning, even on the darkest of days,' Zosime says.

'I don't know how long it will take or how far you need to travel.' My mother wants to give Zosime hope to cling to until they reach land. 'You already have barrels with rainwater, and you know how to catch fish. You survived a big storm already. These boats are more robust than I would have given them credit for.'

'They are small,' Zosime agrees, 'But sturdy. Though I fear another storm would end us. And we are hungry and weak already.'

'We must all end our journey in this realm at some time, Zosime. Try not to fear that,' Geros says. 'But I would more fear not passing on, never reaching the Enlightenment, fading to nothing. Isn't that so, Poppy?'

I feel lightning bolts of pure white terror discharge from me, searing the air around us. Zosime and my mother flinch and cower.

'Oh, Poppy,' my mother cries.

I don't know how to leave you. The magnetic pull towards Geros is not strong enough to overcome what is holding me in the physical world, to my mother.

'Aisling – you only need to let go,' Geros says. 'And embrace your purpose.'

'What is my purpose?' my mother asks, panic rising with neon flashes. 'Without Poppy, I have no purpose.'

'That is your grief talking,' Geros says. 'Our purpose is to be who we are, live the life that we have, tell our story and bear witness to others' stories so we can learn from each other's experiences to be better people – that is our purpose, Aisling.'

At first, his words spark anger in my mother. Who is this old man to tell her what her purpose is? What does he know of her heartbreak? But as quickly as she thinks this, she remembers the trials that Zosime and Geros have survived. He is not simply any old man; Geros has lost everything he has ever had, yet is gifted with wisdom, both from the life he has lived and the enlightenment he possesses, the same enlightenment that was once mine. He is now sharing that with her.

As my mother sees the truth in his words, a heavy weight rolls from her, giving her buoyancy and setting her free. She knows what she must do – live the life she has – and the first part of that is to let me go so I may reunite with the Enlightenment. Her knowing this fills me with joy that spills out to them. It effervesces and dilutes Zosime's fear and my mother's sorrow. When it reaches Geros, it collides with a radiant vigour, far removed from the outward aspect of the physical husk of the old man's body, shrivelled from starvation and gnarled with age.

'I love you, Poppy,' my mother whispers.

My love is wrapped around you, Mother – love never dies. It is eternal, and you absorb it from the moment you receive it. Think of how you love me. You will always feel that way, and I will feel that love, too, always.

My mother's aura vibrates with pinks and oranges as she accepts my love and trusts in my words.

'Go.' This simple word from her is all it takes.

Zosime sees my star wink out.

My mother feels the empty space it leaves.

My spirit surges and intertwines with Geros, like flame and smoke, a frenzy of colour and light, a burst of electricity and magnetism. Energy fluxes, pressure builds, a fluorescence of light and life and love and power until it detonates, discharging, ending pain, dissipating into bliss.

Geros and I are cast into an ecstasy of harmony, adrift in the Enlightenment. We are still with my mother and Zosime, but they do not have the same sense of us. Their sadness doesn't touch us. Emotion does not drag on us. We are aware it is there, but we are free from its effects.

We exist in pure contentment, communing with our ancestors.

Zosime cradles Geros's body, her tears falling on his cooling flesh. When she lifts her head, she sees my mother is still with her, crying with soft sobs and wiping her tears with the back of her hand.

'The star,' Zosime says. 'Who was it?'

She lets the question hang between them as my mother struggles to find her voice. Eventually, she says, 'My baby.'

Zosime's eyes glisten in the dawning light.

'I, too, have stars.'

My mother knows what she means, feels their pain blending together, and nods her understanding.

'Are you stuck here?' Zosime asks.

'No,' my mother says. 'I know how to get back, but I wanted to share this moment with you.'

'This moment?' Zosime is confused. For her, this moment is filled with aching loss.

'Look.' My mother points over Zosime's shoulder to the eastern horizon. There is a sliver of the palest blue tinged with rose gold, a strip between the sky and the edge of the volcanic dust cloud.

Zosime gasps as the first rays of the rising sun spill over the edge of the horizon. Fingers of gold touch the tips of the waves, lighting a path across the ocean, an arrow towards their survival. The rippled undersides of the clouds light up crimson with cerise highlights and mauve hollows.

The sun fills the gap, flooding them with light.

'You know the way?' my mother asks.

'I do,' Zosime says. 'Do you know how my story ends now?'

'I do.' My mother nods. She knows it is better not to say too much. 'Goodbye.'

And she lets go.

CHAPTER 30

Weeping brings me back to myself, my weeping and that of the people around me. As I hear them, it dawns on me that we are still here. I am still here. Geros is in the Enlightenment. I ought not to be sad for him.

But the weeping is not just sorrow. Some are crying out with joy, 'The sun!'

Nereus stands and stretches a hand towards the dawn.

Orient!

There is a breeze, and it pushes towards the Orient. It lifts the tips of our hair to point at the sun. Today is a day to move with the breeze, as the woman with the star, whom I now know as Aisling, directed.

I cover Geros's face, stand up, stagger to the ropes at the pole and pull on one the way I saw the sailors do. The sheet rises up and catches. The craft lurches and starts tipping. Alarmed screams make me drop the ropes. The sail drops and we steady.

'Zosime, what are you doing?' Agis asks.

'We need to go to the sun, or we will die,' I say.

'We're going to die anyway,' Eleni, Yani's wife, says. She is bent over Geros's body, and her children cling to her, sobbing.

My anger flares. How dare she give up on her children's lives? If I had children, I'd never give up. I think of Jaisun disappearing below the waves, how I was immobile with shock and horror, unable to help him. I feel shame at judging my sister-in-law so harshly. I temper my voice with kindness and say, 'Eleni, we have come too far, lost too many to simply give up. We have no choice but to try.'

Eleni nods. 'You are right, sister.' She hugs her children closer.

'Even if we can get this craft to move, how do we know what direction to go to reach the Warmer Lands?' Yani asks.

'Geros told me,' I say. It's the only thing they will believe. I don't try to explain the woman with the star from the future. 'Before he died, he said we should sail towards the Orient. He died as the sun appeared. Surely that is a sign?'

Yani shrugs. 'I suppose this sea cannot last forever. If we choose one direction and stick to it, perhaps we'll find land before we starve completely.'

'We can fish,' Nereus says. 'Now there is sun, it is already warmer. We can take threads from our clothes, make lines.'

His optimism infects others in the boats. They nod in agreement.

'I can make nets and I know a little of sailing, the basics,' Nereus says. 'Enough to get us moving if the wind is not too strong. And we can row. Here …' He pulls a piece of wood from a broken crate and hands it to Yani.

My heart opens in wonder at Nereus. Geros was right. I'd been so wrong to consider him stupid when his head was in the clouds, back when life seemed so easy and I was full of arrogance. In his gentle way, he'd watched the world and noticed how the fishermen in his village had hunted in the water, and he'd watched the sailors and seen how they harnessed the wind.

For the rest of the day, Nereus takes advantage of the better weather and wind direction and employs a combination of experimenting with the sail and paddling.

The sun slides up behind the clouds, but they are edged with an expanding line of blue. The dusk seems to come later and as the strip of blue darkens to navy, then black, I watch as a yellow slice rises from the horizon – the moon! – her one eye sleepy and half closed in a rich golden crescent. When it follows the sun behind the cloud, we are plunged back into darkness.

I lie, listening to the wind rustle in sails and waves whispering on our keel. My stomach gurgles from the lack of food, but I doze off with thoughts of winds pushing us towards blue skies and hope in my heart.

It takes three days of experiments with fishing techniques before we catch anything worth eating. It is a fish I don't recognise, about the length of a man's forearm, with flashing silver scales and unblinking round eyes.

Agis and Yani wrestle it into the boats, and I club it to death with the paddle. Nereus looks green in the face, but when he tastes the translucent pale flesh, he smiles. With the guts tied around splinters of wood and larger jagged bones, we have bait, and the fishing gets easier.

Each day, we sail towards the rising sun, moving slowly out from under the clouds until we can watch the path of the sun for almost its full journey. The nights are clear. I look for Geros in the stars. There are so many; it makes my heart happy to know he is not alone. Perhaps he is with my children, those who, like the star with Aisling, never walked on our land. I feel them in my heart in the quiet moments, and they keep me strong, hopeful.

But if we don't make it to land soon, we will all be stars.

Then, one morning, I realise my journey to join the stars might be a while off yet. The horizon is jagged and dark. I feel weak with relief and gratitude. Even Yani, the most stoic of us, has a tear in his eye as we watch the sun rise above land. The wind is strong, carrying us swiftly to a stretch of white sand and tough grasses. We wade, staggering in waist-high water, dragging the boats until they are stuck fast on the sand.

When we reach the tussocks of grass, there are people on the shore. They look well-fed and strong while we can barely stand under the weight of our own bones. Their welcome is guarded but humane. They help us to their village, lying among enclosures of fat cattle with bulging udders and fields of golden, heavy-headed cereals. I slip my hand into the folds of my tunic pocket, curl my fingers around the little parcel tucked away there and think, perhaps, this is a place where I can plant Kallisto's seeds.

CHAPTER 31

My mother lifts her hand from the scarred oak sample, zapping back to the museum with one hand still in her satchel, touching the ancient bronze axe head.

No time has passed. Professor Baillie is answering questions. Spoons clink off teacups amid the murmur of voices. The air holds the dryness of the indoors, of central heating and dust from the carpet – a far cry from the smell of the ocean and the moist wind she experienced moments ago. Everything is exactly as it was before she touched the scarred oak tree-ring sample. Except for one thing: my mother cannot feel my presence, and my absence lands like a punch to her chest.

No one notices her tears or her leaving. She stumbles out into a beautiful sun-drenched day, wiping her face dry. The air is warm, the sky blue, and the grass on the Mall is verdant, tipped with yellow where the heatwave has dried it out. Groups of people sit in various formations; colt-legged girls folded onto their jackets pretend not to watch sweaty boys chasing a football further down; two women sit on a bench and rock a pram; a man and a dog walk by; three youths dressed in black slouch against the low wall vaping.

On auto-pilot, my mother picks up a brisk pace beneath the leafy chestnut trees, breathing hard, holding her pain close. She has lost me twice now. She thinks of her mother, whom she has already lost to dementia. When Grammo passes, she will have lost her twice, too. Pushing that thought out of her head, she takes the path that cuts across the far end of the Mall.

She wanted so much to have children, to see Grammo play with those children, to teach them about life, to tell them stories, and she will never have that. Geros's words come back to her.

… be who we are, living the life that we have …

She passes a statue of a little girl of about ten, a memorial to the train disaster that happened in Armagh in 1889 that took at least eighty-nine lives, many of them children. My mother knows the story of the ill-fated Sunday school trip but stops to look up at the statue of the little girl with her bucket and spade, set for a day at the seaside. There are yellow pansies in the bucket. Someone has remembered this story recently, remembered these lives.

More of Geros's words drift back to her.

... telling our story and bearing witness to others' stories ...

Then Grammo's voice sounds in her head. Stories are important. They condense what it means to be human. They connect us to past lives, reach out to future peoples.

My mother reaches her car and opens the door, pauses, letting the heat that has built up escape. Gingerly, she eases into the seat, the scorching leather burning through her thin summer dress. She feels like she has lost me, but she realises she hasn't lost Grammo completely. The urge to see her, hold her hand, stroke her cheek overwhelms her. Before she knows it, she is pulling up at the nursing home, parking, and then heading for the entrance.

CHAPTER 32

Nereus closes his eyes and smiles, raising his face to the morning sunshine. The sun has darkened his skin, and his hair glints where the light dances in golden strands. His chin bobs as he chews his grain mash. He swallows, then sighs contentedly. It's only grain mash. We have meat and cheese to eat, too. Even after ten months of good food, we are still grateful for every bite.

A voice calls from the path that passes a little way downhill from our hut. Three wild-haired children run ahead of a woman around my age. It's Febe, who is in charge of planting the crops. Her role is similar to Kallisto's but without the responsibility for livestock. She conducts herself more like Doah, and there's something in her demeanour that makes me think of my sister-in-law, Aleka, as well. I do this – search for my lost people in the new ones I meet. It brings me a strange combination of comfort and pain.

'What is she saying?' She's shouting her words too fast for me to catch.

'She's telling the children not to run in on us without warning us they are approaching.' Nereus has a great grasp of this new language. I still need slow, deliberate words or the hunter's sign language, which I shared when we first arrived, to understand fully.

'It's a courtesy thing,' Nereus explains. 'They're supposed to hail us three times before turning up the hill and leaving the path.'

He shouts something back to indicate we've heard them. I try to grasp his words, but they fly by. So much of a language and customs of a people are intertwined. It was probably the same with us, but we never noticed, not having to examine it or explain it. Our language is fading among us as we switch to that of the village that took us in.

I nod my understanding to Nereus, proud of how smart my husband is, of his talent for languages and connecting with people, a skill I had never seen in him until we arrived here, lost and starving.

Between my hunting sign language and his memory for new words, we were able to communicate with the people who saved us.

The children reach Nereus and fling themselves at him. He lifts them in turn and swings them around. I bathe in their squeals of joy where once this would have caused me to feel the sting of my loss of motherhood. But now, I understand that I didn't need children of my own to nurture others; now, my people are my children; and now, I must help ease them into this new life, as I would any baby born into a world startling and new to them.

Our salvation comes at a price but one we are willing to pay. Their Elders have counted the free food and lodgings, and we must work it off in the fields. Some of us, like Nereus and his weaving, or me with my hunting, can use our talents to pay back our debt for being taken in and given food and lodgings. While it is a fairer agreement than we'd struck with the cruel sailors, which is no longer an issue, it will take years to pay off. We have nothing to call our own. Our huts are borrowed, as is the scrap of land we have been given to grow my seeds. Perhaps our village's children will see a time when they barter as free people, but each day, I feel the sun on my back. I am grateful for its warmth, for life and for the love I share with Nereus.

'Hail,' Febe says, greeting both of us with a hand sign.

We sign back. I smile wide to show I understand her.

'I have something to show you, Zosime.' Her words are deliberate, and I understand easily this time.

I answer with fumbled pronunciation, but she understands I am saying, 'Show me.'

As we three adults walk, the children run in circles around us, chirping questions and exchanging quips with Nereus; he serves up Febe's words when they drop between her saying them and my catching them, and delivers mine when I get tongue-tangled.

Febe walks us to the patch of land she gave us for Kallisto's seeds.

'I think,' Febe says with a grin, 'you will be joining us for the harvest celebration.'

Before us, lines of shoots pierce the crumbly soil, so tiny and fragile, barely more than a rash on the earth. I drop to my knees and, with one finger, touch the new seedling. It bends. I pull my hand away, hardly daring to breathe. But it does not break.

'What is it?' Nereus asks.

Febe and I lock eyes and grin. I shake my head but keep smiling. There was a time I'd have been irritated by Nereus's question, impatient with his lack of knowledge. Now, my heart glows with amusement at the lost look on his face as he takes his turn to grapple for understanding. For all his newly discovered talent, Nereus will never be a farmer or a hunter, but that's fine. I don't need him to be either.

Febe explains, or at least I guess that is what she is telling him because his expression changes from puzzlement to joy.

I wish Kallisto was here to see this. I wish for many things. What person doesn't? But for now, I lift my smile to the sky and give thanks to the sun gently shining on the vibrant green blades, reaching for the light.

We'll survive here, Nereus and I, and what's left of our people, fulfilling our purpose to live the best life we can and telling our story in this new place.

CHAPTER 33

My mother finds Grammo in her room, sitting by the window, wrapped in a soft pink cardigan with a cream blanket over her knees. She turns as my mother opens the door, smiles as the light of recognition flames in her eyes. Then says, 'Maureen! How lovely to see you.'

My mother steps back as if struck,

'Mum, it's me.' Grammo thinking she is Maureen is too much for her. She bursts into tears. I use my energy to guide Grammo back to this room, to her daughter, to my mother. There is only so much I can do from here – it won't always work, but it does this time.

'Oh, sorry, darling, of course, it is,' Grammo says quickly. 'Aisling, sorry. The cardigan confused me. And you know how easily confused I am. Come here.'

Grammo opens her arms and my mother rushes into her embrace.

'There, there, darling.' Grammo pats her back. 'Poppy has gone?'

Another wave of sorrow engulfs my mother. She buries her head on Grammo's shoulder and sobs. Grammo holds her, strokes her hair and rocks her gently. Her tears subside. My mother takes a breath.

'Sorry, yes, Poppy … moved on.' She doesn't quite know how to explain it. 'And then when you thought I was Maureen …'

'I know you have had your issues with Maureen,' Grammo says.

My mother pulls away to look Grammo in the face. 'You do?'

'You've never said anything to me, and you hide it well enough from Jack, especially after he fell in love with her. I know she is careless with your feelings. But she loves you. You're the one person in her whole life she allowed herself to have faith in. To be herself with.'

'Really? I don't understand.'

'She had it hard in ways you can't appreciate.'

My mother wonders if Grammo is confused again. She searches her face but finds only clarity in her eyes. 'Tell me. Please.'

'Maureen never had a good relationship with her parents. There was a lot of alcohol abuse in that house. Things we protected you from seeing, hearing, learning about. But Maureen saw it first-hand and bottled it up, then you befriended her. You changed her story by teaching her about love. Then, she met Jack. Without you, she would never have been able to love him.' She pauses, lets that settle, and then adds, 'I hope your dad and I had a hand in that, too.'

'How could I not know this?'

'Maureen is too proud to ask for help, too ashamed to tell you what she went through. You were school friends, rivals, peers and now family. Maybe she needed one person to see her without knowing about the horrors she experienced.'

'But you've told me now.'

'Yes, but Maureen doesn't know that. And it's time for *you* to see what you two mean to each other. She's your sister-in-law. You might feel stuck with her, but she's not all bad. She loves you to bits, always has, always will. She never learnt how to show it. And you will need her. She'll need you soon enough. When I go to join Poppy.'

'Mum! Please, don't say that.'

'I'm not saying it's imminent – just inevitable. Poppy will be waiting for me. But tell me what happened. How did she go?'

My mother tells Grammo what happened at the museum, finishing with, 'I know it's hard to understand or believe.'

'I believe you,' Grammo says. 'I've seen Poppy. In different realms, too. So, yes, I believe you were there. I believe you changed Zosime's story.'

My mother thinks about the Astropark and what her former student Frances said about her role in young Stevie's life, too – *You really changed his story* – and how good that feels.

As Grammo grows too tired, her mind wanders, and she struggles to stay in the room. My mother, grateful for this time with Grammo, knows she must let her rest, knows she will revisit these moments with her in her mind as she sits beside Grammo when she is not lucid, not in this same room.

She thinks about these lives, these stories she has changed, about the life *she* has, that she wasn't able to change by becoming a mother. Her loss of me pulls hard, tears a fresh strip of pain. She holds the burn of it close, because it feels like she is holding me close when she does this.

Geros's words float in her ears.

Our purpose is to be who we are, live the life that we have …

This is the life that she has. She has no choice other than to accept that. That is her purpose – to accept what she has been given and to make the best of it, change the story where and when she can, for the better.

...tell our story and bear witness to others' stories so we can learn from each other's experiences to be better people – that is our purpose, Aisling.

It is not what she had planned, but it's not bad either. She thinks of how much love she has from my father, from Uncle Jack, from my cousins. How blessed she has been by love, and she thinks of Maureen, deprived of love and functioning only on the surface, in a survival mode that sometimes looked to her like cruelty.

My mother is loved. This is the life that she has – it is rich and full – if she could only embrace it. She'll still feel my loss – the loss of the children she'd dreamed of having – whenever she hears little ones laughing or listens to parents talking of their kids, or gets left out of play dates, or has to navigate Christmas and the magic it once had but is now 'for the children'. She will still feel left out by a traditional family-centric society. But she won't be the only one carrying a broken heart. Perhaps her heart will not be broken forever. She knows, too, she will find other communities, other tribes, where she does fit in. There is always hope if she can hold on long enough and trust the wind to blow her in the right direction.

Being sad about losing me is part of my mother living her life, of fulfilling her purpose. There were never guarantees that it would be easy or without pain, but she knows the joy she's had, too. She has glimpsed the Enlightenment. It is more than most have in a lifetime.

My mother knows what she wants to do next, knows how she'll be able to live her life and bear witness to the stories of others. The marks on the bark told her of a life lived. She wants to retell that story. Maybe she can change more stories for the better if she can tell Zosime's story, show how a changed climate adversely impacted those lives and will do so again if people don't take action. Maybe she can encourage people to change the whole planet's story by rolling back this climate calamity that is now being caused, not by volcanoes, but by humanity themselves.

*

Later, back in her old bedroom at her old desk, my mother flexes her wrists and alternates between making fists and flinging open her fingers. It's been an emotionally exhausting day, but she wants to capture the sense of Zosime before it fades. To be her witness is an

267

honour. My mother takes responsibility for telling this remarkable woman's story, considers it her duty to get it down on paper. If only one other person hears it – my mother thinks of at least four who *will* hear it – then it is told. The story lives.

My mother takes a breath and thinks of Zosime: how she lost her babies, too; how, more than four thousand years later, she shares that same grief; how, despite the wonders of science or how much they now know, humanity is still beholden to both the microscopic whims of fertility and the macroscopic forces of climate.

My mother lets her words flow, arranging them on the screen in front of her:

2354 BC – IRELAND

My stomach cramps. A sour taste rises in my mouth. I swallow hard, but it doesn't help. I have my answer for another moon. Tears sting my eyes in the stench of the slop pit, but I wait until I'm outside to draw a deep breath and compose myself before walking back to our hut and Nereus, my husband …

ACKNOWLEDGMENTS

A talk by the late Professor Mike Baillie in Armagh County Museum in October, 2017, ignited the spark for the idea that became this book. I had been a student and a research associate in the Paleoecology Department QUB under Professor Baillie back in the 1980s and 1990s. I turned up at his talk to say hello and was delighted that he remembered me after almost 25 years. He was always a great storyteller, able to impart his vast knowledge and enthusiasm for his subject in a way that fully engaged the listener. His presentation that day in the museum conjured a vision in my mind. He met with me in person afterwards to discuss my ideas for this book, giving generously of his time and experience, and we enjoyed many interesting conversations speculating on my interpretation of his research. He was my "Geros" in real life – the wise, kind man and teacher. My heart is full of gratitude when I think of him, and remembering him makes me smile.

While I have a grounding in the dendrochronology and environmental science that this book is based on, I am not a historian. The research into the Neolithic period in Ireland was absolutely fascinating, not least because of insights and help from Sean Bardon, curator at the Armagh County Museum. Thank you, Sean.

Thanks also go to Greer Ramsey, the curator of Archaeology, National Musuems NI, for helping me understand the archaeology of Neolithic Ireland and for talking me through ideas for building Zosime's world. Writer friends Gaynor Kane and Lynda Collins also helped me to get a handle on the archaeology of 2354 BC. Thank you, friends.

I'm grateful to Professor Jonathon Pilcher, another mentor from my dendrochronology days at QUB, for helping me with the botanical accuracy of the Neolithic period.

Thanks are due to Heather Alexander and Dr Rok Nežič at the Armagh Observatory and Planetarium for their help and encouragement, which included a tour of the Observatory. They were able to show me what the night sky looked like on the summer solstice in 2354 BC, projected on the Planetarium dome.

Thank you to my friend, Neil Conlon, for educating me on how farmers are affected by climate change today in Ireland, and to Maura and Kevin Johnston for their insights into sailing and how sailors in Neolithic times might have navigated on open water.

Once all the research was done, it was time to write the story. The Irish Writers Centre has been an amazing resource, providing workshops, mentoring and the wonderful 'Writing the Earth' project. Thank you to the Arts Council of Northern Ireland, and the National Lottery, for funding.

To Bernie Mc Gill and Conor Kostick for mentoring. Their advice, support and generous encouragement made all the difference – thank you.

Thank you to Brian Langan for coaching me as an author and for editing the manuscript with tender wisdom and gentle guidance. Thanks also to the eagle-eyed Hanna Nielson for her careful proofreading. To Frances McKenna for her fantastic cover art and painting, inspired by my words.

Thanks to The Belfast Review for publishing the first chapter in the January 2025 issue.

To my wonderful writer friends for their valuable critiques, beta reads, and being a life-raft in a sea of doubt – Tim Hanna, Malachi Kelly, Rachel Toner, Sue Divin, Karen Mooney, Cathy Carson, Fiona O'Rourke, Tanya Mc Ginn, Shannon Hempill, Eva Smith Glynn, Lucy Geever, Cathy Thrush, Martha Engber, Eoin Brady, Sonya Moor, Omaya Nasser, Nina Francus, and Julia Skorcz.

To Frances Moen and Carol Hanna, friends who feel like family, and my sister, Barney McKee, and my mum, Bernadette Grimley, for beta reading and cheerleading. I could not do it without all of you. Last but not least, I thank Allan for holding my heart and helping me live my dream.

ABOUT THE AUTHOR

Byddi Lee is the author of *Rejuvenation*, a speculative fiction trilogy, first published by Castrum Press in 2020, and has published flash fiction, short stories and her novel, *March to November* (Seanchai Books, 2014). She co-founded and manages Flash Fiction Armagh, shortlisted as Best Regular Spoken Word Night in the Saboteur Awards, and co-edited *The Bramley – An Anthology of Flash Fiction Armagh*, Volumes 1 and 2. Byddi also writes for stage and screen and is a member of BBC Writersroom Voices 23. She is an Arts Council Northern Ireland supported writer, and holds professional membership at the Irish Writers Centre in Dublin, and the Society of Authors, UK.

For more information, visit www.ByddiLee.com.

ABOUT THE COVER ARTIST

Frances McKenna is an accomplished Irish artist renowned for her emotionally charged and spiritually resonant works. Drawing inspiration from the profound connections between humanity and the natural world, Frances masterfully blends contemporary and traditional elements to create vibrantly colourful, dynamic compositions to stir emotions and uplift the soul. Frances's paintings evoke the raw beauty of nature, utilizing rich textures and layers, inviting viewers to explore their intricacies. Each piece not only serves as a visual delight but also as a transformative narrative, enriching any space while encouraging reflection and a deeper connection to one's outer world and inner self.

Visit Frances McKenna's world of art at
www.francesmckennairishart.com

Printed in Great Britain
by Amazon

60874059R00160